DATE DUE

DEMCO 38-296

running wild

TRANSLATION CENTER BOOKS SERIES EDITORS

LORI M. CARLSON
FRANK MACSHANE

running wild

new chinese writers

EDITED BY

DAVID DER-WEI WANG

WITH **JEANNE TAI**

NEW YORK

COLUMBIA UNIVERSITY PRESS

The publisher gratefully acknowledges support toward publication given by the Council for Cultural Planning.

Columbia University Press
New York   Chichester, West Sussex

Copyright © 1994 Columbia University Press

All stories used by permission of the authors.
"Divine Debauchery" © Andrew F. Jones
"Transcendence and the Fax Machine" © Jeanne Tai
"One Kind of Reality" © Jeanne Tai
"The Isle of Wang'an" © Kirk Anderson and Randy Du
"Master Chai" © Michelle Yeh
"Ghost Talk" © Charles A. Laughlin
"Mother Fish" © Kristina M. Torgeson
"Festival" © Ann Huss
"Plain Moon" © Michelle Yeh
"I Am Not a Cat" © Amy Dooling
"The Adulterers" © Charles A. Laughlin and Jeanne Tai
"Running Wild" © Kirk Anderson and Zheng Da
"Our Childhood" © Michelle Yeh
"The Amateur Cameraman" © Jeffrey C. Bent

Library of Congress Cataloging-in Publication Data
Running wild: new Chinese writers / edited by David Der-wei Wang with Jeanne Tai.
    p. cm.
    A collection of fourteen stories by various authors, translated from Chinese.
    ISBN 0–231–09648–8
    ISBN 0–231–09649–6 (pbk.)
    1. Chinese fiction—20th century—Translating into English
2. Wang, David Der-wei. 3. Tai, Jeanne.
PL2658.E8R86 1994
895.1'35208—dc20   93–37041
                                              CIP

The Translation Center gratefully acknowledges the generous support of the Council for Cultural Planning and Development in Taipei, Taiwan, in all stages of the translation and preparation of the anthology. Their effort to promote the English version of works that originally appear in Chinese exemplifies the universal desire to be understood.

CONTENTS

1 DIVINE DEBAUCHERY BY **MO YAN** 1

Translated by Andrew F. Jones

2 TRANSCENDENCE AND THE FAX MACHINE BY **YE SI** 13

Translated by Jeanne Tai

3 ONE KIND OF REALITY BY **YÜ HUA** 21

Translated by Jeanne Tai

4 THE ISLE OF WANG'AN BY **ZHONG LING** 69

Translated by Kirk Anderson and Randy Du

5 MASTER CHAI BY **ZHU TIANWEN** 89

Translated by Michelle Yeh

6 GHOST TALK BY **YANG LIAN** 101
Translated by Charles A. Laughlin

7 MOTHER FISH BY **XI XI** 108
Translated by Kristina M. Torgeson

8 FESTIVAL BY **A CHENG** 128
Translated by Ann Huss

9 PLAIN MOON BY **GU ZHAOSEN** 137
Translated by Michelle Yeh

10 I AM NOT A CAT BY **TANG MIN** 158
Translated by Amy Dooling

11 THE ADULTERERS BY **LI PEIFU** 168
Translated by Charles A. Laughlin with Jeanne Tai

12 RUNNING WILD BY **SU TONG** 174
Translated by Kirk Anderson and Zheng Da

13 OUR CHILDHOOD BY **YANG ZHAO** 184
Translated by Michelle Yeh

14 THE AMATEUR CAMERAMAN BY **S. K. CHANG** 197
Translated by Jeffrey C. Bent

AFTERWORD: CHINESE FICTION FOR THE NINETIES 238
David Der-wei Wang

List of Contributors *259*

running
wild

DIVINE

DEBAUCHERY

Mo Yan

(Translated by Andrew F. Jones with Jeanne Tai)

*I*n the early years of the Republic,[1] there lived in Northeast Village in Gaomi County an extraordinary personage, a dashing bon vivant, an elegant free spirit. His family name was Wang, his given name was Bo, and he styled himself Jifan. Later generations knew him as Master Jifan.

My grandpa was no more than fifteen when he began working as a laborer in Master Jifan's household. That is why so many interesting stories and anecdotes about Master Jifan have been handed down from generation to generation within my family. Whenever Big Uncle, my father's oldest brother, recounted these curious tales to us, he would become spirited and expansive, his whole face lighting up with a special glow of pride and satisfaction. Needless to say, this was because Grandpa had had the honor of serving in the Wang family. Big Uncle

---

1. The first republican government in China was established in 1911.

would always begin each story in the same way: "Back when your grandpa was a servant in Master Jifan's household . . ."

One radiant spring day, Master Jifan decided to go on an excursion to enjoy the glories of the season and gave orders for his horse to be readied. The stable boy untied the big roan stallion, sleek as candle wax, gave it a thorough grooming, saddled it carefully, and led it out to the hitching post by the main gate of the courtyard. Sporting a sky blue cotton robe with matching trousers, his feet clad in thick-soled felt-covered shoes, Master Jifan ambled out of the compound, an ivory cigarette holder dangling from the corner of his mouth. My grandpa helped his master onto the horse, and at a signal from him, marched ahead, leading the horse by its halter. When the townspeople heard that Master Jifan was setting out for a ride in the countryside, they all ran into the street to watch him go by. The beggars at Five Mile Bridge heard the news too and immediately sent word to their leader, Li Zixu, who lived in the hutch next to Guandi Temple. By the time Grandpa reached the temple with the roan stallion in tow, Li Zixu, shirtless and shoeless, was down on his knees right in the middle of the road, blocking the way.

"Take pity on me, Master Jifan," the beggar chief implored.

"What's going on here?" Master Jifan asked.

Grandpa answered, "A man is blocking the road begging for alms."

"Tell him the master isn't carrying any money."

"The master doesn't have any money on him," Grandpa shouted.

"Then won't Master Jifan bestow upon this humble creature the robe that his worthyship is wearing?"

"The beggar wants the master's robe," my grandpa relayed back to Master Jifan.

Master Jifan said, "If someone else fancies this robe, it would be a sin for me to go on wearing it. Isn't that right, Han San?"

Han San was my grandpa's nickname. Upon hearing the question, he hastened to answer, "Yes, that's right, that's right."

At that, Master Jifan took off his robe right there in the saddle, shifting his weight from one side to the other as he pulled the garment out from under his buttocks, and tossed it over to the beggar chief, saying, "You lazy bum, what've you done with your life? Can't you even rustle up a robe?"

"Master Jifan, my worthless feet are still bare."

Whereupon the master removed his shoes too and threw them to the beggar.

My grandpa took the halter and resumed the journey, but they had barely reached the banks of Lion's Cove before they were besieged by another horde of paupers.

And so it was that Master Jifan arrived at the honey locust forest stripped to his underpants, sitting astride the big muscular roan and rolling his head from side to side as he chanted verses of classical poetry. Fully clothed, Master Jifan had cut a fine and elegant figure. Now, in his underwear, he was all skin and bones, resembling nothing so much as a monkey perched atop a large fleshy horse. Flocks of children trailed behind them, giggling as they watched this unusual spectacle. Seemingly oblivious to it all, Master Jifan rode on, his eyes half closed, his fingers stroking the tuft of black whiskers under his chin, his face radiating contentment.

Big Uncle said that Grandpa knew what Master Jifan liked without being told, so he made haste to lead the horse into the densest part of the grove. In no time at all they had left the crowd of mischievous kids well behind. The honey locusts, which covered an area east of town of about seventy-five acres, were in full bloom, their emerald green leaves all but invisible under a sea of snow white and pale pink blossoms that swathed every branch and bough. Swarms of bees droned through the air, bustling among the clouds of flowers. It was the time of year when the beekeepers in town were kept busy harvesting their combs every few days, and in the market pale golden locust honey went for as little as fifteen coppers a pound.

Grandpa led Master Jifan's big roan stallion slowly through the locust grove, gingerly picking his way among the dense foliage. The redolent perfume of the blossoms was so heady it made him feel sleepy. The horse trotted behind him, its snout buried in the thick clumps of flowers, munching happily on the tender shoots within its reach. Grandpa was still rather small at that time, with the top of his head reaching only as far as the stallion's haunches, so he was able to move relatively freely between the tree trunks. But he couldn't see much of what lay above the horse's belly. Master Jifan moved through the locust blossoms like someone floating among the clouds. Once in a while, Grandpa would catch a glimpse of his master through a small opening in the foliage. Master Jifan had a spray of locust blossoms dangling between his lips and a dreamy expression on his face, look-ing for all the world like a simpleton. Big Uncle told us that every spring, when the honey locusts were in bloom, Grandpa and Master Jifan would spend days on end wandering through the grove, some-times not even bothering to go home at night. No one in the master's family tried to talk him out of this, because they all knew how eccen-tric he could be. Besides, he was generous and open-handed, and well liked by everyone, so there was little danger of his running into trou-ble with bandits.

Grandpa said that after the moon came out, the scent of the flow-ers would grow even heavier, closing around them like the folds of a tent. An occasional light breeze might momentarily lift a corner of a flap, but the curtains would close swiftly, and thereafter the fragrance merely became more intense. In the silvery glow, the flowers trembled and came to life, shimmering in the moonlight like countless butter-flies fluttering through the air in a mating dance. They swirled and swelled, billowing here, fading there, constantly changing shape, like clouds, like a dream. Now and then the sheen of the stallion's red-brown coat would flash through a breach in the blossoms, gleaming like some newly unearthed treasure. Making the most of the short-lived blooms, droves of bees gathered pollen by moonlight, twinkling through the darkness like tiny shooting stars. Grandpa said that some-times people would come all the way from Sichuan or Henan just to set up their hives in the grove. They would find a clearing somewhere and pitch their tents; at night, their kerosene lamps swayed from the tops of bamboo poles, flickering among the trees like will-o'-the-wisps. At the first sign or whiff of these mere mortals my grandpa would immediately tug the horse and veer off in a different direction; otherwise Master Jifan would have had a royal fit. Deep in the night, as a light dew descended, the flower petals would sparkle even more brilliantly. The moon, glimpsed through an occasional opening in the foliage, was a small and distant object in the vaulting sky, while the ground was dappled with drops of silver that had filtered down through the blossoms and the leaves.

Grandpa said that the locust thorns left bloody cuts and scratches all over Master Jifan's body. After every sojourn into the sea of blooming locusts, the master would remain in a trance for days. He called it his "flower hangover."

Big Uncle told us that every thing in this world, living or not, has a soul and consciousness of its own. There are a few superior persons with extraordinary powers who can commune with every spirit in the cosmos. Master Jifan, beyond a shadow of a doubt, was one such individual.

Grandpa said that Master Jifan kept four tailors on his household staff all year long: one each for winter and summer clothing, one for spring and autumn outfits, and one who specialized in hosiery and cloth shoes. All four tailors worked year-round at their tasks, yet Master Jifan still found himself with nothing to wear. Big Uncle told us that in Master Jifan's day, the best-dressed people in Gaomi were like as not the beggars in the county seat, and the custom has persisted to this day. Beggars who have just come from other counties are always clothed in rags and tatters; the local dogs immediately recognize them as strangers and, snarling, chase them through the streets. Gaomi beggars, on the other hand, would think nothing of selling their own blood to get a new suit of clothes, and when they stroll down the street in their finery, dogs wag their tails in friendly welcome. People would say, "With clothes like that, how come you're still asking me for money?!" To which the beggar would reply, "Master Jifan started it all. He's spoiled us, and now we can't go back to the old ways." In Qingzhou, Jiaozhou and Laizhou, when you want to make fun of someone who hasn't got a red cent but still insists on keeping up appearances, you call him a "Gaomi beggar." In the old days there was even a kind of melon, with a smooth shiny skin but harshly bitter flesh, that was nicknamed "Gaomi beggar." Grandpa said Master Jifan was always impeccably dressed when he went out, only to come home barely clad in his underwear, even in the dead of winter.

Master Jifan was fond of gambling, but he only liked to gamble at night. All the leading figures in town would come to his house to play. A dozen or so large tables would be set up in the main hall, with eight people to a game, and one game at each table. Every table was piled high with stacks of shiny silver dollars. The people who came to gamble were the sort who were too embarrassed to be seen picking up any coins that might have fallen onto the floor. With so many people playing all night long, there would always be at least eight or ten silver dollars that would manage to roll off the tabletops. Later, they were retrieved and pocketed by my Grandpa as a tip for serving tea and refreshments at these gatherings. By the time he left Master Jifan's employ, Grandpa had saved up enough to buy a house in town and farmland too.

Master Jifan never concerned himself with the crops and other business on his estate—his only business was pleasure. But the field hands on the farm were always more than willing to work their fingers to the bone in Master Jifan's fields. Grandpa said that one year, when the wheat was being harvested, one of the farmhands sneaked home a load of wheat on a donkey. When another laborer reported the theft, Master Jifan barked at him: "Idiot! What an idiot! If he thought of using a donkey, why don't you use a cart?"

Miffed, the hired hand threw caution to the wind and took home a wagonload of wheat from Master Jifan's fields. When he learned about it, Master Jifan's only comment was, "He's finally using his head."

Master Jifan had a wife and six concubines in his household. His wife's face was scarred by pockmarks, but each of the six concubines was a bona fide beauty. Big Uncle said Grandpa had told him that Master Jifan always slept alone in his own room. The concubines were all young and in the prime of life, and they found this kind of neglect well-nigh intolerable. Eventually, some of them bundled together money and jewelry and ran off with other men, while others carried on illicit affairs with the farmhands and even had illegitimate children by them. Master Jifan turned a blind eye to all this. The bastard kids were given the run of the estate, and when they caught sight of Master Jifan they would dutifully call him "Dad." He smiled at them without saying a word. Grandpa said that the only child who was really Master Jifan's was the imbecile son born to the pockmarked wife.

Big Uncle told us that one spring, on the very first day of the lunar New Year, Master Jifan decided he would go whoring. Everyone was thunderstruck. The steward urged him to wait until the holidays were over, but Master Jifan said he didn't want to wait till then, he wanted to go right away. The steward said, "This is one piece of business I'm not going to handle for you." Whereupon Master Jifan called out, "Han San!"

"Right here, sir!" replied my grandpa, now a lad of seventeen.

"We're surrounded by boors and louts," said Master Jifan. "Looks like it'll be just you and me, boy."

Grandpa asked, "Will the master be going to the brothel, or bringing the girls back to the house?"

"Back here, of course," replied Master Jifan.

"Shall we summon the girls from the House of Little Lambs," asked Grandpa, "or from the Knockout Club?"

Master Jifan said, "Just bring me every last whore in Gaomi township."

Grandpa swallowed hard but dared not ask any more questions. Perplexed and full of misgiving, he went off to round up the women.

Big Uncle said that at that time there were two red-light districts in the west end of town, one on each side of the Little Kang River. The one on the east bank was called Scholar's Lane, the one on the west was known as Catfish Alley. In those days, going to the brothels was facetiously referred to as "cramming for exams" or "eating catfish." There were five or six bordellos on each street, each housing three to five girls on call. There were also a few so-called half-open doors—little shops that sold dry goods and notions by day and entertained clients behind closed doors at night. Big Uncle said that all kinds of people visited the brothels. There were the regular customers who all but lived in the red-light districts, as well as half-grown boys who had pilfered some money from mom and dad to come and "learn the craft."

At seventeen, Grandpa looked for all the world like one of those "apprentices." It was New Year's Day, and every household was busy paying respects to its ancestors. Even those habitués who were oversexed stayed home. The brothels in Gaomi township observed the New Year by giving the girls the day off. Dressed in their holiday best, the prostitutes whiled away the time eating melon seeds and playing penny-ante games of chance. If the day was sunny, they might even go out for a walk in town, joining the crowds to watch the street shows and festivities. The porters and the tea servers at the brothels had all gone home for the New Year. The madams had been kind enough to give permission for the prostitutes to go home and visit their parents too, but considering the fact that most of them had been sold by their very own parents into this living hell, it was no surprise that nobody took advantage of the offer. So as soon as my Grandpa walked through the doors, he was surrounded by whores all clamoring to teach him a few tricks.

Naturally, Big Uncle didn't say whether Grandpa ever apprenticed himself in this way. What he did say was that before long, Grandpa, who was often seen around town escorting Master Jifan on his horse, was recognized by a sharp-eyed tart, who laughed raunchily as she teased: "Well, if it isn't Master Jifan's junior jockey! Hey, with all those women lying around your master's house, so bored they're rusting between their legs, what are you doing here with us?"

Grandpa told her, "I'm not here for myself, I'm here on behalf of Master Jifan."

Grandpa's declaration caused a joyous uproar among the whores, who chirped excitedly among themselves, "What a windfall! Master Jifan spends money like it's going out of style—if you manage to please him, you'll make a year's worth of pocket money in one night!"

But the madam of the brothel interrupted and said, "It's New Year, a public holiday, and my girls have worked the whole year long. Even if they were made of iron they would have been worn down by the pounding they've taken. Let them rest today."

My grandpa said, "It's not every day that Master Jifan gets an urge like this. Don't be stupid and miss the boat. You know what they say: 'Opportunity knocks but once!' "

The madam forced an obsequious smile and said, "Seeing as how it's Master Jifan who is requesting our services, how can we refuse? But, children, don't accuse me of being greedy and hardhearted!"

The tarts all burst out at once: "Not to worry, Mother dear, we'd be delighted and honored to let Master Jifan pound us with his magical wand."

"So, Little Master," the madam turned to my grandpa and asked, "who'll it be? I've got five girls here—which one does Master Jifan have his eyes on?"

"All of them," Grandpa answered. "Have them wash up, get dressed, and wait outside. I'll send a carriage to pick them up in a little while."

Big Uncle told us that Grandpa took care of the business at hand with his usual efficiency and finesse. In no time at all he had made the rounds of the whole district and picked out twenty-eight whores. Then he went to the main street and hired about a dozen curtained sedan chairs and saw to it that the women were loaded on, two or three to a carriage. At last they were ready!—a dozen sedan chairs, a dozen sturdy mules, a dozen muscular drivers, all lined up single file in front of the county hall. Then they began to march down the street in a grand, noisy procession. So many people milled around to watch that the broad thoroughfare was narrowed into a single lane. Enjoying the attention of the crowds and well aware of whom they were transporting, the drivers got into the spirit of things and worked up a full head of steam, cracking their whips and yelling "Whoa!" and "Halloa!" as they urged their animals on. As the sedan chairs whizzed along, now and then one of the whores would lift up the carriage curtains and smile suggestively at the people watching their parade. From the sidelines some brash and thick-skinned onlooker would call out: "Hey, girls, where are you off to?" And the whores would yell back: "We're off to ring in the New Year with Master Jifan!"

Big Uncle told us that Grandpa was right at the head of the procession, riding atop the big roan stallion until they arrived at the front gate of Master Jifan's estate. Dismounting, he told the women to wait outside and went in alone to report to his master. When he heard that my grandpa had brought back twenty-eight whores, Master Jifan clapped his hands in glee and cried out ecstatically, "Excellent! Excellent! Twenty-eight celestial bodies deigning to grace our humble abode! Han San, you've really outdone yourself. You'll be handsomely rewarded for this. Now, quick! Escort the divine maidens into the house."

Big Uncle said there was a great hall on the estate that could easily seat a hundred people for a banquet—just the right place to hold the Assembly of Celestials. Back then, electric lights were still unheard of in Gaomi, so Master Jifan had Grandpa go out and buy several hundred of the biggest candles he could find—as big around as a person's arm—and place them in every nook and cranny of the hall. Even though it was still light outside, Master Jifan ordered that they be lit immediately. Soon the room was ablaze with an incandescent glow and thick with an oily black smoke, so much so that one might well think the hall was burning down. Master Jifan also had Grandpa send messengers to all the important military and government officials in the county as well as prominent members of the local gentry and literati, inviting them to attend the Assembly of Celestials. By that time the whole town was abuzz with the news that Master Jifan had just summoned twenty-eight whores to his house, and all those eminent personages, like everyone else, were scratching their heads trying to figure out what Master Jifan was up to now. So when the invitations arrived, they of course jumped at the opportunity and could barely contain their urge to rush over to the house right away. A few of the more scrupulous gentlemen might have harbored some brief misgivings about the affair. After all, it was New Year's Day, and one would not want to profane one's ancestors with any improprieties. Then again, if Master Jifan dared host such an event, wouldn't it be unseemly not to attend? And so all of the invitations were eagerly accepted.

That evening, in the brilliantly lit hall on Master Jifan's estate, a host of eminent personages gathered for the Assembly of Celestials. Circulating among the guests, the twenty-eight whores affected a coquettish innocence while exchanging double entendres and lascivious suggestions with the distinguished gentlemen. They carried on with round after round of toasts and drinking games, and before long all the men had taken off their cloaks of propriety and were panting with wolfish lust and excitement. Any thought of their ancestors' spirits had long since been banished to never-never land.

As the night wore on and the candles burned ever brighter, the blush on the women's cheeks deepened with wine. Dissolute with drink and desire, they turned their wanton eyes on their imperturbably elegant and charming host. Some of the more impatient ones began to throw themselves into his lap, entwining their arms around his neck or his waist. Master Jifan instructed my grandpa to trim the candlewicks. Then he ordered that several large rugs be laid out on the floor in the center of the hall.

When all these instructions had been carried out, Master Jifan turned to the whores and said, "Now, ladies, take off your clothes and lie down on the rugs."

Laughing and giggling, the twenty-eight whores wriggled out of their silk and satin finery and lay down on the carpets. Stark naked, they sprawled out in a row of tangled limbs and torsos, twenty-eight wide-open flowers waiting for Master Jifan to sample their nectar.

On that long, cold winter night, huddled around a glowing brazier, we listened raptly as Big Uncle told us the strange tales of Master Jifan's life and times.

"Was he crazy?" I asked.

"Nonsense, nonsense," Big Uncle replied. "From what your Grandpa told me, Master Jifan was a man of superb intelligence, well-versed in all the classics and ancient schools of philosophy, in military affairs and agriculture, in divination and medicine. He knew all there was to know about astronomy and geography, mathematics and accounting. How could a man like that be crazy?"

"If he wasn't crazy, why was he always doing such weird things?"

Big Uncle declared, "As someone who had read all there was to read, Master Jifan had finally figured out the ways and workings of the world. If you want to know what a sage is, you need look no further than Master Jifan."

Actually, we had heard these stories so many times that we knew them all by heart. But we never got tired of hearing them again and would eagerly prod Big Uncle to go on.

"Big Uncle, tell us about the time Master Jifan enlightened our grandpa," my older brother would implore.

Even though Big Uncle was beginning to tire, his eyes would light up again at this request. "Well, one day, when your grandpa was twenty, he accompanied Master Jifan on a stroll through town. Master Jifan turned to him and said, 'Han San, you're twenty years old now. It's time for you to go out on your own.'

"With tears rolling down his cheeks, your grandpa begged, 'Please, master, let me stay a few more years.' But all Master Jifan would say was, 'Even the most bountiful feast must come to an end.' As they walked along, they came to a large honey locust, and at the foot of the tree they saw two armies of ants fighting over a little green worm, pulling it back and forth as in a game of tug-of-war. Master Jifan turned to your Grandpa and asked, 'Do you understand, Han San?' Your Grandpa shook his head and said no. Then Master Jifan lifted one foot and stomped on the ants, grinding them under his heel for good measure. Once more he asked, 'Now do you understand, Han San?' Your Grandpa replied that yes, he did. But Master Jifan said, 'Let it be. In truth, you don't understand. If you don't understand, you have understood.' "

"Did our grandpa really not understand what Master Jifan was getting at?" I asked.

Big Uncle gave me an oblique reply: "If a person wants to understand what it all means, he must study hard and read all the books there are to read. As for you children, you have a long road ahead of you yet."

Next, my older brother asked, "Uncle, did you really watch Master Jifan's photographic memory in action?"

"Why, of course," Big Uncle said. "You don't think I made it up, do you? It was back in the days before our family's fortunes took a turn for the worse, and we were still living in the house in town. One day, I was reading the book *Classics of Epistolary Art* when your grandpa brought Master Jifan over for a visit. Master Jifan asked me what I was reading, so I handed him the book. He took it, leafed through it, and gave it back to me. I said, 'Master, is it true what my Dad says, that you can remember every word you read?' Master Jifan smiled and said, 'Do you want to test me?' I felt embarrassed and grinned sheepishly. He took the book again and read through it page by page. When he had finished, he handed it to me, saying, 'Follow along in the book while I recite it for you.' I listened as he recited back to me every word on every page, from the first one to the last, without a single mistake, without so much as a stutter. When he was finished, your Grandpa gave me a good dressing down. 'You impudent brat, how dare you question Master Jifan! You get down on your knees this instant and apologize to him.' I fell to my knees in a hurry, but Master Jifan helped me up and said, with a chuckle, 'I'm getting old, my brain's not what it used to be.' "

We heaved a collective sigh of awe and admiration. "What a genius! A true genius!" That's what we would always say when we got to the end of this particular episode.

Big Uncle would never tell us the ending of the story about Master Jifan and the whores. He would always get right up to the climax, and then stop right there. But we never pestered him about it. Actually, we already knew what happened after that: the twenty-eight whores took off all their clothes and lay down in a row on the carpets. Dumbstruck with amazement, all the distinguished gentlemen and eminent worthies stared open-mouthed at their host. Our Grandpa said that Master Jifan proceeded to take off first his shoes and then his stockings. Next, he walked barefoot on the bellies of the twenty-eight naked whores, once across the whole row and back again.

And then Master Jifan said, "Han San, give each of them a hundred silver dollars. Now summon the carriages and send them home."

TRANSCENDENCE

AND THE

FAX MACHINE

Ye Si

(*Translated by Jeanne Tai*)

I am thirty-seven years old and single, I work as a research assistant at
the Institute for Cultural Research, and I moonlight at an
accounting firm. In my spare time I like to read the Bible, the
Koran, and Buddhist sutras. My field used to be British and
American literature. But with the emergence of a Chinese
Studies faction among the local scholars and the importance
they attached to bibliographic citations, I, not being on particularly good terms with these people, began to find my
name and my writings excluded from every bibliography and
anthology they had a hand in preparing. As time went by I
began to sense the presence of bibliographies no matter
where I went; no matter what I was doing, there always
seemed to be an enormous pen hanging right over me,
which, with one fell swoop, would make me vanish into thin
air. After that I began reading anything and everything. I even
began subscribing to certain French journals, including

several that focused on religion and literature. Perhaps people involved in the study of religion are more tolerant and considerate; in any case, I would occasionally send them an unsolicited article, and to my surprise they would always respond.

I have remained single for one reason only: I am not very good at interpersonal relationships. Before the age of thirty-five, I used to idealize every woman I met, seeing only the good points and finding plenty of things to love in each of them. And, of course, it always ended in absolute disaster for me. After thirty-five, by way of compensating, I found many faults and shortcomings in every female I came across. Under these conditions I no longer fell in love with anyone. My heart was calm and serene, like a placid lake, and I expected to live like this happily ever after.

But something unexpected always happens.

One drizzly evening I was out with my photographer friend Li Biansheng. Over a couple of drinks, I mentioned to him that I had been invited by some French scholars to submit a paper for their upcoming conference on Literature and Transcendence, but that corresponding with them by mail was time-consuming and very inconvenient. Ah Sheng[1] was convinced that the solution to my problem was to get a fax machine. Later, while we were walking around Causeway Bay,[2] both of us feeling kind of light-headed, he suddenly said: "Wait, weren't you going to buy a fax machine?" And he took me to an electronics appliance store. It was just like what my girlfriends used to tell me: If you wander around aimlessly in Causeway Bay, you'll always end up buying something. Since Ah Sheng knew the manager, it didn't matter that I didn't have a cent on me. By the time I left the store I was no longer lonesome—I was on my way home with my fax machine.

Her looks were nothing out of the ordinary, but somehow they became more and more pleasing to my eye, perhaps because I was growing, uh, accustomed to her face. I understand that a fax machine is just an instrument for the facsimile transmission of documents—nothing to make a big fuss over, really. But ever since the day she came home with me, my life changed. When I finished a piece of writing I would no longer have to wander all over the city looking for a real mailbox among all the toylike receptacles on the street, or stamp my

1. An affectionate diminutive for Biansheng.
2. A busy shopping district in Hong Kong.

feet in frustration in front of the locked doors of the post office, or dodge streetcars while I search for some safe deposit for that bundle of intimate, red-hot confidences I was holding in my hands. No more would I be condemned to roam all creation like a lost soul, stopping in at some telecommunications center or the Foreign Correspondents' Club for a temporary respite, a chance encounter; never again would I dread the emptiness of an endless weekend or an idle weekday. Though the world outside be filled with deception, and communication between people fraught with traps for the unwary, I could be certain of at least one thing when I got home: she would always be there, faithfully receiving, transmitting, ingesting, an absolutely trustworthy connection linking me and places far away.

What a comfort it was to insert a piece of paper inside her and know that its soul would appear on the other side of the world. My beloved written word was now able to stand its ground against the evanescent waves of sound and speech. My most personal musings could be flipped over and, in total privacy, poured into a solitary black earpiece. Even the nastiest customs official was powerless to intercept and examine those electromagnetic waves wafting through space. And wonder of wonders, there was even material evidence of my intellectual intercourse with the world of the spirit: afterwards there would always be a corporeal copy for my files—a facsimile record, a faithful fuss-free summary of my various mental odysseys. Even if my memory were to fail me in the future, I would still be able to retrace with certainty the footsteps of my soul.

Furthermore, I was now spared the trials and tribulations of daily living. No longer would I have to listen to this one's sighs over the telephone or watch tears trickling down that one's cheeks. Pettiness and jealousies were less likely to ensnarl me when conveyed on paper. No more would I have to answer calls from cantankerous friends who were fond of slamming down the phone with a suddenness and vehemence that always left my ears ringing. Indeed, thanks to a simple fax machine, my life had undergone a complete transformation. I could now go to sleep, my mind at ease, and when, in the middle of a dream, I should hear her muffled coos and murmurs, they would sound like a soothing lullaby reassuring me that all was well.

Little by little I became quite dependent on her. It had been a long time since I had opened my heart to anyone, but she looked so innocent and guileless it was almost inevitable that she would become my one true friend. At work, caught in the daily skirmishes of office politics, I couldn't help but think of her, of her cheerful and open countenance, of how she seemed to represent a kind of communion that was more genuine, more real. After work I wanted nothing else except to be with her. I would make a plate of spaghetti or a salad and pour myself a glass of red wine, relieved just to be in her company. Together we would listen to some music or watch some television. She was the only one who supported me in my dealings with the transcendental world. On days when there were no incoming messages, I would switch on her copier mode and feed her what I had written, and it would be reproduced automatically. Expressions such as "the concept of transcendence in Romantic poetry" or "Kant's views on the categorical imperative" would emerge on that special paper bearing her unique scent, and to me it was as though she were voicing her concurrence, perhaps even her compliments, and giving me an enormous boost in self-confidence.

Precisely because of all this, our first tiff came as that much more of a blow. Right in the middle of a transmission she abruptly clammed up, as if in silent protest against the synopsis of my paper. Several pages went swishing through the machine all stuck together—did she find my style too verbose? Quickly I picked up my manuscript from the floor and reread it from a new perspective. Yes, perhaps points two and three could be combined, and the middle section on page two could be deleted. Maybe some of the issues were a little too abstract? And the conclusion, yes, it was rather abstruse, especially for the younger generation (I had to keep in mind that my fax machine was the product of a new generation and no doubt shared many of the values and viewpoints of her peers). Or was my conclusion too definite, too dogmatic, or perhaps too distant? So I sat down and revised the whole thing, cutting it down from four pages to three. When I tried sending it again, the first page went through smoothly, but the second one stopped halfway through the machine. I waited for a long time but finally had to redial and feed it through again. In the same way, the third page also stopped in the middle of the transmission, and once more I had to resend the whole page. After it was all over I got the usual message: "Transmission OK," but I couldn't be absolutely sure that the pages actually got where they were supposed to go. Was my machine protesting something or other by her silence and strike today? Nervous and uneasy, I fell to speculating about all sorts of possible reasons.

After that, things went on pretty much as before, as though nothing unusual had happened—until one day, two or three weeks later, when I tried to send a letter and a bibliography to my usual distant destination. Halfway through the transmission, in the middle of the second page, the machine stopped again. When I pulled out the pages and put them back into the feeder for resending, the paper in the roller began to turn instead: the machine was receiving a transmission from somewhere, abruptly cutting off my devout report. As the paper emerged from the other end and slowly flattened out, I began to see a multitude of messages: emigrants[3] selling their furniture at bargain prices . . . used cars for sale . . . are you in the market for a reliable maid working by the hour . . . *udon* noodles[4] . . . freshly husked new rice . . . a surcharge on taxi fares. They were like installments of a serial, and the story they were telling was not mine. After reading them over carefully, I was convinced they were not some kind of response sent by my far-off correspondents. Most likely my telephone number had found its way onto a master list somewhere, and I was now being sent the gospel according to some advertising agency or communications company.

A practical joke? Maybe. Then again, maybe not. When these messages began coming through a second time, I thought to myself: could there be some special significance, some larger meaning to my being singled out like this? So I studied these faxes even more closely, examining at length each and every sign, symbol, signifier. There didn't seem to be any connection whatsoever between these messages and the texts that I had sent out previously, but on the other hand, maybe there was. Yet what exactly was the nature of that connection? I read and reread the advertisements as they poured out, one after another, in a seemingly endless stream. As for transmitting my own thoughts— well, by then I couldn't get a word in edgewise.

The whirring and humming finally stopped and the communications from the outside world came to an end, for the time being at

3. Since 1984, when the British agreed to return the colony of Hong Kong to mainland China, there has been a widespread trend among Hong Kong citizens to emigrate before the scheduled Chinese takeover in 1997.
4. A kind of Japanese [buckwheat] noodles.

least. I picked up the pages I had set aside earlier and was about to feed them into the fax machine when, for some unknown reason, I began to feel a little apprehensive—I couldn't send them on their way without looking them over once more. But having just read all that other stuff, I couldn't help feeling an urge to revise the discussion of my proposed paper that I had in front of me. I couldn't help thinking that it was not concise enough, that it carried too much intellectual baggage and was too idealistic, that as a result it sounded unfocused, even a little spacey. So I revised it yet again.

But when I faxed my letter to the abbé in Provence, I inadvertently included the advertising circular on plumbing services. Not only that—when I sent a message to the number on the plumbing ad, asking them not to fax me all that junk mail every day, I included, again inadvertently, the letter I had sent earlier to the French cleric. We all work under too much pressure and end up leaving everything to the last minute. Well, it wasn't until after I had hastily transmitted both of my communiqués that I realized what a blunder I had made, but by then it was too late. The reactions on both ends were just about diametrically opposed. The lofty scholar-critics expressed their concern and misgiving over what they saw as my inclination to "superficiality" and "frivolity," because in their view I had introduced mundane and vulgar conceits into what ought to have been a transcendental reverie. The ad agency's reply was predictably terse and impersonal, but even so I could sense the writer's annoyance at having been accosted with meditations on another world, the inordinate gravity of which seemed to embarrass him or her immensely. The respondent didn't quite know what to say, since there were no words in the world of advertising to speak of such things. But the frosty tone clearly insinuated that I was a religious fanatic completely out of touch with reality.

The paper was much more difficult to write than I had imagined, not only because such is the case with most conference papers but also because I was much too entangled in the affairs of this world, so much so that it was next to impossible for me to find an unoccupied corner of my mind in which to regroup and reorganize my otherworldly ruminations. The infighting at the office, my mother's rheumatism, the budget for the next fiscal year that I had to prepare posthaste—I was under so much pressure I could hardly breathe. With the deadline for the submission of papers looming just ahead, one after another the clergymen and the professors sent me anxious faxes asking why I hadn't been heard from in so long. Racking my brains, I laboriously composed an abject, mealymouthed reply explaining my situation. When I punched in the number for the transcontinental call, however, the machine emitted a loud beep but never got through to the other end. It was as if I had sent a series of signals to a planet in a distant galaxy, only to find that, in traversing the intervening vortices of light and shadow and color and sound, my message had somehow gone astray and eventually disappeared without a trace.

I stayed up several nights in a row; even so, I barely managed to finish my first draft the day after the deadline. There were still a few footnotes that had to be checked and several points in the body of the paper that could be further elucidated, but I was already exhausted. Dragging my bone-weary body to the fax machine, I glanced up at the clock on the wall and realized that it was half past four in the morning.

Slowly and tenderly I inserted my manuscript—still warm to the touch, perhaps from the heat of my exertions—into the machine, taking care not to cause her any pain or discomfort. I caressed her dainty, delicate buttons as I gently moved the sheets of paper in and out of the feeder. Afterwards, I lay on top of her, waiting quietly, hoping fervently that nothing would go wrong this time. I prayed that my message would get through to them, and theirs to me. I longed for the moment when the short, shrill notes of her calling mode would modulate into the rapturous and blissful cadences of contact, coupling, communication. In my quest to consummate the connection, I shuffled the pages, shifted them around, tried this, that, and the other position. But alas, it was to be no more than a series of futile knocks, one unanswered call after another, like someone crying out in the wilderness or searching in vain for home in the infinite void of outer space. When all was said and done, some sensitive yet crucial link, some delicate and subtle liaison was never established, and the pearly gates never opened for me.

No matter; we would try again. In my mind's eye I could see those exalted clerics and academics basking in the beautiful Provençal countryside, taking in a glorious sunset or lifting their voices in songs of praise, unencumbered by the toils and troubles that bedevil common people like us. With the echoes from their hosannas reverberating in my ears, I sank into an exhausted sleep. The heady bouquet of a good Bordeaux, the dazzling palette of the impressionists—these things permeated my dreams as I drifted in and out, in and out of a fitful slumber.

My paper on literature and transcendence never did get faxed. Instead, my machine eventually began to flash a series of red lights, followed by a green light, then another red light. Worse, she started making all kinds of strange clucking noises. Finally she spewed out a puff of white smoke. Heavens, she'd come down with something!

I was completely distraught. The deadline was well past, but I still hoped to make it somehow. I really wanted to connect with that sublime transcendental world I so fervently believed in, to communicate my ideals and aspirations to others. At the same time, I felt very strongly that the most important task at hand was to take care of this earthly, earthbound fax machine. In her hour of need, there could be no doubt that my duty was to help her through her crisis and see that she recovered completely.

So I tried everything: I gave her massages and shiatsu treatments, fed her all kinds of mild paper purgatives, took her pulse and checked her heartbeat. To help her clean out her gastrointestinal system, I scooped up whatever sheets of paper were at hand and gave them to her for a diagnostic run-through. That was how a dissertation about transcendence was intermixed with directives on nutritional therapy and plumbing repair. When I took her pulse again, pressing gently against her acupoints, this hodgepodge of a composition went sailing through the machine. I had no idea where those incongruous pages would end up nor what the reactions of those who received them might be. Anyway, such things were not my concern. Caught as I was between transcendence and the fax machine, all I could do was to take care of the most urgent matters to the best of my ability, given the circumstances, and hope that somehow through all this I would be able to find a way out.

ONE KIND

OF REALITY

Yü Hua

(Translated by Jeanne Tai)

1

*T*hat morning was no different from any other morning; that morning it was raining lightly. It had been raining off and on for more than a week, and Shangang and Shanfeng felt that sunny skies were far, far away, as distant as their childhoods.

At the first light of day, the two brothers had heard their mother muttering something about her bones turning all mildewy. Her muttering dripped and splattered just like the rain. Still lying in bed, they listened to the sound of her footsteps shuffling toward the kitchen.

She snapped several chopsticks in half as she told her two daughters-in-law, "At night I often hear sounds in my body like chopsticks breaking in half." The two younger women didn't reply. They were busy making breakfast. She continued, "I know it's my bones breaking one by one."

At that point the two brothers got up. "What a pain!" each

of them muttered as he emerged from his bedroom. They probably meant the never-ending rain, but they may also have been thinking about their mother's rainlike complaining.

Then, as usual, they all sat down around the table to a breakfast of rice porridge and *youtiao.*[1]

The old lady was a strict vegetarian, and on the table in front of her was a small dish of vegetables that she had pickled herself. She was no longer complaining about her mildewing bones. Instead she said, "My stomach feels like there's moss growing inside."

The two brothers pictured the faintly luminiscent green moss, crisscrossed by earthworms, that grew on the rims of wells and in the crevices of dilapidated walls. Their wives didn't seem to have heard what the old lady said, because the look on their faces was as dull as mud.

Pipi, Shangang's four-year-old son, did not sit at the table with the grownups. Instead, he ate his breakfast seated on a little plastic stool. His breakfast did not include *youtiao,* but his mother had added some sugar to his rice porridge.

Earlier, he had climbed on a chair next to his grandmother in order to sneak a few pickles. Right away his grandmother had begun to cry, as she did even now. Over and over she muttered, "You'll get plenty of food in the years to come, I don't have much time left to eat." His father had quickly yanked him back onto the plastic stool. That's why Pipi was feeling rather cranky at the moment. Banging his spoon against the rim of his bowl, he began to yell, "There's too much, I can't finish."

Again and again he yelled, his voice growing louder and louder, but the grown-ups kept on ignoring him, so he decided to cry. At the same time his baby cousin began to bawl. Pipi watched as his auntie carried the baby to one side to change his diapers and went over and stood next to them. The baby was crying very agitatedly, and with each heave of his body what Pipi called "the little thing that pee comes out of" would jiggle back and forth. "He's a boy," Pipi announced to his auntie, quite pleased with himself. But Auntie ignored him and, after changing the baby's diaper, went back to her seat at the table. Pipi stood on the same spot without moving. By this

1. Fritters of twisted dough—a common breakfast dish.

time his little cousin had stopped crying and was staring at him with eyes that looked like marbles. Feeling rather glum now, Pipi wandered off, but instead of returning to his little stool he went to the window. He was so short he had to lift his head high to look out. The rain beat against the window and slithered down the glass like earthworms.

By then breakfast was over. Shangang watched as his wife wiped the table with a rag, while Shanfeng watched his wife carrying their baby into the bedroom. The door was left ajar, and soon she came out again and went into the kitchen. So Shanfeng turned his gaze on his sister-in-law's hand as she cleaned the tabletop. On the back of her hand were several veins that by turns came into and disappeared from view. Shanfeng stared at it for quite some time until he lifted his head, glanced over at the raindrops crisscrossing the windowpane, and said to Shangang, "This rain feels like it's been coming down for a hundred years."

Shangang replied, "Yes, it feels like it's been that long."

Their mother began to mutter again. But now her voice sounded rather faint because she was back in her own room. Then she began to cough, in an exaggerated way, and after that came the noise of her spitting, a noise that sounded kind of rubbery and elastic. They knew she must have spat right into the palm of her hand and was now scrutinizing the phlegm for signs of blood. They could just imagine the scene.

After a while their wives came out of the bedrooms, each carrying two umbrellas. It was time to go to work. The two brothers stood up, each taking an umbrella from his wife, and the four of them went out of the house and down the alley together, as they always did. As usual, the two brothers headed west while their wives went east. Walking side by side, the two brothers seemed like strangers. They moved along in silence until they reached the entrance to the middle school, and then Shanfeng turned onto the bridge while Shangang continued straight ahead. As for their wives, they traveled together only a short while, as far as the end of the alley. Then they ran into some of their coworkers, and, after the usual greetings, joined their colleagues and continued on their separate ways.

A long time after they left, Pipi was still standing on the same spot, listening to the rain. He could already distinguish four different kinds of sound made by the rain. The sound of raindrops as they fell on the roof was like his father's rapping him on the head with his knuckles, while raindrops falling on the tree leaves seemed to be doing a hop, skip, and jump. The other two kinds of sound came from the concrete courtyard in front of the house and the pond in the back; compared to the clear, crisp sound of raindrops hitting the water in the pond, the sound of rain falling onto concrete was heavy and dull.

Finally Pipi turned around, crawled under the table and out the other side, and walked slowly to the door of his grandmother's room. The door was ajar, and Grandmother was sitting like a corpse on the edge of the bed. Pipi declared, "There are four rains falling right now." When the grandmother heard this she burped loudly, and the boy sniffed an awful odor in the air. Lately Grandmother's burps had been getting smellier and smellier. He turned away quickly and headed toward his baby cousin.

The baby was lying in a bassinet, staring up at the ceiling with a smile on his face. The boy told his little cousin, "There are four rains falling right now."

The baby must have heard something, because his tiny legs began to move, and his eyes also began to rove about, but they didn't find Pipi. The boy brushed his hand against his cousin's face and found it soft and fluffy, just like cotton. Then, seized by an uncontrollable urge, he gave one cheek an energetic pinch. With a loud wail the baby began to cry.

The exquisite ear-piercing cry filled Pipi with a nameless pleasure. For a while he gazed at his cousin with a mixture of surprise and joy, and then he gave him a vigorous slap, right on the face. He had often seen his father hitting his mother like this. After being boxed on the ears, the baby all of a sudden gagged. His mouth gaped silently for a long time, and then a noise rushed out like the sound of a violent wind pushing open a window. This sound was loud and pleasing to the ear, and it excited Pipi enormously. But not long afterwards the crying began to taper off, so he gave his cousin another slap. In self-defense the baby clutched frantically at the air, leaving two bloody scratches on the back of Pipi's hand, but the boy didn't even notice them. He only knew that this time the slap didn't make the baby catch his breath; the noise merely got a little louder, and it didn't sound any-where near as thrilling as before. So he slapped the baby again, with all the might he could muster. No big reaction—just more of the same sounds, except that the crying became a little more drawn out. So he abandoned this tactic and, grabbing the baby by the throat, began to throttle him. The baby clawed back desperately at Pipi's hands. When Pipi finally let go, he was rewarded with just the kind of crying he wanted to hear. He did this over and over again, first choking the baby and then letting go, reveling in the explosive screams that burst forth every time. Eventually, though, when he loosened his hands around his cousin's throat, the baby no longer cried with the same intensity and passion. All he did was open his mouth and let out short, tremulous gasps. Pipi soon lost interest and wandered away.

Once again he went over and stood under the window. By now there were no longer any droplets of water running down the windowpane, just the crisscrossing traces of the paths they had taken, like so many little roads. Pipi began to imagine cars zooming down the roads and colliding with each other. Then he discovered several leaves fluttering on the glass, and immediately after that he saw countless little points of golden light flashing on the windowpane. He was filled with awe. Right away he pushed open the window. He wanted to let those leaves come inside and quiver, he wanted those flecks of light to jump in and flutter and dance all around him. And the light did rush in, not in little droplets like rain, but in a flood. He discovered that the skies had cleared, and sunlight now coated him from head to toe. He could see those leaves so clearly now. The elm tree in the yard was reaching out towards him, its foliage a bright shiny green, and each time a droplet of water dribbled off the tip of a leaf there would be a graceful little dance, which delighted the boy so much he burst out laughing.

Then he returned to the side of the bassinet. "The sun's come out," he said to his cousin. By now the baby seemed to have forgotten everything that had just happened and was looking at him smilingly. Pipi said, "Do you want to go see the sun?" The baby thrust his legs in the air and began to call out, "Ah! Ah!" So Pipi asked, "But can you walk?" The baby stopped hollering and began to gaze at the boy, stretching out his arms as if he wanted to be picked up. "I know, you want me to carry you," Pipi said. With a little effort, he picked the baby up from the bassinet, holding him the same way he carried his little plastic stool. He felt as though he had his arms around a slab of meat. "Ah! Ah!" his cousin began calling out again. "You're very happy, right?" Pipi asked. Then, with some difficulty, he carried the baby outside the house.

At that moment the sound of firecrackers came from a house far away, while in the courtyard next door a charcoal stove was being lit, and a cloud of thick dark smoke billowed over the wall toward them. The baby was not interested in the sun, but when he saw the thick smoke he was so pleased he began to squeal and holler. The older boy was not much interested in the sun either; a few sparrows had careered down the roof and come to rest on the branches of the tree, which were bobbing up and down to the sounds of their chattering.

Then Pipi had a growing feeling of heaviness, a feeling that he associated with the thing he was carrying in his arms. So he let go. As the thing dropped to the ground he heard two sounds coming from it at the same time, one dull, the other crisp, and after that nothing at all. Now he felt free and easy. He watched several sparrows hopping from branch to branch, the leaves swaying back and forth like fans with each tremor of the branches. After standing there for a while he began to feel thirsty, so he turned and ambled back into the house.

At first he couldn't find anything to drink. There was a glass on the table in the bedroom, but it was empty. He went into the kitchen, where he found two covered porcelain mugs on the table, but he couldn't reach them to see whether there was any water inside. So he walked out again and came back with his plastic stool. As he was picking up the stool, he suddenly thought of his little cousin. He remembered that he had just carried him outside the house, but here he was all by himself. He was somewhat puzzled by this, but he didn't give it any more thought. Climbing atop the little stool, he pulled the two mugs toward him. Both mugs felt kind of heavy, and he found water in both of them. He took a few sips from each, and remembering the sparrows, he walked outside to see what they were up to. But there were no more birds hopping among the elm's branches. They had all flown away. He noticed that the cement had taken on a whitish tint, and right after that his eye fell on his little cousin. The baby was lying there on his back with his arms and legs sprawled lazily on the ground. Pipi walked over, squatted down, and gave him a little push, but the baby didn't move. Then the boy saw a little pool of blood on the patch of concrete under his cousin's head. He bent down for a closer look and found that the blood was coming from the baby's skull. He also noticed that the blood flowed onto the ground, slowly opening up, almost like a flower. Some ants were scurrying over from every direction, but as soon as they reached the pool of blood they stopped. Only one ant went around it and climbed onto the baby's hair, following a few strands caked with dried blood, and proceeded all the way into the skull, entering it at the point from which blood was trickling. It was only then that Pipi stood up, looked around blankly, and went inside the house.

Seeing that Grandmother's door was still ajar, he walked over to it and found her sitting on the bed, as before. "Little Brother is asleep," he told her. When Grandmother turned her head to look at him, he saw that her eyes were again full of tears. He found her endless crying quite boring, so he went back into the kitchen and sat on the little stool. It wasn't until then that he felt the pain on the back of his right hand. He had to think for a long time before he remembered that it was his baby cousin who had scratched him earlier. Then he remembered how he had carried his cousin outside and had let him go. Remembering was such hard work that he had to stop and rest his head against the wall. Right away he fell fast asleep.

Much later, the old lady finally got up onto her feet. Then she heard the noises inside her body again, noises that sounded just like chopsticks splintering. As soon as they burst out of her sagging skin the sounds would become extremely soft, but even though she was a little deaf, she could still hear them clearly. Her eyes brimmed with tears again. She was certain she didn't have very much longer to live, since every day a few more bones were breaking. Soon, she thought, she wouldn't even be able to lie down, let alone stand or sit. By then she wouldn't even have a complete skeleton, just a pile of broken bones of all lengths, shapes, and sizes, jostling recklessly against each other. By then, perhaps, the bones of her feet would be jutting out from her belly, while the bones of her arms would be boring into her moss-filled stomach.

She hobbled out of the bedroom, and the bone-breaking sounds stopped. But she was still worried and afraid. At that moment the sunshine pouring in from the wide-open window and door almost blinded her. Then she saw something that sparkled and gleamed a little distance away. She couldn't tell what it was, so she walked over to the door. As the sun shone in on her, she noticed that her hands were frighteningly yellow. Then she saw the yellowish heap lying straight ahead. She still didn't know what it was, so she stepped over the door-sill and slowly walked closer. Before she could make out this heap as her grandchild she caught sight of the pool of blood. Terrified, she hurried back into her own bedroom.

2

The baby's mother left work early to get home. She worked as an accountant at a factory that made baby carriages. Just before lunchtime, she had begun for no apparent reason to worry that something bad would happen to her child, and, unable to sit still any longer, she told her coworkers that she was leaving to check on her baby. On the way home she grew intensely uneasy. When she opened the door to the courtyard, her worst fears were confirmed.

She saw her son lying in the sunshine, right on top of his shadow. Now that her fears had come true she seemed to fall into a trance. For some time she stood in the doorway, and after a while she thought she saw a pool of blood on the ground next to her son's head. In the sunshine the bloodstain and the body of her son lying there hardly looked real. At last she walked over and gingerly called out her son's name. There was no response. She felt somewhat relieved, as though the silence proved that that could not possibly be her son lying still on the ground. Then she straightened up and glanced at the sky. It was so bright it made her head spin and her eyes swim. With great difficulty she walked over to the house. When she got inside she found it gloomy and dark; it was also chilly. The door to her bedroom was wide open. She walked inside and stood before the dresser. Pulling open a drawer crammed with sweaters, she began to rummage around looking for something, but it wasn't there. So she opened the closet. Hanging inside were her overcoat and her husband's overcoat, but what she was looking for wasn't there either. After that she opened all the drawers in the desk but only glanced at them before walking away. Sitting in a chair, she began to scan the house. Her gaze skimmed over the closet she had just opened, slid across the glass top of the round table, slanted onto the sofa that could seat three across, then jumped out into the middle of the room. It was only then that she saw the bassinet. Startled, she jumped to her feet. The bassinet was empty, deserted; there was no trace of her son. Suddenly remembering the child lying in the yard, she dashed madly out of the house, but when she reached the body she was again at a loss. At that moment she thought of Shanfeng and turned and ran out of the compound.

Frantically she darted down the alley. She thought she saw some people coming from across the passageway to greet her, but she didn't acknowledge them. Pushing and shoving, she charged toward the intersection. But as soon as she reached it she stopped. A busy street lay in front of her, and she had no idea which way to turn. Her frustration and anxiety left her gasping for breath.

Just then Shanfeng came into view, walking in her direction as he talked with someone next to him. Now she knew what to do. She waited until she was sure that Shanfeng had seen her, and then she finally began to bawl. Not long after that she felt Shanfeng grabbing her by the arm and heard him ask, "What's wrong?" She opened her mouth, but nothing came out. She heard her husband ask, again, "What on earth is wrong?" And again she opened her mouth but couldn't say anything. "Did something happen to the baby?" By now her husband was beginning to shout. At last, and with much effort, she nodded her head. Letting go of her arm, Shanfeng left her behind and ran home by himself.

Now she, too, turned around and started for home. It seemed to her there were a lot of people around her, and many voices as well. She was walking very slowly. In a little while she saw her husband racing toward her with their son in his arms. He brushed against her as he ran by, and she turned around again. She wanted to hurry and catch up with her husband—she knew that he must be heading for the hospital—but she just couldn't walk any faster. By now she was no longer crying. At the intersection she again felt lost, and it was only after asking a passerby, who pointed west, that she remembered where the hospital was. As she trudged along the sidewalk, she felt like a leaf shaking and shuddering in the wind. It wasn't until she reached the department store that she began to recover from the numbness. She knew the hospital wasn't too far away now. But at that moment she saw her husband coming towards her, carrying their son. The stiff, rigid look on Shanfeng's face told her everything, and she began to wail once more. Shanfeng walked up to her and said, through gritted teeth, "Go cry at home." She didn't dare cry anymore. Holding onto Shanfeng's clothes, she followed him home.

When Shangang came home his wife was already in the kitchen. He walked into his own bedroom and sat on the sofa. He had nothing to do while he waited for lunch. Then Pipi came into the room as well. The boy had been awakened when his mother had come home. He was feeling chilly from head to toe and had complained about the cold to his mother. Preoccupied with making lunch, she had told him to just go put something on. He was trembling and shivering when he showed up in front of his father. Shangang was rather annoyed with the way his son looked.

"What's the matter with you?" asked Shangang.

"I'm cold," Pipi answered.

After that Shangang didn't pay any more attention to him. Instead, he turned his eyes away from his son and looked across at the window. When he saw that it was closed, he went over and opened it.

"I'm cold," Pipi said again.

Shangang ignored his son. Standing by the window, he felt very comfortable as the sun shone down on him.

At that moment Shanfeng came in carrying the baby in his arms, with his wife following behind. Shangang could tell from the looks on their faces that something had gone very wrong. The two brothers looked at each other for an instant, but neither spoke. Shangang heard their sluggish footsteps going into their room, and then came the loud slam of the door, confirming Shangang's suspicion.

Pipi said again, "I'm cold."

Shangang walked out of the bedroom and sat at the dinner table. His wife was bringing dishes of food from the kitchen. Pipi was already seated on the little plastic stool. From behind the door came the sound of Shanfeng's bellowing, and Shangang exchanged a look with his wife. "Should we go and tell them lunch is ready?" she asked, as she sat down at the table.

"Don't bother," Shangang replied.

Just then the old lady walked into the dining room carrying a dish of pickles. She never had to be called, she always showed up right on time at the dinner table.

In addition to the hollering coming from Shanfeng's room there was now another sound. Shangang recognized it for what it was. He continued to chew, but his eyes wandered outside through the wide-open windows and door. In a little while he heard his mother complaining next to him. Turning his head, he saw her staring with a worried frown at the bowl of rice, and then he heard her say, "I saw some blood." He turned his face away and continued to look at the sunshine outdoors.

Shanfeng carried the baby into his bedroom, set him down in the bassinet, and with a vicious kick slammed the door shut. Then, turning to look at his wife, who was already sitting on the edge of the bed, he spat, "Now you may cry."

But she stared at him vaguely, distractedly, as if she hadn't heard him. Her wide-open eyes seemed lifeless, though she was sitting up straight and tall.

Shanfeng repeated, "You may cry now."

All she did was move her eyes a little.

Shanfeng took one step toward her and asked, "Why aren't you crying?"

She finally stirred a bit, lifting her head to gaze wearily at Shanfeng's hair.

He went on, "Go ahead, I want to hear you cry now."

Two teardrops rolled out of her vacant eyes and slowly trickled down.

"Very good," Shanfeng said. "Now how about making some noise too?"

But she only wept silently.

Shanfeng finally exploded. Grabbing his wife by the hair, he howled, "Louder! Why can't you cry louder?"

Her tears stopped abruptly, and she stared at her husband with a frightened look.

"Tell me, who took him outside?" Shanfeng bellowed again.

She shook her head blankly.

"Do you mean to tell me the baby walked outside by himself?"

This time she neither shook her head nor nodded.

"You don't know anything, is that right?" Shanfeng had stopped hollering, and was now spitting out his words through clenched teeth.

She thought for a long time before nodding her head.

"So that means the baby was already lying there when you got home?"

She nodded again.

"That's why you ran out to look for me?"

Her tears began to trickle down again.

Shanfeng roared, "So why didn't you take him to the hospital right away? You wanted to let him die!"

She shook her head bewilderedly as she watched her husband brandishing his fist. In an instant she felt a heavy blow to her face and she fell onto the bed.

Shanfeng bent down, picked her up by her hair, and punched her in the face again, knocking her onto the floor. She still didn't utter a single sound.

When Shanfeng yanked her up a second time she covered her face with her hands. But this time he punched her right on the breast. The blow plunged her into a swirling darkness. She let out a sob that sounded more like a gasp as she toppled over.

When Shanfeng went to haul her up yet again he found her extraordinarily heavy, as though her body had fallen into the water and was sinking straight down. So he raised his knee to her belly to prop her up against the wall, and then he grabbed her hair and pounded her head savagely against the wall three times, bellowing all the while, "Why didn't you die instead?" When he finally stopped hollering and loosened his grip, her body slid down against the wall and onto the floor.

After that, Shanfeng opened the bedroom door and charged into the outer room. By they Shangang had already finished eating, but he was still sitting at the table. His wife was clearing the table, leaving two bowls and two pairs of chopsticks for Shanfeng and his wife. Shangang watched as his brother, a murderous look on his face, went up to their mother.

The old lady was still sitting in her seat, quite erect and proper, jabbering away about how she had seen some blood. Her bowl of rice had not even been touched.

Shanfeng asked his mother, "Who took my son outside?"

Lifting her head, the old lady glanced at her son and with a long face said, "I saw some blood."

"I'm asking you a question," Shanfeng screamed. "Who took my son outside?"

The old lady was not interested in her son's questions. She wished he would show some interest for a change in what she had to say, that she had seen blood, and she wished he would show some concern about her appetite. So once again she said, "I saw some blood."

Shanfeng grabbed his mother by the shoulders and began to shake her. "Who was it?"

Shangang, who had been sitting to one side, now opened his mouth. Calmly he said, "Don't do that."

Letting go of his mother's shoulders, Shanfeng turned around and screamed at Shangang, "My son is dead!"

Stunned, Shangang fell silent.

Shanfeng turned to his mother again. "Who was it?"

By then his mother, her eyes brimming with tears, had begun to jabber. "You've shaken me so hard all my bones are broken," she cried. Turning to Shangang, she muttered, "Come over here and listen. You can hear the bones breaking all over my body."

Shangang nodded and said, "Yes, I can hear them." But he didn't stir from his seat.

As if for the last time, Shanfeng bellowed, "Who took my son outside?"

At that moment Pipi, who had been sitting on the plastic stool the whole while, answered in a voice even louder than Shanfeng's: "I did." The first time Shanfeng asked his mother the question, Pipi had not paid any attention to him. Then, attracted by Shanfeng's manner and expression, he had begun to listen to Shanfeng's hollering, although it wasn't easy to understand. When he finally figured out what Shanfeng was screaming about, he cried out right away, unable to hold back any longer. Then, very pleased with himself, he stole a glance at his father.

Shanfeng immediately let go of his mother and headed for Pipi. The ferocious look on his face made Shangang jump to his feet.

Pipi was still sitting there on the stool, intrigued by Shanfeng's bloodshot eyes.

Shanfeng pulled up short in front of Shangang, screaming, "Get out of my way!"

Very calmly Shangang said, "He's still a child."

"I don't care."

"But I care," Shangang replied, his voice still calm and unruffled.

Aiming straight at Shangang's face, Shanfeng struck a fierce blow. Shangang's head bobbed once to the side but he remained on his feet.

"Don't do that," Shangang said.

"Get out of my way!" Shanfeng roared again.

"He's still a child," repeated Shangang.

"I don't care, I want him to pay with his life," Shanfeng said as he hit Shangang a second time. Shangang merely tilted his head again.

The whole scene stunned and stupefied the old lady. Over and over she shrieked, "Help! Help!" But she continued to sit right where she was, since Shanfeng's fists were still some distance away. Then Shangang's wife ran out of the kitchen and called to him, "What's going on?"

Shangang said to her, "Get Pipi out of here."

But Pipi, who was watching Shanfeng's fists with enthusiasm and fascination, didn't want to leave. He was elated that his father had managed to stay on his feet, and when his mother yanked him off the stool he began to bawl furiously.

At that moment Shanfeng turned around to hit Pipi, but Shangang fended off the blow with one hand and grabbed his brother's arms so that he couldn't get near the boy.

So Shanfeng raised his knee and slammed it into Shangang's belly. Shangang doubled over with pain and let out an involuntary moan. But still he held on tightly to Shanfeng's arms until he saw his wife and his son go into their bedroom and close the door. Only then did he let go of Shanfeng and stumble over and slump into a chair.

Shanfeng began kicking the door violently, howling all the while, "Give him to me!"

Shangang watched as Shanfeng kicked at the door like a madman. He could hear his wife calling to him from within the room, her voice mingled with the child's crying, but he sat there without moving. He sensed his mother get up to leave, muttering all the while as if she had a mouthful of cotton.

For some time Shanfeng continued to kick savagely at the door. Then he stopped and stared at it for a long while before finally turning around. Glancing at Shangang, he went over and sat down in a chair too, still nailing his eyes to the door. Shangang continued to sit there, watching him the whole time.

When Shangang felt that Shanfeng's breathing had calmed down, he got up and walked to the bedroom door. All the while he could feel Shanfeng's eyes on his back, piercing through his body. He knocked a few times, saying, "It's me, open the door," cocking his ear to hear if Shanfeng had stood up, but Shanfeng was sitting there without making a sound. Relieved, he continued to knock.

The door opened slowly, and he saw his wife's anxious face. "It's all right now," he said softly. Still, she closed the door behind him quickly.

"Look what he's done to you," she said, lifting her eyes up to his face.

Shangang gave a little smile and said, "I'll be all right in a few days."

As he talked, Shangang went over to his teary-eyed son and, caressing the top of his head, said, "Don't cry." Then he walked over and looked in the mirror next to the closet. He saw a stranger with a swollen and puffy face. He turned to his wife and asked, "Is that me?"

She didn't answer. She just stared at him in bewilderment.

"Bring me all our deposit books," he ordered.

She hesitated for a moment before doing what he had asked.

Lingering in front of the mirror, he discovered that, while his forehead remained intact and his chin was still the same, the rest of his face had turned against him.

His wife handed him the bankbooks, and as he took them, he asked, "How much money is there?"

"Three thousand yuan," she answered.

"That's all?" he asked unbelievingly.

"But we should keep at least a little for ourselves," she argued.

"Bring me everything," he said firmly.

She had no choice but to hand him the receipts for the other two thousand. Shangang put them all together and returned to the outer room.

Shanfeng was still sitting in the same place. When Shangang opened the door and came out, Shanfeng merely turned his gaze away from the door and fastened it onto Shangang's belly. Not until Shangang stopped in front of him did Shanfeng lift his eyes up to Shangang's chest, where he saw his brother's outstretched hand, clutching a dozen or so deposit books.

"Here's five thousand yuan," Shangang said. "Let's put this thing behind us."

"It won't do." Shanfeng's voice was hoarse, his words as hard as steel.

"This is all the money I've got," Shangang said.

"Get lost," Shanfeng said. He couldn't see the door because Shangang's chest was obstructing his view.

For a long time Shangang stood in front of Shanfeng, silently, all the while watching his brother's face, which had a dull, slow-witted look about it. Finally he turned around, walked back into the bedroom, and put the deposit books back in his wife's hands.

"He doesn't want them?" she asked in astonishment.

Shangang didn't answer. Instead, he walked over to his son, patted him gently on the head, and said, "Come with me."

Glancing at his mother, the boy stood up and asked Shangang, "Where are we going?"

All of a sudden she understood. Stepping in front of Shangang, she pleaded, "You can't do this. He'll beat him to death."

Shangang pushed her aside with one hand while with the other he led his son out of the room. Behind him he heard her saying, "Please, I beg you."

Then Shangang walked up to Shanfeng and, pushing his son forward, said, "Here, I'm handing him over to you."

Shanfeng lifted his head and looked at Pipi and Shangang. He seemed to want to stand up, but his body merely twitched a little. Then his gaze veered off and wandered out into the yard. And he saw the pool of blood. In the sunshine the blood glittered and sparkled. It seemed to be giving off a glow, a radiance just like that of the sun.

Pipi stood there, bored and bemused. He looked up at his father, whose face was expressionless, just like his uncle's. Then, peering around, he discovered that his mother had joined them and was also standing behind him.

Finally, Shanfeng got onto his feet and said to Shangang, "I want him to lick all that blood clean."

"And then?" Shangang asked.

Shanfeng hesitated for a moment before saying, "And then that's it."

"All right," Shangang nodded.

Pipi's mother broke in: "Let me lick it, he's just a child, he didn't know what he was doing."

Ignoring her completely, Shanfeng headed for the yard, dragging the boy behind him, and she followed them outside. Shangang wavered for a moment before going back into his room, but then he went over and stood by the bedroom window.

He watched as his wife went down on her hands and knees as soon as she got near the blood. Eagerly, almost greedily, she began to lick it. Then he saw Shanfeng aiming a swift, hard kick right at his wife's buttocks. She fell over on her side, and when she regained her balance, she began to retch violently. The noises coming out of her throat were the kind that made one's hair stand on end. Next he saw Shanfeng pressing Pipi's head down until the boy was sprawled on the ground, flat on his stomach. And he heard Shanfeng say, in a voice that sounded as terrible as his wife's retching, "Lick it up."

Pipi lay there staring at the puddle of blood gleaming in the sun. It reminded him of bright red fruit jam. Sticking out his tongue, he took an exploratory lick, and immediately a brand new taste coursed through his body. He relaxed and began to lick away, though he found the cement a little coarse, for in no time at all his tongue had begun to feel numb. Then a few trickles of red began to run down the tip of his tongue. It made everything taste even better, but he had no idea that it was his own blood.

Just then Shangang saw his sister-in-law come into the yard, battered and bruised all over. Screaming "I'm going to kill you!" she hurled herself at Pipi. At the same instant Shanfeng kicked his foot right into the boy's side. Pipi went flying through the air and landed on the concrete, head first, with a dull, heavy thud. Shangang saw his son's body twitch and quiver once or twice, then, arms and legs stretched out lazily, it became absolutely still.

3

At that moment the old lady heard a loud gurgle, which startled and terrified her. The sound had wriggled out of her belly, as if after having been pent up there for a long time it had finally been released, full of bitterness and spleen. She immediately determined that this was a sign of her intestines rotting away and that this decay had been going on for quite some time. Right after that there were two more gurgles, this time even louder than before, sounding just like bubbles rising to the surface. No question about it, her intestines must have rotted completely away. Though she couldn't quite imagine what color they now were, she could guess what they looked like: a thick, runny mess that gave off bubbles as it undulated and churned inside. Then she caught a whiff of a foul, putrid smell, which was gushing out of her mouth and filling up the whole room. Soon it seemed to her that even the room and the house were rotting away. That must be why she'd had no appetite lately.

She tried to get up, but right away she felt the rotten matter inside her belly beginning to sink down, down, all the way into her thighs. It occurred to her then that eating was really a very dangerous thing to do, since her body cavity was not a bottomless pit. The day would come when every empty nook and cranny inside her would be filled up. Her body would swell and finally explode, scraps of skin and flesh splattering, clinging to the walls like posters, leaving her bones, most of which were already broken, lying jumbled on the ground like a pile of firewood.

Her head—she could see it now—would roll around on the floor like a rubber ball until it came to rest in a corner somewhere.

Her eyes filled with tears again. Now even her tears seemed to be giving off a putrid smell, and as they rolled down her cheeks, they seemed much heavier than usual. As she went over to the door her body felt as heavy as a sandbag. Just then she saw Shangang coming into the house, holding Pipi in his arms as though he were carrying a doll. He wasn't walking toward her, but when he turned into his bedroom, she caught a glimpse of blood on Pipi's head. This was the second time she had seen blood today. This stain wasn't quite as bright as the other one; in fact, it was rather dark and dull. Now she felt she was going to throw up.

Shangang had seen his son flying through the air like a bolt of cloth and then plunging to the ground. After that he couldn't see anything else, but it seemed to him that the whole place had become overgrown with weeds, and somewhere in front of him there was a luminously green well.

By then Shangang's wife had raised her head. She had missed the sight of her son being kicked into the air, but at that very instant the spasms that had been convulsing her stomach had ceased. When she finally managed to lift her head, she saw her son's body stretched in front of her, looking as calm and relaxed as her stomach now felt. The sight puzzled her, and she stared dazedly at her son. Blood was trickling from his head, blood that looked like red ink.

Then she let out a cry. "Shangang!" Turning around, she called again to her husband, who was still standing in front of the window. But he didn't move at all, his eyes half-closed as if he had dozed off. Turning around again, she said to Shanfeng, who was also standing there motionless, "My husband is in shock." Then she said to her son, "Your father is in shock." Finally she said to herself, "What should I do?"

At that moment the weeds and the well vanished before Shangang's eyes, and he again saw his son wafting in the air like a piece of cloth and then falling back onto the ground. He saw his wife standing there staring at him, and he thought to himself, "Why is she looking at me like that?" He saw Shanfeng peer left and right, then saunter to the house, while his bruised and battered wife followed behind. Shangang's son did not get up, however; he was still lying on the ground. Feeling that he ought to take a look at his son, Shangang walked out into the yard.

As Shanfeng was heading back into the house, he heard the patter of his wife's footsteps right behind him. He found this noise extremely irritating, so he turned and told her, "Stop following me." Just as he reached the door Shangang stepped out of it, flashing him a smile—an enigmatic one, it seemed to Shanfeng—and then streaking past him like a gust of wind. When Shanfeng discovered that his wife was still behind him, he bellowed, "Stop following me!"

Shangang walked straight up to his wife. Still in a stupor, she said to him, "You're in shock."

He shook his head and said, "No, I'm not." Then he went over and stooped down next to Pipi and saw that his son was bleeding from the head. He pressed his hand against the gash, but the blood continued to trickle between his fingers. It's hopeless, he thought to himself, shaking his head. When he put his hand in front of the boy's mouth he could still feel a faint breath, but soon it faded away to nothing. He moved his hand down to look for his son's pulse, but he couldn't find any. He noticed some ants crawling over to where he was crouching, meaningless ants. He straightened up and told his wife, "He's dead."

His wife nodded and said, "I know." Then she asked, "What shall we do?"

"Let's bury him," Shangang said.

His wife glanced over at Shanfeng, who was still standing at the door to the house, and said, "Is that all?"

"What else is there?" Shangang asked. He sensed that Shanfeng was watching him, so he looked over at the door, but by then Shanfeng had already gone inside. As if remembering something, Shangang went back over to his son and picked him up. The boy felt very heavy in his arms. Then he headed back toward the house.

As he stepped inside the door, he saw his mother coming out of her room. He heard her mumble something or other, but by that time he had already gone into his bedroom. He laid his son on the bed and covered him with a blanket. Turning to his wife, who was just coming into the room, he said, "Look, he's asleep."

His wife asked again, "Is that all we're going to do?"

He looked at her oddly, as if he didn't understand what she was saying.

"You're still in shock," she said.

"No, I'm not," he answered.

"You're a coward," his wife said.

"No, I'm not," he continued to argue.

"Then go out."

"What for?"

"To get even with Shanfeng," his wife said through clenched teeth.

He began to smile, and, walking over to his wife, he patted her on the shoulder and said, "Don't be angry."

But she only sneered at him and said, "I'm not angry, I just want you to go get him."

At that moment Shanfeng appeared in the doorway and said, "No need to come get me." In his hands were two cleavers. Holding one of them out to Shangang, he said, "Now it's our turn."

Shangang didn't take the cleaver. Instead, he stared at Shanfeng's face. It seemed very pale.

"You look terrible," he said.

"Cut the crap," Shanfeng said.

Shangang saw his wife go up to Shanfeng and take the cleaver from his outstretched hand. Then she brought it over to him. But he stuck both of his hands into his trouser pockets and said, "I don't want it."

"You're a coward," she said.

"No, I'm not."

"Then take this cleaver."

"I don't need it."

His wife stared at his face for a long time and finally nodded her head to show that she understood. She gave the cleaver back to Shanfeng. Turning to face her husband again, she said, "Listen, I'd rather see you dead than see you living like this."

He shook his head, as if to say he had no alternative. Then he said to Shanfeng again, "You look terrible."

Shanfeng finally moved away from the door and went into the kitchen. When he came out the cleavers were no longer in his hands. Turning to his wife, who was cowering in the corner, he said, "Let's eat." Then he went over and sat at the dining table. She followed him and sat down as well.

Shanfeng didn't begin eating right away. Instead, he continued to stare at Shangang. He saw Shangang put his right hand in his pocket and feel around inside, as though he were looking for his keys, then turn and go out of the house. At last Shanfeng began to eat. He brought the food to his mouth and started to chew, but it tasted like mud. His wife, who was sitting next to him, was still quivering. "Why are you trembling?" he demanded angrily. When he finally swallowed the mouthful of food he had been chewing, he turned to his motionless wife and asked, "Why aren't you eating?"

"I don't feel like it," she answered.

"Then get away from the table." Shoveling more food into his mouth, he listened as his wife got up, went into their bedroom, and sat in a chair near a corner. He began to chew once more. This time he actually began to feel nauseous, but he made himself swallow anyway.

He had to stop eating, though, because he soon began panting and puffing from the effort, and his forehead was dripping with perspiration. As he mopped his brow with his hands, the beads of sweat felt like icy pellets. Just then he noticed Shangang's wife emerging from her bedroom. After hovering in the doorway like some sinister spirit, she began walking towards him; it seemed to him that her feet never touched the ground. She glided to the table, then floated down onto a stool across from him. After that she began to stare at him with a look that also drifted and hovered about, a look that he found utterly unbearable.

"Get lost," he barked.

She put her elbows on the table, rested her chin on her hands, and continued to scrutinize him.

"I said get lost!" he bellowed.

She didn't stir. It was as though she had turned to ice.

So he hurled all the bowls and utensils off the table, and then, springing to his feet, he grabbed his stool and threw it violently to the floor as well.

She waited for the clattering and banging to stop before whispering, "Why don't you simply kick me to death?"

By now he was hopping mad. Charging right up to her, he raised his fist and howled, "You're asking for it!"

Just then Shangang walked into the house carrying a big bundle. A little brown dog followed at his heels.

As soon as he saw Shangang coming into the house, Shanfeng lowered his fist and said to his brother, "Tell her to get lost."

Shangang set the package on the table, then went up to his wife and said, "Why don't you go back into the bedroom?"

She looked up at him and asked in surprise, "Aren't you going to punch him?"

Shangang helped her to her feet and said, "You should get some rest now."

She began to walk away, but when she reached the door of their bedroom she stopped, turned around, and said to Shangang, "You've got to hit him at least once."

Shangang didn't answer. Instead, he opened the package on the table, which turned out to be a bundle of soup bones. Again he heard his wife's command: "You should punch him!" After that he sensed that she finally went inside their room.

By then Shanfeng had sat on another chair. Pointing to the floor, he said to Shangang, "Clean this up."

Shangang nodded and said, "In a little while."

"I want you to do it right now," Shanfeng said, glowering.

So Shangang went into the kitchen, got a broom and a dustpan, swept up all the pieces of broken crockery on the floor, picked up the stool that had fallen apart, and took everything out into the courtyard. When he came back, his brother pointed at the dog wandering around the house and asked, "Where did that come from?"

"I saw it on the street, and it just followed me all the way home," Shangang replied.

"Get rid of it," Shanfeng ordered.

"All right." Bending down, Shangang beckoned to the little dog, then scooped it up and went into his bedroom. When he came out again he closed the door tightly behind him and asked, "Anything else?"

Shanfeng didn't answer. Instead, he got up from the chair and went into his room.

His wife was still sitting in the corner, staring into the bassinet where her son was lying, face up, as quietly as if he had fallen asleep. When her eyes fell on the baby's belly, she thought she could see it rising and falling, and she had the feeling that her son was still breathing. Hearing her husband's footsteps, she lifted her head, and then, without knowing why, she stood up as well.

"What are you standing up for?" Shanfeng asked as he too looked into the bassinet. The baby's outstretched limbs made him look as though he were snarling and thrashing about. The image gave Shanfeng such a queasy feeling that he had to go lie on the bed, and his wife sat down again.

Shanfeng felt exhausted. He cast his eyes toward the window, but the view outside seemed at once a topsy-turvy mess and a blank nothingness. So he turned away from the window and began to look around the room. He discovered then that his wife was still in the corner, and it seemed to him she had been sitting there for years. He was very annoyed by that.

"Why do you keep sitting there?" he demanded as he raised himself on the bed.

She looked at him in bewilderment, as if she didn't understand a word of what he had just said.

He said again, "Don't sit over there."

She got to her feet right away, but she had no idea what she was supposed to do after that.

Then he lost his temper and yelled: "Goddamn it, I said don't sit over there!"

She immediately walked away from the corner and over to the clothes rack on the other side. There was also a chair in the other corner, but she didn't dare sit down right away. She looked attentively at her husband, but he wasn't looking in her direction anymore. Shanfeng had lain down again and even appeared to have closed his eyes. She hesitated for an instant before sitting very cautiously, but at that moment Shanfeng opened his mouth again and said, "Stop looking at me."

She immediately averted her gaze, but even in the middle of the room her eyes kept trembling and fluttering; she was afraid that with the least bit of inattention they might slide onto the bed. So she stared at the wardrobe mirror, which, seen at an angle as it was now, looked like a gleaming shaft of light. She didn't dare look at the bassinet; she was afraid her eyes would skitter away from it and leap onto the bed. But then she again heard that angry voice: "Stop looking at me!"

She sprang to her feet, this time without the least bit of hesitation or uncertainty, because she had seen the door. She walked through it into the outer room, where she glimpsed Shangang's back just before he disappeared into his bedroom. The figure she had seen was very solid, but in the twinkling of an eye it had vanished from the doorway. She glanced around the room, then headed for the courtyard.

Outside the sunlight dazzled her and made her head swim. Feeling as if she were about to collapse, she sat on the stone steps in front of the door. Then she noticed the two puddles of dried blood, looking strangely fresh and vivid in the sunshine. They seemed to be still trickling along on the ground.

Shangang didn't bother to rinse the bones. He took them into the kitchen, dumped them into a pot with a little water, and without adding any seasoning set the pot over the gas stove. After turning on the flame, he left the kitchen and went into his room.

His wife was sitting on the edge of the bed, right next to their son, but she wasn't looking at the boy. Her eyes were turned toward the window, just as Shanfeng's had been a little earlier. Her gaze was fixed on one of the leaves outside.

Shangang walked to the bed. His son's head was turned to the right. The wound was still visible, though just barely, but it was no longer bleeding. Underneath, on the pillowcase, was a small blood-stain that looked like a printed pattern. After staring at this for a while, he went over and turned his son's head to the left so that both the wound and the pattern were hidden. The sight of the pattern had made him feel sad.

The little dog crawled out from under the bed, scampered over to Shangang's feet, and began to tug playfully on his trouser bottoms. Shangang was also staring at a leaf outside, though not the same one as his wife. "Why didn't you hit him just once?" he heard her say. Her voice was like a leaf swaying and quivering by his side.

"I just wanted you to hit him once," she said again.

4

The old lady locked the door and gingerly crept back into bed. She piled her quilt underneath the pillow so that she could prop herself against it and keep her body elevated to prevent the decaying intestines from invading her chest. She had made up her mind never to eat again. Really, it was much too dangerous. She knew very well there was almost no room left in her body. In order to keep those rotten intestines from sloshing back and forth inside her, she did not move again. Now it seemed to her as though there were no more noises at all, and that suited her just fine. She was no longer upset or worried; instead, she was quite pleased with herself for being so clever. She began to stare at the rays of light on the ceiling. From dawn to dusk she watched them grow and spread and then wane again. Now, as far as she was concerned, only the rays of light were still alive; everything else was dead.

Early the next morning Shanfeng woke up with a terrible headache. It was so painful he thought his head would split open. When he sat up in bed, the pain seemed to subside a little, but his head still seemed in danger of rupturing, and he knew he couldn't take any chances. So he got out of bed and went to the bureau, where he found a strip of white cloth in the top drawer. This he wound around his head. Now he felt much safer.

While he was getting dressed, he noticed the band of black gauze[2] on his sleeve and remembered Shangang coming into his room with it yesterday afternoon. Even though the pain from his headache was excruciating, he could still recall how Shangang had, very affectionately, fastened the arm band onto his sleeve. He remembered, too, how he had bellowed furiously at Shangang at the time, but he couldn't recall why.

Shangang had gone out later and borrowed a pushcart from somewhere, which he parked right outside the entrance to the courtyard. Then Shangang had carried Pipi out of the house, though Shanfeng

2. A sign of mourning.

didn't actually see that. He only saw his brother come into his room, pick up the baby from the bassinet, and carry him outside. At that point he followed Shangang out through the gate. He walked behind the pushcart with his sister-in-law and his wife. His head was just beginning to hurt. He remembered pouring out a stream of curses all the while, but the object of his abuse was the sunshine, because it was making him so dizzy he almost swooned. He remembered walking down the road, then back again. Along the way he seemed to have seen many familiar faces, though he hadn't been able to recognize a single one. They had all swarmed around, full of curiosity, and the sound of their voices had reminded him of the twittering of sparrows. He remembered seeing Shangang answering their questions. Shangang had seemed rather nonchalant, as if nothing had happened, but he had also looked very grave. By the time they finally got home it was evening, and the two children had already been placed inside a pair of urns. He remembered seeing, from a distance, the tall chimney that reached all the way into the clouds. After that they had walked for a long time until they crossed a bridge and entered a large courtyard full of pines and cypresses.

At that moment a throng of people had come out weeping and wailing, and the sight and sound of it had filled him with disgust. Then he had been standing in a vast hall, with only the four of them there, so that the hall had seemed even bigger, as enormous as an open square. He had been standing there for a long time before he began to hear a very familiar kind of music, music that made him yearn to go to sleep. But after it was over he had no longer felt sleepy. Shangang had turned around to face him and had said a few words. At the time he had understood what Shangang was saying, something about the two children, something about "as a result of two unfortunate accidents," all of which he had found quite ridiculous. Much later, when it was dark, he had finally come back to where he was now. Then, after he had lain in bed and closed his eyes, he had felt as if countless bees were swarming inside his head, buzzing and humming all night long, disappearing only as he awoke a little while ago. By then he had a splitting headache.

After Shangang got out of bed that morning the first thing he did was to go into the kitchen. The two women were already there making breakfast. As usual, they did not say a word to each other, as if nothing had happened, or as if what had happened were already very far away, so far away it was no longer within their memory. Shangang went into the kitchen to check on the pot. When he uncovered it, a pleasant aroma escaped and permeated the room, and he saw that the meat on the bones had already been cooked to a mush. Very pleased, Shangang went out of the kitchen with the little dog close on his heels. It had been barking its head off ever since the aroma began oozing out of the pot yesterday, and its barking had put Shangang's mind at ease. Now he felt even more encouraged when the dog followed right behind him.

Shangang sat at the dining table after he came out of the kitchen and, picking the dog up onto his lap, said to it, "In a little while I'm going to have to ask for your help." Then he squinted his eyes and looked out the window, trying to decide whether to wait till Shanfeng had had his breakfast. The little dog perched very quietly on Shangang's lap. After pondering a while he decided not to let Shanfeng eat after all. "What's the point?" he thought to himself. He got up once more, put the dog on the floor, and headed for Shanfeng's room, the little dog again trotting behind him.

The bedroom door was closed but not locked. Shangang pushed it open and walked in, still followed by the dog. He saw Shanfeng standing in front of his bed with a strip of white cloth tied around his head, looking tired and wan. As soon as Shanfeng saw him coming in he plunked himself down on the bed, his body sinking as though it had just been dropped from a height. Shangang pulled up a chair and sat down as well. Then, at the moment that he pushed open the door and entered the room, Shangang had a premonition that everything would proceed smoothly. "Shanfeng is finished," he thought to himself.

Now he said to Shanfeng, "I put my son in your hands; whom are you going to give me in his place?"

Shanfeng looked at him dazedly for a long time before he frowned and asked, "What do you mean?"

"It's very simple," Shangang answered. "Just hand your wife over to me."

Then Shanfeng remembered that his son had died, and that Pipi was dead as well. He thought that there was something in between the two deaths, though exactly what it was he really couldn't figure out.

He was just too tired now. He only knew that this something connected the deaths of the two boys.

So he said, "But my son is dead too."

"That's a whole different matter," Shangang answered decisively.

Shanfeng became confused. It seemed to him as if his son's death had indeed been an entirely different matter, that it had had nothing to do with Pipi's death. And Pipi, he remembered now, had been killed when he kicked him into the air. But why did he do that? This was another thing he couldn't figure out at the moment. He didn't want to think about it anymore; it would only make him feel dizzier. He thought he heard Shangang saying something, so he asked, "What did you just say?"

"I said hand your wife over to me," Shangang replied.

Shanfeng leaned his head wearily against the headboard and asked, "What are you going to do with her?"

"I want to tie her to that tree," Shangang said, pointing with his finger to the tree outside the window. "Just for an hour."

Shanfeng turned and glanced at the tree. The leaves were glittering so brilliantly in the sunlight he couldn't bear to look at them, so he quickly turned his head back and asked Shangang another question: "And after that?"

"After that, nothing," Shangang answered.

"All right, then," Shanfeng said. He tried to nod but couldn't muster the strength. Then he added, "Why don't you tie me up instead?"

Shangang smiled softly to himself. He had known all along this was how it would turn out. "Should we have breakfast first?" he asked Shanfeng.

"I don't want any," Shanfeng replied.

"Then let's not waste any time," Shangang said as he got to his feet. Shanfeng stood up as well, thinking to himself that his body felt as heavy as a bag of cement. He said to Shangang, "I feel like I'm about to die." Shangang looked back at him and said, "You may be right."

After the two of them came out of Shanfeng's room, Shangang disappeared into his own bedroom for a few moments, and when he emerged again he was carrying two lengths of rope. Holding them out to Shanfeng, he asked, "Do they look all right to you?"

When Shanfeng took the ropes from his brother he found them rather heavy, so he said, "They seem too heavy."

"When they're tied around you they won't feel heavy," Shangang replied.

"Perhaps you're right." Shanfeng was able to nod his head now.

Together they walked out into the courtyard. The sunlight was so dazzling it made Shanfeng feel as though the sky and the ground were both spinning around him. "I can't stand up anymore," he told Shangang.

Pointing to the tree in front of them, Shangang said, "Why don't you go sit in the shade?"

"But it's too far," Shanfeng said.

"Not far at all, only two or three yards at the most," Shangang said as he helped Shanfeng over to the tree. After they reached the shade he gave Shanfeng's body a little push, and Shanfeng toppled over. When he hit the ground his back was leaning against the trunk.

"Now I'm much more comfortable," he said.

"Soon you're going to feel even more comfortable."

"Really?" Shanfeng was straining as he lifted his head to look at Shangang.

"Soon you're going to be howling with laughter," Shangang said.

Smiling wearily, Shanfeng said, "Just let me sit here."

"Of course," Shangang replied.

Shanfeng felt a rope being coiled around his chest, and then he felt himself bound so tightly against the tree that he could hardly breathe. "It's too tight," he told Shangang.

"You'll get used to it in a minute," Shangang said as he finished tying Shanfeng's upper torso.

Shanfeng had a sensation of being wrapped up. "I feel like I've got a lot of clothes on," he said to his brother.

Shangang had gone back into the house, but soon he returned carrying a wooden plank and the pot. The dog had followed him into the yard and was now scampering around Shanfeng.

"Feel my brow," Shanfeng said to his brother.

Shangang reached over and touched his forehead.

"It's burning, isn't it?" Shanfeng asked.

"Yes," Shangang said, "about a hundred and four degrees."

"I'm sure you're right," agreed Shanfeng anxiously.

Shangang squatted and and began to slide the wooden plank underneath Shanfeng's legs. When that was done, he tied the plank and Shanfeng's legs together with the second piece of rope.

"What are you doing?" asked Shanfeng.

"I'm giving you a massage," Shangang answered.

"Well, then, you should massage my temples," Shanfeng told his brother.

"If you like." Shangang had finished securing the legs together, so he stood and rubbed Shanfeng's temples a few times with his thumbs. "How's that?" he asked.

"Much better. How about a little more?"

Shangang took a little step forward and began to massage Shanfeng in earnest.

Shanfeng could feel Shangang's thumbs wriggling amusingly on his temples. He was feeling very happy. Then he noticed two reddish splotches of something or other on the patch of cement in front of him. "What's that?" he asked.

"It's the stain from Pipi's blood," Shangang replied.

"What about the other one?" Shanfeng seemed to remember that one of the stains didn't come from Pipi.

"That's also Pipi's," Shangang said.

He thought Shangang might have been mistaken, so he didn't say any more. After a while, he asked, "Shangang, you know something?"

"What?"

"Actually I was very afraid yesterday, after I kicked Pipi to death I was really scared."

"You weren't afraid," Shangang said.

"No, really," Shanfeng shook his head, "I was very scared, especially when I handed you the cleaver."

Shangang stopped massaging and, patting Shanfeng kindly on the cheeks, said, "You're never afraid."

Shanfeng began to smile softly when he heard this. "You refuse to believe me," he said.

By now Shangang was squatting to remove Shanfeng's socks.

"What are you doing?" Shanfeng asked him.

"Taking off your socks," Shangang replied.

"What for?"

This time Shangang didn't answer him. Instead, after he finished removing Shanfeng's socks, he took the cover off the pot and began to slather the pastelike concoction of meat and gristle onto the soles of Shanfeng's feet. The little dog ran over as soon as it smelled the meat.

"What are you smearing on?" Shanfeng asked.

"Some cooling balm," Shangang answered.

"You messed up again," Shanfeng said, and smiled. "You should put it on my temples instead."

"If you like." Pushing the dog out of the way, Shangang stuck his hands into the pot and grabbed some of the stew, then flung it like clumps of mud onto Shanfeng's temples, a handful on each side. After that he put the lid back on the pot. Shanfeng's face was now an unseemly mess.

"Now you look like a dandy," Shangang said to him.

Shanfeng felt something trickling slowly down his cheeks. "It doesn't feel like cooling balm," he said. Then he tried to stretch his legs, but he found that he couldn't bend or flex them, now that they were tied to the plank. "I'm really very, very tired," he mumbled.

"Why don't you take a little nap?" Shangang said. "It's half past seven now. I'll let you go in an hour."

At that moment the two women appeared almost simultaneously at the door. Shangang saw them standing there in bewilderment. Then he heard a bloodcurdling shriek as he saw his sister-in-law rush at him and grab him by his clothes.

"What are you trying to do?" she screamed.

"None of your business," he replied.

Taken aback, she stared blankly for a moment before screaming again: "You let him go!"

Shangang smiled softly and said, "Then first you have to let me go."

When she loosened her grip, he shoved her aside so vigorously that she fell to the ground. Looking at his wife, who was still standing in the doorway, Shangang gave her a little smile, and he saw that she was smiling back at him. When he turned around again, the little dog was already trotting toward Shanfeng's feet.

Shanfeng had seen his wife come flying out of the house, her body gleaming and sparkling as though bedecked with lights and swaying from side to side like a boat. He thought he had heard her screaming something, and after that, he had seen Shangang push her onto the ground. She had looked quite ridiculous as she toppled over. Then, feeling a little stiffness in his neck, he turned his head to the other side. Again he caught sight of the two bloodstains he had glimpsed earlier. Now he noticed that they were not far from each other and were both glistening in the sun. A few drops of blood had wandered out from each blotch and had run together on the ground in between. Then it all came back to him: the second bloodstain belonged not to Pipi but to his son. He also remembered that it was Pipi who had dropped his son on his head and killed him. And he found the answer to why he had kicked Pipi to death. He realized that Shangang had been deceiving him all this time, and he hollered, "Let me go!" When there was no reply from Shangang, he shouted again, "Let me go!"

But just then a strange sensation began to rise from the bottoms of his feet, slowly at first, then faster and faster as it crawled up through his body, until in an instant it reached his chest. Before he could cry out for the third time, he involuntarily drew his head down into his shoulders, and then he began to laugh as if his very life depended on it. He tried to draw his knees up to his body, but he couldn't even bend his legs—all he could do was swing them up and down. He couldn't move his torso at all, even though he squirmed and wriggled every which way. His head whipped dizzyingly from side to side. His laughter sounded like the grating of metal against metal.

Shangang's face at that moment was a joy to behold. "How happy you are!" he exclaimed to Shanfeng. Then he turned to his wife and said, "So happy it's making me a little envious." His wife wasn't looking at him; she was staring at the little dog as it licked away at Shanfeng's bare feet. In her eyes was a look as hungry and greedy as the dog's. Shangang turned to look at his sister-in-law and discovered that she was still sitting on the ground. Completely befuddled by Shanfeng's peculiar laughter, she sat staring blankly at the deliriously giggling Shanfeng, driven to distraction herself by this inexplicable turn of events.

By this time Shanfeng could no longer muster the strength to swing his legs or even to shake his head. It was all he could do to hold his neck up as he continued to howl. The intense tickling sensation that ran through him as the dog licked his soles made him laugh so hard he could hardly breathe.

Shangang had been watching him with a kind, affectionate look on his face. Now he asked, "What's making you so happy?"

Shanfeng answered with more laughter, interspersed with hiccups, so that the laughter seemed to come quivering out of his mouth in herky-jerky gasps, and with each gasp he managed to suck in a little air. The hiccups were so rhythmic, loud, and clear, that they sounded like the whistles blowing on a parade ground.

Turning back to his wife, who was still standing in the doorway, Shangang said, "I've never seen anyone so happy in my life." His wife was still looking greedily at the dog. He went on: "He's so happy he doesn't even need to breathe." Then he stooped down and asked Shanfeng again: "What's making you so happy?" By then the laughter was no longer rhythmic and steady; it was beginning to sound muddled, disorderly. Shangang straightened up and said to his sister-in-law, "He won't tell me." Shanfeng's wife was still sitting on the ground, a faraway look on her face.

The little dog retracted its tongue, and, arching its back, shook itself once or twice, then sat down on its hind legs, as if it felt entitled to a rest for a job well done. Its eyes, though, darted back and forth, now looking at Shanfeng's feet, now looking at Shangang's face.

By then Shanfeng's head was drooping, but Shangang saw that his brother was still breathing. So he said to him, "Now can you tell me what you're so happy about?" But there was no response from Shanfeng, who was struggling for air, his breathing feeble and unsteady. Shangang went back to the pot, lifted the cover, grabbed another handful of mush, and again slathered it onto the bottoms of Shanfeng's feet. Right away the little dog rushed over and resumed its licking.

This time, instead of laughing uproariously, Shanfeng, his head sagging lower and lower, began to laugh with a whooping noise that sounded like the wind gusting through dark alleys. Gradually the whoops became more and more drawn out until there were almost no gaps in between. But after a while Shanfeng suddenly threw his head up, and the laughter burst out again in a maniacal frenzy. It went on for almost a minute, and then it stopped as suddenly as it had begun. Shanfeng's head dropped abruptly and dangled in front of his chest, while the dog continued to lick contentedly at his soles.

Shangang walked over and placed his hand under Shanfeng's chin. The head felt extremely heavy, and when he turned it up he saw that Shanfeng's face was completely twisted and distorted. He stared at it for some time before letting go, whereupon Shanfeng's head dropped and dangled again on his chest. Glancing at his watch, Shangang saw that it had taken a mere forty minutes. Then he turned around and walked back to the house. At the doorway he stopped, and he heard his wife ask, "Is he dead?"

"He's dead," Shangang answered.

Entering the house, he went over and sat at the dining table. Like an honor guard waiting to greet him, breakfast was still arrayed on the tabletop. As usual, it consisted of rice porridge and *youtiao*. By then his wife had also come into the house. She kept staring at him, but she didn't sit down next to him, nor did she say anything. From the look on her face one would think nothing whatsoever had happened. Then she went into the bedroom.

Through the wide-open door Shangang looked out at the figure of the dead Shanfeng, still sitting on the ground and looking as though he were taking a nap. At that moment a dark shape was crawling toward the dead man, and soon it appeared in Shangang's field of vision. It was his sister-in-law. He saw her stand at her husband's side for a long time before bending down. He imagined that she was talking to Shanfeng. After a while he saw her straighten up and peer around as if she were at a loss. Then she looked through the door and her gaze landed on his face. She stared at him for some time before heading toward him. Walking right up to him, she stared at him a little while longer with a frown on her face, as though she were looking at something that annoyed her. At last she said, "You killed my husband."

Shangang found her voice as harsh and unpleasant as the sound of Shanfeng's laughter. He did not respond.

"You killed my husband," she repeated.

"No, I didn't," Shangang answered her this time.

"You murdered my husband," she snarled through clenched teeth.

"No, I didn't," Shangang said. "All I did was tie him up. I didn't kill him."

"It was you!" she shrieked all of a sudden, almost hysterically.

Shangang repeated, "No, it wasn't me. It was the dog."

"I'm going to report you to the police." She began to weep.

"You'd be bringing false charges, and that's a crime." Shangang smiled softly as he said this.

Seeming at a loss again, she stared at Shangang in bafflement. After a long time she finally said, very softly, "I'm going to report you." Then she turned around and headed for the door.

Shangang watched as she walked away slowly and deliberately. She paused for a while beside Shanfeng and raised her hand to wipe her eyes. "She's finally crying the way she's supposed to," Shangang thought to himself. Then she went out through the gate and disappeared.

At that moment Shangang's wife came out of the bedroom carrying a bulging black bag. Setting it on the table, she said to Shangang, "In here you'll find a few changes of clothing and all the cash we have."

Shangang looked at her blankly, as if he didn't understand what she was saying.

"You should run away now," she explained.

It was only then that Shangang nodded his head. He glanced at his watch, but when he saw that there was still a minute left before half past eight, he said, "Let me sit for another minute." He went on staring at Shanfeng, who was still sitting under the tree, looking as though he had just dozed off. In the meantime Shangang could tell that his wife had sat across the table, facing him.

When he sensed that almost a minute had gone by, he got up without looking at his watch again and went out into the courtyard. By then the little dog had lapped up every last drop of mush from Shanfeng's soles and was licking his temples. Shangang walked to the tree, and, nudging the dog aside with his foot, squatted down and untied the rope around Shanfeng's legs and the one around his torso. Finally Shangang stood and began to walk toward the gate, but before he had taken more than a few steps he heard a dull thud behind him. By the time he turned his head to look, Shanfeng's body had toppled onto the ground. So Shangang went back and picked Shanfeng up, arranging his body so that it was once again leaning against the tree, and then he turned around once more and at last walked out of the gate.

He walked along the alley. It felt dark and gloomy, as if it were about to rain. But when he lifted his head he saw brilliant sunshine, and he was quite puzzled. He kept walking anyway, straight ahead, sensing people going back and forth around him, flashing by, one after another, like the blades of a slowly turning fan.

He didn't stop until he reached the fish store. There were a few people inside, smoking and chatting with each other. He said to them, "This fishy smell is just too much." No one paid him any attention, however, so he repeated himself. This time someone said, "So why are you still here?" But he remained on the same spot; he didn't move away. Then they all began to laugh. Frowning, he said again, "This fishy smell is really too much." He stayed there a while longer, then, feeling a little bored, he continued on his way.

When he reached the intersection he hesitated, unable to decide which way to go. The busy street stretched in front of him, everything running every which way. He saw people and bicycles and cars and minitractors and pushcarts all jostling each other in a mad jumble, like people milling around a theater just before a sold-out show. Then he saw a cobbler sitting under a light pole repairing some shoes. Shangang walked up to him, and, after watching him silently for a while, lifted up his foot and asked the cobbler what he thought of the quality of the shoe leather. The cobbler glanced at it briefly and said, "So-so." This answer evidently left Shangang unsatisfied, because he then insisted to the cobbler that his shoes were made of top-grade cowhide, couldn't he see that? But the cobbler told him that it wasn't cowhide, it was only waxed pigskin. Shangang was deeply disappointed by what the cobbler said, so he walked away.

He was now heading west. He stayed on the sidewalk; he was afraid of the traffic—bicycles and cars and trucks—on the street. Even on the sidewalk he moved along cautiously; he didn't want to be knocked to the ground and not be able to ever get up again, like Shanfeng. After a little while he passed by a public toilet and, feeling an urge to go, walked over to it. Inside several people were standing in front of the latrine pissing away to their hearts' content, so he squeezed up there also, then yanked out his doodad and aimed it at the pit. But although he stood there for a long time, all he heard were the sounds of other people's pissing, while for some reason he wasn't able to do anything at all. The people on each side of him came and went, others took their place, then still others, but he remained on the same spot. Some time later, as if he had just discovered something, he said to himself, "It turns out I didn't come here to pee." Whereupon he went outside again and continued on his way, still hewing to the sidewalk. But he'd forgotten to put his thing back inside his trousers; it was hanging outside, jiggling along merrily with each step he took, keeping time with the rhythm of his stride. He walked along like that for some time, and, incredible as it may seem, no one noticed. Then, as he passed a movie theater, some youngsters walking toward him finally caught sight of it. He saw them suddenly double over, and then he heard them howling with laughter, sounding just like Shanfeng. After he walked through the crowd of young people he heard them calling out behind him, in fits and starts and in an exaggeratedly comical way, "Come—and—look, come—and—look." But he ignored them and kept right on walking. Then he noticed that everyone around him seemed to have undergone some kind of transformation all of a sudden: people were rocking to and fro or swaying from side to side, while some of the women cowered in the distance as if from a gangster. He found it all very funny and began to laugh.

Walking on and on, he finally came to a stop in front of an unfinished building. He looked up and down and examined it for quite a while before entering. It was rather damp inside, but even so he found everything quite to his liking. There were many rooms—though none had any doors yet—and he inspected them one by one before finally deciding on a gloomy little chamber. Stepping inside, he went to a corner and sat down, leaning his back against the wall. He felt that he could now in good conscience get a little rest. He was so very, very tired. He closed his eyes and immediately fell asleep.

Three hours later somebody shook him out of his slumber. He opened his eyes to see several policemen standing in front of him. One of them said to him, "Please put that thing back inside."

5

One month later he was hustled into the back of a truck, escorted by a squad of rifle-toting policemen who surrounded him like a phalanx of bodyguards. He could see people in every direction flocking toward him like sparrows, their heads tilted back as they peered up at him. He lowered his head and stared back at them, and he had the feeling that their faces had all been painted on. After a while, the police car in front of him began to move forward, its sirens howling like the northwesterly wind, but the truck itself simply rattled and snorted a few times and then went dead. Shangang knew in his heart that ever since he had been awakened by someone in that half-finished building, he had been waiting for this moment to come. Now that it had finally arrived, he turned his head toward one of the policemen and said, "Captain, please make it quick and clean."

The policeman looked straight ahead and didn't answer. So Shangang turned his head to the other side and said to another policeman, "Captain, I beg you, just finish me off with one shot." But this policeman also remained unmoved.

Shangang watched as a river of bicycles flowed along in front of him. Suddenly the truck shuddered a few times, and he felt the wind blowing against his ears with a whoosh. The densely packed mass of bicycles parted and began moving to each side in an orderly fashion. Time and again, leaves that reached out from the sides of the road slapped against his cheeks like so many hands. Soon a weed-choked pasture appeared before his eyes, and he knew that in no time at all he would be standing in the middle of that field. Meanwhile a mob that reminded him of weeds had come into view. An ambulance was parked a short distance from the grass, and both sides of the roadway were packed with bicycles leaning this way and that. He had a feeling that the ambulance was there on his account. Perhaps they were only going to shoot to wound, he thought, and then they would rush him to the hospital in the ambulance and bring him back from the brink of death.

While these thoughts were going through his mind the truck shuddered again, throwing him forward so that he banged his ribs against the truck railing, but he didn't feel any pain at all. He felt someone pulling him to one side, and, turning around, he saw some of the policemen jump down from the truck. Then someone shoved him from behind, so he jumped as well, but he landed on his knees and had to be pulled to his feet. Next thing he knew, he was moving forward, swept along by a crowd. He realized that his torso, which was all trussed, was beginning to go numb, though for some reason he could still feel his legs swinging back and forth. He seemed to see many things, and yet there didn't seem to be anything before his eyes. He began to fall into a daze. A little while later he felt himself being grabbed by a number of hands. Unable to move forward, he came to a standstill.

As he stood there, somewhat baffled, with the tall weeds at his feet probing and poking into his trouser bottoms, he began to feel a tickling sensation. He looked down at his feet but didn't see anything. There was nothing he could do except lift his head again while a foolish smile spread across his face. Gradually he began to hear the hub-bub of the crowd, and only then did he notice that he was in the center of a throng of people covering every inch of the field like a mass of reeds. As if waking from a dream, he once again realized the predicament he was in. He knew that his head was about to be blown to pieces.

Then it occurred to him that he knew this place, and he remembered that he used to come here quite often. In fact, almost every time a criminal was executed here he had elbowed his way to the front to watch. This, however, was the first time he had ever stood where he was standing now. The novelty of the situation intrigued him. He searched with his eyes for the spot where he had often stood before, but to his surprise he could no longer find it. Suddenly the urge to urinate came over him again, so he said to the policeman standing next to him, "Captain, I need to pee."

"All right," the policeman answered.

"Please take my thing out for me," he asked.

"Just pee in your pants," the policeman said.

He could tell that people around him were laughing and giggling, but he had no idea what had amused them so. Spreading his legs a little, he began to frown, and a worried look appeared on his face.

After a while the policeman asked, "Are you done?"

"I can't pee," he said in distress.

"Then forget it," the policeman told him.

He nodded, then began to look into the distance. His eyes floated over the hair of the short folks and glided past the earlobes of the tall and eventually came to rest on the asphalt highway on the horizon. It reminded him of a thick vein. Suddenly he felt a kick on the back of his knees, and, his legs crumpling beneath him, he fell kneeling onto the ground. Now he could no longer see the highway with its dark, venous color.

Behind him one of the policemen raised his automatic rifle and took aim. Moments later, a shot rang out.

At the sound of the rifle, Shangang's body tumbled over in a somersault, and then, absolutely terrified, he rolled back onto his feet. Looking at the people around him, he cried, "Am I dead yet?"

Nobody answered him. Everyone was roaring with laughter, a laughter that poured down on him like a thundershower. Panic-stricken, he began to bawl, because he had no idea whether he was dead or alive. His ear had been shot off, and blood was gushing from where the ear used to be. Again he asked, "Am I dead yet?"

Someone finally answered: "No, you're not."

Shangang was shocked and pleased at the same time. He began screaming at the top of his lungs, "Hurry, take me to the hospital!" Then he felt another kick on the back of his knees, and once again he fell kneeling onto the ground. Before he understood what was happening, another shot rang out from the rifle.

The second bullet went in the back of his head. This time, instead of turning a somersault, Shangang keeled over. With a heavy thud his head hit the dirt, lifting his buttocks high off the ground. But he was still alive, his butt trembling and shaking as if he had a bad case of the chills.

The rifleman took a step forward and, putting the muzzle flush against Shangang's head, fired a third shot. As though he had just been kicked in the abdomen, Shangang rolled onto his back. His hands, still tied behind him, now lay underneath his torso, while his legs, crooked up at the knees initially, relaxed a few moments later and also came to rest on the ground.

6

This morning, Shangang's wife saw someone come into the room, someone with only half a head. It was just beginning to grow light at the time. She remembered that she had locked the door very securely, but when he came in she somehow got the impression that the door was wide open. Although he only had half his head, she recognized him right away. It was Shangang.

"I've been released," Shangang said.

His voice droned and buzzed, so she asked him, "Did you catch a cold?"

"Maybe," he answered.

She remembered that there were some fast-acting cold capsules in the drawer and asked him if he wanted any.

He shook his head and said that he didn't have a cold, he was fine, it was just that he didn't know where the other half of his head had gone.

She asked him whether it could have been shot off by a bullet.

He told her he couldn't remember anymore. Then he sat down in a chair and said he was hungry, would she give him some change so he could buy breakfast? She gave him some money and a few ration coupons, and he got up and left. When he went out of the room he didn't shut the door behind him, so she went over to close it, but she was not surprised to find it tightly shut. She undressed and went back to bed.

Just then the sounds of footsteps echoed in the alley outside. They were the footfalls of someone walking toward the intersection. At that moment she woke up. Dawn was just breaking, and she watched as her room began to brighten. In the early morning quiet she could hear those footsteps so distinctly. It was as if they had emerged from her dreams, continued out of the house, and were now about to walk out of the alley.

She began to get dressed. By the time she was finished, the footsteps had disappeared. She walked to the window and pulled open the curtains. Sunlight flooded in right away, sunlight that was still bright red at the moment, although it would soon turn into the yellow of jaundice. After making her bed, she sat down in front of the dressing table. She looked at her own face in the mirror and found it dull and insipid. Then she got up and went out of the room. In the outer room she saw Shanfeng's wife already seated at the table eating breakfast, so she went into the kitchen to prepare her own. She turned on the stove and stood beside it brushing her teeth.

Five minutes later, she carried her breakfast out of the kitchen, and, sitting across from her sister-in-law, began to eat in silence. But at that moment the other woman, having finished her meal, left the table and went into the kitchen. Shangang's wife heard the loud clattering her sister-in-law made as she washed her breakfast dishes. Soon after, she saw her come out of the kitchen, go into her bedroom, come out of it again, then lock the bedroom door behind her before leaving the house.

As she continued to eat her breakfast—with a great deal of difficulty, because she had no appetite at all—her eyes wandered to the tree outside the window. At the moment it looked to her like something made out of plastic. She went on staring at it. Then, remembering something, she cast her eyes back inside the house and began to look around the room. She realized then that it had been quite a few days since she had seen her mother-in-law. For a while she stared at the door to the elderly woman's bedroom, but soon she turned away and resumed looking at the tree outside.

On the morning of the sixth day after Shanfeng's death, the old lady also breathed her last. That morning she woke up with an unusual feeling of excitement. In fact, she could even follow the progress of that sensation as it coursed through her body. Yet at the same time she also felt her body dying, one part after another. She could tell clearly that her toes were the first to go, then the rest of each foot, and next the legs. It seemed to her that the death of her feet had been as silent as snow or ice. Death lingered for a while in her belly, then like the tide it surged up through her midriff, and once past her waist it spread quickly. She felt as though both her hands had gone and left her far behind, while her head was being chewed off, bite after bite, by a little dog. Finally only her heart was left, but death had already surrounded it and, like countless ants swarming from every direction, was now marching toward the center. Her heart began to feel a little itchy. Suddenly her wide-open eyes saw innumerable rays of light streaming toward her through the curtains. At the sight of them she couldn't help breaking into a little smile, which became fixed on her face like a photographic image.

Shanfeng's wife obviously knew what was about to happen that morning. That was why she had gotten out of bed so early. By the time the sunlight was beginning to turn yellow, she had already left the alley behind and was walking along the busy street. She knew exactly where she was going. She was heading for Tianning Temple, because right next to it was the municipal jail. This morning Shangang was to be taken away from there.

While she was still walking on the street, she began to hear passers-by talking about him. In fact, many people were apparently heading for the same place. There had been no executions in this town for more than a year, and today promised to be an exciting day.

For the past month she had gone to the court time and again to inquire about Shangang's case, all the while passing herself off as his wife. Nobody seemed to have noticed that a month ago it had been as the wife of Shanfeng that she had brought the charges against Shangang. Finally, the day before yesterday, they had told her the verdict. She was quite pleased with it and told them she would like to donate Shangang's body to the state, to be used for the benefit of society. The court officials didn't seem particularly overjoyed at her offer, but they told her they would accept it. She knew, however, that the doctors would be ecstatic. Walking along the street, she was already beginning to imagine how they would carve up Shangang, and a smile played around the corners of her mouth the rest of the way.

7

In the middle of this soon-to-be-demolished buildings hangs a thousand-watt electric bulb. At the moment the light is on, casting its incandescent glare into every corner. Below it are two Ping-Pong tables, both of them old and decrepit. Underneath the tables is an earthen floor. Several doctors, some from Shanghai and some from Hangzhou, are standing in the doorway chatting with each other, waiting for the ambulance to arrive. After that they will get to work.

At the moment, though, they seem quite carefree and relaxed as they idly make small talk. And who wouldn't be, considering the surroundings? Nearby is a pond with water lilies floating on the surface and weeping willows all around, and next to it is a vegetable garden radiant with gold and yellow flowers.

The ambulance comes hurtling down the dirt road, sending up a cloud of dust that billows like a tent. It speeds all the way up to the door before coming to a halt, and the doctors standing there finally turn and glance at it. The rear doors of the vehicle open, and someone jumps out. This person turns and pulls two legs out of the back, followed by a torso, and finally a second person jumps out of the truck carrying the rest of Shangang by the arms. As though lifting a sack of potatoes, the two of them haul Shangang into the building.

The doctors continue to stand in the doorway chatting with each other. They don't seem to have the slightest interest in Shangang; they are all preoccupied with the topic of conversation, which has to do with the cost of living.

The two people who have just carried Shangang inside now come out of the building. From time to time these two have gone to the hospital in town to sell their blood. They cannot leave just yet because they have one more task to perform. In a little while they will have to dig a pit, throw Shangang into it, and then bury him. By then Shangang will be made up of things like fatty tissues, muscles, hair, and teeth—all the things that the doctors have no use for. So the two of them walk over and sit beside the pond. They are very pleased with the day's work, because soon someone will hand them some money, which they will then stuff in their pockets.

The doctors stand in the doorway for a little while longer. Then, one after another, they go inside the building and over to the large bags that each of them has brought. They begin to get ready, changing into their surgical gowns, putting on their caps and masks, pulling on their surgical gloves, and finally unpacking and laying out their instruments.

At this moment Shangang is lying on his back on top of the Ping-Pong table, already stripped of all his clothes by the two attendants. Under the light of the one-kilowatt bulb, his naked body glistens and shines as if coated with greasepaint.

The first doctor to finish his preparations walks over to Shangang. He is not carrying any surgical implements at the moment. Having come for Shangang's skeleton, he must wait until after the others have peeled away the skin and hollowed out the insides before he can get to the bones. Perhaps that is why he appears so nonchalant as he saunters over to Shangang, runs his eyes over him, then reaches over to pinch him here and there in the arms and the calves. Afterward he turns to his colleagues and says, "This fellow is pretty solid."

The second one ready is a thirtyish woman doctor from Shanghai. As she walks over to Shangang in her high heels, the unevenness of the dirt floor causes her to swing her hips in a slightly exaggerated manner. She goes up to Shangang's right side, but, instead of pinching his arm, she runs her hand over the skin on his chest, then turns to the first doctor and says, "Not bad."

After that, she picks up her scalpel and thrusts it into the hollow just below Shangang's neck but above his breastbone, then slides the scalpel all the way down to a point below his belly. The incision is perfectly straight, drawing a chorus of admiring gasps from the other doctors—all male—clustered around her, and she casually mentions that she never had to use a ruler for her geometry diagrams in high school. Like a sliced melon, the skin begins to split open along the entire length of the cut, revealing the layer of adipose tissue, which gleams like a mass of golden globules evenly sprinkled with tiny red flecks. Next she picks up a rapierlike dissecting knife and, inserting it under the skin, begins to work it vigorously up and down along the incision. In no time at all, the skin over Shangang's chest and abdomen has been separated from the rest of his body and is laid out across his torso like a piece of cloth. Then she picks up her scalpel again, this time for the skin on Shangang's arms, cutting from the tip of the shoulder to the back of each hand, and after that the legs, slicing from the pelvis to the insteps, finishing the job with the disengaging up-and-down strokes of her knife along each incision. After disconnecting all this skin, she rests for a little while, then turns to one of her male colleagues standing near her and says, "Please turn him over." She slices another straight line down Shangang's back, again finishing off with the dissecting knife. By this time Shangang's body looks as if it has been draped from head to toe with several lengths of cloth. Setting aside the larger knife, the doctor wields her scalpel once more and severs the connecting points between the various flaps, so that one after another, pieces of Shangang's skin begin to come loose. She gathers them up in turn, handling each piece with the attentiveness of a ragpicker plying her wares. After the skin on his back has been removed, Shangang is turned over again, and in no time at all the skin on the front of his body is gone as well.

Having lost its skin envelope, the gold-colored fatty tissue begins to slacken and lose its firmness, first puffing a little like wads of cotton, then oozing out slowly like slush in every direction. To the doctors it seems as if they are once again looking at the sun-dappled vegetable garden they saw a little while ago when they were standing at the door.

The doctor carries her pile over to one corner of the Ping-Pong table and, smoothing out the various pieces of Shangang's skin, begins to scrape them one by one. Using her dissecting knife like a scouring brush, she scrubs at the fat cells lining the skin. The sound made by each stroke of her knife is like the disconsolate whine of a car wheel trapped in sand.

Several days later Shangang's skin will be grafted onto a patient suffering from burns over large areas of his body, but in just three more days it will begin to break down. In the end it will be thrown into a waste bin, then dumped into one of the hospital's toilets.

Now all the doctors who have been standing to the side take their places around the table. Two people who do not manage to squeeze in among the group on the right side hurry to the left, only to discover that from there they cannot reach the body, so they simply climb onto the Ping-Pong table, and, squatting on top of it, join in carving up Shangang. The chest surgeon saws through the cartilage on each side of the rib cage and opens up both halves of the chest cavity, exposing the lungs. The doctors working on Shangang's abdomen have only to scrape off the fatty tissue and cut away the muscles to find the stomach, liver and kidneys lying right before their eyes. By now the ophthalmologist has extracted one of Shangang's eyeballs. Meanwhile, wielding a pair of surgical shears, the oral surgeon has been cutting up Shangang's face and mouth into a pulpy mess to expose the upper and lower jaws, only to find the upper jaw shattered by a bullet. Bitterly disappointed, he mutters to himself, "Why didn't it hit the eyes instead?" If the bullet had slanted upward just an inch or so, the upper jaw would have been left intact, while the eyes would have come to grief. The ophthalmologist, who is in the process of extracting Shangang's other eyeball, cannot suppress a smile as he overhears this lament. He tells the oral surgeon that perhaps the rifleman who carried out the execution is the son of an eye doctor. He seems rather pleased with himself at the moment. After removing the second eyeball, he is about to leave the table when he sees the oral surgeon sawing away energetically at Shangang's lower jaw with a surgical file. "So long, carpenter," the ophthalmologist calls out. He is the first to leave, because he must rush back to Hangzhou this afternoon and perform a corneal transplant in the evening. By now the woman doctor has finished scraping the pieces of skin, and, after folding them up like a suit, she leaves as well.

The chest surgeon has already removed the lungs and is now merrily cutting through Shangang's pulmonary artery and pulmonary vein, followed by the aorta, and finally all the other blood vessels and nerves coming out of the heart. He is really getting a kick out of all this. Ordinarily, when he is operating on a live human being, he must painstakingly avoid all these blood vessels and nerves, which always makes him feel confined and inhibited. Now he can be as careless as he pleases, and he is going at his job with gusto. Turning to the doctor standing next to him, he quips, "I feel reckless." The other doctor can't stop laughing.

The urologist, who has not been able to squeeze in around the table, is pacing up and down waiting his turn. The word *urine* is stenciled onto his surgical mask. As he watches the other doctors fiddling and puttering at the table, he finds himself growing more and more worried. Over and over again he cautions the doctors monkeying around near Shangang's abdomen: "You fellows had better not mess up my testes."

Shangang's chest is the first part completely excavated, followed by his abdominal cavity. One year from now, Shangang's stomach, liver, and lungs, each immersed in a jar of formaldehyde, will be on display at an anatomy exhibit. His heart and kidneys will be used in transplants. The heart transplant will not succeed, and the patient will die on the operating table. The kidney transplant, however, will be very successful, the patient will still be alive more than a year after the operation, with fairly good prospects of muddling along for some time to come. But the patient himself will be querulous and resentful, complaining bitterly that the kidney transplant, which cost him thirty thousand yuan, was much too expensive.

Now there are only three doctors left in the room. Relieved to find the testicles unscathed, the urologist, feeling quite cheerful, is in the process of cutting them off. The oral surgeon is still sawing away at the lower jawbone, but even he is beginning to see the light at the end of the tunnel. Only the doctor who has come for the skeleton is still walking around nonchalantly, so the urologist reminds him, "You can get to work now." But he replies, "No hurry."

The oral surgeon and the urologist leave the building together, carrying the lower jawbone and the testicles, respectively. After this, each of them will perform a transplant. The oral surgeon will remove the lower jawbone from one of his patients and replace it with the one from Shangang. He has the utmost confidence about the success of this type of operation. But the greatest triumph belongs to Shangang's testes. The urologist will transplant them onto a young man whose own testicles were crushed in a car accident. Soon after the operation, not only will the young man get married, but his wife will also become pregnant almost immediately. Ten months later she will give birth to a healthy, robust little boy. Not even in her wildest dreams could Shanfeng's wife have imagined such a turn of events—that in the end it was she of all people who had enabled Shangang to achieve his fondest ambition: a male heir to carry on the line.

The doctor who has come for the skeleton waits until the other two leave with the jawbone and testicles before he gets down to business. Beginning with Shangang's feet, he clears away little by little all the muscles and connective tissue still clinging to the bones, depositing what he has extracted in a neat pile on one side. His work proceeds slowly, but he has plenty of patience. When he gets up to Shangang's thighs, he gives the burly muscles there a good pinch and says, "I don't care how solid and sturdy you are—by the time I bring your skeleton into our classroom you will be the very picture of a weakling."

THE ISLE

OF WANG'AN

Zhong Ling

(Translated by Kirk Anderson and Randy Du)

*D*uring my teenage years, when I wouldn't even talk to boys, I had a dream in which I found myself lying in the stomach of an enormous whale. The whale was rolling and plunging through the waves, but I felt as comfortable as a babe rocking in a cradle. Now, sitting below deck in the cabin of a ferry, I felt as though I really were inside the belly of a whale, but the sense of freedom and security I'd known in the dream completely eluded me. As soon as the *Anyuan* departed from Penghu Island, Qixiong had gone up on deck without me, and I was left alone to battle the sickening churning of the waves and the even more sickening gorge now rising within me.

Suddenly, the middle-aged woman sitting two seats away frantically pulled a plastic bag from her purse and, thrusting her head inside, began spitting up gobs of yellowish gray gunk, her shoulders twitching with each heave. My stomach began to churn as well. I'd better go up on deck too, I thought to myself. It never fails—whenever I need Qixiong, he's never around.

As soon as I got on deck and felt the bracing gusts of the ocean breeze, I began to feel much better. Only a few people were up there, and Qixiong was easy to spot: the tall, muscular fellow in the tan jacket, standing next to the rail. I walked up to him and shouted, "Lin Qixiong, I almost threw up!"

He turned and glanced at me silently with his piercing black eyes. He knew right away that what I really meant was he shouldn't have left me by myself. Pressing his lips together, he gave me a you-have-some-nerve-blaming-me-when-it's-all-your-own-fault look and said nonchalantly, "Look, that's Wang'an Island up ahead."

Well, excuse me! You've come on a pilgrimage to your ancestral home, and now you've finally caught your first glimpse of it. What an important moment this must be for you! How dare I intrude!

Through the roiling swells we could dimly see an island in the distance, bun-shaped and yellowish brown, without a single speck of green anywhere. So this was where he and his mighty Lin family hailed from, this barren godforsaken island.

Actually, I should have said "we Lins." But even though I married into the Lin family three years ago, I have never felt any sense of belonging. Could there be anything more absurd than this trip to Wang'an? Our mission was to visit the grave of Qixiong's great-grandmother in honor of her memory, but not only hadn't Qixiong or his father ever seen her, but even Qixiong's grandfather couldn't really remember what his mother had looked like. And what's more, none of them knew where the grave was located, nor was there a gravestone or marker of any sort. So how were we supposed to visit the grave to pay our respects?

I said, with a snicker, "The mound may well have been washed away by now. How are we going to find it?"

"Maybe it's not altogether hopeless. Last night Grandpa came up with a new clue."

How odd! Qixiong didn't sound at all belligerent. Had he unilaterally decided on a truce? Perhaps it was only because he had changed the subject to his grandfather. Well, yes, in view of Grandpa's current condition, it would have been petty for us to keep fighting. Yesterday, on the roof deck of the four-story Lin family house in Gaoxiong,

Grandpa had sat slumped in his wheelchair, his head of yellowish gray hair sticking up like dead grass amid the crimson sea of roses and azaleas all around him, his hands clutching the armrests of the chair, his shiny black eyes looking at me pleadingly as he mumbled, "Motherfucking bandit, bandit. . . ."

Why was he going on and on about bandits? His mind must have been wandering again.

"What's the new clue?" I asked Qixiong.

"He told me that five hundred paces south of Great-grandmother's grave there was a tomb with a gravestone in the shape of a rectangular pillar. The stone was fashioned out of rock from the local quarries. It's dark gray, and across the top there is a strip banded with yellow and red whorls."

So that's why he was mumbling about *bandit*—he was trying to say *banded*.

"What about the bosom-shaped hillocks he used to tell us about?" I asked again. "Is he sure about those?"

"Yes, he said he's sure about them, that he did bury Great-grandmother in the strip of land right between two small hills shaped like a woman's breasts. But we can't just look for those. It's been over sixty years, and the terrain must have changed a lot. That was what Grandfather overlooked three years ago."

Three years ago, in 1985, three major events happened in the Lin family. In the spring the only son of three generations of only sons married me. The second event took place in the summer. Seventy-one-year-old Grandpa retired from his Wei'an Shipping Company, and Qixiong's father took over the business. The third event occurred just three days after Grandpa retired to a life of growing orchids and raising goldfish: at half past two in the morning he jumped up, put on his clothes and slippers, and took a cab to the Xiaogang Airport, from where he took the first flight in the morning to Penghu and went to Wang'an to look for his mother's grave. What no one could figure out was why, after having left Wang'an when he was fourteen and having lived some fifty years without apparently even thinking of going back, now, three days into his retirement, he could think of nothing but paying his respects at his mother's tomb. To top it all off, he ended up combing the whole island for five days without finding the grave he had dug with his own hands. After he returned to Gaoxiong he became obsessed with trying to remember the location of the tomb, but he couldn't make another trip to Wang'an: a few days after his return he suffered a stroke that left him paralyzed.

Of the entire Lin family—including Qixiong—the only person I liked was Grandpa. Qixiong's father was just a money grubber who seemed to have no thought in his mind other than money and how to make more of it. Whenever he opened his mouth, it was only to talk about how much money he had made on this or that shipment of freight, or about the incredible bargain he had got on one of the specimens in his collection of rare and precious rocks, his only hobby in life. The one thing that confounded me about him, though, was how such a vulgar and uncultivated man had managed to amass a collection of such exquisitely beautiful rocks. I guess, like all natives of Penghu, he was born with a discerning eye.

Qixiong's mother also hailed from Penghu. She was built like a fortress: big-bosomed, with a thick waist and fat hips. As a typical Penghunese mother-in-law, she was biding her time until the day Qixiong and I moved back to Gaoxiong, when she would have me under her thumb and would make my life miserable for as long as she lived.

No question about it, I understood these people from Penghu only too well: I am one-quarter Penghunese myself. My paternal grandfather was from Lugang, but his wife came from Penghu, while my mother was born in Hangzhou. The Lins welcomed me as their daughter-in-law only because of my one-quarter Penghunese ancestry and not for the reasons suggested by my classmates: because my father was a university professor and the Lins wanted the prestige of having some scholarly blood in the family. I considered myself quite lucky, because right after we were married Qixiong took over the Jilong branch of the family business, and we were able to set up house in the Tianmu district of Taipei, far away from Gaoxiong. As a result, I have had to act the daughter-in-law for only eleven days out of the year: seven days during Chinese New Year, two for the Dragon Boat Festival, and two for the Mid-Autumn Festival. I wouldn't have been able to stand it for even one more day. But on those eleven days I had to act meek and subservient, whether I was serving tea to my parents-in-law in the morning, shopping for groceries, doing the laundry, cooking, or cleaning the bathrooms. In the thirty-three days over the past three years that I have played this role, my mother-in-law twice gave me dirty looks but, fortunately, stopped short of scolding or beating me. I can still vaguely remember how, as a little girl, I used to hide behind the door watching my Penghunese grandmother slap my mother on the face again and again. That was after my father had brought my mother and me to live with his parents while he went to Japan to finish his studies.

Qixiong's grandfather was not like the rest of the family: he was like a lion. I first met him five or six years ago, when Qixiong had just graduated from university and was about to go into the army. He brought me back to Gaoxiong, but instead of meeting his parents, we went directly to the Hamaxing District, where the family shipping company was located, to see Grandpa. The headquarters, with about twenty employees, was in an old three-story building painted a kelp green. Grandpa was out, so we waited in his office on the third floor. Presently, we heard a commotion at the bottom of the stairs—some footsteps, and then a sonorous voice booming, "Ah Chai, mother-fucker, go get four ounces of Korean ginseng, now! Then take it right away, motherfucker, to Old Mother Chen in the hospital."

The string of obscenities astounded me. What an uncivilized man! Qixiong took me by the arm as he went forward to greet the tower-ing figure now blocking the door. I looked up in curiosity and met his eyes gazing right down at me. What I saw was a deeply tanned square face, a flat, straight nose, and a shock of white hair that framed his face like the mane of a lion. His eyebrows were two inky horizontal slash-es, and his bright piercing eyes flashed like lightning behind a dark cloud. Abruptly, he closed the door and said to me, "Miss Hu, do you really fucking love Ah Xiong?"

All of a sudden I realized that the swearing was just a habit, no dif-ferent from the mannerisms of some people who sprinkle every sen-tence with "well, well" or "you know." Then I noticed the trace of gentleness playing around the upturned corners of his mouth, and I answered confidently, "Yes, I really do love him."

Back then, I really was in love with Qixiong.

Grandpa gave Qixiong a firm pat on the shoulder and said, "Well done, Ah Xiong, you motherfucker. She's not only pretty, she's also direct!" He let out a hearty laugh that sounded more like a roar, and the windows of the old building rattled. Next thing we knew, he had swept down the stairs like a whirlwind, shouting back to us over his shoulder, "I'm going to the hospital to look in on old Mrs. Chen. You take my car and show her Lake Chengqing."

I asked Qixiong who old Mrs. Chen was and why she was keeping Grandpa so busy. It turned out that the Chens were a family of three brothers from Penghu who all worked for the Wei'an Company as ship captains. Apparently all three of them were out at sea when their mother came down with appendicitis and had to be rushed to the hospital. So Grandpa took it upon himself to take care of her during the brothers' absence. It was a shrewd move on his part—the Penghunese have a long tradition of being very filial toward their mothers, and, forever after, in gratitude for what he had done for their mother, the Chen brothers would have gladly worked themselves to a frazzle for Grandpa's sake. It was this savviness that had enabled him to get where he was: from a child laborer hoisting baskets of fish on the docks of Gaoxiong, he had worked his way up to the owner of ten freighters, each a respectable five or six thousand tons. He was a man used to having his way, but he was also shrewd and full of life.

As the *Anyuan* slowly steamed into the harbor at Wang'an, Qixiong said, "Grandpa told me yesterday that he often dreamed about his mother, and that she always looked sad and anxious in his dreams, telling him that while her neighbors had the roofs of their graves redone every year, her son and her grandchildren have never come to see her. With the wind and the rain beating mercilessly down on her home, she said she was so busy repairing the roof all the time that she has been too exhausted to send babies to her descendants. The reference to having babies was clearly intended for our benefit."

Qixiong threw a barbed look in my direction, and the cold war was on again. What a slow-witted clod I've been! So that was why my mother-in-law had gone to the trouble last month of calling me long-distance and making sure that I would take a few days off to make this trip on the Pure Brightness Festival, the traditional time for visiting the graves of ancestors. And that was why Grandpa had looked at me so beseechingly every time I happened to walk by him. It was all so that I would bear a son to carry on the family line. In spite of myself I burst out laughing. Did they really think that a woman who had been dead for sixty years could help get me pregnant?

The truth was, there was nothing that anyone could do about the situation between us, about the rock-hard chunk of ice lodged between Qixiong and myself. The logical next step for us was separation. How did we ever get to this sorry state of affairs? Well, to make a long story short, I met Qixiong when he was a senior and I a sophomore, and he became my first lover. A young woman in the throes of her first romance lives in a world of fantasy, seeing only what she wants to see. So I saw Qixiong as a strong, bold, and thoroughly masculine hunk who was also a tender and romantic lover. But no sooner did we get married than he turned into a workaholic: he took over the reins at the family company's branch office in Jilong and immediately plunged into a hectic routine of leaving early in the morning for work and not returning until late at night, even bringing paperwork home on the weekends. In the beginning I fussed and complained, but I finally stopped when a certain incident early one morning made me wake up from my girlish fantasies and see Qixiong for what he really was: far from being strong yet tender, bold and romantic, he was in fact very cautious and reserved, a stiff, unfeeling cold fish. So my romantic ardor cooled. Then I got a job at a newspaper, and now it was his turn to complain, often griping sarcastically that even though he was married, he never saw his wife because she disappeared every day. In the past year or so we have gone from having arguments and fights to merely waging a cold war with each other. After that particular incident the frequency of our lovemaking has declined steadily, and, anyway, I have no desire whatsoever to have a baby with him. A woman knows when she is ovulating, and it's not at all difficult to avoid getting pregnant.

Qixiong leaned over and interrupted my thoughts. "No matter what their plans are, we should still do our best to find the grave for Grandpa's sake. What do you say?"

He stared at me intently, leaning into the gusts of the offshore wind, his deep-set eyes squinting a little and crinkling up at the corners. It had been a long time since he had talked to me in such a heartfelt manner.

I answered sincerely, "Yes, of course. It would be wonderful if we could fulfill Grandpa's wish."

Across his shoulder was slung a camera, while a large shopping bag hung from each hand: candles, sticks of incense, and an incense burner in the bag on the left, plates and bowls in the other. I was also carrying two plastic bags full of such offerings as fruits, cakes, a whole chicken, and strips of yellowish brown paper. We waddled down the main street of Wang'an like two penguins from the South Pole. It was the day of the Pure Brightness Festival, and the sons and daughters of Wang'an had all swarmed back to their ancestral home like fish on a flood tide, from Penghu, from Taiwan, to perform the ritual sweeping of their ancestors' graves. Every motorized vehicle in the little town had already been commandeered. After forty-five minutes or so, we finally saw a three-wheeled open taxi come back to drop off its passengers. Qixiong spent a good while haggling with the driver over his rates. By the time we set out, it was already half past four.

As soon as we left the town behind us, my heart began to tighten, and I felt a pall descending over me. I had never seen any place so barren and forsaken. Beneath the heavily overcast sky, with thick black clouds closing in, the rolling terrain of one brown hillock after another stretched all the way to the cliffs that plunged to the roiling waves. In all this vast space not a single person could be seen. Once in a while a few thin blades of grass poked out of the ground, only to be beaten down again by the relentless winds. The strange thing was, in the midst of the wind's howling I thought I heard another sound, a kind of flapping or fluttering, as though made by a multitude of invisible kites flown by a host of invisible hands. Upon a closer look, I noticed the dozen or so gently rising mounds of yellow earth all around me, each topped with hundreds of long strips of brown paper held down by stones and rocks. The yellowish brown streamers fluttered and waved in the wind, looking for all the world like strands of yellowing gray hair sticking out of an old person's wrinkled pate. These were all unmarked graves. Great-grandmother had told Grandpa in his dream: "All my neighbors have their roofs retiled every year." The yellow streamers were the new roof tiles, and I had a big pile of them in my bag.

When I looked further into the distance, I realized there were far more than the dozen or so mounds immediately around us—more like two or three hundred of them, scattered all over the undulating landscape, some covered with tiles, others not. Aside from the two of us and the driver of the three-wheeled taxi, there was not another living soul anywhere in sight, unless one counted the two bony oxen in the distance. The closeness of death was beginning to press in on me, and I turned to Qixiong and said, "For more than a thousand years, the fishermen of Wang'an have either died a watery death or been buried right here. Death is everywhere on this island. The whole place is like one big graveyard."

He shook his head and said, "I don't think it's like a graveyard. It reminds me more of the Colosseum in Rome that you and I once visited."

Surprised, I asked, "Why?"

"Because the people who are buried here led very hard lives. Their whole existence was one long struggle with death, with the sea, with the winds, with life and with loneliness," he said, slowly, as though he were thinking out loud. My mind went back to the day of our visit to the Colosseum: under the brilliant midday sun, the flagstones of the arena stung my eyes with their blinding glare. Suddenly, a vision of bodies torn limb from limb by the fangs of ferocious lions swirled through my head, accompanied by echoing howls of terror. My head began to swim, but Qixiong caught me and held me tenderly in his arms. We were on our honeymoon at the time. But now we were on Wang'an, several years and many battles later. Could that really be Qixiong—the stiff, no-nonsense accounting major—waxing so poetic? Could the two of us—embittered, always at loggerheads—really be having an honest, heartfelt conversation?

The wind rippled through Qixiong's hair, and the skin at the corners of his eyes gathered again into tiny wrinkles. As he scanned the horizon with his piercing black eyes, he bore a surprising resemblance to Grandpa.

The driver, who had a face like a seahorse's, turned to us and said, "That cliff there is Tiantai Rock. You said you were looking for a place about a mile south of the rock. That's right about here."

Qixiong arranged to leave our shopping bags with the driver until we had found the grave site. As we started for the cliff, I was just thinking that we should set up a division of labor when Qixiong announced with a confident air: "Lili, you look for the tombstone and I'll look for the bosomshaped hillocks."

We walked past one earthen mound after another, but most of them were not marked with any headstone. I finally came upon a gray one in the shape of a rectangular pillar, but it was made out of cement. Suddenly I heard Qixiong calling to me from the far side of a little knoll: "Come over here, quick!"

I rushed over and saw him pointing excitedly at two small, round hillocks lying straight ahead, rather like the breasts of a reclining woman. When we ran up to the little depression between the knolls, we discovered that there was indeed an unmarked grave, only it was already covered with strips of yellow paper. Someone had already tidied up and paid their respects at this grave. Great-grandmother had only one son and no relatives, so it was absolutely out of the question that someone else might have visited her grave. What a great disappointment! It had all seemed to fit so perfectly: both the terrain and the grave site matched Grandpa's description of his mother's grave. It even appeared to be about the right age: after all these years the earthen mound had been eroded until it was no more than a flattened protuberance, lying on top of the ground like the nail on a finger.

Dusk was falling, and the clouds were growing darker. A light rain had begun to fall. The wind whipped the shafts of rain this way and that and riffled through the shocks of yellow hair springing out of the graves. We decided to call it a day; we would resume our search first thing in the morning.

In the small double bed in our room at the village inn, we lay down to sleep in our accustomed manner: I on my back, he on his side facing away, our bodies not touching each other's at any point. Like a pair of hands clutching compulsively at an object, the wind was shaking the windows and rattling them relentlessly. I closed my eyes and lay there for a long time, but sleep would not come. The last time we had stayed in a hotel we were in rainy London, on the last stop of our honeymoon.

All of a sudden I felt him turn toward me and run his hands over my breasts and down between my legs. Enraged, I yanked his hand away and blurted, "I don't want to get cystitis again!"

He turned away once more and lay in silence.

It had happened on a chilly morning, in the dark hours just before dawn. At half past four in the morning I was doubled over in pain, feeling the spasms wracking my insides as I stared in fear and foreboding at the streams of blood swirling in the toilet bowl. Why was I urinating blood? I couldn't be menstruating—my period had just ended. Then I was seized by the urge to urinate again, and there was a burning pain when I did so. Afterward, I was stunned to find the bowl filled with bright red blood. What on earth was wrong with me? In a panic, I ran back to the bed to wake Qixiong. I shook him vigorously, but it was a long time before he finally opened his eyes and stumbled groggily into the bathroom. By then the blood in the toilet had long since disappeared. He muttered, "What blood?" and went back to sleep.

I sat down on the bed again. But almost immediately the pain in my abdomen started once more, and I found myself pressing down so hard on my belly to ease the pain it was as though I were trying to squeeze myself off below the waist. I had to urinate again, and again there was blood. Back and forth to the bathroom I went, four times in fifteen minutes. By the end I was so panic-stricken I began to bawl. I was sure that some major organ had burst inside and that I was hemorrhaging to death. Dear God, help me, please! Desperately I shook Qixiong again until he woke up. This time he finally saw the toilet bowl full of blood. Without further ado he called an old high school friend of his who was an intern at Taiwan University Hospital. Then he turned to me and said, with an impatient frown, "It's just a bladder infection. Go to the hospital at half past nine, and my friend will give you some medication."

With that, he proceeded to get dressed and then went off to work! He was my husband—he should have stayed with me and taken care of me. He should have taken me to the hospital. How could he have been so heartless and cold? Later I learned from the doctor that I had come down with "honeymoon cystitis," an infection caused by contusion of the urethra—something for which Qixiong had to bear at least half of the responsibility! Feeling aggrieved and sorry for myself,

I cried for two days. After that I finally woke up from my fantasies about him, and my love for him cooled as well. When this happened we had been married less than a year.

He reached for me again, caressing my hair gently with one hand, while with the other arm he drew me softly toward him. After a long while, my body finally began to relax in his embrace. Then I felt his lips behind my ear, nibbling and kissing me with a wavelike rhythm, and I found myself breathing more and more rapidly. All of a sudden I remembered that he had discovered this erogenous zone of mine on our honeymoon but that he had not touched me there even once during the past year, and I came back to my senses right away. By this time the waves had grown from undulating ripples to a surging tide. I'm stiff and cold, I thought to myself, I'm dry, tight, and unyielding; neither his considerable pride nor his self-restraint would ever allow him to persist in the face of such a snub or to force himself on me. It was my fail-safe strategy for occasions like this. But this time it didn't work. Like an onrushing tide, his passion raged and washed over me, pounding the shores of my reserve with ferocious intensity, and gradually, in spite of myself, I began to moisten, to soften, to let a low, deep song reverberate in my throat, until I finally let out a sharp cry.

He rolled off onto his back, asking me softly, "Was that good for you?"

I didn't know what to say. I didn't want to say yes, but I couldn't lie and say I felt nothing. In the end I gave a slight nod. Satisfied, he rolled over and went to sleep.

Soon his breathing grew deep and even. There we were again, just like before, two people sharing the same bed without connecting. Yet only a few moments ago we had actually managed to connect, to communicate. He wanted me to accept his new self, while his even, untroubled breathing told me that he had already done so without any qualms. The rain continued to pitter-patter outside, dashing against the windowpanes, ruffling the countless heads of yellowed hair. What a strange and wondrous island this was, arousing such feral instincts hidden deep within one's soul!

When I opened my eyes, I found Qixiong staring at me intently, his eyes aglow in the murky gray light that was filtering through a slit in the curtains. Running his fingertips lightly over my lips, he murmured, "Lili, about the cystitis—I've always felt really guilty about that. Back then I had just taken over the branch office and had to prove to my dad that I was capable of running it myself. I was so busy I didn't know which way was up. From now on I'll have my priorities in order. It won't happen again."

Finally, an apology. I didn't say anything, but the feeling of aggrievement I'd had since the incident began to recede like an ebb tide.

He went on: "You probably don't know this, but I've always wanted to start my own accounting firm. . . ."

"Look at you now," I interrupted. "You're already such a workaholic taking care of the family business. If you had your own company you'd be even worse. I think we should just go our separate ways."

He pressed his fingers against my lips. "Hear me out. I'd only do it if we went into it together."

"If we worked together we'd be fighting even more," I argued. But a thought flashed through my mind: if he started his own business we'd never have to move back to Gaoxiong, which means I'd never be reduced to being a miserable Penghunese daughter-in-law.

"We'll discuss it later. Let's get up now. It's already half past seven," he said as he pulled me out of bed.

During breakfast Qixiong pored over a map, planning our strategy for the search: beginning at a point half a mile due south of Tiantai Rock and half a mile inland from the shore, and proceeding south for another two and a half miles we would make a meticulous and methodical sweep of the entire area.

At a quarter of nine we arrived at the spot where we had gotten out of the three-wheeled taxi yesterday. Qixiong left our four plastic tote bags with a cowherd by the side of the road and asked the taxi driver to pick us up at five in the afternoon. We set out with only a camera, a compass, a small shovel, and some sandpaper.

It was still heavily overcast. There were only a handful of people visiting various graves in the distance. Scanning the horizon, I noticed that more than half of the graves had already been covered with yellow roof tiles. That would save us a lot of trouble, since now we would only have to look for those that had not been retiled.

But the morning came and went, and we were still no closer to finding the grave. By then we had already covered more than two-thirds of the area we had planned to search. We sat down under a withered tree and, leaning back to back, ate our sandwiches. Gazing out at the horizon, where steel gray clouds melded into the deep blue sea, I asked Qixiong, "How did Grandpa's parents die?"

"His father went out to sea when Grandpa was two years old and never came back."

It suddenly dawned on me: "Now I understand why this island is called *Wang'an*. It's the prayer of every fisherman's family: May he return safe and sound."[1]

"You're absolutely right. As for Grandpa's mother, our guess is that she died of pneumonia, judging from her symptoms. Grandpa single-handedly wheeled his mother's body in a pushcart out to the slopes, dug a hole by himself, then buried her."

"Poor kid—he was only fourteen." I tried to imagine how the old lion would have looked at that age: probably slim as a bamboo pole, and with flashing eyes.

"Grandpa's widowed mother raised him all by herself. She would gather conches that had been washed onto the beach, pickle them in jars, and sell them in the market. She made barely enough to feed the two of them."

Something puzzled me. "I don't understand. If she was the only family he'd had, why didn't Grandpa visit her grave at all in the fifty years or more since he left Wang'an? Wasn't that rather hard-hearted of him?"

Qixiong patted my hand and burst out in a hearty laugh. "Lili, no wonder you don't understand. This is a man's world, a man's way of thinking. Take a good look at this island. Anyone who grows up in such a harsh and unforgiving environment learns to forge ahead no matter what. You can't look back, you can't have second thoughts. I didn't understand Grandpa either until I got here, but now I'm beginning to understand him a little better."

In the early afternoon we came upon first one, then another twin-peaked hillock, but neither of them had graves matching the descriptions we were given. Then, around three o'clock, I finally discovered a gray, uninscribed tombstone in the shape of a rectangular column, standing in front of an old grave on the leeward slope of a hill. Excitedly, Qixiong took the sandpaper out of his pocket and began to rub

---

1. *Wang'an* can be translated literally as "hoping for a safe return."

one side of the grave marker. Before long he broke into a big grin and pointed to the area, about two inches square, that he had just sanded: "Look, Lili, these little yellow whorls must be part of the banded strip he was talking about. Yes, yes, we're on the right track!"

Hand in hand, the two of us half walked, half ran toward the north, following the small compass Qixiong was holding. In the urban environs of Taipei, "the two of us" were a sight to be seen only in a movie: a young couple running hand in hand across a yellow dirt slope, the sea breeze streaming through their hair; the passion of the night before lingered, slowly melting the chunk of ice that had been wedged between them, and now, their bodies in perfect step with each other, they were counting their strides as they searched for an ancestor they had never met.

At five hundred paces, two small hillocks appeared to our right, not far away. One was higher than the other, and the ground between them was rather flat—not the kind of terrain where one would expect to find any graves. But when we ran up closer, we saw, at the bottom of one slope, a gentle hump of mounded earth—an old, timeworn grave. That's it!

Qixiong let out a whoop: "Grandpa, we found it!"

Suddenly I found myself whirling through the air. Qixiong had picked me up by the waist and was spinning me around in a circle, like a mischievous kid twirling a rag doll. When I finally landed, my balance was thrown off, and I toppled into his arms. I knew this was an important moment for the Lin family, but I couldn't help wishing that it belonged to us and no one else. Like a little kitten, I nestled quietly against his heaving chest. Sensing my tenderness, he caressed my cheek and then, with a gentle chuckle, nudged me away, saying, "Wait here, Little Vixen, I'm going to fetch the incense and candles." It had been a long time since he had called me by that nickname.

Great-grandmother's grave was no more than a gentle rise in the ground, a slight, barely perceptible swelling, like the belly of a woman just three months pregnant. In a little while this grave would also be covered with yellow roof tiles. I began combing the area around the mound for pebbles and small stones with which to hold down the paper streamers, but by the time I had collected seventy or eighty of them, there was still no sign of Qixiong. At that moment the dark clouds in the west began to break apart and a giant red orb popped its head out through the opening, lighting up earth, sea, and sky.—The perfect storybook ending: the grave has been found, the heavens part, and the sun shines forth.

Then Qixiong appeared on the crest of a hill to the east. The rays from the sun shone on his well-built frame and tinted his tan jacket a vivid orange-red. He was walking very slowly, almost ploddingly, and his hands were empty. From his trudging steps and the grave look on his face, I knew something must have gone wrong, and I ran to meet him.

"It's not the right grave," he said wearily when I got close enough. "On my way back I passed by that tombstone again and saw two people who had just arrived to sweep the grave. It was a couple in their sixties, and I chatted with them for a little while. The person buried there was the man's father, who died forty years ago. Our great-grandmother died more than fifty years ago, so Grandpa couldn't have seen that gravestone over there when he buried his mother. Besides, the location of this unmarked grave isn't quite right either. It should be in the hollow between the two breasts, but here it is at the foot of the slope. So it can't be the right one."

Crestfallen and dejected, we resumed our search. There was no more than a quarter of a square mile left, and neither of us entertained much hope of finding anything. And sure enough, even though we combed every last inch of the remaining area, we failed to find a single grave that matched Grandpa's description. It was not yet four o'clock—still more than an hour to go before the driver would pick us up.

"I'm tired, Qixiong," I said. "Let's find someplace to rest awhile."

He looked around and, putting his arm around my waist, led me to the top of a hill nearby. We sat on a west-facing slope, looking out over a vast expanse of ocean.

"If we don't find it, Grandpa will be so upset," I said. "What are we going to do?"

"We'll tell him that Great-grandmother knows we looked all over the island and did everything we possibly could," he answered soothingly.

The glare from the setting sun was hurting my eyes, so I decided to lie down. The ground was a little bumpy but not too hard, since it had rained yesterday, and, thanks to the gusty winds today, it was no longer even damp. Gazing at the flocks of fluffy white clouds, I thought to myself, well, we didn't find the grave, but we did manage to find something—a certain amity, a new harmony between us. Or perhaps it was a new self: for him, a previously dormant wild streak; for me, a reawakened tenderness.

Suddenly an enormous flower dangled in the air above my face, brushing against my cheek like a red-hot flame: a crimson center surrounded by vivid orange petals with bright yellow tips. I shrieked, "What kind of flower is this?"

Qixiong blew into my ear and said, "It's spring already, and this is an early-blooming gaillardia, also called a 'blanket flower'."

Then, tucking the blossom behind my ear, he lay beside me and, clasping my hand in his, said, "Grandpa once told me that in the spring, the entire island of Wang'an is covered with a thick blanket of these flowers. Even the grave mounds are buried under a sea of blossoms, and all at once this desolate island seems to burst into life."

Gazing at me as though I were a blanket of flowers, he smiled at me with his eyes as he pulled me toward him. Then he kissed me. White clouds above, yellow earth below—it was the first time I ever felt a kiss could go on for all eternity, blessed, perhaps, by heaven above and the elements below. Suddenly, he rolled on top of me and, pinning me to the ground, began kissing me with passionate abandon. I could feel the urgency in him, and, fending him off as best I could, I asked nervously, "What are you doing?"

He answered breathlessly, "Don't worry, there's no one around."

In one swift move he pulled me onto my feet and made a broad sweeping gesture with one arm. It was true. Standing where we were on the crest of a hill we could see for miles around, and from the shoreline on one side to the undulating bluffs on the other, not a soul was to be seen. Even if someone were headed our way, it would take at least half an hour or more to get to this hill. In all that vastness there was no one but the two of us and the long-buried folks of Wang'an, perhaps still yearning for a safe return.

His arm around my waist, we stood next to each other for a while, our bodies close and touching. I felt a firmness, a rock-solid strength that emanated from his body and welled up out of the ground beneath his feet. It was the same sense of security I had felt as a child hanging from my father's neck. All of a sudden he pushed me onto the ground and began making passionate love to me, his fingers tugging impatiently at my clothes. Frantically I pried away his hands and gasped, "No, no, not here! Wait till we go back."

He stopped the tempestuous motion of his body and lifting his weight onto his arms and knees, whispered to me hoarsely, "Go back? Where? This is my home, Little Vixen, right here."

I was dumbfounded. Home? Here? But he was right. Wang'an was his home, the place of his roots. This slope could be his bed, a huge bed in the middle of an enormous bedroom. His breathing was the wind that whipped across the island, and I the sea of flowers bending and swaying in the wind, undulating, surging, pulsating, driven before the wind, driven wild with abandon. He was a ship sailing on top of me, his sharp keel plowing through the ocean of my desire, opening up my briny depths. He howled, or was it the wind, mixed with the seagulls' shrill cries? Our whole, vast, sky blue bedroom was filled with the cries and moans of our pleasure. My ears were ringing with the sounds of my own ecstasy, a rich, full-throated song of love that blended with the wind's whistling to weave a silvery net and cast it over the entire island. And then, rushing at me like a wave bedecked with spindrift, he thrusted forcefully, and a low boom like distant thunder resounded in my head. . . .

At the moment of climax, in my swimming vision, the western sky became a velvety curtain of the richest maroon, and instead of the setting sun hovering just above the horizon, I saw a brilliant gaillardia dancing in front of a pitch black stage. In the exalted eyes of God, were we just another blanket flower dancing on this island?

I felt a sharp pain in my skull, on the spot where I had been hit moments ago by a clap of thunder or something. When I touched the back of my head, my hand brushed against something cold and hard—a slab of rock. Turning around to look, I saw the tip of a rectangular block of gray stone poking out of the ground. How strange—its surface was so smooth. Then a thought struck me, and I shouted, "Quick, Qixiong, bring the shovel!"

He leaned over to look and immediately began to dig at the dirt around the stone. It was indeed a stone marker in the shape of a rectangular column. Using the sandpaper, I rubbed vigorously at one of the surfaces and, after a minute or two, wiped off the powdery debris with a wet towelette. Sure enough, the upper part of the stone was covered with a band of yellow and red whorls, ranging in size from that of a large coin to a grain of rice. Looking at each other excitedly, we grabbed the compass and hurried north. At five hundred paces, two gentle mounds appeared in front of us, so low they were almost imperceptible. And when we ran over to the hollow between the two breasts, there it was, an old, worn-down grave! We found it, Grandpa, we finally found Great-grandmother!

But then I heard Qixiong's voice, sounding uneasy and perplexed: "Look!"

At the other end of the hollow about three meters away was another old grave. Which one of the two belonged to Great-grandmother?

Qixiong was lost in thought for a while. Then he said, briskly and cheerfully, "Well, one of the two must be hers, so why don't we make offerings at both graves? Since the two of them are neighbors, I'm sure Great-grandmother would be happy for us to honor her neighbor as well."

So we got to work. I covered both mounds with yellow roof tiles and divided the incense, candles, fruits, chicken, and cakes into two equal portions, setting them in front of each grave, while Qixiong circled the two sites, taking pictures from every angle to show Grandpa. Finally, we both knelt in front of the first grave, each holding the ritual three sticks of incense. Silently, I prayed: "Great-grandmother of Qixiong, this is his wife, Hu Lili. We have come to honor you on behalf of your son, Lin Wei'an, our grandfather. His legs are now paralyzed and he couldn't come himself, but you have always been in his thoughts. We hope you enjoy your new roof tiles and the offerings we brought you today." And then I added, "It would be nice to have a baby with Qixiong."

I glanced at Qixiong out of the corner of my eye. Eyes closed, lips murmuring softly, he wore an open and tranquil expression, a look of unguardedness and contentment I had previously seen on him only at moments of utter relaxation, in bed. The content of his silent prayer must have been more complex than mine; it probably included, among other things, something about his coming of age, perhaps something about our destinies as well. How strange people are! Sometimes you'll suddenly realize he is not at all the man of your dreams, and sometimes he'll suddenly metamorphose into the one you've been looking for all your life. Although today I am not ovulating, who knows? I may yet get pregnant any day now.

A breeze wafted across the roof tiles and rustled them gently. In the gathering dusk, we walked hand in hand and knelt before the other grave.

MASTER CHAI

Zhu Tianwen

(Translated by Michelle Yeh)

A long, long time ago, Chai Mingyi, then thirty-one years old, thought that it would be nice to settle down in Kunming in southwest China in his old age so he could enjoy the area's springlike climate all year long. Were he not waiting for the girl young enough to be his granddaughter, like waiting for an apricot tree to become full of trembling blossoms in early spring chill, he would not have realized that forty years have passed since then. Yes, forty years have passed. Nevertheless, when his skinny but still soft, fair, and extremely sensitive fingers touch the girl's tender breasts, a sharp tremor shoots up from his lower abdomen.

The girl is probably not coming. She lives on the other side of the desert of Taipei Basin, on Rainy Farm Road in the Sesame Hill District. To get here she has to change buses twice, and both rides are quite long. Every afternoon the street-cleaning truck rumbles by his home like a dinosaur, spitting a geyser from its abdomen to settle the steamy smoke and roiling dust. Taipei Basin is a vast desert indeed. As soon as the truck is gone, the overpass construction generates more dust and covers the streets with a film of sand. Construction is going on everywhere. It seems that every time Chai moves to a place, it starts building houses, digging streets, constructing underground tunnels, laying underground water pipes, or building an overpass. He has spent more than half his life in this desert. Yes, waiting for the girl is like waiting for an oasis.

Master Chai—the girl always calls him Master Chai when she phones for an appointment. Every time she knocks at the door and comes in, she always says apologetically, "Sorry to disturb Master's nap." Her voice is as clear as a spring flowing over the parched fields of his memories and feelings. For years he has learned to ignore what he sees and hears around him. But suddenly he finds himself watering the potted plants on the balcony with a white plastic can. The red hibiscus blooms vigorously all year long; its color is so intense that it astounds him. To still be able to be astounded is a nice feeling.

Since Chai yielded to his sons' wishes and moved from the northeast to the southwest of the basin, his patients have multiplied like a sweet-potato vine. According to the Earth trigram in the *Book of Changes,* the southwest is an auspicious direction for meeting friends, whereas the northeast is not. He has great admiration for the wisdom of the ancients; three thousand years ago they predicted his situation. Every Saturday afternoon he goes to the faraway Threefold District; every Tuesday evening he goes to Harmony Road, where there are many pubs. He puts on a winter white kung fu tunic and brings a wooden pole, whenever he remembers, to chase away vicious dogs in the neighborhood. On Monday evenings after his favorite soap operas on TV, he sees Zhang, who teaches at Prosperity Elementary School. They say a man suffers from a bad waist at age forty and bad shoulders at fifty. Sure enough, Zhang's shoulders are as stiff as rosewood blocks. When Chai puts some pressure on them, Zhang screams and squeals, even breaks into tears. Thursday at noon, Young Chen comes. Though young, he already has a pot belly, and his liver is as useless as a piece of rusty metal. Chen usually starts snoring the minute he lies on the wooden bunk covered with a straw mat. When he wakes up from his fifty-minute nap, he has to rush back to work at Taiwan Plastics Company. He always drops a red envelope in the clear acrylic donation box. A sweet scent wafts from the box; these days even the red money envelopes are scented. The scent feels sensual to Chai.

Yes, this is an exciting, barbaric place. Many of Chai's friends have visited the mainland and come back. Only Old Peng decided to stay with his nephews in his old hometown. Chai's sons have applied to the Red Cross for a permit to allow him to visit relatives on the mainland. His disciples in Hong Kong are eagerly hoping that on his way there he will stop by to give them some lessons. Taipei is a city hard to like, but these days he, too, has learned to enjoy the vulgar variety shows as he sits in front of his high-resolution television set. Just now his son came up to copy a videotape. It was an R-rated film that just started showing in the theater last night, but he had already gotten a pirated copy. A naked couple were having sex on the screen, while his granddaughters A Wan and A Li each sat at a corner of the coffee table, one doing math homework, the other practicing handwriting. Displeased, he told his son to erase the picture. A Li gave him a funny look, as if he were some kind of fossil, then lowered her head to resume her homework. Even the children have become accustomed to racy scenes. They say Japanese television even shows women's breasts. Compared to that, the local television is nothing to get alarmed about.

His two sons are even more Taiwanese than their native Taiwanese mother. They both married Taiwanese wives. They and his granddaughters often forget his presence and speak the local dialect in front of him. When Chai landed at Gaoxiong Harbor that year, a tree in the roiling dust with large vermilion flowers shaded half of the sky. Later he learned that the tree that had given him this surprise welcome was called a phoenix palm. On this subtropical island all the plants grow wild. Even fences cannot not keep the hibiscus flowers—some bright red, some peach-colored with pink streaks, some daffodil yellow— from spreading out and staring at the passersby. These days when he goes to Harmony Road to treat Miss Zhong, he notices a virtual jungle of exotic plants and flowers thriving in the shadows of a bar's neon signs. It reminds him of the giant bananas and pineapples, which looked like human heads with spikes, that he saw here for the first time in his life. To a stranger, their exaggerated looks were intimidating.

He is waiting for the girl as though waiting for a familiar home-town accent. His considerate sons partitioned off the living room with panels and turned the upper half into a Buddhist hall for him. The long row of steel file cabinets for storing the sutras takes up a big chunk of the living room, which is not spacious to begin with. He feels sorry about that. In the Buddhist hall two lamps that stay on all day long shine like two large strawberries. Behind them are a pair of scrolls inscribed with his master's teachings. A portrait of his master—who looks a lot like Dostoevsky—hangs in the middle.

Two months after Chai moved in, his sons bought the building next door and remodeled it. New signs were made, with "MTV" spray painted in the frantic shapes and colors of hip-hop. He saw the refurbished building once. The shabby cement staircase has been turned into a tunnel, at the end of which is a red rug glaring in the refracted sunlight. You cannot see the steps when you go upstairs; you have to grope about on the first few steps before you can stand up. A row of neon-painted metallic mirrors makes strange reflections. The tunnel is painted orange and purple, zigzagging along as it leads to holes just large enough for a small coffee table, a love seat, and a twen-ty-six-inch television set.

His sons' business is thriving. Many soldiers frequent the place. There is a barrack on the hillside nearby, the back of which descends below street level by a couple of feet and faces the main street, where five bus routes pass by. He often sees soldiers coming out of the bar-rack, undressed from the waist up, with a tin basin for washing them-selves or doing laundry. Army sweatshirts dry on the lines scattered in the empty lot. From the ventilation window he can see soldiers exer-cising. In deep winter, with luck, he can see them butchering dogs by the long counter. The soldiers used to give wolf whistles as they peered up at the women pedestrians, like models walking on stage, revealing everything under their skirts. It was only recently that the military was given the budget to build a gray wall, which now blocks the nice view. The distant hill with its flat top resembles a loess plateau. A dome-shaped building rises high on Site 107. According to the bus-stop sign, it is a training center; a nuclear-arms battalion is more like it.

Students from the nearby vocational school love to come here, too. For roughly the same price as a movie, they can watch videos and order a soft drink. Sometimes when a hot video is showing, they have to wait for a room. From the newspapers he realizes that something else is going on at MTV. The new regulation stipulates that the door not be locked and a hole be drilled in it to allow a view of the love seat. Still, law is one thing, making money another.

In the narrow living room a black steel rack contains eight shelves from floor to ceiling. On each shelf is a VCR, except on the top shelf where the ancestral tablet sits. Every day he stands on a stool to light the incense and dusts the tablet. His daughter-in-law also climbs on a chair to put fresh fruit there.

During the night he wakes up twice to go to the bathroom diagonally across the living room. The rest of the family are watching a striptease on TV. He chides his grandchildren for staying up so late. A Wan retorts that summer vacation started a long time ago. The air conditioner is roaring. His tiny bedroom does not even need an electric fan. He feels the world is advancing, leaving him far behind.

Waiting for the girl is like waiting for the return of youth. The ancestral spirits occupy a high corner in the room; gods and humans sharing the same space. What is Caesar's does not go only to Caesar, what is the gods' does not go solely to the gods. He is a Taoist, whose heart belongs in the pure land of transcendence. How was it that the sight of the Adidases on the girl's snow white feet sent his heart pounding? He watched the girl open her acrylic pencil box—what a cute pencil box!—in a translucent peacock blue that reminded him of jelly beans, with seven figurines painted in jolly rainbow colors. The girl took out a pen and signed her name in his registration book, drawing each stroke meticulously just like A Li, who just started learning how to write. Written in a childlike style, the characters looked like a bunch of crisscross matchsticks.

The girl met Mrs. Yang when she went to Hokkaido in northern Japan with her parents during Chinese New Year. Mrs. Yang is a formal disciple of his. She looks younger than fifty even though she is sixty-some years old. Once in a while he goes to her house for dinner; its ivory-colored furniture with gold trim has the fragrance of her makeup. Her youngest daughter, Little Zhen, studies French with a French lady under a lamp made of pale seashells. Little Zhen's new client is French. She used to rely on a telephone to conduct her import-business transactions. She had to walk two blocks to use the fax machine at a friend's company. Later Mrs. Yang gave her some money to buy a fax machine and put it in the Buddhist hall, which now doubles as an office. So Little Zhen has little need to go out. She is allergic to the high dust content in the air in Taipei Basin as well to central air-conditioning.

During her trip to the snow country, Mrs. Yang kindheartedly cured her fellow travelers of their colds or gave them transfusions of vital energy. She made a quite a name for herself. After she came back, her telephone did not stop ringing. That day he happened to be having dinner at her place and met the girl; she came to see Mrs. Yang with her elder sister and her nephew, who suffered from a chronic cough. Mrs. Yang exclaimed delightedly, "What a destiny, what a destiny, to meet the Master and have him diagnose you in person!"

After Mrs. Yang brought everyone a mug of Ovaltine, the girl's sister explained that her son caught colds easily. She was worried by the increasing dosage of Western medicine he had to take, and though he had seen several Chinese doctors, none helped. She faithfully exchanged information with other parents about secret cures and geomantic practices, such as changing the direction of the bed and hanging a wind chime, mirror, or a piece of red silk yarn above the door. They did all of these halfheartedly.

The little boy was playing with a transformer and was told to put it down and sit on a stool for diagnosis. He called the girl Little Auntie and said it felt like sitting on a swing, with a lot of smoke coming out of his body.

Surprised, the girl remarked to her sister that she could not see any smoke. Mrs. Yang explained to her with a smile that grown-ups could not see many things, the smoke of a cold being one of them. The girl sneezes like a whale every morning when she wakes up, possibly due to an allergy or dust or who knows what. That day he could not tell that she was wearing fairly strong contact lenses. She has heavy eyelids, slightly tilting upward at the end, and looks people straight in the eye. The girl attributed her sneezing to her eyes' sensitivity to the polluted air. Since in the foreseeable future air pollution in Taipei was only going to get worse, she felt the problem was hopeless.

But she came to his cramped clinic anyway. That day his son came to copy a videotape. On the screen were a bunch of primitive men wrapped in animal skins fighting in a bleak wilderness. It occurred to him that the twenty-first century with its intergalactic exploits seemed no more advanced than the age of the cavemen. Suddenly, a fairly explicit sex scene appeared on the screen, which greatly embarrassed him. He shut the door and the windows and turned on the air conditioner. Soon the newly lit incense from the ancestral table filled the entire room with smoke, making the girl sneeze incessantly. So he turned off the air conditioner and used the old-fashioned electric fan. He just could not figure out how it was that before, when his Buddhist hall was much bigger, quieter, and closer to downtown, he had had few patients and was by himself most of the time.

In his dream, he smells instant noodles. When he wakes up, the bright sun is shining on him. Vehicles drive by with shrill noises and roiling dust. There are many potted plants by the iron railing on the balcony. Every three or four days he rinses them to keep their natural colors. Often when he dozes off on the sofa against the summer mat woven of wooden beads, he can smell the acid scent of the synthetic leather. He awakes and sits there for a while, realizing it is autumn. No wonder the sun pours in even before he has had a good sleep, casting shadows diagonally across the aluminum door and windows in the Buddhist hall. His grandchildren are eating instant noodles and watching a Japanese youth variety show. For fear of waking him up, they keep the volume low. How can they possibly watch like that? During the long, long summer, the routine of the entire family is turned upside down. He is saddened by the thought that he needs a nap before lunch.

He sits in a brightly lit MTV room sipping tea. When he sees some videotapes sticking out on the shelves, he walks over to set them straight. When he notices that the two tapes of a film are separated on the shelves, he pulls them out and puts them back together. There is a large scroll in the middle of the wall with the Buddha character; it is a photocopy of his master's handwriting from half a century ago. His master did not leave any writings behind; this was the only piece. Next to it is a horizontal scroll of calligraphy in the clerical style. An excerpt from a Buddhist scripture, it was a gift from a young Buddhist calligrapher who also mounted it meticulously. On the east wall is a photograph of the former president, Chiang Ching-kuo, on the west wall the present president, Li Denghui. For years he has been a loyal member of the Nationalist Party. His greatest contribution is that he saved a high official suffering from diabetes from the brink of death. Yesterday he drove out an evil spirit from a woman who suffered from chronic hemorrhoids; the spirit turned out to be a fist-sized creature. He has been in the business of exorcism for years. His principle is not to kill, so he let it go with a word of admonition. When the girl came, the television was showing an interview with the singer Fei Yuqing. A few customers sat giggling in front of the set. The plumber who came to fix the leaking faucet was glued to the screen, too. He told the girl that Fei is great at imitating other singers and at his best when he imitates Liu Wenzheng.

The girl makes handmade women's accessories. She tells him excitedly that she has sublet a counter in a shop near Acme Market. She also suffers from hives. Jokingly she says that she is destined to be a wealthy lady because silver jewelry immediately gives her hives, so she can only wear pure gold. When she came out of the bathroom after her sixth treatment, some red spots suddenly appeared on her face and spread quickly. Soon, her face was as red as a chili pepper; even her eyes looked red. Then he learned they were hives. Sometimes when she forgets and wipes her face too hard, her face gets red like that. She has had the problem for a long time; it has become part of her body and she is resigned to it. Chai made a resolution to get rid of it.

For men, the center of vital energy lies in the lower abdomen; for women, in the breasts. Once he treated a woman accountant. Back in school, when cramming for exams was the norm, one of her shoulders was damaged from the constantly heavy book bag. She used to come in the evenings on odd-numbered dates. After three months there was still no improvement, and he felt frustrated. Then, in a moment of inspiration, he asked her for permission to treat her breasts. They were flat like pot-sticker skins, but after a few sessions they grew plumper and plumper. Her vital force became robust, and her sagging shoulder straightened. With that experience in mind, he researched and experimented some more. Later Mrs. Deng, who suffered from vertigo, told him that one day when she was taking a bath, she was surprised to find that all her stretch marks were gone. Master Chai not only cured her disease but also brought her beauty back. A bunch of her close friends came to see him, all eager to become his disciples. Since that fad died, only Mrs. Deng still comes to see him now and then. It gives him a headache every time she reiterates her wish to be his disciple. He is getting old. Often he considers passing on his skills to a disciple, and this time when he goes to Hong Kong, maybe he will find the right one. Two years ago, one of his students was asked to treat a stranger. As the patient deteriorated, his family out of desperation consulted several doctors who prescribed different medicines. When the patient died, they blamed it on his disciple. The lawsuit is still going on.

Waiting for the girl is like waiting for the right disciple. The seventh time she came, he gave her some blessed water to be blended with drinking water at home. He went into the kitchen to look for an empty Coke bottle. When he was rinsing out the bottle, the girl walked up and took it from his hands politely. He poured some water from the kettle on the stove into a tin cup, went into the Buddhist hall, and chanted an incantation. Then he came back in to pour the water into the Coke bottle. The girl took the cup from him, too. The water was hot. Seeing an empty thermal bottle leaning against the wall, she poured the rest of the water into it and put the thermal bottle in a plastic bag before she left.

During her eighth visit, he asked her to unhook her bra, but she was not wearing one because of her hives. A loose-fitting jet black cotton shirt slipped down one shoulder, exposing her collarbones and the two spaghetti straps of the olive top she had on. He reached in and felt her cool, soft breasts. He was suddenly reminded of rainy Jilong Harbor in 1948, where he was taken aback by a blooming tree hanging over a stone wall; its white blossoms were falling in the cold rain and the smoky air. "Cherry Blossoms"—later he found out the place had been a brothel run by a Japanese and was turned into a city hostel after the return of Taiwan to China in 1945.

During her ninth visit, he was determined to improve her eyesight. When she was in the sixth grade, the girl was diagnosed as slightly nearsighted and astigmatic. Every two weeks she went to an optometrist for an examination, medicines, and injections. She did it for a whole year. At the time she could see well enough to play the enchanting "Für Elise," but no matter how hard she tried, she could not go beyond that level. He scrutinized her pale, glowing face and planted a kiss on her forehead.

In the harbor the misty air was filled with coal smoke. Cherry blossoms were blooming by the Japanese-styled house. But the petals did not dance in the air; they dropped to the dark, slippery, coal-spotted ground. A shocking sight. He had come from the south in search of a man named Zhang Longsheng. A few years back they had met in Shanghai. Zhang auditioned four times to get into a theater troupe, whereas Chai was admitted the first time. Later, Zhang moved to Jilong and opened a grocery store. After the troupe disbanded, Chai looked for his uncle without success. The only person he knew on the entire island was Zhang. So he made inquiries, going from one grocery store to another. Just when he decided to take a boat back to the mainland, he spotted Zhang's store on a little street under what is now an overpass. They hugged each other tightly. He moved into the attic and shared the floor with Zhang. During the day he looked for work at the harbor. The store was owned by Zhang and someone else, and though Zhang did not mind taking Chai in, the partner did not even know him.

The steamboats from Shenzhen and Sichuan arrived in the harbor at ten o'clock each night. After a while he learned the secret of the trade. He did not have the nerve to move in on the turf of the red-caps, so he picked those passengers who were in a hurry and did not already have a deal with the porters. He would take them to one side, put their luggage on his shoulder eagerly, and take it to the train station. He let the passengers pay him any amount they liked, anywhere from thirty or forty to seventy thousand. He got a gray cap and pulled it way down to spare himself embarrassment in case he ran into someone he knew. The exhausted passengers were landing in a strange land; his familiar accent was reassuring, and they paid well. In this way he managed to make enough money to buy some pork to take back to the grocery store. Then someone discovered he could write, and he was hired to be an accountant in a restaurant. There, he met a lot of people. The person in charge of money in the restaurant was the owner's concubine. Since he took over her job, she resented him like a needle in the eye, so when his friends asked him if he wanted to open a food shop with them, he agreed. The place was called Penny Profit Steamed Buns and was located in one of the wooden shacks across from the harbor building. Behind it the coal-transporting train never stopped coming and going.

The girl said, "Thank you, Master. Goodbye, Master." Then she ran down the stairs briskly. Her black blouse went all the way to her knees, her white leggings were calf-length, she wore a pair of black sneakers on her bare feet, and a white cotton tee shirt could be seen under the loose-fitting blouse. He was shocked to see that underwear could be worn as outer garments these days. The girl carried a cloth bag large enough to put herself in, but she kept only a few pieces of paper, a purse, and the peacock blue pencil box inside. She took a city bus for half of the journey across the vast desert of the basin and a taxi for the other half. She left like that and has not come back.

The hill looked like a watercolor landscape; on the crest were military headquarters, seemingly sitting among the clouds all year long. An officer there gave him an informant ID card and assigned him to watch the nearby coffee shop. He kept a small notebook, in which he recorded the names of all the customers who frequented the place. Sailors came to Penny Profit Steamed Buns for noodles and left their merchandise at the restaurant for pickups. When he got to know the customs inspectors and military officers well, they let him sell the merchandise and then picked up the cash from him, leaving him a twenty-percent commission. Cigarettes, liquor, pantyhose, and cosmetics were hidden in the crates for dry noodles. When he delivered take-out orders on his bike, he picked up the goods and took them back to his place. Still later he started buying goods from the sailors directly and made a sizable profit. The cash was turned into gold nuggets and hidden in empty Klim powdered-milk cans. When his business got bigger, he used the gold to invest in Chinese herbal medicine. On its way back, however, the smuggling boat was caught by the inspectors. All the medicine was sunk to the bottom of the sea. After that incident, every day he envisioned a pile of gold nuggets shining ruefully at the bottom of a deep blue sea. He left the rainy harbor where he had lived for two years.

He calls the girl's house using the number in the registration book. Her mother says she has gone to her eldest sister's home in Belgium and will be back next month. Autumn is about to pass. In the sunlight in the Buddhist hall, the golden dust of the mundane world roils up and down. Soon, perhaps, Chai will move to Kunming, where there is springlike weather all year round. But his miserable homesickness is for the cherry blossoms in the rain and the lively red hibiscus growing wild by the public rest room.

Will the girl come? The enlarged black-and-white picture of his wife hangs by the door, appropriately taking its place below the ancestral tablet. The dead and the living, gods and ghosts, all occupy the same space and time. The street-cleaning truck comes reeling, sending a foul-smelling gust ahead and leaving a cloud of dust in its wake.

GHOST TALK

Yang Lian

(Translated by Charles A. Laughlin)

*W*hen was it that you stopped using the word *home?* When you talk about this ramshackle old house, you always say *there*. You've also stopped talking about "going back"—what does *back* mean anyway? All you do is go away, again and again, each time a little farther. When you wake up in the morning, you're already a little farther away than yesterday. The distant sea is a glimmering expanse beneath the sunlight, like molten metal or a canyon of light, the chasm yawning ever wider. Soon you will no longer be able to see the string of mountains, now gray, now blue, on the other shore.

You want to speak, yet nothing could be more difficult. Try speaking about the experience of climbing from the first to the second floor—every step of the way, moment to moment. Your toes lead the way: up the first flight of stairs, fifteen steps, turn, second flight, seven steps. There, you did it, but your words sound stiff, formal, like an outline. It's so dark on the stairs, and the balustrade is moldering. There are nails beneath the torn carpeting. There are also two plastic buckets in the middle of the floor, catching leaks. The light's not working, but that's okay; you can feel your way, feel it through the soles of your feet. But you can't say it, because right away, words come into the picture. You can't speak without words—they cut off all the branches and leaves with tiny saws, and you become just a piece of lumber, gleaming white, like a bone. Every day when you go up the stairs, you think, "So this is exile." You must grope your way up every step, lest you lose your footing and the whole world flip over and come crashing down on top of you. You could write a whole canto for each stair and, two flights later, end up with a great epic poem on humankind's exile, but it still wouldn't be you. You can't articulate that elusive feeling, so when someone starts talking about reality, you just want to laugh.

You say you are fleeing, fleeing in this unfamiliar city. From one intersection to the next, all those incomprehensible street names, what have they to do with you? In one hand or the other, whether you read a thousand-page book or flip the only page you have a thousand times, what is the difference? All an exile does is follow a dotted line of footprints, marking time at each point along the way. More painful than standing still—you have been nailed down; hardly a glamorous picture. You remain at one spot only because you don't have the strength to move on, buried alive in days that repeat themselves endlessly—like your poetry, lies about truth. At some point words, like timeworn lacquer, had turned brittle and crumbly and finally had peeled away. Only when you are silent can you hear that terrifying voice—*another day gone!*

Survive. All this just to survive. But why? The sea and clouds here are beautiful, but they imprison you in a clear glass bottle. Water swirls in torrents about your head and feet, swirling beyond your reach, scouring your brain. This is how you have learned to look at the sky. You stare at it all morning long, at the myriad patterns in the air. The old house is tall, so high up you don't dream. You have drowned at the bottom of the sea. A sunken ship, decaying corpses, decrepit bones—once at the bottom you'll have broken the cycle of transmigration.

When you're dead, time hangs heavy, empty. No question about it, it's time for words and speech to be buried. On the seascape in the sky, the clouds' huge feet stomp on you viciously, crushing you, and you look forward with great pleasure to the day when you can avenge yourself on words in just this way.

Your feelings have also changed, imperceptibly. When was it that you suddenly started thinking fondly of all those things from the past? Did the dust of the ages enter your blood overnight? When you talk about your childhood, it is as though you were talking about someone else hiding inside your body. Even that fake antique with the blue-on-white design in the store window catches your eye. When you stare at it, whose reflection is it that glimmers through the glass? An old matchbox suddenly makes your heart throb with pain: a Chinese inscription, a logo that depicts a ludicrously symmetrical mountain, all rendered in a fake imperial style. For thirty years you lived right next door and never once felt any affection for it. How is it that now you wake up in the middle of the night and, with eyes still closed, walk dreamily along the mountain trail, over and over again? Or, in the season of melting snow, revisit that footpath known only to the locals? You conjure the image of your hat tossed carelessly onto the bench, and you feel as though it has been lying there all this time.

In the beginning, you were afraid of forgetting. Afraid that you yourself would forget, afraid that others would forget you. And so, every morning you would speak, write, perform the rituals at your desk. You used your own voice to pursue your memories, trying to fill the growing emptiness inside. You seek a face, many faces, an utterance, a lot of talk that once lingered in your ears. Following the arteries of the wind, you walk a long way, then stop short when you discover that the face had disappeared a long time ago, and what you cradle carefully in your hands is nothing more than a piece of wood, not even worth being called a mask.

Since the moment you parted ways, your memory has stiffened and died. All of a sudden a nail has been driven into the middle of that face. All you remember is that dead face with the unchanging expression, always the same, so frighteningly young. You know it is you who has left the old days and gone over to the other side. In remembering, you have been redacted and rewritten. Even though you keep your fingers tightly clenched, the face begins to melt from the instant you must "remember," trickling away drop by drop. The harder you try to remember yesterday, the more thoroughly you lose today. In fact, there is no difference between the two: death from forgetting is the same as death from remembering.

Eyes wide and mouth agape, you stare as this world slips by you day after day. You are becoming extinct in full view of the multitudes, and now you are truly afraid, afraid of remembering. Those whom you have forgotten or still remember, they have forgotten or still remember you too. Living or dead, they're just two words roaming about, until a day comes when you can no longer remember—do you still remember you? Between you and your shadow, *in that tiny space,* dwell a multitude of lonely ghosts.

So this is the old house, the one you've been living in since last July. Actually it's the room on the second floor overlooking the street. You've even straightened it up a bit; at least you now have a shelter, be it ever so humble. And you have good neighbors: two little animals that live on the roof and run about all night, thundering overhead like a herd of galloping horses; an old wino next door who locks himself in his room and sighs all day. Once in a while, when you run into him on the stairs, his eyes sweep over you as though through empty space. You can hear that gaze crashing into the wall, cracking, and clattering onto the floor. All this time you've been living here, and you still don't know each other's names. Behind the thin plywood walls, you can hear him cursing in some foreign tongue. You curse too, in a different language. You imagine that all those dead soldiers from every nation, whose bodies have been pushed together into one big pile, talk to each other in just this fashion. Your foreign country is on the other side of the thin plywood walls. The other character has nothing to do with you. When there are two lunatics, as long as they crack up under their own portions of the roof, the world is safe.

Then who else can you talk to? What will you say? Only now has the bloodstained umbilical cord been severed. The muddy piece of pottery shard[1] is sharper than a knife. Now you finally know the taste of exile. Something sawing, sawing away every day. It's not until the jagged edges bite into you that they chew you up and break you down into mangled little pieces. Grass is sprouting out of your pores, sharp whiskers burrow under your skin—they itch and they hurt. You feel like laughing; you want to laugh on the street; you laugh at a stranger coming toward you. Chuckling and cackling, you hide before you're noticed.

You finally know what it is like to be chased off the land, to be banished from time; you now know what it is like to be free from care, to be free! A calf that is chased away from the milk bucket, squealing and groaning from hunger—how free it is! You only want to talk to yourself, engage in a soliloquy, but while the calf can repeat the same word every day, you cannot. If you have to ask others to eavesdrop for you, or put on someone else's ears to listen, then you won't be able to fool yourself. What you have to say is said as soon as you open your mouth. The rump of the steer has already been branded. When the red-hot branding iron is pressed against the hide, it makes a hissing noise. It's all quite comical. Others talk about how many pounds of meat they can carve out of the steer.

You listen, listen and wait. Finally things begin to quiet down. You relax and make an eye out of plaster of paris to see whether in the depths of the blank void there isn't a little piece of darkness. In the heart of darkness there has never been anything but a blank void. Your language stops right there. The cell door clangs shut. The warden saunters about behind the walls. But you're locked outside, like water poured beside its container. A freedom that glints and flashes—you know how it feels to be a fish that has just been caught and reeled in from the water. You have come to the end of your life, but you cannot die. You long to hear even the warden's bellows, or the sound of knives being sharpened, yet you can't hear a thing. *Just that tiny space,* but enough to lock you out of all of yesterday. While you plunge headlong into that vacuum known as today.

You're thirty-five, much too old already. Too late to even live your life over from the beginning. All you can do is write, letting each and

1. In olden days a piece of broken pottery was used to cut umbilical cords.

every word fall inkily onto the paper like eggs being laid. Or like flies crashing headlong into a pane of glass—haven't you always wondered whether they crack their skulls and bleed to death? Are they merely answering the call of the open sky when they make such savage fools of themselves? Then what about you? Aren't you fooling yourself as well? In the empty void, you and your poetry inbreed endlessly. Without conceiving, you have brought forth a litter of hideous creatures addicted to unclean blood. They cackle and they bawl. What does an imbecile care about repetition? Your brains have been gouged out, and all of you line up against the wall. You fall in. Attention! Face right! You write emptiness, and so you have been written into emptiness. The hollow words execute you in slow motion; you die so slowly that it doesn't even seem to be death. The old house knows perfectly well that it should admit defeat. Even the walls have suddenly begun to bleed. Before you topple over, you manage to touch the ruins inside your own body.

Silence, that's the only subject left. You should keep silent so you can maintain that look found in the eyes of fish accustomed to salt water. In this world, the victors are those who can live painlessly. You don't like numbness, so you choose defeat. You give voice to the lies buried everywhere within silence. You tell them to the sky. Your lips have already died, but these words ring out posthumously, and you are very pleased; nobody enjoys listening to you proclaim the news of their deaths.

You have no home. What do you need a home for? All day long, cars rumble past in the street below, just like the pedestrians who fleetingly brush past each other. On the desk, sunlight and a poem brush past each other in the same way—each seems unreal to the other. Even you can't understand it: why do you keep decorating and redecorating your room? It's like some kind of hall for commemorating the dead. Are you trying to make today into a yesterday that is worth bringing back? Now you're the only old thing left—unloved, unlamented. Now, you realize that you have already been buried under the yellow earth; when you look up through it, everything is refracted as an upside-down image. Go back? Where to? Beneath this yellow earth there is no such thing as a foreign country or a native land. You are simply born into this place in which you have never existed.

You are not anywhere. This old house has gotten used to all those mysterious noises coming from next door. In an unoccupied room, footsteps thump and clatter. Who knows—who cares—if somebody-or-other's poems are being read? They're just a pack of lies, all ghost talk. People say the place is haunted. Yes, you say, ghosts, everywhere.

MOTHER FISH

Xi Xi

(Translated by Kristina M. Torgeson)

1

A t daybreak the mother fish, looking stately and solemn, was floating on its back on the surface of the water, its entire body
covered with a translucent silvery sheen of extraordinary
luminosity. On each side of the tank were filter tubes shaped
like shepherds' pipes. Out of their tiny air holes sprayed arcs
of water that joined in midair to form a single waterfall, tin-
kling melodiously as it cascaded back into the tank, stirring
up an endless flow of effervescent spume. Silently, this raft of
pearly bubbles held aloft that soul of peerless splendor and
beauty now lying in calm repose.

Since goldfish have no visible sexual organs, we have no
way of determining their sex when they are young. Nor can
their gender be deduced from such traits as gentleness versus
aggressiveness, boorishness versus refinement. Most newborn
goldfish never make it to adulthood. Fluctuations in water

temperature, bacterial infections, and human negligence all tend to contribute to their premature demise. The reference books tell us that, when goldfish reach maturity, the edges of the gills and pectoral fins of the male fan out with tassellike appendages, while the abdomen of the female swells up with spawn. But these features can be seen only in adult fish at least three years old, after they have survived the many perils of life to reach their prime, those years of glorious heroism and heartbreaking pathos.

Across the top of the piano that stood next to the tank, a luxuriant bouquet of lilies sprawled in a rich display, their stems bundled together tightly in an imitation Greek amphora. Here and there a few buds, their heads dangling gently, still slumbered in spring's soothing embrace, while blossoms in full flower spread their cleft corollas to their widest. Stamens thronged around their fairy queen, their bright yellow pollen arousing insects to take wing. The clear bright light of the morning sun made its way onto the terrace and through the tassels of the canvas awning, the tinted glass of the French windows, and the sheer gauze curtains with the lacy butterfly pattern to present, with impeccable timing, the silhouette of a single lily sticking firmly out of one ear of a bust of Beethoven. The delicate fragrance of the white blossoms wafted gently through the air, permeating the room. Against the unchanging, implacable rhythm rapped out by the metronome standing its ground as majestically as one of the pyramids, I could hear the flowers singing their hallelujahs. Flowers, those trumpets of the angels.

I remember the fragrance of lilies.

The box that the Christmas cards came in had a glassine cover. The sides of the cardboard container were printed with illustrations of stories from the Bible—shepherds abiding in the fields, the three wise men from the East, the newborn babe in the manger. The paintings, simulating the effect of needlework, showcased the splendors of folk art and craftsmanship. The wool of the sheep was etched in identical curlicues; the shepherd's staff emerged from a procession of chain stitches climbing ever higher; Joseph's headdress was as ornate as a Persian tapestry; and the face of the infant was presented in bas-relief.

In the background, the boundaries of hills and pastures dissolved into each other. Flowers and leaves were done in delicate petit point.

She scooped the mother fish out of the water with both hands and gently placed it in the box. The fish was still soft and tender to the touch, flawlessly beautiful as always, its eyes gleaming bright and full of life. "I am leaving the goldfish in your care, Sis." Suddenly her mind went back to that beautiful sunny day last autumn, to the airport filled with young people leaving for their studies abroad, and her younger brother, a backpack on his shoulders, smiling cheerfully as he shook hands and said good-bye to all the friends and relatives who had come to see him off.

"Have a smooth flight, Cousin."

"All these people to see you off!" said Grandma.

"Take good care of yourself," said Mother.

"I'm sure they'll be healthy and strong, Sis."

"Remember, you must study hard," said Grandpa.

"I promise I'll send you the biology magazines regularly," said Cousin.

"You'll find the recharger for the dry-cell batteries on top of the bookcase, Sis."

"Come on everybody, let's take a picture together."

"We'll save all the newspapers for you," said Mother.

"You'll come back for Christmas, won't you?" said Grandma.

"You should go see Paris on your vacation," said Third Auntie.

"Everything in the Louvre is a masterpiece," said Third Auntie's husband.

"A batfish looks just like a pine cone in the rainy season, Sis."

"When it rains, make sure you use an umbrella," said Grandpa.

"Let's take a picture over here. The view in the background is really pretty."

"Here's an impromptu present for you, Cousin."

"The credit card is just a backup, in case of an emergency," said Father.

"There are two spare air canisters in the drawer, Sis."

"Who says down jackets make you look clumsy?" said Grandpa.

"They do have central heating at the school, don't they?" said Grandma.

"When it turns cold, remember to put in the heating tube, Sis."

"This present is something the Family Planning Association handed out on the street just now, Cousin."

"The plane ticket is free," said Mother.

"A credit card is not a winning lottery ticket," said Father.

"I'll send you a box of instant noodles every month," said Grandma.

"If you're squeamish about the red worms, just give them fish food, Sis."

"Don't just hang around with Chinese kids," said Third Auntie.

"Make lots of friends and socialize with people," said Third Auntie's husband.

"Write home when you have time," said Grandpa.

"We will call you," said Mother.

"So long, Cousin."

"Thanks for taking care of the goldfish, Sis."

2

As the spell of damp, rainy weather continued into its third week, the pantry began to look like a greenhouse—the garlic and ginger were sprouting, and a bright yellow mushroom burst from a crack in the chopping block. She did not have a single pair of shoes dry enough to wear to school. The droning noise inside the house came not from an air conditioner but a dehumidifier. The city had turned into a gigantic cistern, its citizens groping their way through a miasmal haze. Foghorns called to each other all day long from the ferries plying the harbor, their din finally coming to rest on the motionless sleeves of garments hanging limply on the clotheslines. A long line of customers snaked outside the laundromats, all waiting eagerly to feed the gaping, greedy mouths of the dryers.

She thought it was the weather that was giving her dizzy spells and rumblings in her stomach, as if a road crew were tunneling inside her body. Sometimes these invaders remained in one spot, sometimes they marched single file to their other bases and continued to drill. Grandma wailed that she couldn't see anything clearly, Grandpa hobbled around painfully on joints that seemed to have rusted, and Mother said she felt like a thousand-pound load had been slung across her shoulders. As for her, she became aware of the sharp medicinal odor that hung in the air, overpowering even the smell of the various forms of vegetation growing in the bathroom.

After the second attack of nausea, she suddenly remembered the spur-of-the-moment gift presented to her brother by their older cousin on that beautiful autumn day at the airport. At the time, his baby face had instantly turned a deep pink, and he had insisted on giving the present back to his cousin. All their other cousins had broken into sly, mysterious grins. She had not actually seen the gift, but she knew that it had been something that resembled a rubber glove, except, of course, a pair of gloves would have had ten digits in all. Supermarkets and twenty-four-hour convenience stores all carried this item, prominently displayed on the counter next to the cash register. At first, she had assumed it was a new kind of spearmint chewing gum, or a specially packaged book of matches, like the kind you find in cafés.

It was all very well for the Family Planning Association to hand out these free gifts to all the men passing by on the street, she thought to herself, but the ones who really needed protection were not the adults, nor the lusty young men just beginning to feel their oats, but the callow young maidens still innocent of the ways of the world. In every school and classroom, teachers should convey the facts of life to every girl, so that later their mothers would not have to sit at the breakfast table trying to cajole their nauseous daughters into drinking the scalded milk they have so solicitously prepared.

They were both open cities. It was early spring; the water was still cold, the secluded beach all but deserted. After a little while, they swam back ashore and lay down in the shelter of an abandoned vacation cottage, their bodies coated with tiny grains of sand. They both loved playing in the sand, and soon they were building castles and moats on the beach, giving shape to surrealistic landscapes.

He was wearing a pair of swimming trunks with a marine-life print: crabs and eels and whatnot lurking among coral reefs. Idly, she began to draw shapes in the sand on his back, slowly expanding the universe of the original aquarium until it encompassed all infinity. As the fine grains rustled and rolled across her human canvas, she created thick tangles of seaweed, sunken galleons, rusted anchors, and Spanish doubloons. Under the sun's gleaming rays, she saw Portuguese men-of-war, crabs, seaweed, and eels all coming to life before her eyes.

She could hear the rainlike splashing of the surf as it rolled in. The beach was now completely deserted. The sand felt as fine and soft as pollen. He began drawing pictures on her body—a school of fish, a covey of ever-shifting clouds, a procession of undulating hills, a little house hidden deep within the forest. She could feel him removing the wooden shutters, throwing open the windows overgrown with pink, white, and purple hollyhock blossoms. Gently, he undid the latch on the silent, well-fastened front portal and began to turn the twin rings of the beautiful brass door knocker.

All the starfish, jellyfish, and mollusks she had sketched earlier now floated before her eyes. She herself was ocean and seaweed and coral reef. She felt the slithering of an eel, experienced the shock of a bite from a crab's claw. I love you, I love you. Summer had not yet arrived, its advent no more than a faint drumbeat tapping in the distance. The spring rains had brought mud and a perpetual pea-soup fog.

The mother fish's belly began to balloon rapidly. She stared intently as the docile, long-suffering mother swam slowly back and forth, back and forth, its fan-shaped pectoral fins undulating softly. As it glided along, it seemed by turns to be bearing a heavy, juicy plum; seemed as though its belly had been wrapped around an overripe peach; seemed as though its abdomen had become a pomegranate on the verge of bursting. The skin on its underside looked extremely thin, almost filmy. The overlapping shinglelike scales had all separated, the tectonic plates on the map of its body transformed into continents, permanently adrift. But the mother fish continued to look healthy and happy, its sweet friendly eyes bright and alert, its dainty mouth and gills opening and closing with each serene breath. Its tiny tailfin fluttered elegantly, as though its bulging belly were not big with child but rather a swim bladder filled with air, accentuating the lissome gracefulness of its body. When the air-conditioner repairman—who had brought back the overhauled motor and was reinstalling it—saw the mother fish, he couldn't help exclaiming, "What a beautiful Lanchou!" But right away he sighed, "The delivery could be very difficult."

The mother fish was, in fact, a Lanchou. Her brother was partial to this mutant breed with their torpedo-shaped bodies. They are characterized by the absence of dorsal fins, a short bulbous trunk, a tailfin that looks just like a pair of cotyledons, and a sharp right angle where the back and tail intersect. Prime specimens of Lanchou have well-developed head muscles that ripple and bulge into fleshy protuberances, making them look as if their heads were covered with soap bubbles. After visiting every shop in the fish market, he had picked out eight Lanchous, going methodically from the very first to the very last. He even got out of bed before sunup one morning to check out the specialty market on one of those side streets near the railroad terminal. At each place he stopped and scrutinized every tank, doggedly carrying out his exhaustive search until he had found exactly what he wanted. When he brought the fish home, they were still quite small, each no more than the length of a little finger, and as flat as a willow leaf. But in the blink of an eye, they grew into handsome, elegant adults.

The reference books say that the male fish tend to be somewhat smaller, while the females are generally larger and very robust. Two years later, only one of the eight Lanchous remained small and skinny; the others had all grown to the size of one's palm, at least. At the time, she had been puzzled by that single frail-looking fish. It had seemed healthy enough and quite carefree. Thinking back, she finally understood that it must have been a male. Earlier this spring it had lost its life to the virulent epidemic of white fungus raging at the time. Now, she realized with a start, the inhabitants of the fish tank constituted an all-female kingdom.

3

Easter vacation brought with it a string of family gatherings. There were Pure Bright Festival[1] ceremonies for the grown-ups, April Fool's Day pranks for the teenagers, and general high-spirited play by the children on vocation. All provided an excuse to get together for celebration and fun. Once gathered for one reason or the other, many

---

1. One of the twenty-four solar periods in the lunar calendar which generally falls in early to mid-April. It is the traditional day for people to visit their ancestors' tombs and is also known as Tomb-sweeping Day.

members of the extended family who ordinarily didn't get to see much of each other took advantage of the holiday to continue the festivities at somebody's house. Her home was no exception. By midafternoon on the day of the Pure Bright Festival, the house was teeming with guests.

The living room, dining room, study, and bedrooms had all been commandeered by mah-jongg enthusiasts, who filled the air with the sound of their clacking tiles. Those who couldn't get together a foursome for mah-jongg were watching television. The screen flickered sporadically as it told the story of a girl, thin as a pencil, whose name was Rosemarie and who was just then walking absentmindedly past the colored tiles of the Long Corridor.[2] The younger children were playing electronic games in her brother's bedroom. A steady stream of squeaks and squawks came from the kitchen, where Mother and Third Auntie were bustling about. Was it the vegetables whimpering in the wok, or the clucking of the two women as they chattered about this and that?

She sat down in front of the tank to feed the goldfish. With its bulging belly, the mother fish looked like a balloon floating in the water as it swam back and forth. She wondered whether the fish's stomach would explode like a lighted firecracker. Now whenever she walked up to the tank, the mother fish would swim over delightedly, its eyes turning toward her with warmth and affection. She had been trying to help the expectant mother since early spring, but it was no use; her brother was the only one who knew what to do to save it.

She made her way to the dining-room table and began to cut the chestnut cake into equal-sized wedges, putting each piece onto a paper plate together with a little plastic fork. She poured soda from a liter bottle into glasses and garnished each one with a slice of lemon. She steeped premium-grade oolong in a Yixing teapot, brewed fresh coffee, and prepared tea with milk, English style. Then she brought the beverages and desserts into the various rooms, stopping to exchange a few greetings with the respective parties before broaching the question of how to help a pregnant fish.

With the men, the topic of conversation never strayed from the pros and cons of stereo equipment:

2. A covered walkway in the Summer Palace in Beijing, famous for its brilliantly colored and glazed ceramic tiles.

"What do you think of compact discs?"
"They're small and easy to store."
"They're durable and never wear out."
"But what do you do with the old LPs?"
"(What should I do about my goldfish?)"
"Keep them as antiques."
The women talked about fashion:
"(What should I do about my goldfish?)"
"Pair the gold with the black, it's all the rage this season."
"Are we getting a little too old for patterned stockings?"
"Those gray-and-white outfits by Giorgio Armani are just gorgeous."
The older folks were still grumbling about their health:
"There's no cure for bone spurs."
"There's no cure for presbyopia."
"There's no cure for rheumatism."
"There's no cure for gray hair."
"(What should I do about my goldfish?)"
"There's no cure for any of that."
The little kids were excitedly punching buttons on the video
games:
"(What should I do about my goldfish?)"
"Just gobble up that green flower."
"Jump up on the bricks and knock out that flower."
"When you eat the flower you'll have the strength of Superman."
Several of the teachers couldn't keep their minds off school business:
"Not a day goes by that I don't confiscate a stack of comic books."
"Every other picture shows a skirt hiked up to here."
"Or a chemise unbuttoned down to here."
"(What should I do about my goldfish?)"
"The student who got pregnant went quietly off to Shenzhen."[3]
Suddenly a joyous shout came from the kitchen:
"Third Auntie is going to be a mother!"
"What should I do about my goldfish?"

Mother said, "Why don't you go shopping with Third Auntie?"
Third Auntie was thirty-eight years old and not at all like other
women her age. She was petite, baby-faced, and still childless after fif-

3. A city in mainland China just across the border from Hong Kong.

teen years of marriage. "I don't want to have any children," she had insisted. She was an overage woman-child who refused to grow up and balked at becoming a mother. That was why every grown-ups who heard the cry from the kitchen looked so astonished. At the dinner table, Third Auntie made only one comment: "Just one slip, and you're done for."

They ventured deep into the heart of the shopping center, wandering among its labyrinthine corridors and walkways. Third Auntie had always been more like an older sister to her; they often played tennis and went swimming together. Perhaps this was why Mother had asked her to go shopping with Third Auntie. But she knew nothing about babies and what they needed. The only thing she could offer was a pair of hands to help carry packages.

All the stores had loving, cuddly names: Little Angel, Little Darling, Care For Mothers. No one had any idea that the two women looking over the merchandise were both expectant mothers. Looking was all she could do. The place was full of things she ought to be buying but couldn't; on the other hand, it had none of the things she needed, like a wonder drug, or one of those horrible, grim-looking surgical tools. Third Auntie was in high spirits. All of a sudden she had turned into an honest-to-goodness Little Woman, rummaging happily through racks of tiny pink or blue baby wear and picking over pans, milk bottles, brushes, and diapers. Standing in the midst of this fairy-tale world of little white bunnies and baby squirrels, she, however, felt terribly depressed. What she carried inside her was not a little angel. Those who cared for mothers cared not for mothers like her.

The extravagant trappings of the arcade made it seem ornate yet somehow dissolute. Above the soaring main atrium, in the center of the high ceiling, was a bas-relief of reclining cherubs carved in alabaster; on top of the huge stone pillars in each corner loomed the howling visage of the god of the winds. The colonnades on each side supported domed ceilings, the floors were made of marble, the walls were covered with whorls of gold-leafed sprays. Low-backed sofas upholstered in a richly textured fabric surrounded creamy white coffee tables, each of which held an amber-colored vase graced with dainty pink carnations. The afternoon sun left a yellow glaze over the glass doors, beyond which pedestrians scurried by. Shops and boutiques were arrayed on each side of the atrium. In one of the store windows, a sprig of spring flowers bloomed radiantly atop a bridal veil. The table was set with a sparkling silver tea service. Laid out on lacy paper doilies lining plates of bone china was a colorful assortment of delicacies: ham, tuna, and tomato finger sandwiches; liqueur-filled petit fours; soft and buttery scones studded with raisins; jam and Devonshire cream. The sound of an unseen piano came wafting from the mezzanine. Perhaps it was Aeolus's whistling. I could hear the murmurings of the gods.

I remember the sweet taste of the scones.

This was a course she should be attending.

It was already the fifth session.

The first one was about the prenatal examinations that most pregnant women should undergo.

"I had an amnio, the baby's just fine."

"I saw the fetus on the sonogram. It was like a little kitten, all curled up inside me."

"It kicks me all the time. What a miracle life is!"

The second class was about nutrition.

"You must drink milk every day, you need a lot of calcium."

"Eggs every day, for the protein."

"Drink lots and lots of water."

In the fourth session a movie was shown. It was about the birthing process.

All the pregnant women in the class suddenly fell silent.

The nurse said, "You're all scared now, aren't you?"

4

She decided to make a nest for the mother fish. To get it right, she chose a densely branching alga, a daffodillike stonewort, and a water lily whose miniature leaves looked like little pouches as they floated on the surface of the tank. The reference books say that a fully mature male fish will lure a mother fish to a secluded spot provided by the nest, and, using the pointed end of its mandible as a prod, will nuzzle and poke the female's abdomen. This stimulates the secretion of hormones that causes the ovarian membrane to break so the spawn can be discharged. However, while the tank now boasted a nest, it still lacked a male. It had never occurred to her that the bellies of female fish, even when segregated from the opposite sex, would automatically swell up with eggs. How utterly different from the way females of the human species became pregnant!

When she told him about the mother fish's predicament, he immediately set out to look for a male. Soon vendors all over the market were being called on by two young people urgently seeking a male goldfish. At first they limited their search to Lanchous, but soon they expanded it to include other varieties such as Lion's Head, Paved-with-Gold, Bubble Eyes, Pearly Scales, and Black Peony. But no one could provide them with any clues, not even the fish sellers. In the end, they had to rely on supposition and guesswork when they bought several specimens that looked to them like adult males. Despite their efforts, they did not succeed. The new fish ate voraciously and quickly grew large and stout. Well-fed and content, they swam happily around the tank, completely oblivious to the presence of the mother fish.

She had no choice but to cradle the mother fish in her own hands and gently massage its belly, hoping that this might help it release the eggs. But it was all in vain. As the mother fish's abdomen grew more and more distended, the skin over the belly was stretched ever more thinly, and the distance between the scales grew quickly. While the belly looked tight and firm, it felt exceedingly soft and delicate to the touch, as thousands struggled within for a chance at life. Meanwhile, the other fish in the tank nibbled away at the algae and water weeds, and within three days the nest had disintegrated. So they decided to take the mother fish to a nearby park where they would slip it into the pond when the guard wasn't looking. There were lots of goldfish in the pond, and if the Fates were kind, perhaps the mother fish would get a new lease on life.

When he arrived early that morning to escort the mother fish to the pond, it had already bidden farewell to this world, and the burial had been completed. She seemed utterly grief-stricken. Thinking that her anguish had been brought on by the death of the mother fish, he waited quietly for that memory to fade. But that was not what happened, and her sorrow did not subside. After watching only one of the Easter specials, Werner Herzog's *Nosferatu the Vampire,* she had absolutely no further interest in seeing any of the other movies. Holding her hand, he felt as though he were hanging on to a spirit flitting and gliding through the depths of night. He was stunned at how quickly she had become inhuman.

For her birthday he gave her two records: Horowitz's concert in Moscow and his rendition of Mozart's Piano Concerto no. 23. The maestro was already eighty-two, but his hands were nimble as ever, every note sprang crisp and clear from his fingertips, as exquisite as a string of pearls. Only twenty-two when he fled Russia, money for the journey hidden in his shoes, he had thought he would never be able to return. He did not go back again for sixty years. At the border the guard had recognized him and said to him, "Don't forget your motherland." Now he was a wealthy man: he could afford to have his own piano shipped by air to wherever he was performing; his favorite fish dish was served to him every day without fail. He lived as lavishly as one of the Incan kings in the remote mountains of long ago. But his homesickness was an illness that money could not cure.

She opened the booklet inside the record sleeve and leafed through the gloss photographs—of him visiting the homes of Tchaikovsky and Scriabin, examining the handwritten scores of his illustrious predecessors, of him sitting in front of their pianos, looking as though he had at last found peace. At his triumphant homecoming concert, Horowitz did not perform a signature piece such as Chopin's Polonnaise in A Flat, perhaps because it would have been too passionate, too flamboyant. Instead, he played a short lyrical composition by Schumann, the seventh piece in the suite *Scenes from Childhood*— "Träumerei," or "Dreams." It allowed him to conjure and ponder the early years of his life, reliving those once-distinct experiences.

She adored the way Horowitz performed Mozart—sorrowfully, yet not sentimentally. For the cadenzas, he had chosen to follow Busoni. He played the second movement in five minutes and thirty seconds flat. She was astonished. His tempo was almost two minutes faster than Perahia's. But his style had always been brisk and vigorous; even the melancholy pieces were taken con brio. Perhaps in the end it was Horowitz who came closest to touching the soul of Mozart, whose

works exuded such vitality and life, for whom sorrow always coexist-
ed with joy and grief and happiness were never far apart.

He shared her opinion. What distinguished Horowitz was his bold-
ness and spontaneity. Neither of them believed that a pianist should be
a slavishly faithful interpreter. He said, "Horowitz is a brilliant, asym-
metric pearl."

"Yes," she answered, "extremely baroque."

Slowly, she lost herself in the beautiful world of the music. I could
hear many sounds during the recital other than the piano:—people
shouting "Bravissimo," people hacking and coughing.

I remember Horowitz and Schumann.

5

Downstairs from the office of the Family Planning Association was a
shelter for the homeless. Most of the city's vagabonds, however, pre-
ferred to sleep under highway overpasses, or on stone benches in the
parks, or along the covered walkways by the ferry piers. Rain or
shine, in deepest winter or the heat of summer, they would rather
brave the elements than seek refuge at the shelter. Probably for the
same reason, unmarried mothers were reluctant to go to the association for help. The Family Planning Association was set up to help
those women who were, or were about to be, married and starting
families, she thought to herself. Agencies such as this may say they
want to serve and help you, but in the end the so-called solution they
propose is always the tried and true; "Tell your parents." As soon as
she stepped inside the building she would, in effect, have thrown herself into a net. They would ask for her name, address, age—would all
that really be kept "strictly confidential"? After all, the Family Planning Association was not the Government's Anti-Corruption Unit.[4]
The personnel would say, "It's for your own good." And then, within half an hour, her parents would arrive and take her home; within
twenty-four hours, the school principal and her teachers would all be
counseling her; within three days, all her relatives, friends, teachers,
and classmates would be discussing and passing judgment on her
morals. When news about the pregnancy of someone such as thirty-

4. An agency of the Hong Kong Government that investigates citizens' complaints of official corruption and that promises to keep whistle-blowers' identities in strictest confidence.

eight-year-old Third Auntie was greeted with so much surprise and speculation, what kind of reaction would she—an unmarried seventeen-year-old girl—get?

It was now only two months to Third Auntie's due date, and she had already received many presents: a sterling-silver baby spoon, a backpack for carrying the infant, a portrait of a plump, healthy baby. She continued to busy herself with preparations for the imminent arrival of the little one—decorating the nursery, ordering the baby's bed and bassinet, painting the walls a soft pink. She seemed cheerful and content, full of the joy of motherhood. She even got instructions from Mother about how to make red-dyed hardboiled eggs, how to brew ginger vinegar tea, how to steep ginseng in chicken consommé.[5]

But none of these things concerned the younger woman. She had made up her mind not to have the baby.

She knew of a place: Shenzhen. Every day pregnant women went to this neighboring municipality to take care of their urgent personal problems. If they left in the morning, they could be home that evening, bringing back fresh vegetables, or pottery, or woven bamboo mats that they had supposedly picked up on their outing to the countryside. Shenzhen was an open secret. In the seedier sections of the city, a tangle of signs had sprung from the sides of buildings, overhanging the streets and the heads of passersby. They advertised the services of various medical clinics, all engaged in what had become a flourishing business in the last few years.

Every year on her birthday, her father would give her a gold coin and say, "My daughter's dowry is really building up." And, indeed, the price of gold had risen tenfold in the last ten years. She decided to spend one, two, even ten of the gold coins in exchange for her once-lithe and -graceful body, her former carefree self. She had never imagined that her dowry would be spent not on her wedding but on something like this that was nevertheless so intimately related to marriage. What concerned her was not the cost of the operation but its consequences. What if she went to Shenzhen, only to depart forever? Would she end up like the mother fish, floating belly-up and all alone

---

5. Red-dyed hardboiled eggs are customarily given to friends and relatives in celebration of a safe childbirth. Ginger vinegar tea and ginseng steeped in chicken consommé are both considered tonics in traditional Chinese medicine.y

on the surface of the water? She decided she would take the risk, alone. She would put away her Hong Kong identity card and give a false name and address, so that if something went wrong, nobody would know who she was.

In the presence of the stranger, she would lay bare her beautiful young body. Once she had faced the prospect of death, she was suddenly filled with courage. She could see the gloomy room with its sickly green walls and dirty gray ceiling high above, lit by a hanging lamp coated with dust and grime. A rancid, putrid odor filled the room. In a peeling enamel tray, metal clanged against metal. Instead of the soft caress of warm, tender flesh against her own, she would feel the coarse, slimy, toadlike skin of a large, hideous snake as it thrashed about at will across her body, sinking its sharp fangs again and again into her flesh and veins.

She remembered a news story about a young couple who got into an accident while riding in a taxi. In the collision the wife received a blow to her forehead, and her husband and the driver both jumped out of the cab to get help. But every car on the road whizzed by without stopping, until the two men managed at last to flag down a passing truck. After demanding an exorbitant price, the owner of the truck diddled and dawdled before finally driving the injured woman to the hospital. By the time the husband had completed all the forms, complied with all the requirements, and rushed to the appropriate office to pay for the blood transfusion—in advance, please—the wife had slipped into a coma from loss of blood. Even after she was put on a respirator, the husband had to stay by her side and manually operate the pump to make sure it was working properly. Six hours later, the woman, who had originally received only a minor injury, died without regaining consciousness. That was exactly the kind of place she would be lying in.

Every day at the appointed hour, she fed the goldfish, using a little measuring spoon to scoop out the proper amount of fish food. The flakes smelled vaguely like dried seaweed and, once scattered onto the water, fluttered slowly toward the bottom of the tank. All the goldfish swarmed around the sinking flakes, sometimes sticking their heads into the nooks and crannies among the pebbles that lined the bottom, their upturned tails resembling flowers stalks swaying in the wind. While she fed the fish, she examined them for signs of injury and disease: were the tips of their fins broken or split, were their scales falling off, were there any cuts or scratches on their gills, were their backs covered with a thin gray film, were there white spots on their bulbous heads?

By now she had become not only a nanny to the goldfish but their doctor as well. She regularly cleaned the tank, the filtration system, and the pebbles. On really cold days, she even brought the water to room temperature by warming it on the stove before refilling the tank. She knew that a fish that swam off and stayed by itself must have come down with a disease, while one that wheeled about was suffering from an attack of worms. She had also learned how to set up a little tank as an infirmary, where she would immerse the ailing fish in a saline solution, and she knew how to apply medication directly to infected areas.

She was no longer stumped by any of the afflictions that goldfish were subject to, except for one, pregnancy. There were still seven Lanchous in the tank, and since they were all female, each would become a mother sooner or later. At some point their bellies would swell rapidly, and then they would die from the complications of labor. In a letter to her brother she said: "Life and death are so close to each other, yet there's not a thing I can do. Mother said, 'Don't worry, just three more months and your brother will be back.' Father said, 'Don't take it so hard, it's only some fish.'"

It was not the fish. But Father could not have known that. They saw her with strips of litmus paper day after day, sometimes red, sometimes blue, and they assumed she was checking the water quality in the tank. Was it acidic or alkaline? Was it positive or negative? Locking herself in the bathroom, she too waited for the result. The instructions said that red meant the test was negative, yellow meant it was positive. She had already done the test many times, holding a glass tube in one hand as she measured droplets of the reagent with her other hand. When it came out yellow the first time, she felt as though all heaven and earth were spinning around her.

She should not have done the test in the afternoon. Also, she was not supposed to have had any milk, spinach, fruit, or vitamin pills. So she performed the test again in the morning. Several days in a row, in

fact, she carried out this onerous task. When she saw a tube of rasp-
berry-colored liquid, she was relieved. But why did it turn yellow at
some times and red at other times? The colors confounded her.

6

He went with her to buy cigars for Third Auntie. On the telephone
Third Auntie had said, "Oh dear, I forgot to get cigars." They went
to Davidoff's and carefully reviewed every brand on display. Which
kind should they get? He vetoed the Grand Cru series. He said,
"Davidoff's biggest mistake was to name cigars after French chîteaus.
After all, cigars are not wines." She didn't like the Bouquet assortment, because those were not hand-rolled. They read out one name
after another: Larrañaga, Partagas, Juan Clemente, Bolívar.

"Bolívar sounds good—he was a great Latin American hero."

"If you were the father, which brand would you choose?" she
asked.

"Monte Cristo No. 1, of course, because of the story, and because
of Alexander Dumas. What about you?"

"Romeo and Juliet, because of Shakespeare, and because of a rose
by any name," she replied.

What she really liked were not the cigars themselves but the boxes
they came in—all made out of plain unvarnished fir with not a speck
of paint, even the ornate lettering seared into the wood with a dark,
smoky tint. Some had rolltop covers, others came with brass-plated
latches. Suddenly she remembered the Christmas-card box that had
become the mother fish's coffin. After paying for their purchase, they
headed home along the embankment by the harbor. Hugging the box
of cigars, she broke into tears and began to sob inconsolably. He finally found out why.

"Don't be so sad, silly girl," he said. "Why don't we just get married? We're just in love, like other people; we're just going to be parents, like other people. Why do something stupid? Shenzhen is out.
That's no way to deal with this situation. A child would be wonderful—we both love kids. I am nineteen; I will make a good husband, a
good father. Let's get married and have the baby. We'll go to the baby
boutique and buy baby clothes and little toys, just like your Third

Auntie did, and we'll also buy cigars to give to our friends and relatives. We'll give cigars even if it's a girl. If it's a boy we'll give Monte
Cristo No. 1, if it's a girl we'll give Romeo and Juliet. We'll still go to
the university. We'll bring the baby to class. We'll both study hard,
and after graduation we'll get good jobs and have a cozy little home
of our own, where we'll keep a big tank with lots of male goldfish.
On our vacations we'll bring our child along. We'll go to Florence to
see Botticelli's *La Primavera*."

"I'll go up by myself," she said.

He knew it was pointless to argue with her further, so he stayed
downstairs and waited. Glancing at his watch, he told himself that if
she didn't come down within half an hour, he would go upstairs to
look for her. He looked up and saw the overhanging jumble of sign-
boards and shingles that cluttered the space above the alley. Coming
here was her idea. He didn't agree with it but thought they could give
it a try. He watched as she stepped into the elevator and then turned
around to give him a wave. He knew that she was scared but had put
on a brave front.

She had to ring the bell twice before a middle-aged woman
answered the door. The place was set up like an ordinary residence,
but there was no one else in the living room, and imprinted on the
glass door was a red cross. "I am here for a test," she said, beginning
to relax once she realized she would not have to give her name and
address after all.

"Did you come alone?"

"He's waiting downstairs."

"You don't want a baby, is that right?"

"I'm always feeling nauseous."

"Do you have problems with your stomach?"

She came out of the bathroom and gave the jar to the woman, who
poured it into an array of smaller containers and performed one test
after another, carefully examining each reaction. During the rainy
season, when water was running and dripping everywhere, her body's
canal had dried up. Now that summer was here, the sun burned off
every last bloom of mildew in even the darkest nooks and crannies.
And now here, in this unfamiliar room, she suddenly discovered to
her great astonishment that her waterway was once again flowing.
Outside the window the sun shone very, very brightly.

She came out of the elevator and saw him running toward her. The lobby appeared to be deserted except for the two of them. Throwing her arms around his neck, she blurted out, "I'm okay, I'm okay." Then, like exuberant little sparrows, they tripped out of the narrow alley overhung with signs that blocked out much of the light. Looking up, she pointed to one of the signs and said, "I thought I'd have to go to one of those places and I'd never see you again." And the tears came streaming down.

I am your *tousheng*,[6] your firstborn, born out of your head. I am your fantasy. Most *tousheng* creatures are but fictional characters created by writers, brought into this world for the sake of the story. I do not belong to the story, nor did you create me in order to write a story. It was as a result of love's taking shape that you conceived and gave birth to me.

Writers take loving care of their *tousheng* characters, bringing them to maturity, breathing life into them, displaying them proudly before all. Most mothers are like this too. But you, you have spared no pains in your effort to stow me away, to keep my existence a secret; you stand ready to destroy me, because I represent darkness and shame. This is your sorrow, the sorrow of the female sex. Why do you continue to submit to a life of such humiliation and self-abasement? Out of nothingness into being—it should have been a process of discovery, of creation, of propagation. Birth should have been the greatest joy of all—why turn it into tragedy?

It has been only three months since my birth, yet I have already lived with you awhile, through sunshine and stormy weather. Since you gave birth to me out of your head, before all else, I have become part of your memory, your consciousness, a spray of ever-flowing spindrift in the ocean of your mind. I wish you health and happiness; I pray that you will grow ever stronger, mother. Love is nothing to be ashamed of. I love you, and I love my father. He is the precious male fish.

6. Firstborn; also a pun on its literal meaning, "born out of the head."

FESTIVAL

A Cheng

(Translated by Ann Huss)

1

The wheat was just about to ripen when the grown-ups got a bunch
of guns from somewhere.

It was the first time Xiao[1] Long had seen a real gun. Until
then all they'd had in the village were those old-fashioned
ones, the kind where you had to stuff the black gunpowder
into the barrel. You also had to make sure the powder didn't
get wet, because it wouldn't catch, and then you'd have to dry
it by stir-frying. You did this by taking an iron skillet and
heating it over hot coals, then setting it on a cool surface
before pouring in the damp gunpowder. Next you stirred it
slowly, steadily, until there were no more wisps of steam.
Finally you poured it out, and it was ready to use. One time,

---

1. "Little." All the children's names in this story are prefaced with "Xiao," a common
diminutive.

before the Cultural Revolution, Xiao Rong's father was drying gunpowder when someone called him. He turned his head to look, and the powder exploded, leaving one whole side of his face permanently charred. Not only that, but the eye on that side looked like a rabbit's, and the ear like a tree fungus.

After that, the children were no longer allowed to watch, but the chickens could still run around the iron kettle as the powder dried.

Nor were the children allowed to go into the hills with the grownups to watch the hunting and risk being attacked by an injured animal. The people of Pingzhen took good care of their children. If something unfortunate happened, what good would it do to cry or carry on after the fact? If an accident could be prevented, then it should be.

But the children were allowed to watch executions. Pingzhen was not too far from the county seat, and right outside the village was an open stretch of land on the riverbank. A criminal sentenced to death in the county court would be brought over in a big truck and flung down onto the floodplain by the river. A guard would check him over and make him kneel with his head down on his chest, waiting for the final order. The children would cover their ears, but they could still hear the shots ring out. Afterward the prisoner would fall onto the ground, blood streaming from his gunshot wounds. Sometimes a person who had been shot dead would still twitch and turn, slowly, until a man in white walked over and did something to the body, and it would lie still. Xiao Long was really curious about how the man in white did this, but he could never slip past the guard who blocked the way.

Once, just before the order to fire was given, a prisoner suddenly got to his feet and began to run. The firing squad was accustomed to shooting at stationary objects at close range. So, while the convict kept running, not a peep came out of the guns. The crowd that had gathered to watch began to jeer. Then shots rang out. But they missed their mark. More shots—but still no hits. By this time seven or eight rifles were firing away, but the prisoner was already beyond their range. Everyone on the riverbank was hysterical with laughter, even the other convicts waiting to be executed. The squad leader and two of his men went after the escaped prisoner and finally brought him back. Holding back their guffaws, the soldiers carried out the execution. The incident was later retold and passed along in many different versions. What Xiao Long remembered was how the man had stumbled as he ran, hobbled by the big round stones on the floodplain.

So this wasn't the first time Xiao Long had seen a real gun. It was just the first time he had seen a real gun up close. While his father wasn't looking, he even touched it. It felt cool.

2

When it came time to test the gun, Xiao Long's father looked around for a target. Xiao Long's mother told him to aim it at the sky, so he wouldn't hit anyone. But he told her that's what guns were for—hitting people.

Xiao Rong's father came looking for Xiao Long's father, saying, "Hot damn, this time we've got the real thing. Those Red Rev Rebs[2] are going to be in for it!"

Rubbing a bullet head against his pants leg, Xiao Long's father answered, "Yes, but I hear they got hold of some guns too."

"Not even close," Xiao Rong's dad countered. "Besides, the Fifth Detachment is on our side. That Captain Hu—you know, the chubby one, joined the Eighth Route Army[3] back in 42—he keeps the higher-ups informed about what's going on."

"I hear the other side's got people with good connections too," Xiao Long's father said as he pressed the bullet tip against his cheek.

Losing his temper, Xiao Rong's dad cocked his head to one side and shouted, "Whose side are you on, anyway, the Red Reb Central's[4] or the others'?"

Xiao Long's mother stood in the doorway and said, "Don't argue when you've got guns in your hands. Why are you arguing while you're waving those guns around?"

2. Short for Red Revolutionary Rebels. Political struggle during the Cultural Revolution in China (1966–76) often devolved into factional fighting, with each faction seeking to distinguish itself from its rivals by, among other things, assuming a "more revolutionary than thou" rhetoric that was reflected in its name. Such names were often abbreviated in daily usage.

3. The army led by the Chinese Communist Party during the War of Resistance against Japan (1937–45). Soldiers who fought in this army were accorded great respect and prestige after the Communists assumed power in 1949.

4. Short for Red Rebels Central Command, another typical name for one of the many factions operating during the Cultural Revolution. At times such groups became the only administrative authority in given localities.

The two men picked up their guns and went outside, shifting their weapons from one hand to the other as they rolled up their sleeves. Xiao Long began to follow them out of the house.

"You come back here this instant!" screamed his mother.

Startled, the two men stopped and turned around to look. Xiao Long's mother ran over and grabbed her son, muttering angrily, "Haven't you seen enough killing already?"

The two men broke into laughter and went on their way.

The Red Rev Reb gang was the first rebel organization in the county, but it took only three days for people to figure out what was going on and to set up their own groups, one after another. Because it was close to the county seat, Pingzhen was a natural target for organizing, first by the Red Reb Central, a newer group, and later by the Red Rev Rebs, the original gang. So now all of Pingzhen's accumulated problems—from the most piddling to the most pressing—and the resulting bad blood among the villagers found new channels and champions for its expression—by force, if necessary. Because each side swore allegiance to Chairman Mao, the confrontations had intensified and escalated until, finally, guns entered the picture.

The children of Pingzhen were not allowed to watch grown-ups drying gunpowder or hunting, and now, they were also forbidden to play with the children of those who belonged to a rival faction. When the Red Rev Reb controlled Pingzhen, their children could go outside to watch demonstrations, rallies, and members of the Red Reb Central gang being paraded in the streets as counterrevolutionaries and beaten with sticks and chains. And, of course, when the Red Reb Central wrested control of Pingzhen, *their* children could go onto the streets to watch demonstrations, rallies, parades, beatings of Red Rev Reb members, and so on.

3

At the moment Xiao Long was quite bored. He looked around at the chickens, then up at the birds and the sky, all the while hoping to hear a few gunshots. A long time passed, but he heard nothing.

Slowly he sidled over to the courtyard gate and stopped. Then he stepped outside and, again, stood still for a few moments. Leaning against the door frame, he stuck his hand under his shirt and nonchalantly scratched himself on the back for a little bit, then on the belly. Suddenly he darted from the door. When he didn't hear his mother calling after him, he began to walk more confidently down the deserted street, hugging the wall just in case.

Not much had changed on the street. As usual there were some new slogans plastered over the old ones, and, as usual, a chicken was foraging among the globs of rice glue at the foot of the wall. Stomping his feet, Xiao Long ran a few steps closer. The chicken quietly darted away, cocking its head as it eyed Xiao Long. Angry that the chicken hadn't even bothered to cackle, Xiao Long stood by the wall and wouldn't let it get back to its meal. Unfazed, the chicken strutted casually to the other side of the street. Spreading out one wing and one leg, it stretched itself languidly and shook its feathers a few times while leaving a pile of droppings on the ground. Then it began pecking at the feathers on its chest and back.

Pretending his hand was a gun, Xiao Long was aiming it at the chicken when, suddenly, a shot rang out from far away. Absorbed in its grooming, the chicken was oblivious to this. Xiao Long, though, was so excited he began to shout: "Xiao Rong, Xiao Rong, my dad's shooting a real gun!"

In the twinkling of an eye Xiao Rong came running out of the gate next door, followed in hot pursuit by the screams of his mother: "You little bastard, go ahead, just die in front of my eyes, you brat. That crazy dad of yours, he's going to get shot one of these days. Go ahead, run, you little son of a bitch."

As the two boys raced through the village, a sense of life began to stir in the street.

4

A big locust tree stood at the edge of the village. In summer, caterpillars dangled from its branches, gnawing at its leaves until they were full of holes. Next to the tree stood a smithy, and inside the shed was a brick furnace. When the blacksmith was at work, the coals glowing in the furnace grew brighter, then dim, with each blast from the bellows. The children loved to watch the sparks fly from the anvil every time the hammer struck the red-hot metal. They watched until the blacksmith set the hammer on the ground, upright, and, without casting a glance at anyone, muttered: "Let's rest a while." Although he could easily have boiled water over the fire in the furnace, he never had to, because one of the children would always dash home and bring back a kettleful of boiled water. It was a great honor to have the blacksmith accept one's offering of water. When the break was over, the donor, puffing with pride, would invariably assume he had a right to stand closer to the action, so the blacksmith would have to yell at him to get out of the way.

Xiao Rong ran into the shed and scooted onto the top of the furnace to catch his breath. Xiao Long joined him, also puffing and panting. It had been a long time since the shed had been used as a forge, and the place was now filled with a stale, musty odor.

"My mom and my dad had a big fight," Xiao Rong told his friend. "He even slapped her hard on the face."

"Your dad and my dad went shooting together," Xiao Long replied. "Did you hear the shot my dad fired?"

"That shot was fired by my dad!" Xiao Rong argued.

"No way!" countered Xiao Long. "My old man would get to shoot before yours did!"

"You're full of shit!"

"YOU'RE full of shit!"

Suddenly a voice behind them said, "Are you guys playing a game?"

Turning around, Xiao Long and Xiao Rong saw that it was Xiao Qin, whose house was right behind the forge. They fell silent. Xiao Qin's father belonged to the Red Rev Reb gang.

Leaning against the door, Xiao Qin lifted her leg and fixed the strap on her shoe. Then she set her foot down and stomped it a few times for good measure. Neither Xiao Long nor Xiao Rong said another word about the guns. Instead, they stared straight ahead at the road leading out of the village.

"Look, my mother made me some new shoes," said Xiao Qin.

Xiao Long took a sidelong glance. "What's so special about new shoes?"

Xiao Qin replied, "They're for the festival tomorrow."

Drawing a blank, Xiao Long asked, "What festival?"

"It's Children's Day, silly!" Xiao Qin replied.

"Look, if there's no school,[5] there's no Children's Day," quipped Xiao Rong. "You can only have Children's Day when you have school. When the teacher says it's time to celebrate this or that, *then* we have a holiday. That's the way it always was, don't you remember?"

This reminded Xiao Qin of something else. "Hey, I heard that Teacher Zhang's leg is still broken. My mom says that if they can't fix it, he'll become a cripple."

"You mean Baldy Zhang? He was beaten by that teacher who came down from the county. Did you guys see the beating?" asked Xiao Long.

"Yes, I saw it," Xiao Rong replied.

"So did I. Boy, he hit him harder than my father beats me," Xiao Long tittered.

"What are you guys going to do tomorrow to celebrate?" Xiao Qin wanted to know.

"Us?" Xiao Rong hesitated for a moment before waving in the direction of the fields outside the village. "We're . . . we're going to play in Deep Gully, right, Xiao Long?"

Xiao Long answered gleefully, "Right. You've got to celebrate a festival with special games. That's much better than new shoes."

Pleased with themselves, the two comrades jumped down from the furnace and, arm in arm, began to head for home.

Xiao Qin called after them, "Can I come too?"

Xiao Long stopped. He hemmed and hawed but didn't say anything.

"Please let me come," Xiao Qin pleaded. "I promise I won't tell my parents."

"OK," Xiao Long finally agreed.

"Can Xiao Liang and the others come along too?" Xiao Qin added.

This time it was Xiao Rong who answered: "OK, but you guys will have to listen to us, because we're in charge. We'll go there tomorrow night. And make sure the grown-ups don't find out!"

5

That night, at dinner, Xiao Long's father announced: "We're going to see some real action. Those Red Rev Rebs want to take over all the

5. During the Cultural Revolution schools were closed in many places for long periods of time.

water in the irrigation ditches, including what we need for our wheat fields. We told them no way, that water is ours, and they can just forget it."

Xiao Long's mother said, "Well, we've gone through this before, threats and all. But now, with all these guns . . . why don't you stay out of it this year?"

Xiao Long's father didn't reply. He took a mouthful of food and began munching noisily.

Xiao Long took the opportunity to pipe up, "Ma, tomorrow's a festival."

"What festival?"

"It's Children's Day, don't you remember? Xiao Qin was already wearing new shoes today."

As soon as he mentioned Xiao Qin, Xiao Long wanted to kick himself. But neither his father nor his mother seemed to have noticed. They just said, "Oh." His mother added, "You're right. Well, then, tomorrow you can wear the jacket you got for New Year."

6

Only the chickens and the dogs knew that the children of Pingzhen had sneaked out of their houses and were now walking along the riverbank. When Xiao Long pointed out that the grown-ups might still see them there, Xiao Qin reminded him that he and Xiao Rong had said they were going to play in Deep Gully. So they all crept through the wheat fields and made their way to the big irrigation ditch.

By then the setting sun had lit up the top part of the eastern bank and was bathing it in an orange-red glow, but the other side of Deep Gully had already let off the heat of the day. Even the grass was beginning to perk up. The water in the ditch splashed and gurgled as it flowed along. Down in the gully the children could shout and holler and not be heard by anyone, so they screamed and screeched to their hearts' content as they ran along the slopes of the canal. Their only other companions were the insects that buzzed about and the swallows swooping from one place to another.

Then the moon's reflection in the water grew smaller and smaller, and darkness settled in. Three or four stars twinkled steadily in the sky, while many more fireflies flitted here and there.

Suddenly, Xiao Qin exclaimed: "I lost my flashlight!"

"You brought a flashlight along?" Xiao Rong asked incredulously.

"Didn't you guys say we were going to play night battles?" Xiao Qin retorted. "That's why I brought a flashlight. If I don't find it I'm going to be in big trouble, because my dad and mom will find out I've been here."

Everyone got all excited and began to feel around on the ground, looking for the flashlight. When Xiao Liang found it, they all crowded around.

"How does it work?" asked Xiao Long.

"You push it this way, and the light comes on. Pull it back, and it goes off," Xiao Qin told him.

"Let me see," said Xiao Long as he grabbed the flashlight. A little flick, and a beam of light gushed forth. "Wow!" he cried as he aimed it at the sky. Insects caught in the glare became blurry streaks of white.

Suddenly shots rang out.

Stunned, the children fell onto their stomachs. Bullets whizzed overhead, each trailing a thin, bright strand of light, to be met by another barrage from the other side.

Much later, the shooting finally stopped.

Xiao Long was the first to find his voice. "I bet they can't hit us down here in the gully!"

Xiao Qin burst into tears and said, "Let's go home!"

"Let's do it one more time," countered Xiao Long. He pushed the switch again, and once more the threads of light stitched back and forth across the night sky.

"It's like at the blacksmith's!" cried Xiao Rong.

"It's like firecrackers at New Year's!" Xiao Liang chimed in.

In their excitement and glee, the children sprang to their feet and flicked the switch again.

Xiao Long thought he heard a stone ricocheting against the side of the gully. Turning to look, he saw that both banks were suddenly awash with the red glare of a setting sun. Only this sunset was full of noise.

The flashlight flew way up in the air. When it finally hit the water, it was still shining. Gradually, a school of small fish, bathed in the red glow, began to nibble at the round lens.

PLAIN MOON

Gu Zhaosen

(Translated by Michelle Yeh)

1

R ich Garment Manufacturer was located in western Chinatown, in a cul-de-sac where even devils would not go. Seen from the outside, it looked like Berlin after Allied bombings in World War II. Inside it was dilapidated too, with the acrid stench of piss coming from the corners under the staircase and trash strewn about.

The roomy cargo elevator, with chipped paint and rusty scars, went straight up to the sixth floor. As the door opened, one could see three rows of glaring fluorescent lights illuminating the entire factory so that it looked like a snow-lined cave. Sewing machines of all kinds stretched in long rows, lined up closely together. Bits of thread and fabric covered the floor.

Most of the machines were occupied. Gray- and hoary-haired heads bent down as the machines thudded along.

When the women saw Plain Moon coming up, they greeted her in a chorus, without even stopping what they were doing. "Morning, Little Moon!" "How are ya, Little Moon?"

Mrs. Lai, with her born-sad face, stopped the girl. Even when she smiled, the outer corners of her eyes drooped down, making her look pathetic. "Come here, Little Moon. I've got a present for ya. Happy birthday!" She shoved a big box of white tree fungus and a small box of dried dates into Plain Moon's arms.

After much polite refusal and good-natured insistence, Plain Moon accepted the gift. Mrs. Lai was a widow in her late fifties and dressed in black all year long. Although she was supported by her children, she could not stand staying home and had been working here for more than a year. Because she was not very skilled, she was mostly given jobs cutting threads and ironing. During lunch break, Plain Moon sometimes would take time to give her some tips. Probably because of her age, she could not handle the five-thread machine. She always ended up tying the wrong threads or sewing on the wrong lining. Behind her back, many younger workers poked fun at her, but Plain Moon, who even fed stray cats, helped her whenever she had the time. For this, Mrs. Lai was truly grateful. She only regretted that she didn't have an unmarried son left for Plain Moon.

Plain Moon walked up to her usual machine and took her seat. Mrs. Lin, who was sitting next to her, leaned over and said, "Little Moon, later I'll take you to lunch at Phoenix to celebrate your birthday."

Plain Moon waved her hand, saying, "Don't be so extravagant. There's a birthday every year. No need to waste money."

"I've rounded up quite a group already—Mrs. Wang, Mrs. Lai, Julie in the Pattern Department, Little Chuan, . . ."

"That's right," Mrs. Wang added. "We're all going together. It won't cost much. It's for your birthday!" Taking a look around the floor, Mrs. Wang shifted back to her role as the unit head. "I've got to turn in the jacket today. Help me rush it out!"

After Mrs. Wang had walked away, Mrs. Lin turned around and quickly got a canteen of chrysanthemum tea from her handbag. She took a sip and pouted. "It's hard to get by working on wool jackets. I get only eight cents for each. It's all bones and no meat, what shall I live on?"

Plain Moon tied a knot on the thread and tapped the pedals a few times before she replied, "It's not every day that you get to enjoy steamed chicken! The more work you do, the more you make."

Mrs. Lin shook her head: "You young people sew fast. I'm afraid there're only bones for me!"

The women's wages were based on the number of pieces they sewed. Those who were slow made about twenty dollars after a whole day of sewing. Deduct the income taxes and the trimonthly union fee, and there was not much left. Many young workers quit after a short time. The older ones, what with language barriers and a lack of education, were more inclined to stay. The unit head, Mrs. Wang, sighed more than once, "Young people these days can't endure any hardship!" At the same time, she praised Plain Moon for her youth and maturity as well as her skills: "Little Moon, you're terrific. It's just a matter of time before you're the unit head." Her tone revealed a tinge of being threatened. But each time Plain Moon kept sewing with her head bent low, as if she had heard nothing.

2

Hours passed in the factory without a trace. Immersed in her work, Plain Moon forgot time. When she heard the noise outside the elevator, she glanced at her watch and realized it was almost noon. She raised her head and saw several Caucasian men in white shirts coming her way, shouting loudly in English.

"The inspectors are here again." Mrs. Lin let out a sigh. "With the penalty so stiff, why would our boss hire illegal aliens?"

Plain Moon nodded in agreement as she took her labor card from her purse and waited for the immigration officers. Four years before, after the amnesty law was passed, a new law was instituted forbidding employment of illegal aliens and imposing a heavy penalty on violators. Since wages were not based on hours, there was little need to exploit unskilled workers; illegal aliens were rare. After the accident a few years before, the boss avoided this kind of trouble like the plague. The year Plain Moon first came was the turning point. One day the immigration officers raided the place, and a few employees without papers scrambled for the storage room at the back. An overseas student's wife slipped and fell from the fire escape on the sixth floor. She was dead on impact. Afterward, a rumor that the storage room was haunted lasted for two or three years.

As soon as the immigration officers had left, the workers took a break. With Plain Moon at the rear, the group walked to the restaurant down the block, boisterously exchanging horror stories about immigration raids.

As Plain Moon entered the restaurant, she noticed that a young man with a bag of take-out food was holding the door for her. She blurted a thank-you and cast a quick glance at him as she quickened her steps. He gave her a big grin, showing a tiny protruding tooth on the upper left of his mouth.

They sat down at a round table. Julie said, "That guy must be new. I've never seen him here before. Not bad-looking, huh? Pretty cute."

Little Chuan gave her a shove. "So what if he *is* cute? You're married already. Aren't you afraid your husband would kill you?"

"What's wrong with looking? So, only my husband gets to gawk at pretty girls?" Julie said, rolling her eyes. The two friends started giggling.

Mrs. Wang frowned as she turned the pages of the large red menu. "Little Moon, order whatever you like."

They finally reached a consensus: two orders of shrimp dumplings, one plate of pan-fried rice noodles, an order of salted shrimps, a deep-fried flounder, and a vegetable dish. For dessert, they ordered egg custard.

The shrimp dumplings came first. Plain Moon bit into one and took a sip of 7-Up. That young man, she said to herself, was really good-looking. She was right. He had a fair complexion, slender eyebrows like two gladiolas, a pair of big, clear eyes. His lips were ruby red, his hair dark and full, hanging low on his forehead—he probably cut it himself. He was lean, maybe four inches taller than she. Not really tall, but tall enough . . .

Lost in thought, she suddenly heard someone calling her name. She was startled and blushed for no reason. It was Mrs. Wang speaking. "Little Moon, you are twenty-five years old. With your high standards, you'll never get married!"

They were discussing her marriage. Working as hard as she did, they thought she must have a lot of money. After all, not only did she own an apartment, but they were sure she had a fat bank account. They all agreed that whoever married her would be a lucky man.

A few friends had tried to match her up with likely prospects, but nothing came of it. Usually, Plain Moon felt the man was not good-looking enough. She had a point, most of the men she had been introduced to were truck drivers or worked in restaurants. They tried to look wordly but only ended up looking ridiculous. Some even had pierced ears and wore gold earrings or had permed hair—a man with a perm, ugly. Plain Moon thought her ideal lover should look like Zhang Guorong, the Jon Bon Jovi of Hong Kong. At least he should wear tortoise-rimmed glasses. Of course, he must not be too near-sighted. A man with glasses as thick as the bottom of a wine bottle would not be right, either. A student would be perfect. She knew, however, that she could not afford to be picky much longer. She was not ugly, but she was no beauty, either. She had a face as round as the full moon, a tiny nose, and two tadpole-shaped eyes a little too far apart, which gave her a slightly startled look. When seen separately, these features might be fine; when put together, they made a mediocre face. But she was still young and had been able to support herself since her mother had passed away. She wasn't in a great hurry to get married, but it was on her mind. On Chinese New Year, she had secretly gone to the Buddhist temple to ask for her fortune about marriage. She drew the worst of the worst. The last couplet of the divinatory verse read: "Wutong leaves fall apart; / Loving husband and wife do not last till winter." The blood had drained out of her. The gloomy temple with its depressing electric candles, the overcast day, and her fortune had run together in her mind. In the incense smoke, the chantings of Buddhist Sanskrit sutras from the cassette player had sounded like the tragic heroine Yingtai wailing at her lover Shanbo's grave. As she had listened to the intermittent sounds of fire-crackers outside, she had begun to shake all over.

At the end of lunch when egg custard was served, there was a tiny red candle on hers. The waiters gathered round and sang "Happy Birthday," the English mixed with Cantonese. Amidst the singing and laughter, Plain Moon felt happy.

3

The next day, helping Mrs. Wang count jackets made her run late. By the time she left the factory, it was quite dark. She walked hurriedly on the street, and just as she made a turn, she heard a bicycle screeching to a halt. She screamed, more out of reflex from real danger. When she composed herself, she threw an angry look at the bicyclist. It was him!

"I'm sorry!" He spoke Mandarin. "Did I hit you?"

She pretty much figured out what he was saying. With her hand on her bosom, she asked, "Do you speak Cantonese?" He pushed the bicycle along and replied in awkward Cantonese, "I can understand a little, but I can't speak it."

She could not help smiling and switched to English. "You didn't hit me."

His long eyebrows arched. "I'm sorry I startled you. I was in a hurry."

His English had a heavy accent, but he pronounced his words carefully, like a child reading from a textbook. There was a touch of maturity in his childlike tone. Each word made her heart feel like melting.

When they reached Phoenix, it was time to say good-bye. In the street's yellow light, she hesitated. Finally she said, "I work in the factory on the next block. My name is Plain Moon." She opened her left palm and wrote the Chinese characters on it.

He nodded. "My name is Li Ping." He gave her a cheerful smile.

Plain Moon walked all the way home before she realized that she had forgotten to buy dinner.

In the next few days, whenever she got a chance, whether during lunch break or after work, she rushed to Phoenix like a nail to a magnet. She bought chow mein to go or ordered a lunch special and ate at a corner table as she looked around. If Li Ping happened to be working, he would come up to say hello. Although their conversation was limited to weather and the most perfunctory greetings, which seemed even more impersonal when spoken in English, she felt excited every time she saw him. She would go over their chats again and again afterwards, as if there were something between the lines waiting to be discovered.

Plain Moon wore the same type of clothes as that of her older coworkers. They all dressed comfortably, usually wearing absorbent blue cotton blouses and pants. But now she put on a floral dress and some blush and lipstick. The first time Mrs. Lin saw her made-up face, she cried out in surprise, "Little Moon, you look so pretty today! Are you going on a date?"

She spent more and more time in front of her mirror every morning. The more attention she paid to her looks, however, the more depressed she became. How wonderful it would be if she were prettier! As she stared at her round face that seemed to fill the entire mirror, she yearned to change what she saw. She didn't have to look like those beautiful movie stars. If only her face were a little smaller, her skin a little lighter, her eyes bigger! Who knows, then maybe Li Ping would ask her out.

On Saturday she worked an extra day. She left her apartment early in the morning, and all day she bent over the sewing machine absent-mindedly. The only thing she could think of was the lunch break that would free her to go to the restaurant. She was even unaware of her sloppy work with several shirts. Mrs. Wang could not believe that Plain Moon could mess up. She picked up two of the lopsided shirts, came up, and asked Plain Moon, "Are you not feeling well today?"

Plain Moon was flustered. Despite the huge fan sending up a cool breeze from the corner, she felt warm all over. She paused and apologized hastily, "Yeah, yeah . . . I am a little . . . but I'll be more careful."

Mrs. Lin cast a meaningful glance at her. She did not say a word, but a smile rippled her face. Plain Moon felt as though she had been hit with a clap of thunder. Her whole face burned.

That day she somehow restrained herself from going to the restaurant. Instead she lost her appetite completely and did not eat anything. She returned to her apartment and walked up the staircase in a daze, turned on the stereo, and pushed a button without thinking. "My Dearest Love" by Zhang Guorong flowed out softly. She looked up at Zhang's poster on the wall, feeling like an empty shell.

That poster had been brought-back from Atlantic City many years ago. What a night that had been! A group of high-school girls took the bus to Atlantic City to watch Zhang's midnight show. They were too excited to sit still. Those who were bolder rushed up to the stage at the end of the show and hugged and kissed him. The timid ones, such as Plain Moon, only huddled under the stage with their arms crossed in front of their chests and screamed like a bunch of startled monkeys. On the way back, they were as boisterous as turkeys on a farm, routing about Zhang as if he were their common boyfriend and they could share their hearts.

But she had no one to share her heart with now. Some of her friends were married; some had moved away, and she had lost touch with them. She had been working in the factory for six years, but she did not have much to say to her older coworkers. Instead, they confided in her. Having kept quiet for so long, she didn't know how to open her mouth.

Plain Moon lived close to the Manhattan Bridge, but until this night she had never been aware of the cars honking all night long. She felt as though she were back in the countryside in Kowloon where she spent her childhood. In midsummer, frogs sat by the pond, croaking incessantly till the break of dawn.

4

Even though it was Sunday, Plain Moon woke up at dawn out of habit. Having tossed and turned all night, she did not know when she had drifted to sleep. She felt lazy as she lay in bed, and she refused to budge. She picked up a novel from the nightstand—*Once I Loved,* by Yi Shu—but she got bored after a few pages; her usual enthusiasm for this sort of trashy romance was gone.

The window to the left of the bed was open, and the noise of traffic and pedestrians floated in. The breeze was cool for this time of the year. Between spring and summer it was hard to tell if it would be warm or cool. She glanced outside the window and saw an overcast sky sandwiched between two buildings. She could not tell if it was raining.

Finally, Plain Moon got out of bed and rambled here and there in the apartment. Wandering into the kitchen, she opened the refrigerator and stuck her head inside it for a long while, but she couldn't remember what she was looking for.

Maybe going out would help, she thought. She washed her face, tied her hair in a ponytail, and put on a loose-fitting tee shirt with "I Love New York" written on it in Chinese. When she put on her jeans, she found that they were getting too big for her.

The streets were still wet from the night's rain, and there was a big puddle by the street corner. Plain Moon walked aimlessly and stopped at a fruit and vegetable stand, but even after staring at one red apples for a while, she still could not make up her mind whether or not to buy some. She kept walking and joined the flow of weekend shoppers in Chinatown. Jostled by the crowd, she began to feel lonely and empty. When she stopped and looked up, her back was all sweaty—she was at the door of Phoenix!

She mustered her courage and pushed the door open. The owner's wife, by the cash register, gave her a smile as sweet as a date: "Are you working today?"

Plain Moon shook her head and took a quick glance around. Li Ping was not in. She was slightly disappointed but somehow relieved.

"I came to buy some food to go. My older brother just came from upstate." The fact was, they hadn't spoken in two years, since their mother's funeral.

Leaving with a box of roast duck and barbecued pork, she finally felt a little hungry. Half a block down the road, she heard someone calling her, and when she turned around, she nearly dropped the bag. It was Li Ping, sitting on his bike with one foot on the ground, wearing a white tee shirt and black pants. A strip of white cloth was around his forehead, making him look like a wounded soldier. There was some crimson paint on the white cloth.

"What's going on?" She went up to him briskly and realized that the crimson paint was a few simplified Chinese characters she couldn't understand.

"I'm going to the Chinese consulate"—he leaned his head to one side and tried to fish for the right English word—"to demonstrate for democracy!"

Plain Moon was confused. Although she understood his English, she could not figure out what he meant. She rarely watched American television. She read Chinese newspapers, but she only browsed through the entertainment section and paid little attention to world news, big or small. She looked at him in surprise. "Today?"

"It's been going on for days. I demonstrate whenever I can. Do you wanna come?"

His question exploded in her mind. He wants me to go out with him! That means he doesn't have a girlfriend! "Okay," she blunted.

It started to drizzle. She opened her umbrella and waited for him to lock up his bike in front of the restaurant. He turned around and walked up to her. She held out the umbrella to shelter his dark hair already glistening with raindrops. It was such a familiar gesture, as if she had practiced it many many times before—holding an umbrella as bright and yellow as a full moon to ward off the wind and rain blowing through time and waiting for him to come to her in this life and the many more to come.

5

On the subway to the Chinese consulate, he summarized his life for her. He came from Shanghai, from a small family. His father had retired, his mother had passed away a long time ago, and he had two younger brothers. He was studying computer science at the city college on a government scholarship and lived in a rented basement in Brooklyn with a few Chinese students. His English was barely intelligible, with many grammatical errors, but it did not stop Plain Moon from listening with great interest.

When it was her turn to talk about herself, she didn't know where to start. Between pauses, she talked about her childhood in Hong Kong. How the neighbor's dog gave her a big bite on her thigh; how she went to a Chinese school run by Catholic nuns, and how, when she was fourteen, her family emigrated to New York. Her father had worked as a chef in a restaurant, her mother had worked in a garment factory, and she had gone to high school. As they walked out of the boisterous subway station, she sighed, "It's been more than ten years. Both of my parents have passed away. I have never had the chance to go back to Hong Kong."

"Your English is so good," Li said clumsily.

Her ears felt warm and her heart pounded—so there was something about her that he admired after all!

In front of the consulate, police had set up blue wooden barricades, separating the shouting crowd from the tightly shut building. Many banners, fists, and umbrellas waved in the drizzling rain. Shouts coming from hundreds of mouths converged into a powerful torrent: "Reform! Democracy!"

She stood close to Li and could feel the warmth from his arm. She asked him: "Do you know these people?"

"A few," he replied.

"Your roommates?"

"No, they're afraid of getting into trouble, so they didn't come."

The excitement was contagious. She got worked up all of a sudden. Putting her bag down, she shouted with a raised arm until she became hoarse.

Li had to go back to the restaurant in the afternoon, so they left before the demonstration ended. As they pushed their way out of the crowd, he held her hand. She completely forgot about the bag of take-out food lying by her feet.

Like exhausted soldiers coming home from the battlefield, they were silent on the way back. Li took off the strip of white cloth on his forehead and twisted it around with his fingers. She sneaked a glance at him. He seemed lost in thought, his brows tightly knit. She felt like smoothing those brows with her hands. Before they parted in China-town, she asked hesitantly, "Are you going to demonstrate next week? . . . Is it okay for us to go together?" She caressed the wet umbrella in her hand as she spoke.

She wrote her telephone number with a trembling hand. To save money, he did not even have a phone.

Plain Moon got up earlier than usual the following Sunday because Li had said he would call in the morning. After she freshened up, she stood in front of her mirror, undecided about the two dresses she had picked out the previous night. At last, she chose the white dress with red dots.

She fixed her hair in a big braid and tied a red satin ribbon on it. She used an eyebrow pencil to fill in her sparse brows, put on some red lipstick, and sprayed Calvin Klein's Obsession on her bosom. By the time she finished, it was already ten o'clock. She sat by the phone, waiting for it to ring.

By two o'clock the phone still had not rung. She got up to go to the bathroom and suddenly the phone rang. Panic. But it was only a magazine salesman, and before he could say the second sentence, she hung up with a bang.

It was getting warmer and warmer in her apartment. She twisted her hands in a daze and drifted from one room to another, trying to guess why he hadn't called. Had he forgotten? Was he sick? Had he been in an accident? There were so many knots in her head she couldn't begin to untangle them.

Close to five, the phone rang again. She jumped on it and knocked the phone onto the floor. When she picked up the receiver, she heard Li's voice. She was short of breath and didn't know if she should smile or cry.

"I'm really sorry," he said slowly. "My roommate was mugged on his way home this morning and got shot twice. I stayed with him until the operation was over before I remembered to call you."

"Is he all right?" she stammered.

"He's out of critical condition. But it's too late for us to go today."

"It's okay." She calmed down a little. "I'm tied up with something anyway. But do be careful when you go home tonight."

"I will. We'll go next Sunday, okay? I'm really sorry."

6

Early in the morning she was awakened by the phone. Half-consciously she reached out her hand and picked up the receiver.

"Did you hear the news?" It was Li, who sounded agitated.

"What news?"

"Last night the army drove into the Tian'anmen Square and shot thousands of people!"

"What!" she was completely awake now.

"They use tanks to kill their own people!" he exclaimed suddenly in Mandarin, crying a little.

She sat there in a daze, not knowing how to comfort him. Quickly they made a date. Li was coming to pick her up, and they would join the students to demonstrate in front of the Chinese consulate.

She washed her face and took a shower. She had barely changed when Li rang the doorbell downstairs. His eyes were bloodshot and his face looked pale. He was like a dark cloud moving in.

"It's a small place. Have a seat here," she said apologetically.

He was taken aback. "You live in this huge place all by yourself? Wow!" He looked around, saw her television, and asked her to turn the news on. "I heard about it yesterday after I got off work. I listened to my radio all night long but couldn't figure out all the details."

On the screen, flames were reaching the sky, machine guns were shooting like firecrackers, and tanks were arriving one after another. A tank that got separated from the troop was set on fire. Terrified faces, blood-dripping bodies on galloping carts, flattened bicycles . . . then they were both stunned. On the screen, a man wearing a short-sleeved white shirt and carrying a bag in his hand stood in front of the troop of tanks. He climbed on the one at the head. You couldn't tell what he was saying. Then he climbed down. The tank steered to the left, he moved to the left; the tank steered to the right, he moved to the right, refusing to retreat.

Li jumped up in the air, waving his fists: "Great! This is a real man! What guts!"

She stood by his side amazed, her eyes brimming with tears. The images on the television twitched excitedly through her teary eyes.

They tied strips of black cloth around their arms and joined thousands of people walking from the consulate to the United Nations on forty-ninth Street. In the surging sea of people and banners, she held Li's hand tightly. Halfway through he let go of her hand and put his arm around her shoulder. She wept silently. At that moment, she felt they had become one.

Li worked on Sunday afternoons, but that day he did not go. They had a simple dinner and went to the memorial in the square in front of the United Nations.

Frail candles flickered before the faces against a surrounding darkness that seemed immense. Amid the small flames, they sang songs Plain Moon didn't know. She looked up. In the dark blue sky there was a crescent moon next to the giant shadow of the United Nations building.

7

Now Li called frequently. Even though their conversation was mostly about demonstrations and the student group he was involved in organizing, to Plain Moon it was as sweet as lovers' talk. When the news of Wu'er Kaixi showing up in Hong Kong came, he cried and shouted excitedly on the phone, as if he had found a long-lost family member. She was happy too, not so much for Wu'er Kaixi as for Li.

On a few weekends he stopped by her apartment before he went to work. Sometimes, he sat there complaining. The money he made on deliveries was not steady. There were times when he pedaled more than ten blocks to deliver a twenty-some dollar dinner only to be tipped fifty cents! Plain Moon was indignant for him and cursed even more vehemently than he did.

Yet they did not make their relationship public. She had never met his roommates, and in the factory her good mood made her coworkers roll their eyes and laugh as she hummed a song and sewed. But Plain Moon was like Scrooge, who counted his fortune only in the middle of the night. No matter how much Mrs. Wang and the others pried, she would not divulge anything. For two months New York City was as warm as a steamy spa. Ten minutes at the sewing machine would give her a salty film of sweat on her back, but Plain Moon didn't even notice. The ten hours in the factory flew by. All she thought about was Li's phone call every evening.

On a stormy night in August, the phone rang as usual around half past ten. She brushed aside the hair on her forehead and picked up the phone with a smile.

"It's me. Can I come over? I have something to discuss with you."

She was taken aback. He never visited her at night, but she replied instinctively, "Sure. Why don't you come after you get off work?"

When he arrived, he sat to the right of the floor lamp, his face half hidden in the shadow. His back arched, he held both hands between his knees. Panic was written in his round eyes; like a child who has lost his way, he made her heart ache.

"My scholarship has been canceled."

"Why?"

"Someone turned me in to the consulate. My name is on the blacklist. If I drop out of school now, I'll have visa problems."

"Who did that?"

"I don't know."

"What about the money you've saved from working?"

"I've sent it all back to Shanghai."

"I'll go get something to drink. Would you like a 7-Up?"

Plain Moon got up and walked into the kitchen. She pulled open the refrigerator door, took out a two-liter bottle, and poured soda into a glass, overfilling it. A thought flashed through her mind. She guessed he was here to borrow money for tuition, but she had a better idea. When she lifted her head, she caught sight of a grinning face reflected in the windowpane above the sink. She quickly rearranged the expression on her face.

She sat down beside him. Patting his hand with hers, she comforted him, "Don't worry, we'll think of something."

Obviously he had difficulty asking to borrow money. When he left, he still had that helpless look on his face. She insisted that he take her yellow umbrella. That night, lying in bed, Plain Moon listened to the rain beating on the windows and went over and over her idea. She virtually fell asleep with a smile on her face.

Two days later, she asked him out for lunch at a small Chinese restaurant.

"I've thought this over in the past two days," she said, putting down her glass of iced tea. She peeked at him, then dropped her eyes and said calmly, "You'd better find a citizen to marry."

They sat face-to-face in the booth, surrounded by the noise of ordering and serving around them. She could not help feeling that this was the wrong place to discuss marriage.

"Marry?" Li cried out in surprise, making the customers at the next table turn around to look. He lowered his voice right away. "Marry? Who should I marry?"

Plain Moon picked up her glass and took another sip of the sweet and bitter tea, then she said slowly: "Me. I'm an American citizen. After we get married, you can apply for temporary residence. Two years later, you can apply for permanent residence. Once you get your green card, you'll pay resident tuition at the city college, which won't cost much. You can also get a student loan."

Li's mouth dropped open, as if he did not understand a word she was saying. After a while, his mouth opened even wider. Obviously he had caught on. "But, but how can we . . .? We . . . don't know each other . . . very long . . . I . . ." he stuttered in broken English.

"Why don't you think it over? I think this is the best way, and it's a lot easier than applying for political asylum," she said softly.

"Why are you doing this?" At last he succeeded in making a complete sentence.

"Don't you know?" Then she realized she was being coy. Embarrassed, she bent her head down. Li was shocked.

That day when she got off work, he was waiting for her outside the factory. Looking down at the ground, he said, "If you don't think I'm beneath you . . ."

8

The addition of one person in the apartment didn't make it seem as small as Plain Moon had expected. Li, after all, was used to living in a cramped space. He knew how to stay out of the way. His luggage was simple, too, consisting of some clothes, two pairs of old shoes, twenty or thirty textbooks, a worn toothbrush, a portable radio, and a Russian felt hat.

The apartment had been newly painted; the living room was light blue, the kitchen pale yellow, the bathroom azure, and the bedroom pink. Zhang Guorong's poster had been taken off the wall and stuffed into the closet.

They went to a studio to have wedding pictures taken. She had planned to sew her own wedding dress, but when she considered the fact that she would only wear it once, she thought it better to rent one. Makeup alone took two hours. She had a full facial, which made her face slightly sore. Scotch tape was pasted over her eyelids, making her eyes appear larger and deeper; her hair was trimmed to shoulder length and permed in large curls; foundation, eyeliner, blush, lipstick, . . . By the time she put on the lacy wedding gown, pinned the silk flowers of various colors in her hair, and picked up the bouquet of long-stemmed red roses, Li had dozed off in his suit.

When she saw the pictures, she could not believe her eyes. Had it not been for Li standing next to her, she would have thought that the studio had given her the wrong photos. The bride in the pictures was as beautiful as a television star! For months after the wedding, each time she saw those pictures, she was amazed that she was that beaming beauty.

Although Li thought it was excessive to hold the wedding banquet in a fancy Chinese restaurant, Plain Moon insisted. She invited all her coworkers from the factory, and at the banquet Mrs. Wang made the bride tell them all about her romance. They all felt betrayed by their best friend, who had gotten married without hinting that it was coming.

Afterward, they discussed it in private and came to the conclusion that they had never seen a bridegroom so glum.

Although it was her first time, sex was not as painful as she had expected. There was no pleasure, either, of course. She only held on tightly to his skinny, mildly perspiring back.

Li had used a condom. "It's not the time to have a baby," he explained. "I haven't finished school yet."

His underwear was frayed. The elastics on two pairs of underpants were completely loose, and they looked old and yellow. Without saying anything about it, she bought new underwear during her lunch break and threw out all the old ones.

Three days after the wedding, she went back to work. Her friends still called her Little Moon instead of Mrs. Li.

When she went home from work, Li had dinner ready: a plate of shredded beef and bell peppers, a plate of pickled cabbage with dried tofu, plus a sparerib and lettuce soup. Plain Moon was taken by surprise. He shrugged his shoulders. "I'm the oldest in the family. My mother died a long time ago, so I did all the housework."

When she asked about his past, he said little. He always answered her questions tersely.

They hired a lawyer to submit his application to the immigration and naturalization office. She paid all the fees.

School started. She persuaded him to quit the delivery job at Phoenix, and she gave him money to send home to Shanghai every month. She had figured it all out; evenings and weekends, she could sew thirty to fifty pieces at home. That would bring in a few hundred more dollars every month.

At Thanksgiving her boss gave every employee a turkey that weighed a good ten pounds. By the time she hauled it home, her arms felt as if they would fall off. Seeing the big bird, Li muttered clumsily, "I . . . I don't know how to do this."

Plain Moon smiled. "We'll bake it in the oven. I know what to do."

Five hours later, the turkey was overdone. It was as tough as tree bark. Neither of them ate much, but he would not let her throw it away. For two days he prepared turkey in a variety of ways. She was sick and tired of it, and at last, deaf to his pleading, she dumped the bird, bone and all, into a garbage bag and threw it away.

In the Chinese newspapers there was news about Wu'er Kaixi—some members of the democracy movement accused him of mismanaging the funds. Li got so mad that his face turned blue. "Chinese people just don't know how to work as a team!" Plain Moon poked fun at him for taking it so seriously, and for the first time he lost his temper.

At the end of the year, a letter came from Shanghai. After reading it, Li was silent for a long time. He would not answer her questions and tore the letter into pieces.

Usually when Plain Moon got home, the evening news would be over. But now that he was home, she, too, heard about the fall of the Berlin Wall, the collapse of the Communist government in Czechoslovakia, the execution of Nicolae Ceausescu of Romania, the new Solidarity regime in Poland. . . . Concentrating on a piece of sparerib or deep-fried tuna that Li had prepared, she remarked every so often, "Oh, really!"

Apparently Li had little interest in sex. Their encounters had dwindled from once a week to whenever she took the initiative. One day, as she looked at the wedding picture on the nightstand, she suddenly exclaimed, "I'm thinking of getting plastic surgery to make my eyes bigger. What do you think?" She pressed a toothpick on her eyelid and stared at her new look in the mirror.

He was shocked. "Why?"

"Because you have heavier lids!"

"Are you kidding?"

She decided not to do it after all.

Near Chinese New Year, the factory had to rush out the spring fashions. The employees worked overtime almost every evening. For days, by the time Plain Moon got home through the deep snow, it was close to midnight. Most of the time Li had already gone to bed. She quietly undressed in the dim glow of the nightstand lamp. As she gazed lovingly at his profile, his eyelashes, and his slightly curved upper lip, she wanted to cry.

The factory was closed on Chinese New Year, so they went to see *The War of the Roses*. They had expected a comedy, but it turned out to be about the double deaths of a divorcing couple. Slow on American humor, Li did not quite understand what was going on. When they walked out of the theater, Plain Moon only felt sad.

She suddenly sensed that he stared at her a lot, especially when she was busy sewing. When she asked him, "Why are you staring at me?" he always denied it. This only made her more alert. Sometimes when she sewed with her head down, her back seemed to be burning, as if she were walking alone at night and someone were following her step by step. When she lifted her face abruptly, she would catch Li's strange, prying look. Then he would turn his face away, pretending he was reading a book or taking notes.

9

By the time word reached her, it was an open secret in the factory.

One day Mrs. Lai took her hand and pulled her into the women's room. Leaning on the door, she whispered, "Little Moon, you may think I'm nosy, but I have to tell you this. Your husband is seeing another woman. Several people have seen them having lunch together."

"I trust him. You must be mistaking him for another man."

"No mistake. I saw them with my own eyes last Sunday. You'd better watch out."

Plain Moon got a chill, but she retorted, "Last Sunday he went to Wu'er Kaixi's lecture. Of course there were men and women there. Having lunch together is no big deal!"

"Wu what? No, no, it was just your husband and a woman! She's probably from mainland China. Don't you believe him!"

Although Plain Moon denied it fiercely, her defense was partly to calm herself down. For the past two months, she had sensed there was something wrong with Li, but however she pried, she could get nowhere. It was like sewing with your eyes closed; no matter how good you are, you just can't do it. More than that, she suddenly realized that she did not understand him at all. All she knew was that face of his. All day long, Mrs. Lai's words played over and over again in her ears. Everyone's eyes seemed knowing and full of pity, making her so miserable that she thought she would lose her mind.

Plain Moon left work two hours earlier than usual. When she walked out of the factory, it was still bright. There was not a cloud in the sky, and there was an elusive sliver of the moon visible in the distance, so pale it was almost transparent. She thought about how to confront him, but all of a sudden, her English seemed limited; she could not find the right words.

When she reached the intersection near her apartment, she hesitated. She wanted to turn around and pretend nothing was happening, but just at that moment, two people sitting in a remote corner in a little diner caught her eye. She recognized the man's back right away. The woman sat facing the exit; in the sun, her skin looked pale, making her eyes deeper and her short hair darker. She was weeping as she spoke, and once in a while she raised her hand to wipe away her tears.

Plain Moon felt weak in her knees; she almost sank to the ground. She composed herself and dragged herself home. Thirty-six minutes later, Li walked in. Startled by the sight of her sitting stiffly on the sofa, he panicked. He couldn't hide the alarm on his face and could only mutter: "You're home."

"Who is she?"

He wrung his hands together, his lips opening and closing silently, like a goldfish in an aquarium.

"Who is she?" Plain Moon persisted. "Don't tell me she's your younger sister!" Suddenly she hoped it was true.

"She's . . . my fiancée from Shanghai."

Plain Moon felt like jumping up, rushing up to him, and pouring out a thousand questions or strangling him. But all she did was sit there dejectedly, saying: "What?!"

His explanation was fragmented, but eventually she pieced it together. He had been engaged a long time ago to his childhood sweetheart. After the Tian'anmen Square massacre, he thought she would never escape, but she got a student visa and arrived in New York earlier that year.

"You've hid it from me on purpose, isn't that right? The money I gave you was all sent to her?"

He looked at her with wide-open eyes, neither admitting nor denying.

"What do you plan to do now? Divorce me or give her up?"

"I . . . I don't know," he sank to the floor and started weeping, with a hand covering his face. Intermittently he muttered, "I owe you too much, but . . . she and I . . ."

Disgust and pity suddenly surged up in Plain Moon, like the kind of disappointment you feel after having too much to eat—you are no longer hungry and so full that you feel sick. She stood and walked to the end of the living room to be as far away from him as possible. She heard herself speaking shrilly: "No wonder you use condoms; you want to avoid complications in the future. Isn't that right? Maybe you planned to hide it from me for another year so you could get your permanent residence and take off. Well, then you should've been more careful about not being seen by my friends. Okay, stop crying. Don't worry. We'll get a divorce once you've gotten your green card. I guess I owe you for your companionship for the past eight months. But you must move out right away." She paused a moment, then said solemnly, "You've never loved me, have you?" Spoken in English, it sounded even more self-righteous.

She felt as though she had just been reborn, like the beautiful and proud heroine she often read about in romances—holding her head up high, making a grand, courageous gesture with a wave of her hand.

Like an English aristocrat, she kept her cool until he walked out the door with his bag. She even remembered to ask him for the yellow umbrella back. But when the door shut, she threw herself at it and gasped for breath, though no tears came.

That night she sat in a daze in front of the window until the break of dawn. Although her eyes were wide open, she saw nothing. When she stood up, ready to go to bed, she suddenly noticed a bright full moon sandwiched between two buildings. Several large buds were visible on a magnolia tree, glistening in the moonlight. "Spring is here," she casually observed.

10

Plain Moon put away all the wedding pictures and hung Zhang Guorong back on the wall. Soon she quit her job at Rich Garment Manufacturing Company, and with her experience she easily landed a job at a Jewish shirt company.

Plain Moon arrived at and left work right on time. She rarely opened her mouth; some coworkers even assumed that she was mute. She worked eight hours a day and got paid by the hour. She always met the stipulated quota of one hundred shirts a day, not one more, not one less.

I AM NOT

A CAT

Tang Min

(Translated by Amy Dooling with Jeanne Tai)

1. My Cat and I

*N*o one ever seems to question the idea that being a woman means one should have children.

Having children appears to be the fundamental duty of women. If a woman can't have a child herself, she must at least find one to adopt. Women and children, mother and child—these belong together as naturally as heaven and earth, the bonds between them as inviolable as natural law. If any woman were to assert that she did not want children, she would probably be condemned by all her compatriots in the sisterhood of women. In China, in particular, having children has become mandatory for women. Those who can have children are held in greater esteem than those who cannot; what's more, those who have boys can carry themselves more proudly than those who have girls. When people encounter a married couple, the first thing they want to know is always, "Do you have any children? A boy? A girl?" No one ever asks, "Do you love each other? Do you get along well?" It seems that loveless marriages are quite acceptable, but childless ones are looked upon as abnormalities that strain the social fabric.

Naturally, it's even more improbable that anyone would ask whether a baby's mother had a difficult time during her pregnancy, or whether the birth itself was physically or psychologically stressful.

Even women themselves say, "If you become a wife, then of course you'll have to become a mother too. Yes, it's hard, and a lot of work, but it's the same for every woman, so why all the fuss? It's your fate as a woman, and you might as well accept it."

Nowadays, urban women go to hospitals or clinics for regular checkups during pregnancy. Especially since the One Child Per Family policy came into effect, young couples today take great pains to ensure that the fetus is genetically sound, and some even test those newfangled theories about beginning the child's education in the womb. All this is done for the sake of the child, not for the well-being of the woman. No matter how miserable the pregnancy or how torturous the childbirth, women have no alternative but to suffer through it. The pain and agony they endure have never been taken seriously by society. Indeed, women who have adverse reactions to pregnancy are viewed as sissies or fakers. Women working in factories continue performing their tasks even as they are throwing up, and still they are subject to such comments as "why couldn't you hold it in?" or "why didn't you run outside?" So, waddling about with their huge bellies, they haul themselves to work and then drag themselves home. Only when the baby is born are they finally excused from their jobs and allowed to go on maternity leave.

As the ancient saying goes: "A white horse is not a horse." Adapted for us women, it becomes: "A childless woman is not a woman."

All female animals share this misery. Let me tell you about the time our cat and I both became pregnant.

Exhaustion from my unrelentingly stressful job had led to a bout of acute nephritis. That came on top of a severely weakened condition caused by years of chronic overwork. So frail that even my clothes seemed to overwhelm me, I weighed barely ninety pounds, and the nephritis brought me to the verge of total physical collapse. Then, as if this weren't bad enough, I became pregnant too. It couldn't have happened at a worse time.

Not two days after I discovered I was pregnant, I began to throw up unremittingly. Food, water—I couldn't keep anything down. Coincidentally, our cat also began exhibiting symptoms of acute morning sickness. Both of us would be hunched over while we turned our insides out, both emitting guttural noises that were more animal than human. Afterward, we would lie there like cadavers; the violent heaves of our emaciated chests were the only sign that we were still alive. There were times when I couldn't even make it to the bathroom and ended up puking right on the floor, just like the cat. A few times I even spat up blood.

When we got married, I had told my husband that to be able to devote all my energies to writing, I wanted to wait a couple of years before having a child. At the time he had agreed but had added the stipulation that if I did become pregnant, we would have to go through with it and not get an abortion. When I actually got pregnant, however, he broke down even before I did. "You can't go through with this! If this keeps up you'll die before the baby is born!"

The doctor told me that as someone with kidney disease, I should not have become pregnant in the first place, and, furthermore, that the large doses of antibiotics I was taking would be extremely harmful to the fetus. I agreed to have an abortion, because I was afraid of having a child with birth defects. My husband, on the other hand, agreed to it because he hated the fetus I was carrying.

"He's going to kill you!" he ranted. "Only one of you can survive, and I want you, not him! Even if you make it through the pregnancy, you won't survive the childbirth. What if you die while you're giving birth?"

We had to keep the abortion secret from our parents and relatives, because we knew that once they found out they would have vehemently opposed our decision. They would have argued, "How can you be so sure that you would die in childbirth? How do you know that the baby will have birth defects? If we believed everything the doctors said, we would all have been dead a long time ago! Once you're pregnant, you should have the baby!"

But if my husband and I had a physically deformed or mentally handicapped child, what would that do to us—our dreams, our hopes for happiness, our lives . . . ? Has anyone bothered to consider the pain and grief entailed in all this?

Such is the pressure produced by the combined weight of social custom and traditional moral precepts. The result is to impose a kind of servitude on women, who become conscripts dedicated to "perpetuating the family line." In the face of this forced labor, women are not even allowed to plead ill health or some other disabling condition. Getting married is tantamount to obtaining the "legal right to bear children," and whoever dares to give up this right will be execrated and damned in this world and the next.

When women are forced to carry out the task of propagating the race, it becomes nothing less than a life sentence: pregnancy, birth, parenting, education, pulling strings to find a good job for your child, scrimping and saving to pay for your child's wedding, taking care of your child's child—one after the other, each chore falls unmistakably and inevitably on the shoulders of every woman. There is no escape. Yet society seems perfectly at ease with this state of affairs and considers it as natural as the sun's rising every morning in the east. And while women carry this heavy burden, they still have to work and make a living just like the men, all in the name of "equality between the sexes."

I was lucky enough to have a good husband who could not bear to see his wife suffer. Together we exercised our veto power against "women's servitude." As a result of our decision, he has had to endure countless accusations and denunciations, all the while emphatically insisting, "I was the one who didn't want the baby! Anyway, what's it to you?!"

Yet so many people, including some husbands, give no thought at all to a woman's health. I once met a woman who was diagnosed with breast cancer right after she was married, so it was clearly inadvisable for her to have a child. But the families on both sides decided that she should take a chance anyway and try to get pregnant. They felt that since she was already married and was now diagnosed with an incurable disease, it was quite logical and all the more important for her to try to leave behind an offspring. The result was that by the fifth month, the fetus had become another breeding ground for cancerous cells, and she had no choice but to have an abortion. One month later, this woman quietly passed away. Her family and friends were all very surprised. "She seemed so healthy after the operation. Why did she die all of a sudden?"

Why? It was a mother's grief at losing her child that had devastated her. Once a fetus begins to grow inside her body, a woman can never forsake the affection she has for this new life. This maternal love is the only thing that enables a woman to endure all the pain and hardships of motherhood. A serious illness will not always result in a woman's death, but the anguish of losing a child can take a woman's life.

Once, after my cat gave birth to a dead kitten, she tried in vain to nurse it, staying by its side all day long, stroking and petting it over and over. When my husband and I disposed of the kitten, the mother cat flew into a rage and leaped about, trying to recover the remains. If even animals feel the loss so deeply, how much more so the human heart? This inextricable bond to one's flesh and blood—can it be something beyond the comprehension of men?

The night before I was to have the abortion, my cat had a miscarriage. Amid the puddles of amniotic fluid and blood were three semitransparent embryos, each no bigger than a broad bean. So weak she could barely even mew, the mother cat nevertheless struggled to sniff and stroke them. That night, in a state of extreme anxiety and anguish, I had a vivid dream in which I saw an X ray of my fetus—a bluish, transparent baby boy sound asleep in my womb, his hair undulating in the ripples of his watery environment. . . .

When I came home from the hospital the next day, I saw the image of this baby every time I closed my eyes. Lying in bed, I wailed and cried my heart out. My whole life seemed empty after the loss of my child.

2. I Am Not a Cat

I have heard countless women who have had abortions talk about the mental pain and shock they suffered during the operation. I offer the following account of my experiences in the hospital to you, my readers, so that you may know what else love entails.

My abortion was carried out at the largest obstetrics and gynecological clinic in the province. The patients were either pregnant or suffering from some gynecological problem, and the outpatient clinic was filled with wan, sickly women. There was hardly a single presentable-looking one among them—no trace of the comeliness one finds in normal, healthy women. The prospect of being examined while naked from the waist down further aggravated the general sense of unease and foreboding. Addressing those who had come for an abortion, the doctor would ask: "First time? Second? You pay twenty yuan for the first, ten if it's the second. Get a receipt from the cashier, then get in line in front of the operating room."

The unfortunate women waiting for abortions all looked extremely nervous and apprehensive, like convicts just before their execution. But strangely enough, we all wanted to be at the head of the line, as though we were shoppers waiting to buy scarce fresh vegetables in the middle of winter. There were eight of us in the first group. After changing into hospital slippers, we entered the disinfecting room. The middle-aged nurse in charge, who reminded me of one of those robust, no-nonsense vendors in the market, briskly ordered us to take off our pants and line up to be scrubbed and disinfected. It was a cold day, and everyone scrambled to get one of the cotton bathrobes hanging from the clothes rack to wrap around our bodies. But there weren't enough robes to go around, and those who came up empty-handed had to wait until someone took hers off just before climbing onto the operating table.

For the nurse, who must have performed this same task countless times, day in and day out, the whole procedure had long since become routine. Crisply, nonchalantly, she directed these distraught and distracted women to get on and off the disinfecting table one after another, asking each one in turn, "Abortion? IUD?" Those who had come for an IUD were merely cleaned and scrubbed, while those who were about to have an abortion had their pubic hair shaved as well. The swiftness and dexterity with which she carried out these procedures were positively awe-inspiring. I was reminded of the practiced motions of those women workers who wash bottles in recycling plants or who peel potatoes in canneries. By the time the nurse was done with our group, we were all privy to the information that seven of us had come for abortions while one woman was waiting to have an IUD inserted. I couldn't help noticing that this last patient had a curious but unmistakable look of superiority on her face.

From the time I walked into the outpatient clinic to the time I entered the operating room, no more than two hours had passed, but for me they went by more slowly and more agonizingly than twenty years of hard labor.

I was among the first group of four to enter the operating room. To my amazement, the minute I walked into the room the nurses inside began commenting on my appearance, talking loudly among themselves about what a good-looking outfit I had on. True, I was wearing a rather pretty sweater that day under a fashionably chic ski jacket. But how they found any aesthetic appeal in the clothes of a woman who was naked from the waist down was quite beyond me.

I walked over and lay on the operating table, breathing in the frigid air as I looked at the worn, antiquated furnishings in the room. How many unfortunate women had had to undergo the most painful episode in their lives on this very spot! At moments like this, love, so prized and esteemed by the world, seems but an iniquitous crime, a shameful vice. Yet it is only the woman who must suffer this punishment by fire!

The doctor who was to perform the operation seemed quite young. Looking around the room with her attractive large eyes, she turned to me and said, "You're not getting any younger. This is your first pregnancy—why aren't you keeping it?"

Fearful of what she might say if she found out I had become pregnant while suffering from kidney disease, I decided to lie. "I want to go back to school—I've just been accepted into a special study program."

"You mean you'd rather go back to school than keep your baby? What kind of woman are you?!" She paused in her tongue-lashing, then sneered and said, "Well, with someone like you, who knows if you're even married?"

"Yes, I am," I shot back, "and this *is* my first pregnancy."

"If you're lying, I'll find out as soon as I take a look."

"I'm not lying, this *is* my first time!" I screamed, unable to control myself any longer.

The nurses, who apparently were not used to finding themselves with a patient as unruly as I was, hurriedly chimed in, "Yes, it's true, we can tell just by looking, you know. If you've had an abortion it would be obvious."

I was so angry I almost jumped up from the operating table. "Go ahead, look, look! I have nothing to hide!"

After that I had to wait for almost twenty minutes, a seeming eternity, as I twisted and chewed on my handkerchief. During that time, I heard another doctor scolding a woman who had become pregnant shortly after giving birth, and yet another doctor interrogating a young woman, also there to have her first pregnancy terminated, about whether or not she was really married.

And so it went. The only person treated with kindness and concern was a doctor on the staff of the hospital, who had come to have her IUD removed. She was allowed to keep her pants on until the operation.

My pride and self-esteem lying in shreds, I was barely conscious of the horrible reality of my child being mangled and crushed into bits and pieces that were then aspirated into a tube. All I could focus on was my desperate desire to get out of this place.

When I finally staggered out of the operating room, the doctor fired a parting shot at my back. "Don't come crying to me if you can't have a baby later on!"

Something made me look up the doctor's name in my medical record. I found out that this beautiful doctor was named after an even more beautiful flower. But to me she was a diabolical figure whom I will never forget as long as I live.

Afterward, as I was getting dressed in the changing room, an eighteen- or nineteen-year-old girl walked in. She was the only truly healthy and beautiful woman I saw in that hospital the whole time I was there: an exquisite figure, a rosy complexion, a thick head of lustrous black hair, and a pair of shapely long legs traced by her blue jeans. She approached me and, in a touchingly innocent manner, asked: "Does it hurt much?"

"Have you also come for . . . an abortion?" I replied.

"Yes. I'm so scared. I've heard that it's really painful."

"Well, actually, it's . . . not all that bad. Just grit your teeth for a while and you'll be all right."

She broke into a fetching little laugh, "Oh, that's wonderful! Now I can stop being scared."

I watched as she deftly took off her pants and continued to follow her with my eyes as she walked over to the bottle-washing, potato-peeling nurse. This poor girl was going to meet her fate armed with nothing more than her naïveté, but perhaps that was just as well.

I shuffled into the waiting room just in time to hear my husband jovially telling a friend of mine, who had also come to the hospital with me, "Yes, my sister-in-law is a doctor too, and a lot of women also go to her hospital for the operation. They're taken inside, they scream and holler for a while, and next thing they know, it's over."

That was when I lost whatever self-control I had left. Tears poured down my cheeks as I held on to my friend for support. With my other hand I slapped my husband. Then I fell sobbing onto the bed in the recovery room. Panic-stricken, my husband stammered: "Was it, was it really painful? Here, hit me again, hit me. . . ."

It was not until some time later that he finally realized my tears had nothing to do with physical pain. But when he asked me why I was crying, I found myself at a loss for words to express the myriad thoughts and feelings swirling inside me. In the end, all I managed to say was, "The doctor said she didn't believe I was married."

"You should have made her come out to see me," he roared, outraged. "I even have our marriage certificate right here!"

The recovery room began to fill up with women who had all been put through the wringer. Some were weeping, others moaned softly, while still others heaved and retched. Here and there a few women chattered away compulsively, telling anyone who would listen about how the birth quota for their factory this year had already been filled, how they had missed getting a permit, how they had been told to wait until next year to have a baby.[1] The whole scene was like a tableau straight out of hell.

Four days later, I suddenly had an attack of sharp pains in my lower abdomen, followed by massive internal bleeding and a cold sweat that drenched me from head to toe. Because the lovely doctor had failed to completely remove the embryo and the adjoining tissue, I was once again plunged into that living hell. Late in the day I was rushed to the hospital and, in the gathering dusk, underwent a second dilatation and curettage. The pain was many times worse than the abortion itself, and I couldn't help screaming in agony. It began to dawn on me that there was a good chance I might never

---

1. Under China's One Child Per Family policy, state-owned enterprises such as factories are assigned an annual quota of allowable births. Married women working at such factories must obtain official permission to have a baby or face penalties in the form of lowered salaries, and loss of benefits or even jobs.

be able to become pregnant again. For a long time I wailed and howled like a desolate beast—was it in anger? remorse? hatred? I'm not sure I knew the difference.

Meanwhile, the hubbub of the bustling streets below, mixed with the roar of firecrackers welcoming the new year, surged through the window like waves and crashed all around me.

THE ADULTERERS

Li Peifu

(Translated by Charles A. Laughlin with Jeanne Tai)

*I*t was almost daybreak, but the night was as restless as ever. The band saw in Jiuxiang's house was screeching away, grating on the senses like a splinter stuck under the skin. The tarp factory in the west village was in full swing, its machines banging and rattling incessantly. Now and then a minitractor would chug along the main road, its rumbling bearing down on the nerves like a steamroller. The dogs were all barking their heads off. And the moon—the moon was no more than a blurry figure, skulking among the clouds like a burglar. Even the pigsties were jumpy. After the recent disappearance of another two pigs, some villagers had taken to sleeping in the pens. At the smallest sound, some dark shape would leap up from the straw-covered floor of a stable and shriek, "Who's there?"

The brothers Tongchui and Tiechui were crouched furtively beneath Mingtang's window, listening intently to the darkness around them. The night was chilly, but they were burning inside. For some time now, Tongchui's wife had not been sleeping at home, claiming she had to keep watch at the pen. One night, feeling horny, Tongchui had groped his way to the sty, but all he found were the pigs. What a lot of work it is to get a woman! he thought to himself as he tugged his pants on and went out into the night. He looked all over, only to find her fast asleep back in the sty at home. Confused and bewildered, he couldn't quite bring himself to ask her about it. She was very fair-skinned and as tall as a foreign-bred horse. He, on the other hand, was short, dark, and skinny as a cur. If they hadn't been betrothed as toddlers by their parents, she never would have married him. There were many similar incidents after that, and Tongchui, growing more and more suspicious, began to follow her around at night. But his wife, savvy and nimble as a cat, always managed to throw him off her trail. He tried eavesdropping at this house and that but always came up empty-handed. Eventually his suspicions began to focus on Mingtang, and, needing an eyewitness, he had asked his brother to come along and help him catch the adulterers.

It was past midnight when the two of them crept to Mingtang's house and squatted beneath the window. They thought they could hear something going on inside, but Tongchui didn't want to do anything rash. He licked the window paper and made a peephole, but all they could see through it was a murky blackness. Although he was seething, Tongchui restrained himself until he could find out for sure what was going on.

After a long, long time, they finally heard a soft voice murmuring in the darkness inside. It was answered by a low, deep-voiced growl, followed by the rustling of clothes. Then, click!—a light was turned on, and there was Tongchui's wife, sitting on the edge of the bed, her face flushed with color as she turned and said, "I have to go."

The man she was talking to, a brawny fellow lolling stark naked in the bed, was none other than Mingtang. Stretching himself lazily, he answered, "Fuck, what's your hurry?" Then he turned over, pulled out a wad of money from under the pillow, and tossed it over to her, saying, "Here, take this."

Tongchui's wife was stunned. With a look of outrage, she swung her hand high as though she were about to hit him, then slowly lowered it again as she stammered, "What—what is this, after all these years? . . ."

Mingtang yawned, no less lazily than before, and drawled, "Here's a thousand. Take it."

Tongchui's wife glanced at the money flung down on the bed and looked over at Mingtang again, but she couldn't think of anything else to say, so she mumbled once more, "Look at this, after all these years. . . ."

Mingtang made no reply; he merely glanced at her out of the corners of his eyes. Suddenly Tongchui's wife seemed overcome with shame, and she hung her head in silence. Flustered, she groped around until she found her shoes, then fumbled and struggled before she finally got them on. But plopping herself on the edge of the bed, she dawdled as she combed and pinned up her hair, trying hard not to glance at the money. The look in her eyes undulated and swayed, now shimmering with her genuine feelings for her longtime lover, now glinting with thoughts of the creature comforts at last within her grasp, and for a while she was lost in reverie. In the end, she reached over with a trembling hand and took the money. Then she mumbled nervously, "Well, I'll be going now."

Outside, two shadowy faces peered over the window ledge, a sinister green flame blazing in their eyes. Tiechui arched his back and hissed: "Come on, let's go in!" But Tongchui clenched his teeth and, letting out a deep breath, answered, "No, wait. . . ."

Inside, Tongchui's wife was about to go out the door when Mingtang rolled over and said, "Qin, wait. . . ."

She turned to look at him, her heart thumping. Without realizing what she was doing, she glanced at the money in her hand and all of a sudden felt a sense of loss.

Fixing his eyes on the ceiling, Mingtang said nonchalantly, "Qin, don't bother to come tomorrow."

Tongchui's wife stared blankly at Mingtang, her body trembling in spite of herself. It seemed as though she had understood everything, and yet she didn't seem to understand anything at all. Her palms were clammy with sweat, but her heart was chilled through and through. In an instant, the beautiful memories of all those tender nights had been turned into something tawdry. Tears streaming down her cheeks, she stammered, "Is there—is there someone else?"

Mingtang said nothing.

"You're so heartless . . . you, you've found someone else. . . ." she sobbed.

Mingtang remained silent, but it was all very clear. As a manager at the tarp factory, he had been making good money these last two years and was no longer penniless. Tongchui's wife raised her arm again, and, steeling herself, seemed ready to fling the money back at the callous wretch. How satisfying it would be to throw it all in his face! But once again she lowered her hand, slowly, ever so slowly. Those moments of splendor and passion were gone forever, but at least she could look forward to days, perhaps years, of prosperity. But what about all those sweet words she had murmured to him through night after night of their illicit affair: "I don't want anything else, I just want a real man, a man who loves me. . . ." And all the tender, loving things he, the tomcat, had whispered in return. His passion for her had seemed ardent enough to melt her entire being.

She stood there silently, trying to summon those happy moments, but she could not find the words. In the end she could only repeat, "You're so heartless!"

Outside, Tiechui was burning with impatience. "Hey, what are you waiting for? Let's do it!"

But a pale green fire gleamed in Tongchui's eyes, and his breathing became more and more rapid. Slowly, he sat down on his haunches and rubbed his head against the brick wall. Finally, in a hoarse voice, he muttered dispiritedly, "Let's—let's just forget it."

"Fuck, what do you mean forget it?"

"The son of a bitch said no more, he wasn't going to see her anymore," Tongchui rasped, sweat pouring down his face as he knocked his head savagely against the wall, again and again.

Bang! The door slammed behind Tongchui's wife as she came running out like a gust of wind.

The night was thick and heavy, the air fetid. The chickens were all asleep in the trees, a cluster of browns and blacks here, a clutch of reds and greens there. The moon bobbed among the clouds, now bright, now dim, so that the night seemed even more shadowy and confusing. Silently, sullenly, the two brothers stumbled homeward, their heads sagging, their breath coming in gasps like a dog's on a sweltering summer day. Though their faces were hidden by the night, their shame hounded them with every heartbeat. Tongchui knew full well how thoroughly he had humiliated and disgraced himself, and he let his head droop, unable to look his brother in the eye. They both knew it was because of the money, the thousand yuan. How important that was to him! For quite some time now he had been planning to go in with a partner on a minitractor, but he could never scrape together enough money. The thousand yuan would just about do it—but what about his wife's virtue and good name? Well, her virtue's gone, but he still wanted the good name—*his* good name. Not to mention that he wanted to save face. After all, face is what a person goes by—it's how one is known, what one lives behind. His heart raged. One minute all he could see were the colorful bills fluttering before his eyes. The next instant all he could imagine were those long, ivory legs spread on the man's bed, shuddering and thrashing in front of him until he couldn't stand it any longer. Oh, how he hated it! Heaven, and earth, his wife, that man, himself—he hated them all!

On and on they trudged, until at last Tiechui broke the silence. Stomping his foot and breathing heavily, he cried out, "Tongchui!"

His older brother swayed unsteadily before lowering himself onto his haunches and crumpling himself into a little knot. His face glistening with sweat, Tongchui whimpered, "Go ahead, brother. Curse me, curse all you want. I'm a worm, not a man."

Tiechui's eyes blazed with a terrible light, and he was shaking so much even his teeth clattered. Swallowing hard, he appeared on the verge of speaking but seemed to change his mind. Instead, he stomped his foot again, then stood there like a man transfixed. But in the end he couldn't hold it in any longer and suddenly blurted, "Let me have a go at her too!"

Tongchui shot up and grabbed his brother by the throat, screaming, "What did you say?! You son of a bitch, what did you say?!"

Tiechui hung his head. He hesitated for a while and finally said, "Well, that . . . that guy already got her, so why not me too?"

Tongchui seemed to have had the stuffing knocked out of him. Perspiration streamed down his face like raindrops as he slowly turned and headed for home again, trudging with leaden steps.

Tiechui caught up with him and begged. "Tongchui, listen, listen to me. She's already a piece of trash. I'll . . . I'll pay you too. Let's put it all on the table. Just name your price."

The raging balls of green fire crashed into each other, and in the conflagration the two brothers suddenly became strangers. Tiechui, already thirty years old but still single, with no prospects of finding a woman soon, was consumed with one thought: he must have a taste of her! If none of this had happened, he might have been able to control himself. But after all this, after he *saw* her, *saw* everything. . . .

Falling to his knees, he pleaded, "Tongchui, please. . . . She did it with him—why, why not with me?"

How Tongchui wished he could strangle his brother right then and there! But there was nothing he could say. He had only himself to blame for bringing his brother along on this night. His head drooped lower and lower and he finally muttered, "She . . . she wouldn't."

"Never you mind. I'll . . . I'll handle that," Tiechui replied hastily.

For a moment Tongchui's eyes flickered. Then he resumed walking, slowly, ploddingly, looking as though he had suddenly aged ten years.

Tiechui stayed close on his heels. "Tongchui, I'm . . . we're family. How about fifty?"

Tongchui continued on for a few more steps. Then, through clenched teeth, he hissed: "Sixty!"

"Not fifty?"

"Sixty!"

"All right, all right, sixty."

"Never mind whether she wants to or not. . . ."

"Go, go for a walk," Tiechui panted. "Take a long walk, take your time." With that, he bounded off in a frenzy.

The bottomless night closed around Tongchui, pickling him in its briny depths. He thought to himself, Why not go take a look at the vegetable plot, make sure no one's been stealing anything? So he set out. But he couldn't feel his limbs moving. Instead, he had a vague sensation of some empty shell of a body floating along, a body that had no connection with his own. It was only when he bumped his head into a tree that all of a sudden he came back to his senses. Then the fire engulfed him once more and he charged home, intoning as though reciting a mantra: "Kill, kill, kill!"

The next morning Tongchui's wife was nowhere to be found.

RUNNING

WILD

Su Tong

(Translated by Kirk Anderson and Zheng Da)

*W*hen the wind howled, house and earth floated together in darkness. Somewhere far away, or perhaps even right inside this old, tile-roofed house where Yu slept, some invisible creature was creaking. The wind outside was so violent that Yu felt some unknown fear. He pushed the coarse mosquito net aside. Outside the window was a purplish blue sky scored with the shadows of a few trees. All was peaceful and quiet. Yu guessed a huge monster might be making that noise in the night, but he didn't know what to call it. Even with his eyes wide open, he couldn't see where it was hiding. There were too many things Yu didn't understand. For a country boy, he was unusually weak and feeble. Since the headaches started, Yu had not left the courtyard of his house.

When the color of the morning sky brightened, Yu hurried out of bed to go pee. When he passed Grandma's room he pushed the door open and saw Grandma sitting on the toilet groping under the bed for toilet paper with one hand while clutching her chest with the other, coughing loudly, as usual. It seemed like Grandma had been coughing like this all her life. Yu spoke into the room, "I'm going to pee." As he passed Mother's room, again he pushed the door open. Mother had already gotten up; she was looking in the mirror on the wall doing her hair. Her long, black, shining hair had been rolled into a bun at the back of her head. Yu said, "I'm going to pee." Then he hopped up on the doorstep and peed outside onto the frosty ground. As Yu was tying his pants, he saw the circular skyline of the village become gradually lighter, slowly growing distinct. The cowherds had already reached the pond. The fresh smell of grain wafted from the threshing ground.

Sometimes Yu would sit on a haystack on the threshing ground watching a flock of chickens pecking at the fallen grains. But this normally happened later in the morning. On their way to the fields, the villagers all saw Yu seated motionless on the haystack. In his hand was half a leftover pancake, on which a few flies rested.

"Do you have another headache, Yu?"

"No," said Yu, "I'm eating a pancake."

"Yu, is your daddy coming home soon?"

"Yes, he'll be home for New Year."

In the sun Yu's body shed a light that was the same faint yellow color as the haystack. After he swallowed the last bit of pancake, he felt a headache coming on again. Yu climbed down the haystack and heard his mother calling him loudly from the door. "Yu, come here to take your medicine." While Yu stumbled across the threshing ground he saw someone walking down the road. It was a carpenter with his tool bag slung over his shoulder. Yu stood looking at the person, who looked very much like his father. That was because of the way he walked and the saw, hatchet, and ink marker he was carrying. Actually, Yu didn't know him. That's not my daddy, Yu said to himself. He spat in the carpenter's direction, then dashed back home.

Yu was taking the puckeringly bitter herbal medicine. Following folk tradition, Mother collected these herbs in the mountains. She stacked the stems and leaves in a shallow bamboo tray and dried them in the sun. When they were dry, Mother ground them into a powder and kept them in a basket. Every day Yu's mother took a handful of herbs from the basket and made a tea for Yu to drink. Yu feared the tea's bitter taste and poured it into the swill bucket in the courtyard for the dog to drink. The dog wagged its tail and walked away. Yu thought, if the dog won't drink this, then why should I? After his mother discovered what he had been doing, she would sit in front of Yu watching until he finished the medicine. She said, "You should listen to me. When you're sick, you should take medicine. If you don't, you will die. Do you understand? How horrible it is to die! Aren't you afraid of death?"

Someone was standing at the door. Yu recognized the carpenter who had been walking down the road. Yu also noticed that Mother knew the carpenter. They stood near the door chatting for a while. The carpenter stepped into the house, sat on a bench, and asked for something to drink. Yu saw his tool bag, as tattered as his father's. Through a hole the sharp edge of a plane was exposed.

"This is your uncle." While mother dipped a ladle into the barrel, she raised her head and said to Yu, "He's Daddy's good friend. He's come to our house to do some work. Do you remember him?"

No. Yu shook his head and replied, "I don't remember anything."

"Your daddy went to the Northwest to work, and he won't be back for New Year." Mother handed the ladle to the carpenter. With an amused smile on her face she said, "Yu, your father has sent money back home. He made a lot of money this year."

With a grimace Yu finished the medicine and set the bowl facedown on the table. He said, "I'm done." Yu raised his head and looked at the carpenter and Mother suspiciously. They looked back at him the same way. The carpenter's face was full of pimples and lumps, with a big mole. Suddenly the carpenter smiled at Yu, exposing his soy-sauce-brown teeth. He said, "Come here, I'll give you some candy." Yu responded, "I don't want any. I'm going out." As Yu walked toward the door, he heard Mother say apologetically, "The boy doesn't know how to behave. He has a strange temper. It's all because of these damn headaches."

Yu leaned against the wall listening to the conversation between the carpenter and Mother, but they didn't say anything else. Afterward

Mother led the carpenter into Grandma's room. They were apparently discussing something, but Yu still couldn't catch what they were talking about. He could vaguely sense that it had something to do with him. What were they really up to?

The carpenter, named Wang, stayed at Yu's house. The next day he took down the door of Yu's room and laid it across two benches to make a table. Yu screamed at the carpenter, "What are you doing here at our house?" The carpenter responded, "Go ask your mother." Yu ran to his mother and asked, "He took down my door—what's he doing?" Mother said, "He's starting his work. He can't work without the door." Yu said, "My daddy's a carpenter too. Why didn't he come home to do the work? Why did you have to let that guy come?" Mother was a little impatient. She nudged Yu with her elbow. "Yu, didn't you hear me? How many times have I told you? Daddy's gone far away to work, and he won't be back home this year." Yu didn't say another thing. After a while he asked, "Is he going to make us a dresser?" Mother responded, "What do we want a dresser for? He's not making a dresser; he's making a coffin." Yu's face paled instantly. He turned around to look at the tools in the living room. Yu grabbed his mother's arm. "Why is he making a coffin? Who's going to sleep in it?" Mother was washing the rice. She seemed to have been in a bad mood that whole day. Yu saw his mother throw the bamboo strainer down with a clatter. She said, "You're really an annoying child. I can't stand it. Who's going to sleep in the coffin? It's for you, for you to sleep in!"

Horrified, Yu stared at the rice scattered on the floor beside the water barrel. Mother was really mad. She was wearing a cotton print jacket and blue khaki pants, her sleeves and cuffs rolled up. Her face was red with anger. Yu saw sweat bead on her forehead, and light blue veins emerged like worms. All this seemed unexpected to Yu. He murmured, "What did I do? I haven't done anything wrong. I just don't like that carpenter."

Mother then bent over, scooped up the rice, and continued washing it. Mother said, "Yu, I didn't mean to get angry with you. I'm just tired. I don't know if this will be enough rice for him.

Our rice barrel's almost empty, and your father hasn't come home."

The carpenter's plane zipped back and forth from morning to night. The ground was covered with sawdust and curls of wood shavings. The fresh smell of wood changed the musty smell in the air. Yu was always awakened from his dream by the noise and the smell of wood. The door to his room was gone. Now, lying in bed, he could see what was going on in the living room. The carpenter bent again and again, smoothing the plank. Tucked behind his ear was a red and blue pencil. A bottle of wine was on the table next to him. Every so often the carpenter stopped what he was doing and took a gulp from the bottle. When he drank the wine, peacefulness resumed at home. Yu heard Grandma's ancient cough and spitting. Mother was in the courtyard calling the chickens to feed.

Yu picked up a wood shaving from the floor. He cut two holes in it with a knife and put it over his eyes. Afterward Yu sat beside the stove. Staring through these two holes, he examined the carpenter named Wang. The carpenter was planing the plank forcefully. His movements were mechanical and full of power.

"Hey, why did you come to work here?" Yu asked. "Why don't you go to other families?"

The carpenter didn't reply. He just worked. He rarely opened his mouth to talk.

"My family doesn't need a coffin, so why did you come here to make one?"

The carpenter turned to glance at Yu, his face expression less. Yu saw his two fingers pull a nail from the plank and toss it on the floor.

"Even after you're done it will be useless," Yu said to the carpenter. "Nobody in our house wants to sleep in the coffin—unless you want to yourself."

Yu heard the carpenter burst into laughter. He straightened up and walked around the plank, kicking sawdust into the corner. The carpenter ran his hand over the plank, which was gradually becoming smoother, and said, "Once the coffin is done, there will be someone to sleep in it. This coffin is made of the best wood in the world. When you grow up you'll understand." Having said this, the carpenter suddenly sat down on the plank and slowly reclined. The carpenter's body lying there seemed huge beyond comparison. With the smile still on his face, he said to Yu, "How comfortable it is to lie on a coffin plank. You'll understand when you grow up."

When the carpenter jumped off, Yu couldn't help but back up a few steps. The carpenter's piercing, fiery eyes frightened Yu. Yu saw the carpenter open his arms to him and say, "Boy, I'll lift you up. Try the taste of sleeping on the coffin board. It's the best bed in the world. Much more comfortable than your little bed." Yu leaned against the wall. Almost in tears, he cried, "No. I don't want to." But the carpenter's powerful arms pulled him in. Yu felt like a seed falling gently onto the coffin board. The board was ice cold. The fresh smell of pine was heavy and thick. What followed was a fateful dizziness. Yu passed out on the coffin board.

In half an hour Yu woke up and saw his mother and the country doctor, as well as his sickly grandmother, around his bed. Mother's eyes were very red. She must have been crying the whole time. Grandmother ran her chicken–claw-like hands repeatedly over his forehead. The country doctor felt relieved. "It's all right now. He just had a fright."

"I can't sleep. Don't make me sleep in the coffin." Yu told his Grandma that he felt very weak, as if he had really been dead.

"My poor boy, how can you sleep in a coffin?" Grandma said, "This is my coffin. I am old. I will be in the coffin soon."

Yu sat up in bed and saw the carpenter named Wang still working in the living room. The carpenter's back was to them, and no one could see the expression on his face. Yu's mother said, "How could Wang scare the boy like this? I don't know what to say."

"Don't make me sleep in the coffin." Yu clung to his mother, saying, "I'm scared. Promise not to make me sleep in that coffin."

"Look how you scared the boy," Yu's mother said, weeping. "Yu, don't be scared. Didn't you hear Grandma say that this is her coffin? Your daddy respects Grandma, and he invited uncle Wang here especially to make this coffin."

"But I feel like I'm dying. My head is going to explode," said Yu, clutching his head in pain.

Yu no longer slept alone. He went to sleep with Grandma. Grandma's old, bitter, sour smell accompanied Yu as he fell asleep. Her annoying cough lasted from midnight through early morning. Yu often awakened suddenly and saw Grandma's mouth opened slightly, like a dark cave. Her opaque eyes flashed bright and dark in the moonlight. Outside in the living room, the carpenter named Wang snored loudly. Yu wanted to stuff a rag in his mouth. He grumbled, "Why can't they sleep quietly for a while? It's going to be light soon. When it's light, we'll have to get up."

This very autumn night was strange. Late at night Yu saw Grandma standing by the door, clinging to the wall. Her weak old body was rocking back and forth. Yu jumped off the bed to hold her up. He said, "What do you want to do, Grandma?" Grandma replied, "I'm going to the bathroom, leave me alone." Yu drowsily went back to bed and heard Grandma curse between her teeth in the darkness. "Bitch, shameless bitch." Yu didn't know who Grandma was cursing. He wondered to himself, who was the bitch? Whoever doesn't sleep well is a bitch.

The unfinished wood of the coffin took shape very quickly. Half of it rested on the door, the other half was propped up against the wall. Grandma often came out to check on the carpenter. She used her cane to knock on the side of the coffin and said, "Too thin. But since I didn't earn good luck in my previous life, it'll have to do." The carpenter never responded. He just gave senile old Grandma a sarcastic look. His eyes had an undisguisable cold cruelty. These eyes made Yu deeply afraid and sad.

Yu's subsequent shocking deed was aimed at the carpenter named Wang.

By chance, Yu found half a bottle of pesticide in the storehouse. The red characters and the skull and crossbones on the label meant death. Yu recalled that that very year someone in the village had swallowed that kind of pesticide and died. The thought flashed through Yu's mind, then he poured the poison into a cup, which he put on the table. He knew that the carpenter named Wang had gotten used to drinking water from the table. It was noon. The carpenter was sweating as he connected the joints of two coffin boards. Yu peered through the window. He saw the carpenter wiping the sweat from his brow, then stretching to grasp the cup from the table. Yu's heart started beating wildly. He crouched suddenly, covering his eyes.

The carpenter named Wang screamed wildly in the living room. The cup flew out the door, falling to the ground. Yu ran immediately. He didn't dare look back until he reached the playground of the village school. The playground was empty. Only a few haystacks rustled in the wind. Yu found a hole in one of the haystacks, so he climbed inside, then blocked the hole with a few bundles of hay. Everything became infinitely dark. He could faintly make out the sound of children reading aloud inside the school. Those were the kids who didn't suffer from disease or catastrophes. This morning they were reading. None of them knew what Yu had done.

Yu heard the school bell, and the children stormed out of the classroom, crossing through the playground past the haystack where Yu was hiding. One of the kids pushed the hole open. Surprised, he exclaimed, "What are you doing hiding in there? Are you taking a shit?" Covering his face with his hands, Yu wept, saying, "I have a headache, a big headache."

In the evening Yu crept out of the haystack. His face pale, he walked back home unsteadily. In the distance he could see smoke rising from the chimney. Mother was in the garden picking vegetables. It seemed as if nothing had happened. When he reached the front door, Mother asked, "Yu, where have you been all day?" Yu stood there, extending his finger to pick the paint off the door frame. Mother continued, "You look so scared. Has someone been mean to you?" Yu shook his head and said, "I have a headache, a big headache."

Yu shivered as he stepped through the door. The carpenter was alone at the table drinking wine. The carpenter's eyes, sharp as knives, pierced Yu's heart. Yu bowed his head and kicked the wood shavings on the floor. He heard the carpenter's chuckle. The carpenter said, "You're back? Your mom has been looking for you all day." Yu said, "Why was she looking for me?" The carpenter responded, "No reason. My work is done. I'm leaving tomorrow." Yu raised his head and saw the coffin standing on end against the wall. He had never seen a coffin so close up. The surface of the newly made coffin was smooth and clean, and the room was filled with the fragrance of wood.

"Is this a good coffin?" asked the carpenter.

"I don't know," said Yu. "Anyway, I don't want to sleep in a coffin, no matter how good it is."

"You are a clever boy." The carpenter walked over and laid a hand on Yu's shoulder. The other hand pinched Yu's cheek as he said, "This is the best coffin I've ever made. Sooner or later someone in your family will sleep in this excellent coffin."

The next morning the carpenter named Wang left the village. He never said anything about the pesticide. This surprised Yu. A deep confusion would shroud Yu's life from then on. Yu could not ignore the tracks and shadows that the carpenter named Wang had left in his home.

Autumn and the falling leaves were swept away together by the wind.

The gigantic coffin rested on one side of the living room. One corner of the coffin was illuminated by the sunlight coming through the window, while the other half was covered by irregular shadows. That was during the day; when night came, Yu never dared to look straight at the coffin. He was afraid it would open its cover unexpectedly and trap him inside. Late at night Yu could still hear something creaking in the house. He suspected the noise came from inside the coffin, a most secret, dark place.

Mother had said that Grandma's illness was getting worse daily and that she probably wouldn't survive the fall. Grandma herself had said this, too. But fall had passed, and Grandma was still alive. Wearing a cotton overcoat with a hand warmer on her lap, she sat on her bed, coughing continuously. Grandma's temper had also become strange and unpredictable. She often sat on the bed cursing Yu's mother loudly. Yu didn't know why. He often saw tears welling up in his mother's eyes. Yu also didn't know whether or not Grandma would die. He didn't want her to die, but once Grandma died she would sleep in that coffin, and the coffin would be moved out of the living room and buried in the cemetery on the river. That's what Yu hoped.

Yu no longer dared to sleep with Grandma at night, and he began to spend nights in his mother's room. This made Yu sleep deeply, with sweet dreams. Once Yu saw Mother put a balm on her belly. She used a lot. Yu asked, "Why are you putting on so much?" Mother replied, "I have a stomach ache; the balm soothes the pain." This is the detail Yu recalled long after that eventually helped him comprehend the cause of his mother's death.

One bitterly cold, windy morning Yu found his mother on her back on the storehouse floor. Beside her was the bottle of pesticide that Yu had used before. Yu smelled something that made him choke—an almost suffocating combination of pesticide and balm. He struggled to pull his mother's hand, which felt very cold and stiff.

Yu's mother's body was in the house for three days. The villagers who came for the wake whispered among themselves. They asked Yu baffling questions, many about the carpenter named Wang. Yu just wept as he said, "I don't know, I don't know. I thought Grandma was dying. I didn't know Mother would die." The villagers said, "The boy's still too young to understand. If his grandmother doesn't explain it to him, who will?"

Yu's father didn't come home for the funeral. Everyone knew he was also a traveling carpenter, and no one knew where he was.

On the fourth day, Yu's mother was placed in the coffin. The coffin was its natural color, still unpainted, for all this was unexpected. Death is never predictable. Yu walked toward the riverside behind the four pallbearers. That was early in the morning, when the frost fell. Snow white frost fell silently on the coffin and on the heads of those in the funeral procession. The fields and trees also became covered in frost. The landscape of the village looked as usual—tranquil, solemn, suitable for any kind of funeral.

On a road a few steps away from the cemetery Yu halted suddenly. He gazed down the road, where a carpenter with a tool bag over his shoulder appeared. The funeral procession also stopped and looked in that direction. Someone said, "Could it be Yu's father?" They soon realized that it was not Yu's father. Traveling carpenters often came down this road. The one who appeared that morning was just another carpenter.

I'm scared.

At that moment Yu let out a shrill cry. The white funeral band around his head, he pushed through the funeral procession and ran wildly down the road. In the distance he looked like a wild white-maned horse.

OUR

CHILDHOOD

Yang Zhao

(Translated by Michelle Yeh)

1

*W*hat was our childhood like?

It was days filled with sunshine. On the nearby school playground, the boys played cowboys and Indians. Their hullabaloo sounded subdued despite the clamor. It was as if it came from the earth, making you want to lie down and lower your ear to the same level as the sound.

It must have been afternoon. Grown-ups were napping in their cement houses. Only the hyperactive boys were out playing. I don't know what the girls were doing. Our childhood never quite explained how girls spent their afternoons after school.

Our childhood stood on a hillock that emerged gradually at the edge of the campus and rose abruptly beyond the dirt road for about a hundred feet to form a dull angle. The hillock belonged to the soldiers. Every few days the soldiers from the nearby barracks came here to drill. They rushed to the top of the hill with rifles in their hands, making strange sounds.

Through the classroom window I could see their clumsy movements. Most of them stumbled halfway through. Those who failed to run to the top had to roll downhill with their rifles—which reminded me of rubber balls—and start all over again.

When the drill was over and they were returning to the barracks, the soldiers passed through our village. Our childhood loved to watch the young men go by. She would wait in front of Granny's grocery store and as they marched by, exhausted and singing a military song out of tune, shout, "Soldiers eat big steamed buns, can't get it up when they see girls." After they were gone, Granny would run out of the store to beat our childhood, mumbling as she chased, "Why don't you drop dead, for a young girl to say such vulgar things?"

On afternoons when the soldiers did not show up, there was no one in sight on the hillock. Our childhood sat on the top and pulled up blade after blade of wild grass.

Patiently she waited.

2

When Meihua and Meijuan get together, they seldom talk about stocks, though they meet every morning to take the bus to the stock market and later have lunch and spend most of the afternoon with each other.

They are just not used to talking about stocks. It's hard to say exactly why. Maybe it's because they are still novices; and their rapidly growing wealth takes them so little effort to gain, and somehow they feel undeserving and awkward. Or maybe it's because the stock index is escalating unbelievably, from five thousand to eight thousand points. No matter how lousy a stock may be, they still end up making money; there is no reason to be preoccupied with the market, and they hardly ever get excited over it. Or it may be because they have seen too much of the naked greed those middle-aged wives seasoned in the stock market hide under the robe of social graces, and they simply wish not to become like them.

3

Our childhood waited on the hillock. She jumped up at the slightest sign and stared at the train crawling slowly into view. It is hard to say which came first, image or sound. Presumably, she heard the sound first, then she stood up and saw the dark shadow of the train gradually emerging in the misty air. But once seen, the train seemed to be transposed to the realm of sight, as distance made sound elusive. It took another moment before, all of a sudden, the fast, rumbling rhythm grabbed the bottoms of her feet and her ears, as if erupting from the earth.

Our childhood knew no heavy-metal rock 'n roll. There were only two kinds of metallic percussion in her life. One was the annoying intermittent target shooting coming from the barracks, which made her want to hide. The other was the beat of the train wheels rolling on the railway, which made her want to dance.

As it came closer and closer, the rhythm took over her heartbeats, which became so heavy that she began to pant. On the hilltop our childhood swayed wildly, with the waves of the rhythm. As the volume increased, her arms and legs swung faster and faster, her whole body immersed in the excitement of dancing.

Then it all ended inexplicably. Maybe her heart could not keep up with the speed of the train anymore, or maybe the muscles of her body became so sore that her nerves finally snapped. Or it could be that the metallic percussion just vanished with the wind. It's hard to say which happened first; all I know is that at a certain point our childhood collapsed in total exhaustion, lying in the clumps of wild grass listening to her irregular breathing and pounding heart.

It took her a while to gather enough strength to sit up and examine the bloody cuts inflicted by the mugwort here and there on her legs.

Then she waited. She kept waiting patiently.

4

Meihua and Meijuan started talking about their families only when they became close friends. Even though people have little else to talk about, we tend to avoid difficult topics at the start our friendship. Because the two women had been neighbors in the same apartment building for three or four years and had seen or heard about each other's family problems, the subject was hard to handle. Only when people feel certain that telling the truth will not cause any displeasure do we gradually shift from trivialities about others to our own stories.

Meijuan tells Meihua that she doesn't like her own name at all. She feels bitter every time she thinks of the word *mei*—beauty—in her name.

Meijuan has been out of work since she graduated from a business vocational school six years ago. Right after graduation she looked for a job and applied to several companies. Almost without exception, she passed the written test but was turned down at the interview.

She realizes that she is not good-looking. But when she was a child, she believed that looks were not that important. Grown-ups told her that as long as one tried, one could become somebody or, at the very least, have a nice, happy home.

In elementary school she knew that none of her teachers liked her, but she always thought it was because she did not study hard enough and her grades were not good enough. Besides, girls who were teachers' pets often got fondled on their behinds, which seemed to her nothing to be envious about.

After junior high, when she entered vocational school, she discovered her own strong points. The teachers still did not like her, but they called on her whenever they needed help. She was attentive to details and skilled with her hands. Every teacher who had given her assignments said so.

Before, she had been in the lower half in her class, but after she entered vocational school, her grades shot up dramatically. She read some statistics showing a seventy-eight percent employment rate for graduates from her school, and she was in the top ten percent. She felt confident.

How could she have known that they would not even give her a chance to prove her ability? A horrible fate.

5

Our childhood waited at the hilltop until evening came, until the boys were done playing and about to leave the campus.

She rushed down the hill and stood up straight at the street corner outside the campus walls, waiting for them. With the wind blowing on her face, she envisaged herself to be the swordsman hero in the only kung fu movie she had ever seen. Though she did not have a sword at her waist, fitted skirt of her uniform flapped properly in the wind.

Without saying a word, the boys who saw her and were willing to race her lined up with her on the street corner. The others, interested in seeing the result, yelled, "Get ready—get set—go!"

They ran along the pebbled road, which got narrower and narrower as it led to the village. The first fifty yards was the key to victory, after which the road abruptly turned into a ridge barely one foot wide. It was hard to overtake someone on the ridge, and it was less than ten yards from there to the finish line.

Our childhood had great explosive power. They had raced here many times, and she was seldom behind when they stepped onto the ridge. But she had her share of losses, too. Usually they happened because she slipped on the ridge or was pushed off into the rice paddies by someone overtaking her.

She had a tough time whenever she went home with mud all over her. Her mother would peel off her clothes and yell at her as she washed them, and her father would whip her naked buttocks with a broom handle.

She always had scars on her body, scabs on her legs, or bruises on her buttocks, but she did not seem to mind.

For our childhood, dancing and running were the true center of life.

6

Meijuan resents the men who interviewed her. They never criticized her looks, but they put on a righteous facade. "Our company hires people based on their ability alone," they said. They picked on her ability because they could not comment on her looks. They always came up with one or two little excuses—her handwriting was not elegant enough, her English was not good enough, her accounting was poor, she did not have filing experience, etc.

After she saw her schoolmates who had been poorer students land jobs one by one, she refused to look at want ads. Later, she felt nauseous whenever she saw the tiny print in the employment section of the newspapers. Eventually, she stopped reading newspapers altogether.

She could not take any criticism from anyone. When her father suggested that she take computer classes to get an edge in the job market, she cried all night in her room. She felt that her father did not like the way she looked, either; the computer was just an excuse. How come her better-looking sister did not have to study computers? The more she thought about it, the angrier she became. Before dawn the next morning, she locked her bedroom door and cussed and yelled to her heart's content.

At the dinner table her mother remarked that her cooking was too salty. She catapulted from her chair and screamed, "If you don't like the cook, just say so. Don't beat around the bush about my cooking!" Then she threw her chopsticks at the wall and ran into her room.

Out of work for a long time, she realized that she had little chance of having a family of her own. All doors were closed to her. Her temper could not be worse; eccentric and lonely, she often created havoc at home.

A while back her mother had been thinking of setting her up with someone. Then about two months ago, her sister, who had been married for only a year or so, discovered that her husband was having an affair. Naturally it caused a furor in her family. At first her sister insisted on getting a divorce, but her mother-in-law came pleading. She pulled Meijuan's mother into the kitchen and pulled out a picture of the other woman, sighing, "She is so pretty, and aggressive, too. How many men could have resisted a woman like that?" Meijuan's mother brooded on it and had a good cry. It made a lot of sense to her that her daughter compared unfavorably with that other woman. In the final analysis, there was no one to blame except the parents, who did not endow their daughter with a more attractive face. By the time the whole thing blew over, Meijuan's mother had lost the heart to play matchmaker. If even her pretty daughter could have marriage problems, how much worse it would be for the ugly one?

Meijuan is like an undernourished chick too weak to peck open its shell; no matter how hard it tries, it can never touch the world outside.

7

Except for dancing and racing, our childhood's life was pretty boring.

She did not play with the girls, who got all excited over nothing. When she showed her panties while flipping on the balance bar, they tattled to the teachers. She would have loved to play cowboys and Indians with the boys, but they wouldn't let her. Neither would the teachers.

So she spent most of her time by herself. Still, the boys called her names behind her back. Some said that because she was pretty, she enjoyed hanging around with the boys and seducing them. Others said that she only played boys' games because she was ugly and looked like a boy. Ironically, she was both the prettiest and the ugliest girl in her class.

Later on, even racing ceased to be part of our childhood's life. One day when she was running, she fell about halfway through the race. By the time she got up, her opponent was already on the ridge. She ran as fast as she could, completely ignoring the pain of her scratched knees. The boy ahead of her was the proudest boy in her class. Head of the class, he looked down on, yet was secretly admired by, the girls. She could stand losing to anyone but him.

Since he was not really a fast runner, especially on the ridge, she had no problem catching up to him. She figured that as soon as they got off the ridge, she could overtake him.

Panicking at the sound of footsteps close on his heels, the boy lost his balance and fell into the newly sprouted rice to the left. Not expecting this turn of events, she could not react in time to dodge his flying feet, and she fell into the muddy field next to him. Neither one winning or losing, they looked like two mud balls.

She did not escape a sound whipping when she got home. In the middle of it, the boy's mother came to her house with him, blaming her for pushing her son into the mud. Without waiting to find out the truth, her father yanked her out of the house while she was still undressed and gave her another beating in front of the guests. The whole time, he cursed, "He's a boy. It's okay for him to be on the wild side. You're a girl. What are you competing with him for? Don't you know where you belong?"

After class the next day, the boys in her class grouped in twos and threes and whispered and giggled about her tits and thighs. She never raced with a boy again, never.

8

It's Meihua's turn to tell the story of her family.

In this big city, who knows how many women each year discover that their husbands are having an affair? There are too many novels and TV soap operas about extramarital affairs already—everyone jokes about their lack of imagination. Women who are going through the crisis themselves feel so typical that they are at a loss as to how to deal with it.

Meihua is one of those women. After three and a half years of marriage, she found irrefutable evidence that her husband was having an affair. Yet, contrary to the situation of Meijuan's sister, the other woman turned out to be unbelievably unattractive.

Meihua doesn't know how to handle it. She swings from mood to mood. Sometimes she gets so upset that she starts an all-out fight. Sometimes she feels that acting this way is silly and is reminded of those unlikable characters in soap operas, so she calms down. Sometimes she cannot swallow the fact that her life is ruined, and she grits her teeth in hate. Sometimes she tells herself that she is making a mountain out of a molehill; many women have been in the same situation, it's a common occurrence, so what is there to be angry about?

Her mood swings have a lot to do with her husband's attitude. He seems humiliated by the way he has desecrated their marriage. At the beginning, whenever her face changed colors, he immediately repented and apologized. He swore the affair was over, and her temper tantrum was usually short-lived. Yet, later, when she saw her husband acting as if nothing had happened and falling back into his old habits—such as sitting on the couch concentrating on the newspaper and laughing for no reason at all—she couldn't stand it. Is that it? He has made a big mistake, but he can go back to reading newspapers just like that? What an injustice!

Her moods have gone through many cycles like this. Her husband has tried his best to placate her. He has apologized, sworn, guaranteed, even gotten down on his knees and broken into tears. Afterward, she feels better. She begins to believe that this is all part of the necessary therapeutic process, at the end of which her marriage will be back to normal.

9

Life was hard to bear without racing. Of course, she could run by herself, but without opponents running was a drag. The moment she stopped, the bleakness of the world overwhelmed her, making her feel ten times worse than when she had lost. Our childhood was beginning to understand how important competition is.

On those aimless afternoons, she could only drift about. She did not have anything to wait for. Our childhood roamed from the bamboo shades on this side to those on that side, at a loss as to what to think.

One afternoon she dozed off under a beefwood and did not wait for the train on the hillock. It was the train that came looking for her.

It was like hearing herself breathing in a dream. For a long time it was calm and regular. Then she could suddenly hear her breathing turning into snoring, which kept getting louder and louder. She worried in her dream about how shameful it was for a girl to snore like this. Anxious and embarrassed, she felt the blood rushing to her face and woke up flustered.

On awakening she jumped up, realizing the noise wasn't her snoring but the rhythm of the train. She galloped toward the source of the sound. The railway stretched past the pigpens and the fish pond. She ran as hard as she could toward the train. The rumbling sound transformed the surroundings into a volcano about to erupt, a volcano crater at the apex of the world.

The moment she saw the engine, she turned around and posed as if she were racing with the train. She chased the train with all her strength, gradually sensing that her steps were synchronized with its wheels. The sound of the train enveloped her like a warm skin, wrapping her tightly. There was not a sound from the outside world, only a peacefulness that made her forget her ears. It was a brief moment of security, and, while she was still lost in it, the last coal black freight car overtook her. With the fading of the metallic jangling, the outside world came tiptoeing back.

Our childhood glared at the world as she lay next to the tracks.

10

Meihua does not know if it is she who stubbornly prolongs the therapeutic process or if it is her husband who lacks patience.

Suddenly one day, her husband refused to placate her. The truth was, by then her anger had subsided and her husband had pretty much explained everything. There was only one question left to which she had not found a satisfactory answer: Why did he fall for a woman far less attractive than she?

She asked that question over and over again and the man finally exploded. She had no idea that a man could be so loud—more frightening than thunder—and change so quickly. One minute he was kneeling by the bed, begging her for forgiveness, and the next minute he was pointing his finger at her and shouting and screaming. She was stupefied, oblivious to what he was saying. He probably didn't know either. She was too scared to utter a word; she was only praying that the tornado would blow over soon.

It did eventually. Her husband curled up in a corner, exhausted and glum. After a while she began to feel that his behavior was uncalled for. How dare the culprit yell and scream like that? So she picked another fight.

In this way, she started a new cycle. She yells until her husband explodes. Then he starts shouting and she quiets down. Then he stops. Unable to swallow it, she starts yelling again. . . .

Her voice is too feeble, though, and she is too timid. Every time they fight, the moment he raises his voice, she can do nothing except listen quietly. He finds all kinds of excuses to justify his behavior and shouts them out. There is no way for her to yell back. After many repetitions, he comes to believe his excuses. Then she is shaken, too. Those excuses gradually become the authoritative explanation for his affair.

The gist of the explanation is her good looks. The mistake all began with her beauty. Because she is pretty, she was wooed by many men before their marriage. She was pampered and became vain, so vain that she would not bother to acquire the common virtues and skills of an average wife. Because she is pretty, she attracts men easily. Before their marriage, he was completely spellbound by her beauty. He exhausted all his resources to defeat his rivals in love, so he never had a chance to really know her, to know her sloppiness and incompetence in housework. Any girl who was less pretty would make an effort to improve her temper and learn to do house chores. Because she is pretty, when they make love, she does not feel the need to take the initiative or pay some attention—she believes too much in the power of her attractiveness. Because she is pretty, in many ways she is irresponsible. Even now he hesitates to raise a family. What kind of marriage is it if after three and a half years they still don't want to have a child? She is pretty, so how could he *not* have an affair?

She has shed many tears over his explanation. She begins to dislike her name. How sarcastic is the middle word *mei?*

11

Our childhood had found the pleasure of running again in racing against the train.

Of course, she could not beat the train—that is, if they ran in the same direction. After a few hopeless tries, she invented a new game. When the train passed the border of the village, it crossed an intersection. There was no barricade or signal light, only a triangular sign. That was the finish line of the race.

The starting line was in front of the earth-god shrine. In the afternoon, she sat on the long bench under the banyan tree in front of the shrine and waited for the train to give the signal to start. When the train passed the beefwoods by the rice paddies owned by A Ping's family, she stood up and got ready for running. When the engine lined up with the steel tower of the power company, she shot toward the intersection like an arrow.

Her goal was to cross the intersection before the train did or to reach it at the same time as the train. At first she heard the wind howling in her ears. Gradually the metallic rhythm of the railway joined in, weaving a louder and louder percussive melody. In the final rush, there was no wind, no footsteps; she felt as if she were gliding on the railway. She crossed the intersection and stopped. The train overtook her in a wink, and she turned around to see it off. Then she could walk back to the outside world fearlessly, savoring the taste of triumph.

12

There is no more story to tell. Sitting by the window in a fast-food restaurant—its glass shining yet allowing not a ray of sunshine to come in—Meihua and Meijuan don't know if they should pity each other or cry for themselves.

Pity and crying are useless, though. Besides, the first time the story is told there is some excitement. After the second time there is nothing but sheer sadness, sadness so deep that it seems absurd.

On an afternoon when there is nothing to talk about, Meijuan suddenly brings up her childhood and her races with the boys. Meihua utters in surprise, for she had similar experiences.

Having discovered a new topic, they start talking about their childhoods enthusiastically, each trying to tell her story first. We can only catch the beginnings—"My childhood . . ."—and we cannot tell to whose story it belongs.

There is only "our" childhood.

13

Again and again our childhood enjoyed the pleasure of defeating the train. Again and again she challenged it eagerly. She knew her relationship with the train was changing gradually. It was no longer her dance partner and the jukebox that played the dance tune. It was not the skin enveloping and isolating her, either. Now the train was a tough competitor, an opponent she must beat over and over again to build enough confidence and courage to face the world.

She did not know when she started sensing the sneer that puffed out of the train's nose each time she beat it. She finally realized what it was sneering at. In a dream the train told her that since she had made up the rules of the game, there was nothing to be proud of when she won. She had no right to make up the rules of the game in the first place.

When she woke up, her teeth were sore from grinding. She began to push back the starting line of the race or to start running when the train was closer. She wanted to prove that without the advantage of making up the rules, she still could win.

14

Meijuan and Meihua quibble over what happened to their childhood. Still confused as to which is Meijuan's voice and which is Meihua's, we only know that one sighs, "She was run over," while the other says, "No, that can't be."

One says, "Our childhood could never beat the train. She kept shortening the distance between the intersection and the train until one day she couldn't dodge the charging engine and was knocked down and killed. Her mother came to the railroad and chided her even as she wailed, 'What are you, a girl, competing for? A girl . . .' "

The other says, "If our childhood was killed by the train, then how could we be sitting here talking about it?"

"So what? What can pretty or not-so-pretty women do in this society anyway?"

"That's not how it happened. Our childhood was not knocked down by the train. Why did it have to be killed by the train? Our childhood kept running and running. The train came whistling. When it was about to reach the intersection, our childhood took off and flew into the sky. She flew over the train, the village, and just kept flying . . ."

"Where did she fly to?"

"To paradise, where nobody paid attention to looks, nobody cared how she looked. She flew to paradise."

"I got it. She flew to the stock market, where nobody pays attention to looks, nobody cares how you look."

15

When we see Meijuan and Meihua again, they are in the middle of a heated discussion about stocks, all kinds of stocks. There is a special glow in their eyes.

THE AMATEUR

CAMERAMAN

S. K. Chang

(Translated by Jeffrey C. Bent)

1

*W*u Ziqiao had secretly been thinking about killing his wife for at least four or five years. The first time he had gotten the idea, she had just been promoted to a managerial position within the company and was entertaining guests at their home. There was no place for Wu Ziqiao to hide—he had had no alternative but to get dressed up and mingle with all the Americans who would be coming. He thought he'd been the perfect host; who would have thought that as soon as the guests had left, his wife would start berating him from the bathroom?

"Wu Ziqiao, what's wrong with you tonight? You were a lousy host. What did you think you were doing, anyway?"

"What do you mean, I was a lousy host?"

Wu Ziqiao looked on as his tall, heavyset wife took off her clothing item by item, and, like a big white walrus, delicately slid into the bathtub. He just stared at her stupidly, and only after a while did he open his mouth to say, "The whole time I was in the living room chatting with your boss, I didn't try to sneak off, even for a second."

"Sure, but you completely forgot who you were talking to. Why were you talking to Bill about photography? I thought you were going to bore him to death. Plus, you backed him into a corner, where he couldn't escape. The reason they're called cocktail parties is because everybody needs to be moving around nonstop like a cock's tail; it's the only way they can get the full social benefit of mingling with everybody at the party. After you trapped him in the corner, I wouldn't be surprised if he thinks you're a homo trying to hit on him."

She didn't pull any punches, Wu Ziqiao thought to himself. He looked at his wife through the clouds of steam, as if from afar. The pure white pile of flesh in the bathtub looked like a snow-covered mountain. What kind of a person would lie in her bathtub and call her own husband a homo? Only his wife. Looking at that great Mount Fuji, Wu Ziqiao suddenly had an idea. This idea was so bizarre that it shocked him. He promptly turned and left the bath-room, a plume of steam and his wife's voice following him as he left. "Wu Ziqiao, where do you think you're going?"

"I'm going to take out the garbage."

"Don't forget to put a big rock on the garbage-can lid, or a raccoon is going to come along in the middle of the night, pry it open, and make a rotten mess."

In the middle of the night, the raccoon came as predicted and was banging around outside the kitchen. Wu Ziqiao's wife forcefully shook him awake.

"Wu Ziqiao, go out and scare away the raccoon."

"Scare what away? The lid's on tight and the raccoon won't be able to get in. Even if I go out to scare it off, it'll just come back."

"What, and let it start riot out there? Out! Go scare it away."

There was nothing he could do. Wu Ziqiao went barefoot into the kitchen and turned on the outside light. There were two glossy black-furred creatures, one large and one small, standing motionless for the moment in the light, fixing Wu Ziqiao with their bright eyes. After a while, the two raccoons started to jostle the trash cans again. Wu Ziqiao knew that the raccoons really weren't afraid of him and thought, "It'd be easy with a gun. Fire it once, and even if they weren't dead they'd be scared off."

Thinking of the gun, his idea from earlier in the evening mysteriously came back to him, as if it were put back in his head by some supernatural being. Wu Ziqiao scared himself with his own thoughts and just stood by the kitchen window, at an impasse with the raccoons outside. The two raccoons were unable to pry open the garbage can and, fortunately for him, decided to leave. Just as it was about to go, the bigger raccoon looked back at the house; Wu Ziqiao could have sworn that the damned beast gave him a contemptuous wink before it left.

2

Wu Ziqiao wasn't really planning to kill his wife, but he definitely liked thinking about it. He wasn't the kind of person who liked to argue with his wife; if he were really pressed, he would simply state, "A gentleman doesn't fight with a lady." But this wasn't a point he could afford to bring up often; if he did, Helen would argue all the more.

"What do you mean, a gentleman doesn't fight with women? You're living in American society now. You can't not fight. If you don't fight, how will you be able to persuade anyone of anything? If you don't fight, how will people know what your strong points are? If your opponent's a man, you have to fight with a man. If your opponent's a woman, you have to fight with a woman. 'Gentlemen don't fight with women' is only an excuse, that's all; besides, have you ever even fought with another man? If you don't fight, you'll be an accountant for your whole life—is that really all you want?"

What Wu Ziqiao said was that he didn't care. Of course, in his heart he did, but he couldn't change one of his lifelong philosophies. He'd been fairly unmotivated for as long as he could remember; probably the only time that he had ever been really stirred up had been when he courted Helen. But it had been so long ago. At that time, Helen Hu was a college basketball star. Wu Ziqiao's hobby was photography, and he followed the team around everywhere they went, taking pictures of the girls and doing odd jobs for them. Originally, he didn't much care which one of them he ended up going out with, but since Helen was the captain, he did a little more for her than for the

1. In the original, Helen used the English word *chance* in this sentence.

others. Gradually, everyone began to think of them as a couple. Even now, when she got angry, Helen would bring up those days.

"That was when you trapped me, when you spoiled all my other chances. All I could do was marry you. I guess it's just my luck. What happened to all the vitality and persistence you had in those days? Why don't you wake up and try to act like you did back then?"

Helen hardly needed to bring it up; even Wu Ziqiao found it kind of strange. The only explanation he could think of was that Helen had completely exhausted all that energy. The same Helen who with her powerful build shook the basketball court and slam-dunked her way to fame now applied that same spirit and stamina to her work. No wonder all the Americans were amazed by her. Helen had advanced to assistant manager; Wu Ziqiao was still a mere accountant. Except for a slight increase in salary, his position was exactly the same as when he had entered the company ten years ago. His wife's salary was already twice as much as his. The thing that really annoyed him was that it was through his introduction that she had gotten the job in the first place. He'd just meant to get her a small job to while away the time; who would have thought that in just six years she would become an assistant manager? She didn't even have a master's degree!

Wu Ziqiao definitely wasn't planning to kill his wife, but starting from that night when the damned raccoon had given him that look, it was as if he were possessed. Thinking back on it, he realized that the moonlight had definitely been a bit odd that evening. Americans said that there was always something eerie about the full moon. The raccoon's intentions in coming to his house hadn't been good; for all he knew, it might have been a devil in disguise. Wu Ziqiao's downfall started on that night of the full moon.

3

On another night with a full moon Wu Ziqiao resolved to start writing a diary.

When he was young, Wu Ziqiao hadn't snored. Or maybe he had but hadn't been aware of it. Snoring is really quite a strange physiological phenomenon; usually, the thinner one is, the louder one snores, as if the volume of the snore were in inverse ratio to one's body size. Wu Ziqiao was getting thinner and thinner as his snoring was getting louder and louder. Chinese people who live in America for an extended period of time, eating an American diet, usually find that they put on weight and begin to look more like their American counterparts. Not Wu Ziqiao. Helen, though, had gained at least forty pounds. She had been large to start with, so she gained weight especially quickly. She was fortunate in that she had put it on in the right places, so she was voluptuous rather than fat. She resembled a beauty of the early Tang dynasty—large, fair, and plump, with the grace and carriage of nobility. In comparison, Wu Ziqiao seemed like a shrunken Stan Laurel or like one of the commoners from the ink paintings of Feng Zikai.[2] Even an accomplished flatterer would be hard-pressed to come up with an appropriate way to say that they looked good together.

Of course, after they had been married, there had been a certain honeymoon period. Even now, Helen really wasn't all that bad to Wu Ziqiao. The fact that she, a former basketball center, yelled at Wu Ziqiao about this or that wasn't really anything unusual. And even though she asked a lot of him, Helen did most of the household chores herself. Strictly speaking, Helen couldn't really be considered a shrew. There was, however, one thing that she truly couldn't stand, and that was Wu Ziqiao's snoring. At first, when he snored too loudly, Helen would shake him awake. Later, she found that when Wu Ziqiao slept in a sitting position, he didn't snore. Although her undergraduate degree had been in international trade, her thinking was still more scientific than Wu Ziqiao's. She demanded that he sleep sitting up to avoid disturbing her sleep, and with science behind her, Wu Ziqiao had no way to say no.

Sleeping sitting up became natural for Wu Ziqiao; he often sat on the bed propped up with a pillow and passed the drawn-out night in a dreamy half-asleep, half-awake state. He didn't have a very high-pressure job, so he could usually pass the day in a half-asleep, half-awake state as well. Day and night gradually became indistinguishable to him, but he discovered an advantage to sleeping while sitting up— you could rest up and think about things at the same time. At first, his

2. An accomplished artist in the modern period. Born in 1898, he was a proponent of the new cultural movement and of things modern. Besides being a painter, he was also a music teacher, the author of more than 150 books, and a translator of both Japanese and Russian works into Chinese.

thoughts and dreams got muddled together, but later he had it per-
fected to the point where he could sleep for a few minutes, wake up,
think, sleep again, wake up, think again, and still maintain consisten-
cy in his thoughts. Helen didn't believe that he could really do this at
first, but slowly came to admire him for it.

Of course, if Helen had known what Wu Ziqiao was thinking
about, she probably wouldn't have admired him for it at all. Sometimes he thought about work; sometimes he thought about photography tricks; but most of the time he thought about ways to kill her.
At first, thinking about killing Helen had made him feel like he was
transgressing some moral code, but he gradually overcame his guilt
and handled it purely as a matter of photographic technique. His musings on how to kill her were like reflections on the layout of a photograph. He pictured Helen lying in the bathtub, that pure white pile of
flesh like a snow-covered mountain. Anthony Perkins rushes in and
with a virgin dagger stabs the snowy mountain; the snowy mountain
collapses and slides to the bottom of the tub. Ah, but when to release
the shutter button and take the picture? As the wicked knife pierces
her white, white flesh? Click-click. As the snow-covered mountain
collapses into the tub? Click-click. Or when the blood comes oozing
out? Click-click, click-click, click-click.

In his half-asleep, half-awake state, Wu Ziqiao came up with one
after another ingenious plan for killing his wife. He sat on his bed,
three pillows behind his back propping him up, with Helen beside
him in deep sleep, the sound of her breath rising and falling evenly.
Sometimes, the sound of her breathing would suddenly stop, and Wu
Ziqiao would get nervous and uncomfortable. Only when she murmured something in her sleep and moved around a little, and the
sound of her even breathing reappeared, would Wu Ziqiao be able to
relax again and continue pondering yet another way to kill her.

One night, when the moon was full, Wu Ziqiao's creativity soared,
and he thought up five different ways in a row to kill his wife. He
couldn't sit still on the bed and decided he might as well take his pillow
and go sleep in the living room—he knew Helen had an important
meeting early in the morning, and he didn't want to disturb her pleasant dreams. The living room was a bit cold. He lay down on the sofa
and looked through the window at the moon. The full, bright moon
reminded him of an old children's song, and he began to hum it softly.

Spring's flowers,
How fragrant they are!
Autumn's moon,
How bright it is!
I in my youth,
How happy I am!
Beautiful she,
What's happened to her?

He remembered Helen at the Armed Services Arena during the finals of the women's basketball championship. With twelve seconds left to go in the game, she made a jump shot from outside the key. He had released the shutter and had captured the instant of the ball just leaving her hand. It was a fantastic shot, click-click.

"If only I had been holding a shotgun, it would have been like hunting pheasant; an even better shot!"

The cool, majestic moon looked down upon him and suddenly appeared to make a bobbing motion, as if nodding approval of his marksmanship. Even though he was in a half-asleep, half-awake state, Wu Ziqiao still caught sight of its movement. From that time on, he resolved to start writing a diary and to carefully record all the methods he thought of for killing his wife, one by one.

4

"Wu Ziqiao! Wu Ziqiao!"

Wu Ziqiao heard the muffled sound of someone calling him and quickly took off his earphones. His wife, all dressed up, was standing in front of him.

"You idiot. You listen to music all day long. Aren't you bored with it by now?"

Wu Ziqiao chuckled and was about to put his earphones back on, but Helen knocked them out of his hands.

"Hell, Zhou Xuan would kill herself if she knew how much you were listening to her tape. Let's go."

"I'm not going."

"You're not going? It's the general manager's party and you're not going?"

"No."

His wife stood with her arms akimbo. She looked particularly elegant this evening, wearing a low-cut black evening dress with a double chain of pearls around her neck; it served all the more to bring out her fair skin and the fullness of her breasts. Wu Ziqiao mumbled and quietly applauded her beauty.

"What?"

"Nothing."

"You really aren't going to go?"

"No." Wu Ziqiao pointed to a stack of tales of knight-errantry[3] on the table beside him. "Practicing martial arts at home is a lot more interesting than yakking with all those whiteys."

"You loser. You never go to any social functions; how will you ever make it in American society?"

"I've never said I wanted to make it in American society. You did."

"You'll never get anywhere, you recluse." His wife walked downstairs and, as she went out the door, yelled back, "Don't forget to take the trash out, and cover the lid with a rock. You really have no future. Marrying you would be anybody's downfall."

Wu Ziqiao put his earphones back on and picked up the small green notebook hidden under the kung fu novels. Nature in her mercy nurtures man, and man is powerless to recompense, kill, kill, kill, kill, kill, kill, kill![4] The green notebook was densely packed with characters the size of a fly's head; when Helen was reprimanding him, he had thought of yet another ingenious plan for killing her. Helen's car must be on the highway by now; at the first big loop before the bridge, she steps on the brakes and suddenly discovers that they aren't reacting at all. She screams, and the car, speeding like an arrow, smashes through the guardrail of the bridge. Click–click, the BMW is suspended in midair; the photo is laid out so that the bridge is in the left corner, and in the lower right corner is a stand of small trees; the

3. Tales of knight-errantry, *Wu Xia Xiao Shuo* are a form of popular literature originating in the Han dynasty and continuing to this day. They involve a central figure who acts outside of the law to help those unable to help themselves, similar to the Lone Ranger, or Robin Hood without the band of Merry Men.

4. "Nature in her mercy nurtures man, and man is powerless to recompense, kill, kill, kill, kill, kill, kill, kill!" is a famous poem written by Zhang Xian-chong, c. 1605–47, a powerful and cruel robber baron who made himself king of Szechuan Province for two years during the close of the Qing dynasty. This poem was carved on a stone monument (near Chengdu?), called the Seven Kills Monument to commemorate his many massacres.

composition is perfect. Click-click, the front end of the car, falling vertically, enters the water, which sprays out in every direction. Click-click, click-click, click-click, click-click.

Wu Ziqiao had written yet another plan in his green notebook. In a seductive voice, Zhou Xuan sang a song about flowers to him alone.

"KILL!" Wu Ziqiao yelled. "Beautiful flowers are short-lived, kill, kill, kill, kill, kill!"

The Little Dragon Girl, the heroine of the novel he was reading,[5] turned to him and smiled. Wu Ziqiao laughed aloud, "Love is never having to say you're sorry, kill, kill, kill, kill, kill, kill, kill!"

He took the garbage outside by the kitchen, found a rock in the bushes, and put it on top of the lid. It looked as if there were a pair of green eyes secretly peering at him from inside the grass pile. Damned raccoons, just waiting for a chance to raise hell. If only he had a gun. He'd shoot them on the spot. They wouldn't give him much trouble then. He took a hoe out of the toolshed and in the last rays of the setting sun dug out the weeds growing next to the sidewalk.

As the round red sun sank weakly beyond the horizon, Wu Ziqiao's shadow stretched across the lawn. Helen should have made it to the party by now; he could picture her thrusting forward her ample bosom and charging right into the midst of everything. Someone asks her why T. C. didn't come, and she just laughs and shrugs her shoulders. No, that's not right, nobody would ask why T. C. didn't come. Who would care whether T. C. came or not? Wu Ziqiao looked out over his long long shadow extending across the lawn, and at his side, Zhou Xuan sang, "After tonight's parting, when will you come back to me?"

"After tonight's parting, kill, kill, kill, kill, kill!"

He swung his hoe toward the skinny shadow, and the blade hit something hard—dong!

"Kill!"

Helen is at the party. She lifts her glass and finishes the drink in one gulp; suddenly, her blossomlike face pales, and the wineglass falls to the floor, click-click. She falls into the embrace of her American boss, Bill. Click-click, click-click. Close-up: her hand clasping at her throat, her lips going into a spasm, her face turning from white to purple, click-click, click-click, click-click.

5. The Little Dragon Girl, Xiao Longnü, is the heroine of a tale of knight-errantry, *Shen Diao Xia Lü* by Jin Yong.

"When will you come back to me? Kill, kill, kill, kill, kill!" Helen's head drops to one side, and life leaves her. The fragrance disperses, the jade falls. Her soul returns to the Heaven of Painful Separation. Click-click.

5

"You've gone mad."

"No, I haven't."

"After writing something like this, you still say you haven't gone mad?"

"Give me back my notebook. You have no right to look through my private stuff."

"I would never have thought you were this kind of person. You hated me like this all along. I'm really hurt."

"Give me back my notebook."

"Closet sadist. You need to see a psychiatrist."

"Who needs to see a shrink? This is my creation, don't you get it? It's a novel. They're all fictitious stories."

"One hundred seven ways to kill your wife—that's a novel? Don't give yourself so much credit.[6] You don't have a single artistic cell in your body. All you can do is play with cameras, the simplest kind of toy, the most fitting for you."

Wu Ziqiao's gaze focused on his wife, and he thought to himself that it wasn't 107 ways anymore—now it was 108.[7]

"Still, for you, it's pretty amazing," his wife laughed bitterly. "In the thirteen years we've been married, this is the first time I've seen you really work hard at something. It's obvious there's still hope for you. It's also obvious how much you hate me. Who would have imagined."

"Give me back my notebook."

"Fine, I'll give it back to you." Helen threw the diary back into his arms. "What have I done to make you hate me so much? Everything I've done has been for us, and still you hate me like this. Forget it, I've just been blind. Just leave. Get out."

6. The expression used in the original, literally rendered, is, "Don't attach gold foil to your own face," a reference to a practice among Buddhists to show devotion by rubbing a sheet of gold foil onto the face of a statue of Buddha.

7. The number 108 has mystical significance; it is also the number of bandits who live on a hill in a tale of knight errantry, *The Water Margin*.

Wu Ziqiao was silent. Years before, his mother had said the same kind of thing to him. Silence is golden; when facing a cruel wife, you should stay composed.

"Go. Leave. Make it a clean break. I can't tell you how disappointed I am in you."

Wu Ziqiao stayed silent.

"Really. I thought marrying a man would be the biggest event in my life. Who would have thought I'd end up married to a heartless beast? I'm truly disappointed."

Silence. Helen is walking on the sidewalk. Suddenly, from out of the sky comes an unexpected disaster—a block of concrete falls off the scaffolding of a tall building, click-click.

"What have I done wrong? Tell me! Other husbands do whatever their wives tell them to do. This one not only doesn't love his wife but secretly plots to kill her and lies by saying he's only writing a novel."

His wife falls into a pool of blood, a big gash in her head, click-click, click-click.

"He can't fit into American society—all he does is listen to music and read knight-errantry tales, and he decides to kill his wife to vent his frustration. And you still have the nerve to just stand here? A divorce! I want a divorce! Get out of here! Go! The farther the better! Get out!"

His wife went into the bedroom and threw out Wu Ziqiao's pillow and blanket.

"Get out of here by tomorrow morning!"

She slammed the door shut but shortly opened it again and said, "Before you leave, take out the trash, and put a rock on the lid."

She slammed the door shut again. Wu Ziqiao waited for quite a while, until all was silent inside the room, then picked up his blanket and pillow.

Early the next morning, when the lawn was still covered with dew, and before the garbage truck came, he really did leave.

6

At the entrance to the toy store there was an oblong glass fish tank on display, with plastic, camouflage-colored frogmen swimming in it. Every time Wu Ziqiao passed the toy store, he saw the frogmen bumping their heads into the glass and paddling around without stopping. One time he couldn't help but fish one of them out of the water; the alert sales clerk quickly walked over.

"Why don't you buy one to take home for your kid?"

"What happened to this frogman—why isn't it moving anymore?"

The sales clerk, a fat, red-haired girl whose face was covered with pimples, snatched the dripping frogman out of his hand and put it back into the fish tank.

"The batteries died. All it needs are new ones."

The sales girl's intention wasn't to change the batteries, however, but instead to watch Wu Ziqiao, like a buzzard waiting for prey. How could she think she would make a sale with an attitude like that? He pretended he didn't care about it anymore, put his hands in his pockets, and walked away. After half an hour, he made it a point to walk by the entrance to the store again. The pimply-faced sales girl had already gone in, and the grass-green frogman was floating motionless in a rigid, bent position. An electric frog had been added to the tank, and it was swimming back and forth in a lively manner.

That evening, Wu Ziqiao called his sister. Bao Zhu wasn't home; her daughter Betty answered the phone.

"Mom took Bobby out. Uncle, why don't you come over for dinner this weekend? We all miss you a lot."

"I can't. The company is sending me to Los Angeles to audit an account. Tell your mom that I'll be over the Sunday after next. I've bought a pair of Calvin Klein jeans for you, and some toys for Bobby. I'm sure you'll like them."

"Thank you, uncle. Don't forget to bring the receipt, so I can return them if they don't fit." She then blurted, "Uncle, Debbie's mom is here to pick me up. I have to go now, bye-bye."

Wu Ziqiao hung up the phone, and dutifully started searching through everything for the receipt for the jeans. Last year Betty wasn't nearly as tall as Bao Zhu, but she had sprung up overnight and was now only half a head shorter than her mom. She'd become a young woman; she had Bao Zhu's people skills and even resembled her, too. Where had he put that receipt? Wu Ziqiao searched wildly through his room and finally started taking all of Bobby's toys out of the paper bag one by one. Wu Ziqiao took out the frogman hiding at the very bottom, and, as if in fear of punishment, its hands and feet suddenly started to shake. As might have been expected, the receipt was wedged under the final present.

He put the frogman in the sink. It made a few forced strokes until its head collided with the white porcelain, and then it stopped, floating motionless like a corpse.

"Damned clerk. It obviously wasn't a problem with the batteries," Wu Ziqiao swore as he looked at the grass-green plastic frogman floating bent over in the water. Tomorrow he'd go find that pimply-faced sales clerk and return it; as Betty said, as long as you keep your sales receipts, there are never any problems.

He put the toy and the jeans back into the paper bag and then put the bag away out of sight in his closet. Besides two chairs, a small round table, a TV set, and a single bed, his room was completely empty. The landlady said he could ask for more furniture anytime he wanted, but Wu Ziqiao didn't see the need. He hadn't brought in anything the entire two months he'd been here. He had spent most of his energy getting used to his new job. As soon as he got home, he just collapsed on his bed—he didn't even have the energy to watch TV. Fortunately, his sister lived on the east side as well and invited him over for a home-cooked meal on the weekends. Bao Zhu had been classmates with Helen; she'd known from the beginning that they wouldn't make a good couple. This time when Helen kicked him out, his sister didn't say anything and didn't try to patch things up for them. He was extremely thankful to her for this, and he spent most of his weekends at her home. Bao Zhu's husband, Zhou Zimin, was an engineer. He was kind and broad-minded, and he enjoyed recreational photography as well. Wu Ziqiao felt completely free to be himself at their home. Occasionally Bao Zhu would mention Helen, but Wu Ziqiao would either pretend that he hadn't heard or change the subject.

Actually, on infrequent occasions Wu Ziqiao would talked to Helen over the phone, usually about the house. Sometimes if Helen couldn't find something, she called him. On the phone, they treated each other with great mutual respect. Helen had never asked about his new job, and he had never asked how things were for her either. In all their years of marriage they had never been so tacitly considerate. Sometimes Wu Ziqiao had doubts about whether his moving out had really been a wise decision, but never for more than an instant. His departure had been a release for Helen. He could tell from her tone of voice that she didn't miss him or want him to come back. He knew she didn't think much of him, and he had moved out determined to make it on his own, earning back a little of her respect in the process. Go back with his tail between his legs and plead forgiveness? Why bother?

When Wu Ziqiao felt bored, he took out his diary and admired it. Since he'd moved out, though, he hadn't written another wife-killing entry. Unless he was in a particularly nasty mood, he didn't hate Helen anymore. Now that he had his freedom, what could he do? What did he want to do? This was something that couldn't be written in his diary.

7

Wu Ziqiao called Jin Lihe as soon as he got into Los Angeles. Jin Lihe wasn't home; it was Xiao Jiling who answered the phone. "Jin Lihe went to San Jose and won't be back until late," Xiao Jiling said. "Leave your number and I'll have him call you when he gets in tonight."

Wu Ziqiao left the hotel number. As expected, at half past ten Jin Lihe called and, without so much as a hello, bluntly asked him, "What are you doing in Los Angeles?"

"Auditing an account," Wu Ziqiao said. "Tomorrow's Saturday. Why don't we get our old classmates together and have a little reunion?"

"Of course. We'll see them all at the funeral."

Startled, Wu Ziqiao asked, "Funeral? What funeral?"

"Xiao Jiling didn't tell you? It's "Camel" Luo-tuo's funeral. All our classmates are going. Do you have a car? I'll give you the church's address. It's at nine o'clock, don't be late."

Jin Lihe had always been on the taciturn side; even after not seeing Wu Ziqiao for five years, he hung up after only a few sentences. Wu Ziqiao had no alternative but to take out his address book and look up Lao Chen's telephone number.

"It was lung cancer. You know that he smoked like a chimney. Even when his illness had reached the critical stage, he still wouldn't quit. It went on for more than a year. He just passed away last Monday. We told all our classmates who are living in California now. You say you just got in from New York? Want me to pick you up? In the morning, 'Monkey' Houzi and I are going to the flower shop; it wouldn't be any trouble to pick you up on the way."

Wu Ziqiao said that it wouldn't be necessary, that he had rented a car and it would be equally convenient for him to drive himself. He hung up, and after a bit Jin Lihe called again.

"I've thought about it. It'd be best if I pick you up."

"Really, there's no need. I have a car."

"I'm not just being polite. On the road we'd have a chance to talk. Xiao Jiling probably already told you—we're moving to San Jose soon. I'm getting ready to go into business for myself, and I wouldn't mind hearing what you have to say about it."

Xiao Jiling hadn't mentioned it. He hadn't expected that Xiao Jiling would adopt Jin Lihe's philosophy of silence being golden. Fifteen years before, when Wu Ziqiao had just come to America to study, Jin Lihe and Xiao Jiling had been the first of their classmates to get married. Wu Ziqiao had ridden Greyhound for three days and three nights to get from South Carolina to Los Angeles in time for the wedding. On the eve of the wedding, Xiao Jiling had still been in Jin Lihe's apartment chattering away like a happy sparrow, loud enough to give everyone a headache. After a while, Camel had been able to take it anymore and had told her that there were only a few hours left to Jin Lihe's bachelor days; the fact that she was still there was a little out of keeping with tradition. Xiao Jiling had said she didn't care what the American tradition was. Laughing, Camel had asked how, according to the Chinese tradition—in which an unwedded bride didn't leave her parent's home before marriage—one would evaluate the conduct of one who was staying at the bridegroom's house before their marriage? Angry and embarrassed, Xiao Jiling had ranted at Camel and stormed out. . . .

"So does that settle it?" Jin Lihe said. "I'll come get you tomorrow morning at eight o'clock."

Wu Ziqiao turned off the light and lay down on the bed with all his clothes on. Camel. He almost couldn't remember what Camel looked like. The spirit of memory was like the spirit of Aladdin's lamp; you needed to polish industriously before it would appear. He thought about it over and over; all he could come up with were the faces of the annoying people in the office. "Camel," Wu Ziqiao, rubbing the lamp of his memory, quietly intoned, "where are you?"

Camel's appearance gradually became clear, a silly grin exposing his two buck teeth. The four brothers in Camel's family were all crowded into a narrow wooded shack in a village for military dependents. Within his memory, Wu Ziqiao once again saw that rickety wooded shack with Camel inside, mouth wide open in a silly grin, and his three younger brothers, who looked as alike as peas in a pod. In the darkness, he couldn't help laughing, and recited from memory a poem by Ku Ling.[8]

8

"Did you sleep well last night?"

Wu Ziqiao climbed into Jin Lihe's Mercedes Benz. Jin Lihe was wearing dark sunglasses, and Wu Ziqiao noticed that his hair was graying at the temples.

"Where's Xiao Jiling?"

"She doesn't feel like coming. We'll be moving soon, and there are a lot of things that need taking care of."

"Why are you moving to northern California all of a sudden?"

"Why not? Everyone who's interested in starting a business should move to Silicon Valley. You should come, too. We could go into business together."

Wu Ziqiao mumbled an incoherent response. Jin Lihe added, "Lao Chen just quit, too, and started his own trading company."

"Really? He didn't mention it yesterday."

"You didn't ask."

Wu Ziqiao thought Jin Lihe would continue to discuss the prospects of their going into business together, but, surprisingly, he didn't say anything the rest of the way. Only when they had nearly reached the cemetery did Jin Lihe say, "Just about all of our classmates have come today. In all the years since we graduated, this is the first time we've gathered together enough people to hold a class reunion."

Jin Lihe was right. The tiny church was packed with their classmates. Wu Ziqiao stood by Du Jian's side. Du Jian, with his protruding belly and glistening red face, lowered his voice and whispered to Wu Ziqiao, "Aren't you living in New York?"

8. Ku Ling is a modern Chinese poet.

"I just happened to be here to audit an account. Aren't you living in Taipei?"

"I just happened to be on the West Coast for a meeting." Du Jian continued, "Camel wanted us to come, and we all came."

Wu Ziqiao knew that Du Jian wasn't joking. Of all their classmates, Du Jian had been closest with Camel. Without having made arrangements beforehand, when Camel's coffin came out, they all spontaneously proceeded to the altar to act as pallbearers. Outside the church, the southern California sun was dazzling. With soon wonderful sunshine, it didn't seem like a day for sorrow. Camel had been a straightforward, upright person; it was only fitting that he depart on such a bright day as today. "Camel," Wu Ziqiao said softly, "Camel, my brother, go in peace."

His eyes became moist. Du Jian walked in front of him, while on the other side of the coffin were Jin Lihe and Monkey with their heads lowered, Monkey making unusual blubbering sounds. Wu Ziqiao had never heard Monkey cry before; it actually made his own emotions settle down a bit. Such brilliant sunlight! He softly hummed John Denver's old song.

Du Jian's shoulders were really broad. He had never realized Du Jian's shoulders were that broad. Du Jian walked forward stolidly. Perhaps it was the stance of one who had spent many years as a flag bearer in basic training. Wu Ziqiao wondered what he was thinking about. For a while Camel and Du Jian had been at odds. Their political opinions were on opposite ends of the spectrum, and they had argued whenever they had seen each other. What would Camel think if he knew that Du Jian had come all the way from Taiwan to send him off?

9

"Uncle Ziqiao is here, Uncle Ziqiao is here!"

Bobby charged forward to meet him. Wu Ziqiao hoisted him up; his two chubby legs were kicking so hard that Wu Ziqiao almost couldn't hold him.

"Bobby, don't kick your uncle!" Bao Zhu scolded. Wu Ziqiao put him back down, pulled out the toy inside his paper bag, and gave it to him. Bobby took the Transformer robot that Wu Ziqiao had bought him and immediately started to disassemble it on the living-room floor.

"Bobby." Bao Zhu smiled, shaking her head. "He's quite a mischief maker."

"That's all right. Where's Betty?"

"She went with her dad to watch a ball game. Last week we made dumplings and waited for you, but you never came."

"I went to Los Angeles to settle an account—didn't Betty tell you?"

"She must have forgotten. She's a lot of trouble for such a small kid. Ever since she's had a boyfriend, she hasn't taken anything seriously. It's only a year until she starts college, and I haven't seen her study yet. I'm really worried she won't get into a good school, but I can't even complain. As soon as I start yelling at her, she leaves the house. We were never like that as kids!"

Wu Ziqiao had sunk into the soft sofa and was watching Bobby roll around on the carpet. He was standing on his chubby arms in a handstand when he slipped, hit his head on the floor, and burst out sobbing, all the while keeping an eye on his uncle. Wu Ziqiao took a lollipop out of his pocket.

"Don't cry, Bobby. Boys as big as you shouldn't cry—shame on you."

"Don't give him any candy. He won't have any appetite for dinner."

When Bobby saw that he wouldn't get any candy, his fake sobbing turned real. Bao Zhu shook her head.

"It's all your fault, Ziqiao. You have to stop spoiling him. Every time you come, I have to spend three days straightening him out."

Wu Ziqiao smiled and nodded his head. He and Bao Zhu were only three years apart. When they were young, they were both skinny. After marriage, Bao Zhu had put on more than a little weight. In these last two years especially, she had begun to resemble a balloon.

"Ziqiao, have you been in touch with Helen recently?"

"I called her before I went away on business, but I haven't talked with her these last two weeks."

Bao Zhu looked as if she had something she wanted to say but then held herself back. Wu Ziqiao knew what she wanted to say and thought he might as well come out directly and say it first.

"I got the letter her lawyer sent me yesterday. She wants a divorce."
Bao Zhu looked at him. Wu Ziqiao shook his head.

"Obviously I'm not giving my consent. Divorce? Hah."

"Have you told Helen yet?"

"Not yet. Tomorrow's Monday; I'll find a lawyer to call her lawyer."

"Why get a lawyer? Why don't you just call her directly and talk it over? After being husband and wife for so many years, what is there that you can't talk about face-to-face?"

"*I* wasn't the first one to get a lawyer!" Wu Ziqiao's anger boiled up inside him, and he struggled up out of the sofa. "I had just gotten back from Los Angeles, I was in a terrible mood, and then I saw her lawyer's letter. What do you think, was I annoyed? I didn't move out, you know. She forced me out. In these past few months, I've sent her money to pay the monthly mortgage bills, just like before. When the pipes were clogged, I rushed back to fix them. I've done everything I could to accommodate her. After all this, she's the one to strike the first blow!"

Wu Ziqiao was angry enough to get sharp pains in his stomach, and he paced back and forth in the living room. Even Bobby could sense his uncle's anger and took his robot and quietly sneaked off to the TV room.

"She's picked up American bad habits, getting a lawyer at the drop of a hat like that. She thinks that American laws can rule me, but I won't stand for it. A divorce, oh, how she wishes. She's out screwing around with that American boss, and she still thinks I don't know." Wu Ziqiao turned to Bao Zhu and continued, "Before we came abroad, she wasn't like this, as you're well aware. Before, her temperament was bad, but at least she was reasonable; she's not a bit reasonable now. I really regret bringing her. Once abroad, women change entirely."

"We've all changed," Bao Zhu said. "Ziqiao, everyone grows up. Helen has talked it over with me quite a few times—it's not that she didn't want to save your marriage, but the things that you did hurt her too deeply."

"You two have discussed it? What did she say?" Wu Ziqiao's voice became rushed. "Whatever you do, don't believe any of her one-sided arguments."

"Are they one-sided? Helen says you've wanted to kill her for a long time and wrote a whole diary of ways to kill one's wife. It was only after you scared her that she forced you out."

"Why would I want to kill her?" Wu Ziqiao forced a laugh. "Kill my own wife because I have nothing to do after dinner? In the thirteen years we've been married, have I touched a hair on her head? She always considers Americans to be superior to Chinese. Sure, Americans' English is better than Chinese people's, but when an American beats his wife, he doesn't just stop when her face is bruised, he keeps going until he's beaten the living daylights out of her. Have I ever hit her? She didn't fulfill her duties as a wife, and I moved to the living room to sleep without even a murmur of complaint. She wanted me to get lost, and the next day I moved out of the house. I even quit my job. Would I kill her?"

"Of course you wouldn't," Bao Zhu consoled. "Ziqiao, you're my brother, I know what your temper's like. She was angry because all you wrote in your diary was that you wanted to kill her. I know you were going through hard times, but why did you write all of that down? If there's really a lawsuit, you'll never beat her."

"I'm not afraid of a lawsuit." The muscles on Wu Ziqiao's face were taut. "A gentleman fights with words, not with fists. Moreover, my diary is a work of art. Anybody who looked at it would know that the stories are fictitious. All the neighbors were well aware of how she mistreated me. Before, when we only had one car, if she got off work late, I took the subway home and cooked dinner. In the evenings before her classes at the community college, when she thought the parking lot would be too crowded and she wouldn't be able to get a space, she sent me there an hour early to stand in a space and wait for her to get there. It was OK in the summer, but in the winter? I've suffered like this for her and never complained. Would I kill her?"

Bao Zhu sighed, pulled on his arm, and pleaded with him, "Why, Ziqiao? You're both almost forty, and you've been through this many years, even if it has been a constant fight. If tomorrow you go to Helen and have a talk with her, quietly and calmly ask for her forgiveness. That'll fix it. Like you said, you've suffered so much for her, why blow it by trying to act tough?"

"It's not an act," Wu Ziqiao replied. "She's really picked up Americans' bad habits, finding a lawyer to intimidate me. Divorce? Never!"

10

After three days, Wu Ziqiao finally mustered enough courage to call Helen. Over the phone, Helen's voice was cold and distant. It made Wu Ziqiao wonder whether or not caving in and being the first to apologize was a wise move. Nevertheless, Helen didn't refuse to see him. He arranged for them to meet at half past five at a Western restaurant, but before three he lost his patience and left work early. When he arrived at the restaurant, there were hardly any customers there. He chose a seat in a corner and ordered a martini.

The restaurant had just turned on the lights which gave it an air of majesty. This was one of the classier restaurants in midtown. Helen would certainly appreciate it, but Wu Ziqiao regretted that it was so expensive. He had never had much of a liking for Western food, but Helen, following the native traditions, had suddenly developed a remarkable appetite for steak, eating it blood rare. The previous phase she had gone through was an infatuation for French cuisine, especially bouillabaisse. Wu Ziqiao wouldn't touch it with a ten-foot pole. Helen made fun of him for not understanding how to enjoy life. She would always say that since he didn't have any kids, he ought to learn how to live it up a little; did he think he could take his money with him to the grave?

Wu Ziqiao gulped down half the contents of his glass. The icy liquid stopped in his esophagus and stayed there for a while before entering his stomach. He noticed he was starting to warm up, but his stomach hurt a bit, too. He liked to drink, but recently his liver had been acting up, so he rarely did anymore. Today, though, he needed the soothing effect of alcohol.

He couldn't say he didn't regret not having a child. If they had had children, maybe things would have been different. Of course, they might have been even worse. If they were going to separate now, at least no innocents would suffer. He thought of the three half-grown children Camel had left behind. It was fortunate that his wife was strong; after all, she had grown up in a military dependents' village as well. At the funeral, Du Jian had started a collection on the spot for Camel's kids' tuition. Du Jian really had initiative, and his activities in the Taipei political arena in the last two years had proven successful.

"Sorry to have kept you so long."

Wu Ziqiao was startled; he couldn't believe that Helen could be so refined and polite. As soon as she sat down, though, the old Helen resurfaced.

"Drinking again? Are you trying to kill yourself? What a loser."

"I've only had one glass," said Wu Ziqiao, smiling amicably. "Is there a lot of traffic outside?"

"It's all right. I didn't drive, I called a cab." Helen had lost some weight, but her face was still glowing with well-being. "Yourself?"

"I took the subway. There's something wrong with the car's transmission, and I just took it to be fixed. I have the feeling we're going to be extorted for another lump of money."

"Speaking of the car . . ." Helen fished around in her purse and pulled out an envelope. "The car's insurance expires at the end of the month. Since we're living separately, the cars should be insured separately as well. Will you call, or shall I?"

"Here, I'll take care of it." Wu Ziqiao took the envelope and took advantage of the situation to say, "I have something to give you, too."

"What?"

Wu Ziqiao took the green notebook out of his briefcase and handed it to Helen.

"What do you mean by giving this to me?" Helen looked as if she'd touched a poisonous snake. "I don't want it."

"You can have it if you like. Burn it. Keep it for evidence. Do whatever you want."

"Who would want to keep this for evidence?" Helen raised her voice in anger. "Wu Ziqiao, if you think that this wipes the slate clean, if you think that this is repenting for your mistakes, then you can go stick it!"

"That's not what I meant."

"Then what did you mean? That dog-shit diary of yours. I get the shivers just looking at it. I can't believe you had the gall to bring it!"

Wu Ziqiao knew he'd messed up again. How was it that he didn't think to buy a dozen roses or something? He had never sent Helen flowers before; he would never be able to do so now.

"You've lost your senses! You don't have even the most basic sense of decency. If you had any sense, would you still continue to think of ways to kill your wife every night? How pathetic."

"Certainly it's pathetic," Wu Ziqiao told her. "They're all fake, vulgar, fictitious stories. Who would actually want to kill his wife?"

"You would!" Helen opened the green-covered book and read, "'Uxoricide method number 47: In Haiti there is voodoo magic, by which one can stab a little doll with sharp needles, causing one's wife to ache everywhere. Every day she'll have a headache, stomachache, a sore liver, a sore heart, a sore waist, sore shoulders; there won't be anywhere that doesn't hurt, until finally she dies of pain.' You're truly cruel to think up this kind of torture. Have you any decency left?"

"Actually, I was thinking about myself when I wrote that. At night my liver often hurts. I wrote that entry because it hurts so bad I can't sleep."

"Is that because I used voodoo to get you? Because of this you want revenge and want to use voodoo to get me, too? Even the Khmer Rouge aren't as cruel as you. I always hoped I could get you to give up drinking. I was afraid you would get cirrhosis of the liver, and here you are, biting the hand that feeds you!" Helen stood up and threw the green-covered book at him. "Wu Ziqiao, this is the knife that cuts us in two. I'm telling you, don't bother trying to save the situation, because there's nothing left to save. Anyone who could think of these venomous plans to kill his wife, feel no remorse, and think they're 'interesting' is someone with an abnormal psyche. Divorce! Believe me, we will be divorced!"

"Helen," Wu Ziqiao stood up as well and pleaded, "all the stories are fictitious."

"Fictitious stories can be acted out. I won't be giving you the opportunity." As she left, Helen had a final comment to make. "Hurry up and find a lawyer. I want this strictly by the rules."

But Wu Ziqiao didn't look for a lawyer. The next day, just after he had reinsured the two cars, he was sent to the hospital in a state of confusion. He couldn't even remember how he got there. All he could remember was that as he came out of the bank, his sight grew dimmer and dimmer and his legs became weak and wobbly. After that he couldn't remember anything. Looking back on it, he thought it was interesting, like a gradual fadeout in a movie. It was surprising that in life one could have such a perfect montage. If he had passed away then, it would have been like the last curtain call. When he woke up, his stomach had been cut out; the success rate of American hospitals in saving people had always been admirable. He stayed in the hospital recovering for eight days and didn't call Bao Zhu or anyone. His sister thought he had gone off on business, and, surprisingly enough, Helen's lawyer hadn't come to bother him, either. These eight days should have been a good opportunity for Wu Ziqiao to repent for his misdeeds, but in the end he didn't repent and instead had another strange encounter.

11

Her English name was Wendy, and at first Wu Ziqiao thought she was Vietnamese. There weren't many Asian nurses in the hospital—most of them were ungainly old women of indeterminate ancestry. At first Wu Ziqiao, in his weakness, let them handle him. Every time they changed the sheets, he didn't know which way was up or down. Once he regained some strength, he did all he could to get off the bed himself. Every time the stout, black, head nurse saw him sitting primly in the chair at the head of the bed, she would laugh like a braying donkey and say, "Mr. Wu, have you come to visit yourself again? Sorry, he's gone to have an operation, try again tomorrow."

Wu Ziqiao detested the head nurse's jokes. He didn't think they were a bit funny. One time Wendy happened to be bringing his medicine, saw the expression on his face, and whispered to him, "Don't mind her, Barbara's just like that. She's the same with patients who have a terminal illness, cracking stupid jokes. That's her way of cheering them up."

Wu Ziqiao forced a smile and replied, "I know, but if the patient were a lonely old person and had been made fun of like this, would he be able to stand it?"

Wendy gave him a wink, picked up the medicine tray, and left.

The next day, Wendy's shift came, and, as usual, she took Wu Ziqiao's pulse and blood pressure, then left. It was only after she left that Wu Ziqiao noticed that a bottle of yellow flowers had been added to the room. It was a long wait until Wendy came back, and Wu Ziqiao, all choked up, thanked her. Wendy chuckled and, switching to Chinese, said, "You'll be all right. In another two days you'll be out of here."

Wu Ziqiao, who had been counting the days until he could leave, now felt rather differently about the whole affair. He started to daydream about the story of the Girl with the Red Whisk and Li Jing.[9] He was sorry that Wendy didn't come by again before the day he was released. After he finished the hospital check-out procedures, he dressed himself nicely. When the male nurse wanted him to get in the wheelchair to escort him to the front door, Wu Ziqiao signaled to him that it wouldn't be necessary. Now that he could get around by himself, there was someone he wanted to find. Where was she?

"Wendy? Isn't she on leave?" said one nurse to another. "Didn't she go on vacation?"

"She took a week off. From what she said, her mother was coming from Taiwan, and she wanted to take her sightseeing."

Wu Ziqiao got a taxi and returned to his temporary residence. Everything was still the same: the same old bed, broken table, and two rickety chairs. Wu Ziqiao swept and cleaned the room, found himself in a sweat, and sat down on a chair to rest. Although it didn't seem that anything had changed in the room, he definitely sensed some slight, almost imperceptible differences. What had changed? He remembered that when he had just moved in, he had felt a bit uncomfortable, but he always felt a little bit at odds with his surroundings. Later, the room slowly accepted him, like a woman accepting a man. There was always a mutual acclimatization process between room and tenant. He wondered, was it possible the room had been hopefully waiting for him to come back?

Wu Ziqiao slowly settled down. At least something was still waiting for him. He thought of Wendy. He had asked her what her Chinese name was, but he hadn't heard her answer clearly. It seemed to have been Fan something–qiao. Fan Xiaoqiao? Fan Wenqiao? Fan Aiqiao? He had mentioned how his name ended in -qiao, too. When he told Wendy this, she grinned, showing her teeth. Her teeth weren't straight; they tended to stick out in different directions. She was quite tall, almost as tall as Helen, and slender, a southern Chinese natural beauty. People who were that thin were usually Southerners. It was no surprise her mother had come from Taiwan to visit her. From the fact that she was willing to take her mother around, you

9. These are characters from a Tang dynasty tale of knight-errantry, "The Curly Bearded Hero." The girl with the red whisk packs her belongings and leaves her job to be with Li Jing, a historical future minister to the founder of the Tang dynasty. See Cyril Birch, *Anthology of Chinese Literature*.

could tell that she was a good filial daughter, and you could also tell that she hadn't married yet.

Sitting in the chair, Wu Ziqiao slipped into a befuddled state of consciousness. In his half-asleep, half-awake state, Helen pointed at his face and cursed him for being such a loser. He suddenly woke up, startled. The light inside the room had dimmed. It was dinnertime, but Wu Ziqiao didn't feel especially hungry and fell back asleep. He was standing at the entrance to the hospital, waiting for the long-legged Wendy to get off work. Finally she came out, and she grinned when she saw him. When he escorted her home, it was already getting dark. The apartment, having only a single female occupant, gave off a faint aura of sorrow. Like his room, it only had one old bed, a broken table, and two rickety chairs. What was she doing living in a place like this? Wendy smiled and shook her head. The next-door neighbor was making a racket, moving tables and chairs around for no reason, making a "bam bam" sound. Ah, Wendy, Wendy, beautiful Wendy, why do you live in such a place? Bam, bam, the next-door neighbor was still making a racket. Wendy smiled and sat on the side of the bed. Wu Ziqiao tried hard to recall her proper name. Fan Xiaoqiao? Fan Wenqiao? Fan Aiqiao?

Bam, bam, bam.

Wu Ziqiao gave a start; someone was knocking at the door. He turned on the light and opened the door. Two policemen were standing outside, and the landlady stood behind them, sneaking glances at him. The husky policeman who was in front took out his identification.

"Mr. Wu? You're Mr. Wu?"

Wu Ziqiao nodded. He began to understand why there were some slight and almost imperceptible differences to the room.

"Ziqiao Wu," the policeman said to him, "You're under arrest."[10]

12

"Ziqiao, are you all right?"

Bao Zhu's face was slightly pudgier; Wu Ziqiao wasn't sure whether it was because she had put on weight again or because she had been crying. He was disinclined to pursue the question and instead said to her, "I didn't kill Helen—it's all a misunderstanding."

---

10. The policeman, not aware that Chinese surnames precede the given name, has reversed them.

"I know you wouldn't do something like that," Bao Zhu comforted him. "We want to get a lawyer for your defense."

"I didn't kill her. Would I kill my wife just because I had nothing better to do after dinner? In any case, I had just left the hospital. Does someone who's just had half of his stomach removed have the strength to kill someone?"

"Why didn't you tell us you'd been hospitalized?" Bao Zhu was breathing in jerks and began to cry. "If only you'd told us sooner, it wouldn't have come to this."

"Come to what?" asked Wu Ziqiao in shock. "It's not like I killed anybody. I'd just come out of the hospital. Where would I get the time and energy to go kill someone? America has a good judicial system. They won't falsely convict me. Poor Helen, to have been butchered so cruelly by some burglar. Have they found . . . her head?"

Bao Zhu shook her head and started crying again, and then it was Ziqiao's turn to comfort her.

"Don't cry. I'm not in such bad shape."

"You really don't remember anything that happened?"

"Remember what?" Wu Ziqiao bellowed. "You still don't believe me? Helen and I had our problems, but it wasn't as bad as all that. As the Chinese say, for every night a husband and wife spend in wedlock, there come a hundred days of affection. How could I kill her?"

"But your diary . . ."

"They're all fictional stories, the plots to novels! My God, how is it that none of you can tell fact from fiction?"

"Helen really died." Bao Zhu swallowed slowly and said, "Ziqiao, listen carefully. Helen is really dead. She died in her own bedroom. She died a horrible death—the murderer cut off her head, and they still haven't been able to find it."

"Why talk to me like this? I'm no psycho. You think I'm nuts, don't you?"

Bao Zhu didn't answer. Wu Ziqiao sighed. He realized that the situation was serious; even his own sister didn't believe him. How the hell had it come to this? He carefully recalled what had happened the day he left the hospital. In the morning, he completed the outpatient procedures at about ten, no, eleven o'clock. It must have been approaching eleven, because he saw the food cart in the corridor. He'd probably wasted another half hour looking for Wendy. Afterward, he took a cab home. By the time he got home, it was close to one. He cleaned the room and then sat on the chair and napped. By the time the police arrived, it was already dark. The police records said it was eight o'clock. He had actually slept seven or eight hours sitting in the chair! But after an illness, with your body weakened, it's easy to fall asleep. The judge should believe him.

Wu Ziqiao broke out in a cold sweat. He urgently needed evidence that he hadn't been at the scene of the crime. Too bad nobody had seen him come home. Perhaps if he found the cab driver who had driven him home that day, he would testify for him? But, that probably wouldn't be enough. He could have taken another cab to do the deed, rushed home after killing her, and still have made it on time.

"My thinking is still quite clear," Wu Ziqiao announced, pondering and speaking aloud in a loud voice. "This will prove that I'm not crazy. If I'm not crazy, I couldn't unknowingly run out and kill someone. I don't sleepwalk, so I couldn't have killed anyone in my sleep. Therefore, I didn't kill anyone."

Bao Zhu listened to his analysis and burst out laughing. Wu Ziqiao laughed, too. When they were little, they used to tease each other. Wu Ziqiao liked to blurt out a big pile of nonsense to trick Bao Zhu, and every time, Bao Zhu was intimidated into believing him. She took out her handkerchief, wiped her tears, and said to him, "Ziqiao, all the evidence is against you. They've found your diary and are looking for someone to translate it right now. Helen had also told her boss that you wanted to kill her. He was furious; he said that it didn't matter how much the company would have to pay in legal expenses, he wanted to see that you receive the punishment you deserve."

"It figures it would be her lover." Wu Ziqiao explained, "Of course he'd love to get rid of me. They'd be rid of a thorn in the eye; they would be free to do as they pleased."

"But Helen was slaughtered. It's only natural that her friends would want to avenge her." Bao Zhu quickly added, "Sorry, I wasn't accusing you."

"I want to avenge Helen as well. Don't think that I don't hate her murderer. His method was too brutal, just too brutal."

Hearing Wu Ziqiao say this caused Bao Zhu to get worked up and start crying again.

"How could this happen? I just don't get it, such a good person butchered like that . . . I really don't get it."

Wu Ziqiao couldn't get it either. After Bao Zhu left, he was taken back to the detention center. This was the first time in his whole life that he'd been jailed, and, surprising enough, he stayed calm and cool. If he had moved directly from his old home into jail, he might have felt uncomfortable. But after having lived away from home for half a year, he found that the differences between his little room and the jail were not that great. The decoration was equally simple, and the meals were just as hard to swallow. Being in jail made Wu Ziqiao finally realize that, since he had been forced out by Helen (or, that is, decided to move out on his own), he had never been free. Why? Before, he hated how Helen yelled at him to do this and that and just wished that he could kill her. Now, he hadn't even gotten to sample freedom's pleasures. All the media hype about how single yuppies lived the high life seemed to have no bearing on him. Damned yuppies, Wu Ziqiao thought, they're imprisoned, too—it's just that some people know they're in prison and some people don't, that's all.

Actually, he didn't mind being in jail. No need to go to work, no need to deal with those boring nincompoops; it wasn't bad at all. Wu Ziqiao just wanted to clarify that he didn't kill his wife. Afterward, if they still wanted him to live here, he really wouldn't object.

The whole thing was still a mystery to Wu Ziqiao. He didn't have a newspaper, but he could imagine the headlines: "Corpse of Voluptuous Asian Found Headless, Suspect Husband Under Arrest." Even the Taiwan newspapers would make this into a big story: "Study-Abroad Student Kills Wife." No, his student days were long over. They would say, "Overseas Chinese Bumps Off Wife!" "Chinese Kills Wife!" "Taiwanese Kills Wife!" "Chinese American Knocks Off Wife!" "Scholar Slays Spouse!" He liked the last one the best. After having suffered through all these years, he should be considered a scholar. Two years ago he was almost invited to attend the National Reconstruction Council.[11] That's it. "Scholar Slays Spouse"—that should be the headline.

Pity that the news broadcasts had it all wrong. He hadn't done it. The fact that the police had taken away his diary left him defenseless. He wished he had burned it a long time ago, but burning it wouldn't necessarily have helped any. Helen must have told Bill early on that

11. The National Reconstruction Council, *Guo Jian Hui,* is a meeting of overseas Chinese intellectuals and professionals who return to Taiwan to counsel the government on domestic policy.

her husband had come up with 108 ways to kill her. Didn't she realize that if someone could come up with 108 ways to kill his wife, he must have some talent, so why would he bother to kill her?

He hadn't killed his wife, but still his wife had died because of him. Whoever set him up must have read his diary or at least have known that they weren't getting along. Who would want to frame him? Wu Ziqiao thought it through over and over. He didn't have any enemies. Perhaps Bill wanted to get rid of him, but he wouldn't take it this far. In the company, he was a low-level employee; there were people who picked on him, but he certainly didn't get the opportunity to pick on anybody himself. Maybe the companies whose accounts he'd audited were unhappy with him, but that was business; they wouldn't take it out on his family.

Wu Ziqiao thought for a long time and couldn't help but admit to himself that there wasn't anyone who would kill Helen just to set him up. In that case, could it be that it was Helen's enemies who had killed her? Helen was blunt and outspoken. She was the only person in the company with enough nerve to yank the tiger's whiskers and yell at the bigwigs. The Westerners were all somewhat intimidated by her. But he didn't find it plausible that someone would kill just for this, either.

The most logical explanation was simply that burglars had killed her. But the police had taken him with them to comb her house, and nothing was missing. Besides, the coroner's report said that she hadn't been raped, so neither greed nor lust could be established as motives.

So who could it be? Bill couldn't be completely eliminated as a suspect. Maybe he really *had* had something going with Helen, and they'd had a fight. He couldn't satisfy her demands, so why not kill her and frame Wu Ziqiao? If that was truly it, then this American was a real brute.

Of course, there was still the last potential killer, the possibility Wu Ziqiao least liked to consider, the unfortunate possibility that the real killer might in fact be who the police had determined it to be.

13

"Your case isn't hopeless. At the very least, there's still a possibility for defense. However, you have to trust me completely and cooperate with me."

Wu Ziqiao hadn't liked this lawyer all along. He was a typical Jew, big nose, wire-thin lips, the very picture of some louse who wanted both his life and his money. When Bao Zhu selected this lawyer, Wu Ziqiao argued with her, but Bao Zhu only said, "Your judgment is too subjective—you have biases against every kind of person. Here in New York, if you don't get a Jewish lawyer, what kind of lawyer are you going to get? Would you rather get a Chinese lawyer?"

That one phrase was enough to shut him up; there was no way he was going to get a Chinese lawyer. At least this Mr. Cohen didn't know who he was. As far as Cohen was concerned, Wu Ziqiao was just another yellow-skinned, slanty-eyed, slightly wacko Oriental. Even if Wu Ziqiao was sentenced to life imprisonment, he wouldn't necessarily be interested. This Oriental would rather entrust his life to a Jew who was not willing to see him electrocuted, although he still might be a Jew who would nail him to a cross.

"You've got to cooperate with me. It isn't a pretty situation—that diary, . . ." Cohen wagged his head back and forth and clucked continuously. "Too bad. Too bad. I hate my wife, too, but I would never be stupid enough to write a diary about how to kill her. You know how I unwind?" Cohen lowered his voice and said, "Fishing! When I catch a big saltwater fish, I take the knife in my own hand, slice open its belly, and rip its guts. As I cut I say, 'Paula, this knife is for you. Did you hear me? Paula, this knife is for you!' Ha ha!"

Cohen laughed aloud, and it caused Wu Ziqiao to think of that head nurse at the hospital with the weird sense of humor. These Westerners had all gone crazy, but instead, they thought *he* had gone crazy. What kind of world was he living in?

"I did not kill my wife. My diary cannot be used as evidence for homicide."

"But it's enough to explain your motives for doing so and your mood at the time."

"I didn't kill her!"

"The primary objective of our defense is to prove that on the afternoon of September 14, 1986, you went crazy for a short period of time—that is to say, had temporary insanity—and so are unable to take responsibility for your actions."

"I didn't kill her!"

"I didn't say you killed her. Although this is the crux of the matter, it is not the crux of our defense. The most important thing is to prove that sometimes you can't take responsibility for your actions."

"I didn't kill her, and I didn't lose my sanity." Wu Ziqiao continued, "How many times do I have to say it before you'll believe me? On the afternoon of September 14, 1986, I went home, put my room in order, and then sat in my chair and fell fast asleep. I slept until evening."

"Did anyone see you sleeping?"

"No."

"In that case, how do you know you were sleeping?"

"Because . . . because when I woke up, it was already dark out. Besides, I remember the dreams I had."

"What were they?"

Wu Ziqiao suddenly realized he'd slipped, but he couldn't avoid going through with what he was saying. "My wife was calling me a loser. But this wasn't the only dream, this was just the last dream. I've forgotten all the dreams I'd had before. You must have had the same experience, only remembering the last dream before you wake up."

"Aha," Cohen said. "You dreamed of arguing with your wife, and when you woke up, it was already dark out. This doesn't conflict with my defense at all. In fact, it perfectly supports my primary argument."

"But I didn't go crazy."

"You don't *think* you went crazy. But strictly according to what you said, you don't even remember what dreams you had, so how could you remember what happened in your dreams?"

"I am not insane, and I did not kill my wife. Maybe I can't present any strong evidence that I wasn't there, but the opposition can't present any evidence that I was there, either. Why don't you make that the focus of your defense?"

Cohen fixed his gaze upon Wu Ziqiao like a hawk and after a while responded, "I considered it, but then decided that it wouldn't work."

"Why not?"

"Because although the opposition still can't prove that you were there when your wife was killed, they can prove that you were at the scene of the crime on the day it occurred."

"Nonsense! Of course I've been to my house before, but on the day it happened, I did not go to see Helen."

"In that case, how do you explain the fact that the police found your diary at the scene of the crime?"

How could that be?! Wu Ziqiao was dumbfounded. The green-covered diary had always been by his side. Hadn't the police found the diary when they searched his room? Mr. Cohen seemed to sense his confusion, and he continued, "You thought the police found the diary when they searched your apartment, didn't you? That's just it— that's what they hoped you would think. That way, during the cross-examination in court, they could take you by surprise and ruin my defense. But the advantage of having asked a brilliant lawyer like me to defend you is that no one can deceive me. Not the prosecution and not even you, ha, ha."

"That's not possible. The diary was clearly in my room," Wu Ziqiao mumbled to himself. "I've never taken it out. How could it have gotten to my wife's? It's completely impossible."

"In this world, nothing's impossible." Mr. Cohen closed his briefcase and stood up, saying, "The reason God is willing to forgive man is because man doesn't know what he's doing. Relax, I'm getting more and more confident about this case. I'll come again to see you tomorrow. In the meantime, just get some rest."

14

Of course, Wu Ziqiao wasn't able to rest. He could not believe his diary had grown wings and flown home. He remembered things quite clearly. That day in the restaurant Helen threw the diary back at him. He took the diary home, hid it in his wardrobe, and the next day he passed out in the street and was sent to the hospital. Before he came out of the hospital, no one knew where the diary was hidden.

Who had sent the diary to Helen's? He couldn't have done it himself, could he? Cohen had repeatedly insinuated that he wanted Wu Ziqiao to confess that he had temporarily lost his sanity. It couldn't be that he had really gone crazy? Wu Ziqiao began to worry. He distinctly recalled that he had dreamed of Helen. Perhaps he hadn't been dreaming? Perhaps he really had taken the diary and rushed over to

Helen's house. He had apologized for his mistakes again,[12] but Helen still wouldn't accept his repentance, and he, in a fit of anger, had killed his wife.

Ever since he had been arrested, Wu Ziqiao had managed to keep his cool, but he suddenly felt extremely frightened. He wanted to scream but was unable to make a sound. It was as if he were possessed by a demon and could only lie paralyzed on the bed. No matter how he struggled, he was unable to stand up. His face was covered with tears, and although he was unable to emit a sound, he still repeated to himself over and over, "I really killed her! I really killed her!"

Everything was clear! The 108 ways to kill one's wife were just a rehearsal for the tragedy. The unseen supernatural force caused him first to record all the ways to kill one's wife, and in the end one was destined to be carried out. He thought that he had been daydreaming, that they were fictitious stories, but actually he had been fated to be his wife's executioner.

Poor Helen. Since it had happened, he had been calling for justice to be served. Even though Helen's head and body had been separated, he had felt no pain or contrition. Now, he suddenly was overcome with remorse towards her. Helen!

Suddenly he was able to move his hands and feet again, as if the demon had loosened his bonds. Wu Ziqiao struggled up, kneeled in front of the bed, and prayed for his soul. He didn't know how to pray; he just intoned again and again, "Helen, please forgive me. Helen, please forgive me."

"Helen! You died such a horrible death, please forgive me."

He kept up this attitude of prayer until he fell asleep from exhaustion.

15

By the time court opened session, Wu Ziqiao had already agonized to the point where he hardly looked human anymore. When Bao Zhu saw how Wu Ziqiao had to be slowly led into the courtroom by the bailiffs, she couldn't restrain herself from bursting out sobbing. Wu

---

12. The expression used in the Chinese here is, "To bear thorns and ask for forgiveness." This is another reference to *The Men of the Marshes,* a tale of knight-errantry in which the character Li Kui begs for the forgiveness for doubting the bandit leader Song Jiang by flagellating himself repeatedly with thorns.

Ziqiao's hair was all dried out, and his eyes had sunk into his head. He had the look of one who saw death as a release.

The cross-examination went smoothly, with no great highs or lows. It was only when the prosecution interrogated the Chinese specialist who had translated Wu Ziqiao's diary that the defense attorney stood up several times to protest. Wu Ziqiao listened to the entire testimony without any expression on his face, as if he had completely lost hope.

When it came time for Wu Ziqiao to testify, Bao Zhu's sobbing became too excessive, and she was taken out of the courtroom by her husband. Wu Ziqiao looked all around. In the entire courtroom there was no one he knew. Was it these people who would judge his crimes?

But he didn't care about these people anymore. He knew he was only the puppet executioner of an unseen power. As he could be used, so could these people be used; they were all fate's straw dogs. Wu Ziqiao answered the prosecution's questions according to Cohen's instructions. He didn't believe that Cohen's ingenious plan could save him, but this was no longer something he was concerned about. Even if the law didn't punish him, he still wouldn't be able to absolve himself. Who had told him to go out and kill his wife?

Wu Ziqiao thought of rugged Helen, who used to gallop around the basketball court. At that time she was something to see, able to sink baskets from midcourt with ease. She ran back and forth on the basketball court, and he took his camera and ran back and forth along the sidelines, the good husband following his wife wherever she performed.[13] Their golden years were when they had just been married and were living in Kaohsiung. She got up early to go running, and he followed behind on a bicycle, while she hollered, "Wu Ziqiao, hurry up! I'm running and you're riding, and still you can't catch up. What do you think you're doing?"

She had always liked to shout, but after leaving Taiwan, the quality of her yelling had gradually changed from an intimate tone to one of scorn. Was it she who had changed? Or was it he? If he had known it would turn out like this, he would never have come to America.

Wu Ziqiao looked around again. There were quite a few people in the court—who knew what rock they had all crawled out

13. This is a reversal of the usual expression, "The good wife following her husband wherever he performs."

from under? Perhaps some were reporters, perhaps some had come purely to see the excitement. Helen's boss, Bill, sat primly and properly in the third row. In the last row there was a woman shrouded in a black veil; Wu Ziqiao couldn't see her face clearly. It was almost as if she were a close acquaintance of his, but it also seemed as if she were a stranger. He didn't think he had seen her earlier. Why had she suddenly appeared? Why was she wearing a veil? Why?

He mentally struggled with this question and almost didn't hear the prosecuting attorney's question.

"Mr. Wu, please pay attention. What is this notebook?"

In his hand, the lawyer held up the green-covered notebook that was the source of his misfortune. It really was strange. He had clearly hid it in his wardrobe—how had it gotten to Helen's room?

"My diary."

"Why do you keep a diary?"

"When I can't sleep at night or I'm feeling depressed, it's my custom to get up and write in my diary."

"You say that this is your custom. However, previously, you didn't have this custom, right?"

"Right."

"When did you acquire this new habit?"

"About a year ago, on a night with a full moon."

"Mr. Wu, can you tell me what the contents of the diary are?"

Was it he who had brought over the "flying diary"?

"The contents of the diary are all fictitious stories."

"What kind of stories?"

"Stories about how to kill one's wife."

"Mr. Wu, when most people keep a diary they record actual events, but you say your diary is all fictitious stories. Is there such a thing as a fictitious diary?"

"Perhaps it shouldn't be called a diary. It's the scattered thoughts that I had every day and casually wrote down. You could call it a novel, a novel written for myself to read."

"Regardless of whether it was writing a diary or writing a novel, you certainly had an objective, didn't you? What was your objective?"

"I just answered that. If I couldn't sleep well at night or was in a bad mood, I wrote in my diary."

"Mr. Wu, please read this section of your diary." Wu Ziqiao read the selection the lawyer pointed out. He had never read Chinese in front of foreigners before, and it came out very awkwardly.

" 'March 15. Uxoricide method number 68. Put a leather bag on top of the wife's head to catch the blood, and in one swift move cut off the head.[14] Afterward, splash on some hydrochloric acid, and in no time the head will have dissolved into a clear liquid. The leftover corpse won't bleed a drop of blood.' "

"Mr. Wu, of course we don't understand with you reading in Chinese, but fortunately, just now Mr. Meier translated for us. Now, please explain for us, in your own words, what is the meaning of the passage you just read?"

"It doesn't mean anything. As I've already said, the whole diary is only fictitious stories. This story comes from a Chinese tale of knight-errantry. . . ."

"Mr. Wu, I am not the least bit interested in Chinese tales of knight-errantry. I would just like you to explain in simple terms the sixty-eighth method you wrote for killing one's wife."

"It's just to cut off the head, and then use a chemical to dissolve it. This is a tale of knight-errantry. . . ."

"Your honor!" The prosecuting lawyer addressed the judge. "From this it can be seen that the accused had premeditation from early on, and this sixty-eighth method of killing one's wife is the evidence."

"Objection!" Wu Ziqiao's lawyer, Cohen, immediately stood up and shouted. "It remains to be proven that the defendant killed anyone. The prosecution is trying to distort the defendant's testimony."

"Objection sustained." The judge went on, "Continue the cross-examination."

"Mr. Wu, why did you want to cut off your wife's head?"

"Objection!" Wu Ziqiao's lawyer shouted again.

"All right, let me rephrase the question. In your diary, or novel, or god-damned-who-knows-whatever-the-hell-it's-called, why did you want to cut off the wife's head?"

Why? Why would the killer use this cruel and heartless method? Why was it that the police had never found the head? Why?

14. This is another reference to "The Curly Bearded Hero," in which one character carries the head of an adversary in a leather bag. In the story, the man whose head it was, was "unrivalled throughout the empire for mean ingratitude," according to his killer, who was a hero and a model of the Confucian virtue of yielding.

"Mr. Wu, please pay attention and answer my question."

Why couldn't they find the head? Why?

"Ziqiao Wu," the judge said to him, "you have to answer this question honestly."

Who was that woman shrouded in the veil sitting in the back row? Unless . . .

"Ziqiao Wu!"

"I didn't kill my wife, I didn't kill anybody! The person who died wasn't my wife Helen Hu, and that's why you can't find her head. This is an old Chinese story—no, two stories. The old switcheroo—"Using a Plum to Replace the Peach," and "Switching a Cat for the Crown Prince."[15] If you don't understand, I'll explain it for you. The dead person isn't my wife at all. She's still alive and living well, and she may be enjoying this farce as we speak. She arranged the corpse. She arranged to have the diary placed right next to it as well. She's fooled you all."

Wu Ziqiao stood up excitedly. The prosecuting lawyer looked completely dumbfounded and helpless. Wu Ziqiao's lawyer, however, slowly sat down, and his mouth shifted into a satisfied smile.

"I didn't kill anyone! The deceased is not my wife!"

"Your honor," the prosecution attorney said to the judge, "what's going on today? Are we investigating a murder case or taking creative writing class?"

"Ziqiao Wu, I order you to sit down immediately!" the judge commanded. "If you lose control of yourself again, I'll have to instruct the bailiffs to restrain you."

"I've got it, I've got it all figured out! The person who died simply isn't her. This is called "The Golden Cicada Sheds its Exoskeleton"[16] plan. If you don't understand, I can explain. . . ."

"Mr. Wu, we're not as dumb as you think," the prosecuting attorney said. "You say the dead person isn't your wife. In that case, who is she?"

15. These expressions, known in Chinese as *Li Dai Tao Jiang* and *Li Mao Huan Tai Zi,* are both representative of stories in which one thing is replaced with another. "Using a Plum to Replace the Peach" is from a poem in the Record of Music from the Song Records, describing how a worm who was going to eat the roots of a peach tree ate the roots of a plum tree instead; it is a reference to the closeness that should exist between brothers. "Switching a Cat for the Crown Prince" is a Yuan dynasty Judge Bao detective story in which two rival queens in the Song dynasty compete to have the first male heir, and one switches the other's boy with a cat to humiliate her and gain status.

16. Personified later by a character in *The Journey to the West,* the cicada is originally referred to in a poem by Guan Hanqing in the Yuan dynasty.

"I don't know, but it's not Helen Hu."

"This is America, it's not China. Would it be that easy to find an Asian woman who was tall and built completely alike to take her place?"

"Perhaps some hospital just happened to have the corpse of an Oriental woman who died of an illness. You can buy corpses. . . ."

"Weaving stories again! We're sick of hearing your stories. Mr. Wu, the court deputies accompanied you to examine the corpse, and you didn't have any objections then. Wouldn't you notice any special marks on your wife's body? Mr. Wu, if you're telling the truth, can you tell us of any defining mark on your wife's body to prove that the corpse isn't her?"

Wu Ziqiao was speechless. He thought carefully but couldn't come up with any type of mark on Helen's body. It had been too long since they had been together; all his recollections of her seemed hazy. He thought a good while, but without any result, and was left completely shamed. The prosecuting attorney looked at him scornfully. The jury was listening, but there was nothing he could say. He noticed that the woman with the veiled face had already walked to the entrance. Although he couldn't see her face, he was still able to perceive the air of supreme desolation emanating from her eyes. The woman in the veil! Wu Ziqiao jumped up again.

"It's her! Don't let her get away—she's Helen Hu, my wife. Somebody stop her, don't let her get away!"

He wanted to leave the witness stand, but the bailiff immediately grabbed him from behind and held him fast. The judge pointed at him and started to bawl him out, the prosecuting attorney was yelling, and his own lawyer stood up and shouted as well. By the time all the clamor had subsided, the woman was already gone.

16

"A brilliant performance, even better than I had expected." Cohen said smiling, "Who would have thought you'd come up with a trick like that? Now no one can doubt that you're schizophrenic and have a tendency to lose your sanity temporarily on occasion."

Wu Ziqiao had no reply. His hands had been cuffed, and he was in despair. The woman with the veiled face . . . it must have been Helen, she looked too familiar.

"Don't be disappointed," said his lawyer, patting his shoulder. "We've won. They can't establish the murder charge against you. At most, you'll get fifteen years. Of course, you'll be sent to an asylum to be treated, but if everything goes well, in a few years you'll get parole and regain your freedom."

"I'm not crazy, and I don't want to go to an asylum."

"It's still a lot better than being put away for life," said Cohen. "Mr. Wu, it's been my honor to work with you."

She didn't die, Wu Ziqiao thought to himself. Not only didn't she die, she still had the gall to come back and attend her own murder trial. This was just like Helen. Whenever the women's basketball team made trouble, Helen was always in the lead. There had never been anyone who could control her no-fear-of-heaven-no-fear-of-hell attitude. Even the coach gave her some free reign. Wu Ziqiao had spent a lot of his energy courting her; he'd labored especially hard scrape up enough money to buy a motorcycle. There were only a few in all of Kaohsiung at the time. Cruising around town, darting amid the safflower trees aflame with blooming red flowers, was like flying in heaven.

"Mr. Wu, you definitely have creative talent. Once you're out of the cuckoo's nest, you should give up your boring job as an accountant and take up a new profession."

She wasn't dead. Wu Ziqiao said to the lawyer, "I want to appeal to a higher court. I'm innocent."

"Save it," Eichmann answered him. "No one will believe you."

"You don't believe me?"

"I believe," he said, "I believe that you *think* you didn't kill your wife. As to what actually happened, only your wife knows."

Wu Ziqiao thought there was some truth to that and said, "We can summon her to appear in court to give testimony."

Eichmann looked at him with a surprised expression and waited a while before responding.

"I didn't want to admit it all along, but I can't avoid saying it anymore: you need to go to an asylum. You're not feigning insanity, you're really insane."

But Wu Ziqiao knew he wasn't insane. Sometimes he was still extremely worried that he might have actually killed his wife in a fit of insanity, and at these times he would kneel and pray with an inexpressible feeling of grief. Most of the time, though, he believed that Helen hadn't died, that this was all her plot, and that he was completely innocent. She was a woman who could never be killed by a man. Still, he didn't hold a grudge toward Helen. At the end of their life together as husband and wife, the one who wasn't crazy had been sent to an asylum, and the one who hadn't died had been forced to live incognito, and this was tragic enough in itself. He would often think of the air of despondency in the eyes of the veiled woman. He knew he would never see Helen again. It wasn't until that last glance in the courtroom that she really departed from the world of the living.

Upon entering the sanitarium, Wu Ziqiao's behavior was excellent, and he became the model patient for the entire clinic. Every two months, Bao Zhu would come to see him and bring canned food and beef jerky. She never brought the children, to spare them from knowing that they had a crazy uncle. On days when Bao Zhu came to visit him, Wu Ziqiao was always waiting for her in one of the iron chairs out on the patio, playing with his camera and humming a tune. . . .

> Spring's flowers,
> How fragrant they are!
> Autumn's moon,
> How bright it is!
> I in my youth,
> How happy I am!
> Beautiful she,
> What's happened to her?

The moral of this story is,
The man who fears his wife is a real husband,
the man who kills his wife is a barbarian.
Another moral of this story is,
If you're really set on killing your wife,
don't keep a diary.

CHINESE FICTION

FOR THE NINETIES

David Der-wei Wang

*T*his anthology contains fourteen Chinese short stories and novellas
written in the late eighties and early nineties. The writers of
these stories are from mainland China, Taiwan, Hong Kong,
America, and New Zealand. By grouping these stories together under the category of contemporary Chinese fiction, the
anthology intends to posit a new image of China, a China
defined not by geopolitical boundaries and ideological closures
but by overlapping cultures and shared imaginative resources.

Traditional anthologies of modern Chinese literature are
too often regionalistic, corresponding to the reality of a China that has been divided into politically exclusive realms. It is
not uncommon to find that a criticism or the works of a certain anthology of Chinese fiction are drawn exclusively from
mainland China or Taiwan.[1] But at a time when mainland

1. Michael Duke's *Worlds of Modern Chinese Fiction* (New York: M. E. Sharpe, 1990) repre-
sents perhaps one of the first attempts to anthologize modern Chinese literature on a global scale.

the embrace of its vast neighbor, any attempt to define Chinese literature in terms of the old geopolitics will risk instant anachronism.

Events in the late eighties and early nineties have pushed Chinese literature toward irreversible change. In mainland China writers are fighting to reclaim the ground lost after the 1989 Tian'anmen Incident; in Taiwan unforeseen political upheavals and financial successes have caused a substantial shake-up of the traditional literary market; in Hong Kong, the specter of the end of Hong Kong's separate existence in 1997 has driven writers to write about the end of the century as if it were peculiarly their own.

During this period Chinese writers have also traveled overseas more frequently than ever before, thanks both to the easy access of transportation, and, ironically, to the cruelty of politics. The expatriate experience is one of the major themes of twentieth-century Chinese literature. The latest exodus of intellectuals from mainland China has added a new and poignant dimension to that tradition. Pessimists are again announcing that the Tian'anmen Incident has brought an untimely end to the development of modern Chinese literature. But mainland Chinese literature bounced back vigorously after the bloody crackdown, impressing us with its more somberly sophisticated discourse. Meanwhile, in Taiwan, Hong Kong, and overseas Chinese communities, literature has been undergoing booms and metamorphoses. It's safe to predict that the last decade for twentieth-century Chinese fiction will be just as exciting.

The changing landscape of contemporary Chinese fiction is related to political dynamics, but it is also a result of postmodern technologies. With computers and global telecommunication systems, writers and publishers are able to contact each other instantly; works considered unpublishable for political or commercial reasons at one publishing house may quickly appear in print somewhere else. For instance, writings by Mo Yan, Yu Hua, and Su Tong—three of the most talented mainland Chinese writers—now often receive their first publication in Taiwan and Hong Kong. The inventive Hong Kong writer Xi Xi, though unpopular among local readers, has won great acclaim in Taiwan, so much so that she was once mistaken for a Taiwanese writer by the Hong Kong government.[2] Where fashionable

2. Zheng Shusen [William Tay], introduction to the special issue on Xi Xi, *Lianhe wenxue* [Unitas] '99 (January 1993): 117.

Marxists discern signs of technocratic incursions on China's authentic existence, Chinese writers see new ways to disseminate their own truths and myths. As Ye Si's "Transcendence and the Fax Machine," a short story about a bittersweet affair between a religious scholar and his fax machine, indicates, transcendental truth now mingles with mechanical reproduction; the global and the local impinge upon each other's territories.

Overseas writers constitute a major force in modern Chinese literature. Around the time of the Tian'anmen Incident, many important mainland writers left China and have since formed a new expatriate voice clamoring for attention. A Cheng, one of the most celebrated "root-seeking" writers of the eighties, has settled in the United States; the dramatist and novelist Gao Xingjian is sojourning in France. Bei Dao, poet and founder of the controversial *Today* [Jintian] in the late seventies, is now taking refuge in Sweden, while Yang Lian, one of the most brilliant of the young Chinese poets, has made New Zealand his new base. Exile may eventually deprive these writers of the native experience their works were nurtured on, but for the time being at least it provides them with a different perspective from which to think and write about China.

Little surprise that some of the most powerful writings about the Tian'anmen Incident are written by mainland Chinese writers in exile. A parallel case can be found in Ping Lu, a writer who lives in the United States but writes most vividly about the Taiwan status quo, thanks to her consistent concern about and frequent visits to the island. Already situated outside their homeland, overseas writers find it both a condition and a result of narrating China that their works must cross established physical, formal, and conceptual boundaries. The new generation brings to mind names of an older generation, such as Lu Xun, Lao She, and Yu Dafu, the May Fourth writers whose experiences abroad helped them modernize Chinese literary discourse seven decades ago.

All the foregoing observations about the contemporary Chinese literary world—its cultural/political turmoils and technological innovations and the diaspora of mainland Chinese writers—make us think afresh about a theoretical scheme for characterizing the nineties. The fictive map "center versus margin" has to be redrawn for the new strategy.

While works by mainland Chinese writers still claim most of our attention, the old questions will be asked, such as: What are these writers writing about? For whom are they writing? Where are they writing? How does one classify a work produced on the mainland and published in Hong Kong with a Taiwan sponsorship, which receives its first acclaim from readers in the United States? In answering these questions, one comes to realize that literature from mainland China—the "center" of traditional geopolitics—is becoming decentralized. Some writers "inside" literature are politically outside. Literature from Hong Kong, Taiwan, and overseas—the "marginal" Chinese communities—is to be taken seriously because its readers are already living, economically and culturally, inside modernity.[3]

However, this should not be taken to mean that the marginal can occupy the center, as if the old notion of dialectic struggle were being revived. Instead, it points to a landscape where dialogues between many different Chinas become possible, a negotiation that does not establish a republic of Chinese letters but rather creates a real heterogeneity of contemporary Chinese literatures.

A reconfiguration of Chinese literature from different regions further questions the concept and practice of realism and representation. By *representation* I refer not only to the aesthetic meaning of mimesis but also to the political implication of legitimacy. In claiming to transcribe an objective reality, *realism* became the genre of privilege as early as the twenties, and until after the Great Cultural Revolution it dominated Chinese literary theory, be it called humanitarian realism, critical realism, or socialist realism. It is significant that the mid-eighties saw the decline of realism on both sides of the China straits along with the disintegration of authoritarian regimes.

When ideological truth proves to be fiction, when realism proves to be an art not of revelation but of formulas, the celebrated realist canon "art reflects life" also has the ring of a political slogan. In writing, representation leads to new questions: What kind of work re-presents popular consensus that doesn't represent governmental policy? What nonrealists were sent into internal exile when only realism could be acknowledged or written? Why can't expatriate writers' works be representative of a national capacity to write? Why can there

3. See also Leo Ou-fan Lee's discussion in "On the Margins of Chinese Discourse," *Daedalus* (Spring 1991): 207–26.

be only one foreign mapping of the (post)modern and not several Chinese versions? Chinese writers' efforts to go beyond realism are therefore no more aesthetic gestures than they are radical historical gestures, gestures against the old systems of truth by power and the old myths of representation by centralization.

The best contemporary Chinese fiction cannot be classified as realistic in a traditional sense. For those used to seeing modern Chinese fiction as a supplement to social history or as a predictable Jamesonian "national allegory" of sociopolitics, the fiction produced since the late eighties may tell a different story. It shows that literature in the post-Tian'anmen period has not harked back to the old formulas of reflectionism. Precisely because of their refusal either to remain silent or to cry out in an acceptably "realist" way, the new writers see life as an ongoing process, a conglomeration of possibilities and impossibilities. Precisely because of their inability to believe in the one true path through realism to modernism and then postmodernism, or in any melodramatically predictable path through history, contemporary Chinese writers promise new and lively beginnings for the end-of-the-century Chinese imagination.

There is another aspect of representationism. In opposing the totalitarian Maoist regime to the relatively more open post-Maoist society, critics and scholars have coined a new term, *Maoist discourse* (*Maoyu, Mao wenti*, etc.), to summarize the coercive rhetoric that once controlled humanistic activities in China. The term has historical validity, particularly in insinuating the irony that a Marxist society could reproduce the superstructural tyranny it set out to overthrow. But the term may have also created an easy way out for critics, generalizing an otherwise complex issue. By uncritically contrasting the Maoist and the post-Maoist eras as two distinct or even dialectical discursive paradigms, and by asserting in retrospect the total, irresistible power of Maoist discourse, one actually risks succumbing to the double bind of representationism. A verbal reenactment of Maoist purges will neither redeem the deaths and the resentments of millions of Chinese nor properly represent the dark force of Maoist tyranny and the hidden power of a million unutterable questions. Only by continuously refusing to speak summarily of the past can we remember the past.

To launch a retroactive protest against Maoist discourse, one has to learn not to affirm the lie of its omnipotence, because it was not an undivided whole that erased all other voices—it merely suppressed them. This is an ironic strategy, but it is based on an ethical imperative rather than mere rhetorical play. Had Maoist discourse been perfect at both the technological and ideological levels, all critique of it from within would have been unthinkable. We know, however, that even at the darkest moments of the Cultural Revolution, thousands of Chinese uttered dangerously nonconformist speeches—and this accounting does not include those who protested mutely, often through suicide.

To speak of Maoist discourse in the nineties as if it had been an unquestionable, total power, therefore, indicates less a critical indictment of it than a complicity with its pretensions. It eschews the real intellectual labor that would have thwarted Mao's brand of historicism and therefore dissipated its spell.

Extrapolating from these observations, I propose a different way of reading contemporary Chinese fiction, in terms of the following three configurations: *familiarization of the uncanny; lyrical appropriation of the epic; flirtation with China.* Each heading refers not only to a theme that pervades contemporary Chinese writings but also to a polemic stance that has been adopted by Chinese writers as they have set out to reconfigure China.

1. Familiarization of the Uncanny

One of the most fascinating phenomena in Chinese literature of the late eighties has been the radicalization of traditional realist discourse. Writers in mainland China, as in other Chinese communities, have explored materials hitherto considered untouchable and rendered them in a wide range of forms: stream of consciousness, metafiction, magical realism, etc. Particularly in mainland China, this rejuvenated creativity has become a powerful critique of Maoist discourse, the formidable literary and political rhetoric that prevailed in China for more than three decades, suppressing all hope of free literary expression. But now, by turning the world into a realm of fantastic and uncanny elements or by identifying normalcy with the grotesque and insane, writers awaken their readers from aesthetic and ideological inertia, initiating them into a new kind of reality.

Defamiliarization—aesthetic and conceptual distancing of a familiar subject in order to restore its perceptual newness—has been frequently used by critics to describe this phenomenon. But the term cannot really cover the new Chinese rhetoric, especially the political rhetoric composed on the eve and in the aftermath of the Tian'anmen Incident.

Defamiliarization presupposes a perceptual diminution of life to a banal, repetitious continuum, an aesthetic malaise from which readers can only be rescued by a regimen of parody and disruption, till these readers lose confidence in tradition. With the artificiality of the old realism exposed, the imagination of the real can start again, fresh and new. In China, this recipe must appear ironic at best and perhaps even cruel. Who else, after all, is more competent (or decadent) than the Chinese Communist propaganda apparatus in sending its people through the same ideological hoops again and again by defamiliarizing that which is all too familiar? Who else is more imaginative than the party at churning out a new set of slogans, campaigns, and enemies and at reenacting the old cadre games in the guise of yet another people's revolution?

Moreover, the Chinese people, who have gone through so many calamities over the past half-century, have seen no shortage of grotesqueries and disruptions in their everyday lives. Amid the continual parade of the absurd and the abnormal, they might be thought to have hoped for a year or two of routine and repetition. Reality *was* already more eerie and unthinkable than anything that fiction could conjure.[4] Insofar as it aims to "make strange" things that otherwise seem familiar, defamiliarization would have to mean, in the Chinese context, not an outrage or a revolution to subvert the tedium of the familiar but either a refamiliarization of the trivial or a creative deformation of the unbearable.

I suggest *familiarization of the uncanny* as one key to Chinese writers' handling of defamiliarization. Precisely because reality is already too bizarre and grotesque, the writers' greatest challenge lies in how to make it more plausible rather than more strange. Whereas for Freudians the uncanny means "something familiar and old-established in the mind that has been estranged only by the process of repression,"[5] there

---

4. For more discussion on the discourse of the grotesque, see David Der-wei Wang, "Jirenxing" [A parade of the grotesques], in *Zhongsheng xuanhua* [Heteroglossia in modern Chinese fiction] (Taipei: Yuanliu, 1988).

5. Sigmund Freud, "The Uncanny," in *Studies on Parapsychology,* Alix Strachey, trans. (New York: Macmillan, 1981), 47.

is an additional dimension to the Chinese uncanny. In China, repression is not just an individual defense mechanism; a governmental mechanism represses individual responses and legitimates that repression as something necessary and reasonable. The horrors and unpredictabilities of ordinary experience are legitimated; the temptation to see these everyday events as uncanny is repressed. This second repression is made possible by public exposure of the private, by normalization of the unnatural. To talk about the Chinese uncanny, therefore, is to explore the paradoxical question as to why things that would be seen as dreary and therefore repressed in a Western, Freudian context have ever been taken as natural in China. If the majority of works appearing in the early nineties can be called uncanny, they are so merely as a preparation for, or an evocation of, the incomprehensible, which nevertheless manifests itself everyday.

Accordingly, the contemporary Chinese uncanny can be seen in the paranoia and megalomania that have alternately possessed China's two hostile regimes and their peoples: the horrors and absurdities of the Cultural Revolution, the deification of Mao Zedong, even triumphant consumption of human flesh in the name of "Mao thought"; a national campaign of abuse of woman's body, through mandatory abortions of the most primitive kind; stock-speculation mania involving millions of people, first in Taiwan, now in mainland China; and the brutal bloodshed of Tian'anmen Square, televised all over the world, followed by cynical rewritings of the Incident by People's Republic of China officials—no bloodshed, no massacre, just "a tiny handful" of bad elements.

There are four genres of stories that rely on familiarization of the uncanny: grotesquerie, fantasy, the gothic tale, and the animal allegory. Yu Hua's "One Kind of Reality" is an example. The novella chronicles the way in which a family quarrel turns into a series of family murders. Few readers will be undisturbed by the discrepancy between the bloody family feud and the matter-of-fact style with which Yu Hua narrates the incident. One can almost discern macabre humor when the narrator catalogues the ways the family members humiliate, torture, and mutilate each other—a veritable museum of Chinese cruelty. One of the most talented avant-gardists in mainland China, Yu Hua has been praised (or criticized) for his desolate view of life, his violent deformation of language, and his penchant for the neurotic. But personal idiosyncrasies aside, all Yu Hua does is to lay bare the horrors that Chinese are used to in life but would rather find incredible when encountered in art. Yu Hua purports to record merely a slice of life, a story about nothing. Can the sadomasochist festivity of the family murders still be seen as uncanny when the bloody national carnival of the Cultural Revolution or of the Tian'anmen Incident is an unrepressed everyday affair?

The mode Yu Hua uses to deal with human neurosis and grotesquerie can also be seen in Su Tong's "Running Wild," a story about a child's obsession with death, which ends with unexpected misfortune. But whereas Yu Hua opts for almost barren narration, Su Tong, one of the most charming storytellers of the early nineties, displays a rich, elaborate symbolism and an ornate vocabulary. Su Tong is at his best in writing family melodrama with a gothic touch; looming behind the facade of his domestic tales are decadent motives and unspeakable desires. As "Running Wild" opens, something infamous has already happened to the family; we witness, from a child's perspective, its utter downfall amid disappearance, adultery, madness, and murder/suicide. But do these incidents really "mean" anything? Do they really "matter"? "Running Wild" is as dazzlingly elaborate and inscrutable as "One Kind of Reality" is bothersomely simple and literal. Beyond its stylistic exuberance, however, one finds in the text a hollow center. The verbal intricacy of the text cannot hide the banality of its evils.

In Yang Zhao's "Our Childhood," comic fantasy is used as a perspective from which to examine the social/cultural problems of Taiwan. In a fantasy, the real and the illusory mix with each other; the impossible becomes possible. This syndrome is illustrated in "Our Childhood," a story about a fantastic outcome of the Taiwan stock speculation frenzy in the late eighties. The two women speculators in the story have been losers at life's game until they find new hope in the boundless optimism of stock-market speculation. They not only consume the fortune they have yet to make but also manage to redeem their real unhappiness with an investment in imaginary nostalgia. They fantasize their childhoods in the same way they speculate on stocks, to the point where money and memory become interchangeable tokens. Nostalgia, after all, pays a dividend, in entropic speculation and fictitious dealings.

S.K. Chang's "Amateur Cameraman" is a black comedy about a man's secret desire to murder his wife. In many ways the novella combines the uncanny and the fantastic. One of the most popular overseas Chinese writers, Zhang has tried his hand at genres ranging from science fiction to fantastic romance. He is best known, however, for his series of sarcastic stories about the war between the sexes. Situated in an American city, the novella introduces a middle-class Chinese couple trapped in marital crisis, which is followed by the murder of the wife. The husband is charged with the killing. Did he really commit the crime? Was he set up for having merely fantasized on paper about killing his wife, as he claims? Was his wife really dead? Mixing mystery and black humor into a surprise ending, the novella completes its dizzying attack on militant feminism and male chauvinism.

In the anthology there are two gothic tales, "Ghost Talk" by Yang Lian and "The Isle of Wang'an" by Zhong Ling. Both stories borrow from the genre of the gothic tale, using such conventions as ghostly atmosphere, macabre plotting, mysterious reincarnation, and an ambiguous moral schematization. Writing at the turn of the nineties, however, Yang Lian and Zhong Ling convey the paradox that accounts about our reality cannot be related except as gothic tales: the ghosts looming in their works are not supernatural beings of the other world but phantoms of *this* world.

In Yang Lian's "Ghost Talk," a lonely soul is heard speaking to himself in an empty house; the response he receives is a cluster of chilly echoes of his own voice. In Zhong Ling's "The Isle of Wang'an," a woman launches a desperate search for love and sexual fulfillment on a desolate island under the auspices of the ghosts of her family ancestors. Why are these characters deprived of their authentic existence? Why are they doomed to be wanderers outside the arguable "human" world? Who are these ghosts? Perhaps they are expatriate poets whose voices have been reduced to meaningless rambling; political exiles who have lost the grounds on which to fight for their ideals; women whose desire for sexual fulfillment has been repressed as obscene. In their attempt to contact the human world, to overcome social taboos and indifferences, these ghosts find they have always been habitants of the human world, which remains part of the ghostly unknown.

Whereas Zhong Ling is inspired by ghost stories in her portrait of a modern Chinese predicament of sexual fulfillment, two other women writers in the anthology, Tang Min from mainland China and Xi Xi from Hong Kong, turn to animal imagery in dealing with the issue of womanhood and motherhood in two different Chinese communities. Tang Min's "I Am Not a Cat" records in a tone of journalistic apathy the way in which mainland Chinese women are forced to have abortions under the most primitive medical conditions; Xi Xi's "Mother Fish" renders a poignant portrait of women's desire for and anxiety about marriage and maternity. Despite their differences in style and concern, both writers compare their female characters to animals. In so doing they seem to proclaim that in a representational system prefigured by men, one way to make women's fate "intelligible" is to translate the established code of mimesis into an animalist mimicry.

Mimicry implies exaggeration, dehumanization, and simplification. For these women, this is exactly where the politics of their animal allegories start. The Chinese women in Tang Min's "I Am Not a Cat" are treated worse than cats when they are ordered to wait in line, pants off, to await their abortions. Xi Xi, the more sophisticated, sees in her "Mother Fish" an ironic parallel between an unmarried teenage girl's fear and desire when she thinks she is pregnant and a pregnant fish's painful death before delivery, in the absence of her male partner. The story also contains a subtext in which Xi Xi juxtaposes women's unfulfilled motherhood and female writers' aborted creativity. For both writers, animal allegories are less literary devices than literal testimonials to the fate of Chinese women. To read these stories is to familiarize oneself with the uncanny that is the real.

2. Lyricization of the Epic

The second direction this anthology indicates is contemporary writers' highly subjective approach to history. In response to the drastic political changes since the late seventies, writers on both sides of China have raised questions about the authenticity of traditional historical discourse: what valorizes the appearance of truth in history; who legitimizes the "voice" of history; how history exerts its power over our view of the future. Because History has been sanctioned by Communist theoreticians as a holy text, one that prefigures China's destiny in the Socialist millennium, mainland writers' efforts to rewrite history in fictional forms deserve special attention. Facing the hiatus between what happens and what should have happened in accordance with official historiography, these writers try to make sense of the broken past by personal accounts. Instead of offering a new narrative closure, however, their stories are often marked with an ironic awareness of the contingency or even absurdity of any human effort to recapture the past.

Almost half a century ago, Jaroslav Průšek commented on the rise of modern Chinese literature by pointing out its lyrical inclination. By *lyrical* Průšek means a subjective and individualistic discourse that the first generation of modern Chinese writers formulated, a discourse that derives its conceptual and enunciative format from classical poetic tradition.[6] This lyrical inclination enables modern writers to articulate their nonconformist feelings against feudal literary and ideological canons. For Průšek, however, the lyrical mode cannot generate a powerful literature until it is complemented by writers' epic sensibility, i.e., a sense of shared communal fate at a changing historical moment. Writing in terms of Marxist ideology, Průšek sees in the lyrical and the epic, or the mode of the individual and the mode of society, a dialectic tension, one that appropriately constitutes the subtext of modern Chinese (literary) history.[7] Implied in his theory is a view that the lyrical and the epic would reach their happy (re)union in a Marxist era. People's Republic of China literature from 1949 to 1979, however, shows that the lyrical mode was erased from a discourse dedicated to writing the (Socialist) epic. Only in the eighties does one see a resurgence of the lyrical in Chinese narrative discourse.

If Průšek's paradigm makes sense to us today, it is not because the lyrical and the epic still function as two disparate modes, perennially negotiating the "total" inscription of national fate, as Průšek would have argued. Rather, the lyrical and the epic have undergone a mutual displacement, which has reshuffled their inherent aesthetic and ideological expectations. History is still the primary concern of contemporary writers, but its literary manifestation, epic discourse, can be conveyed only by its *lyrical other.* Writing at a time when the master narrative of history is already fragmented and anachronized, Chinese

6. Jaroslav Průšek, *The Lyrical and the Epic: Studies of Modern Chinese Literature,* Leo Ou-fan Lee, ed. (Bloomington: Indiana UP, 1980), 1–29.
7. Leo Ou-fan Lee, introduction to *The Lyrical and the Epic,* vii–xii.

writers can only approximate (rather than authenticate) historic meaning through a lyrical evocation. The forces at work in the dark realm of the political unconscious can be simulated only through a language that transgresses generic boundaries between the real and unreal.

While the lyrical appropriation of the epic may point either to the new capitalist desire to make personal what used to be public or to the schizophrenic syndrome of broken historical subjectivity, as suggested by some critics, a deeper motivation has to be spelled out.[8] With its emphasis on the figurative landscape that language can construct, the new lyrical mode points to a critical position that refuses to be confined by the referential imperatives of epic (or historical) discourse. If literary representation is substantially a rhetorical performance rather than the outcome of logical or ideological prefiguration, then the text can be liberated from the iron prison of referential determinism to make its own figurations of the real. This emphasis on language and poetic expression is a confirmation of human choice in "figuring out" the world. In this regard, the predilection for the lyrical recapitulates the critical lyricism evolved for Chinese literature by Shen Congwen, the great modern Chinese nativist writer, half a century ago.[9]

Yu Hua's and Su Tong's stories offer access to the margins of war and history, away from the official depravities of the center. They emphasize a microlevel, the level of seemingly insignificant happenings, the empty space between the significant disruptions of historic events. The grand epic narrative dissolves into fragmentary impressions, fortuitous events, and pointless monologues. These bits and pieces serve as poetic incantations, ushering us here and there in the cavern of history, sending flashes of light down some of the darkest passages.

In A Cheng's "Festival," history is lyricized by another personal style. Though dealing with an impending bloody clash between two factions during the Cultural Revolution, the story is nevertheless narrated from the innocent perspective of three children. These children

8. See, for example, Wang Jin, "Benweihua qingjie yu dayuejin xintai" [The complex of egocentrism and the mentality of "the Great Leap Forward"], Zhang Xudong, translated, in *Jintian* [Today] 3–4 (1991): 26.

9. For more discussion of Shen Congwen's "lyricization" of history, see David Der-wei Wang, *Fictional Realism in Twentieth-Century China: Mao Dun, Lao She, Shen Congwen* (New York: Columbia UP, 1992), 203–10, 224–33.

are taking a one-day vacation in celebration of their own holiday, Children's Day; they play together, not knowing their parents are about to begin a deadly combat against one another. The situation all too easily recalls the story in which Lu Xun founded modern Chinese literature, and its famous slogan: "Save the children!" But A Cheng refuses to continue the mode of shouts and slogans that had become the rule in the intervening decades, instead favoring understatement and quiet, just-visible symbolism. In "Festival," A Cheng's narrative rhythmically blends sensory images from the natural and the human environments into a contrapuntal whole until one cannot ignore their harmonic resonances. One can, of course, talk about A Cheng's ironic intention, which reveals the absurdities of the adult world by lyricizing it with the innocent eyes of the children. But I suspect the polemicist's dilemma with a story such as "Festival" lies in the fact that it draws the reader's attention without any specific investment in the subject matter and without any conviction that the work is a definitive treatment of anything. The narrated event and the narrative event demand equal attention.

Mainland writers' lyrical inclinations reach an apogee in Yang Lian's "Ghost Talk." A poet taking refuge in New Zealand after the Tian'anmen Incident, Yang Lian makes a radical move in dealing with the subject of exile. Exile indicates not only physical or psychological displacement but also a break in the symbolic chain that used to make sense of one's existence. Yang Lian's story foregoes elements thought necessary to a coherent narrative, instead piling up images and impressions, murmurs and silences. The result is a story that reads like rambling, a narrative turned against the narrative premise of verisimilitude. Perhaps this is the poet's most vehement indictment of History; for all his effort to remember and narrate the unspeakable historical event, he manages only to utter something that erases the line between the lyrical moment and the epic event. As the story's title suggests, "Ghost Talk" is nothing but a phantom voice that is forever doubled in its own echoes.

Taiwan writers have shown a similar tendency to see and write history as if from a subjective angle. In Yang Zhao's "Our Childhood," one finds two interlacing arrays of narrative segments—one realistic, one fantastic. Whereas the realist segments point to the dreary continuum of life as it is lived, their fantastic counterparts bring forth a past where dreams and desires can be found. When "childhood" is personalized as a girl, when nostalgia is crystallized by the girl's contest with a galloping train, poetry is evoked as the redemption of time from pain and ressentiment by fantasy.

Zhu Tianwen's "Master Chai" exhibits a lyrical rewriting of the epic narrative no less ambitious and eccentric than her mainland counterparts'. The story has only one character, an aging masseur who runs an underground clinic in a dubious district of Taipei, and one event, the masseur's waiting for a young patient who is coming for her last treatment. What really "happens" in the story is the masseur's remembrances of the past narrated in a kind of litany: his escape from mainland China when the Communists took over; his involvement in smuggling; his desolate marriage and family life; and his decaying business and health. We thus see a life that has been wasted and a figure whose existence, in a society that cannot wait to deny its historical ties with the mainland, seems only a useless decoration, a relic of some almost-forgotten event. Zhu Tianwen's story intrudes into the most unlikely life an epiphanic moment, one that casts a sudden light on the pathos of one generation's fate. The innocent patient embodies for the masseur an escape to the realm of youth and hope. Through massaging (or fondling) the girl's naked body, the masseur undergoes an erotically charged ritual of spiritual rejuvenation; each touch leads him closer to the forever-exiled past, recalling, obscenely or rhapsodically, one generation's dreams of sorrow and meaning.

3. Flirtation with China

The discourse of modern Chinese literature from 1919 to 1989 is burdened with writers' heavy concern for the Chinese nation and eager readiness to reform Chinese society with a program of literary admonishments. "Obsession with China,"[10] the phrase coined by C. T. Hsia in his ground-breaking study of modern Chinese literature, has been widely used to describe the general tendency of modern Chinese literature. Chinese writers are so committed to their country's salvation that their sole mission is to excoriate social malaise, provoke or resolve national crises, and contemplate if not actually hasten

10. C. T. Hsia, "Obsession with China," in *A History of Modern Chinese Fiction* (New Haven: Yale UP, 1961), 533–54.

the nation's future. In practice, the obsession with China has led fiction writers to "hard-core realism,"[11] another phrase of Hsia's, meaning a raw, even brutal exposé of Chinese misery that spurns pretensions, aesthetic or intellectual. China is considered so afflicted with spiritual disease that there is no way to save it from degradation except through extreme measures. While this obsession has generated a moral ethos rarely seen among other national literatures, it has also enticed writers into ideological fetishism, one that makes China sanction their unwillingness or their inability to deal with issues beyond immediate political concerns.

One might talk about the sadomasochism in Chinese writers' insatiable desire to write about the pain of their mother country and to share in her despair, as one contemporary critic notes.[12] But one must face the issue of the morality of form. For writers of both the post–May Fourth era and the early People's Republic of China regime, writing is a political act, and any literary re-form must yield to the agenda of overall reform. History, however, has shown us how postponing questions about the form of the idea has led over and over to ideological emptiness and moral capitulation. The more that post–May Fourth writers wrote about the mindlessness of their compatriots, the more they threw doubts on their own writings and on the mindless way in which they captured and then changed reality. The continued celebration of the new Communist utopia by early People's Republic of China writers turned out to be transparent self-exposure, a reenactment of the fable of the emperor's new clothes. In both cases, writing starts out confident of its refreshed moral vision but ends up declaring its complicity with a decadent reality.

Chinese writers since the beginning of the nineties have tried to break away from hard-core obsession with China by reducing what they do to a *flirtation with China*. While its undertone of frivolous yet harmless eroticism is intentional, *flirtation* refers not to the new writings' treatment of sexual subjects but to their attitude toward or approach to any "serious subject"—above all, to the most serious serious subject, China.

11. C. T. Hsia, "Closing Remarks," in *Chinese Fiction from Taiwan: Critical Perspectives,* Jannette L. Faurot, ed. (Bloomington: Indiana UP, 1980), 240.
12. Rey Chow, *Woman and Chinese Modernity* (Minneapolis: Minnesota University Press, 1991), 121–69.

Writing in a postmodern era, Chinese writers have come to realize that writing does not have to be equated with political action and
that literature cannot solve all social problems, as Lu Xun's successors
expected it to. Writing now becomes a facetious gesture, a playful
action, that titillates rather than teaches, flirts rather than indicts.
Instead of the conventional "tears and sniveling" or "call to arms,"
contemporary Chinese writers exhibit a much wider range of emo-
tive skills, from crying to clowning, in accord with a subtler relation
to society. And beyond the single standard of hard-core realism, they
are ready to try on a variety of styles, old and new, classical story
telling or modernist collage—whatever best fits their slimmer
expectations.

The state of unbearable lightness suggested by contemporary Chinese writers' flirtation with China, however, must be treated with no
less caution than the deadly gravity of literature from earlier generations. From one angle, it reflects writers' self-ironic contemplation of
literature's position in a postmodern multimedia network, one in
which images deconstruct realities and morals boil down to mere
manners. But from another angle, flirtation with China informs us of
the writers' strategic repositioning vis-à-vis their volatile political surroundings. Through their "light" writings, writers either tantalize the
formidable organs of censorship or tease the apparent solemnity of the
state and thus redeem their readers as well as themselves, however ten-
tatively, from the old cycle of obsession with China. For some critics,
this may represent the demise of the modern Chinese literati, a sign of
end-of-the-century dissipation and self-indulgence. But at a time
when writers themselves refuse to treat writing as a crusade, those
critics who insist on the old ways are sick with the most dissipated and
self-indulgent of Chinese diseases: an obsessive desire to consume
writings that show an obsession with China.

Five stories about love and lust, drawn from mainland China, Taiwan, Hong Kong, and America, illustrate this point, though in fact
flirtation with China does not have to be understood in romantic
terms. The transition of style in some of Mo Yan's recent work, such
as "Divine Debauchery," is an example. Mo Yan was praised as one of
the most brilliant writers of the eighties, and his popularity among
readers and critics climaxed with the publication of *Red Sorghum*
(1987), a fantastic mixture of national romance and family saga. In the

wake of the Tian'anmen Incident, one would have expected a writer like Mo Yan to produce powerful works that exposed Communist atrocities at either a literal or an allegorical level. But the best works he has produced are a series of anecdotal stories, such as "Divine Debauchery," that relate quaint customs, fantastic happenings, and eccentric personalities from the old days. "Divine Debauchery" deals with a rich man's strange sexual behavior: he brings home all the prostitutes in town, plays with them by walking over their naked bodies, then sends them away. Be it called a bawdy joke, an erotic fantasy, or an account of sexual perversion, this is a story about a sexual tease that leads nowhere, a story that ends before anything real (hardcore?) happens. One can certainly infer from the aborted sexual action an allegorical reading, but I would rather argue that Mo Yan's unabashed attachment to the surface of his subject matter is the story's driving force. Insofar as the absence of allegory is a new kind of allegorical manifestation, "Divine Debauchery" is symptomatic of contemporary writers' facetious tactics in playing with their subject matter, whatever it is.

The misery of the peasantry is a sanctioned theme of modern Chinese fiction, but in Li Peifu's "The Adulterers" the theme finds an expression that combines both irony and sensuality. The story may look like a remake of a conventional farce, with a farmer setting out to catch his unfaithful wife and her lover in flagrante delecto. It is not. Overhearing that his wife will be deserted by her lover after all her passion and self-sacrifice, the farmer starts to feel sorry for her. His jealousy gives way to compassion, and his anger with his wife's unchastity is replaced by fury at her lover's ungratefulness. But a sentimental solution is the last thing Li Peifu intends; his story takes yet another turn. The farmer's poor bachelor brother, taking his brother's forgiving attitude for a signal, now begs to sleep with his sister-in-law, perhaps for a modest fee! At a time when the democratic movement was going strong in the capital, what preoccupies this group of Chinese farmers is the necessity not of revolution but of (prudent) copulation. "The Adulterers" does not contain any political comment, but through muffled laughter it permits a word on behalf of the libidinal needs and perverse hopes of the people.

Overseas Chinese writer Gu Zhaosen's "Plain Moon" is the only story in the anthology that bears directly on the aftermath of the

Tian'anmen Incident. But Gu's intention lies less in glamorizing the movement than in deflating the heroism and tragic hyperbole that constitute most narratives about the movement. The story does not even take place in Beijing, where the incident happened, but in New York; it details a marriage of convenience between a former student leader of the movement, who is desperately seeking permanent-resident status, and a mediocre Chinese American woman, Plain Moon, who yearns for marriage. Though the Tian'anmen democratic movement is sufficient cause to bring the two together, the pressure of life in America will not allow either of them time to look back sentimentally at the Incident. The marriage is soon in crisis, as our heroine Plain Moon discovers that her husband's sweetheart has come to town. Thousands of miles away from Tian'anmen Square, Plain Moon becomes a belated victim of the Incident. Gu Zhaosen makes a parody of the "revolution plus romance" formula that governed modern Chinese literature from the thirties to the seventies, revealing heroes and heroines that ultimately are captives of either vanity or the survival instinct. His indignation at the bloody outcome of the Incident and his sympathy for his characters are undercut by his ironic tone and black humor.

In Zhu Tianwen's "Master Chai," sexual perversion and historical pathos are mixed with each other in Master Chai's caressing his patient's body. Zhu Tianwen rewrites the genre of tearful obsession with China, turning it literally into a bizarre piece of erotica about an old man's obsession with a young woman. As Zhu Tianwen's character caresses his young, innocent patient, so Zhu teases the total body of nationalist literature. Zhu's vision of Taipei deserves equal attention. Taipei is envisioned as a city that has almost forgotten its days as the center of the Nationalist crusade to restore a lost China, or as the stopover for those mainland emigrés who yearned to go home. Taipei at the end of the twentieth century is a city where post-martial-law politics mingle with post modernist fashions, a place where memories of the past and desires for the future meet and cancel each other out. Zhu's end-of-the-century aesthetics tells us: time wears out one's will; all lofty ideas of nation and history must succumb to decayed senses and sensibilities.

In Hong Kong writer Ye Si's "Transcendence and the Fax Machine," a professor finds himself more and more isolated from his colleagues while his tie to a group of theologians in France gets increasingly close, thanks to the advent of fax communication. His fax machine silently and obediently takes his theoretical treatises and sends them to somewhere far away; it functions as tamely and subserviently as a woman. This "romance," however, is endangered one day when the machine acts up and starts to produce junk messages from all sorts of sources. Ye Si lavishes feminine images on the machine, at the risk of seeming a male chauvinist, but in so doing he manages to dramatize Hong Kong life torn between seduction and despair, one drawing ever nearer to the double perils of 1997 and 1999. Through the fax machine, concepts such as religion, history, and nation are turned into mysterious signaling systems; the transcendental telos that the professor searches for and receives is always in danger of proving itself to be a phantasm, a ghost in the machine. By the end of the story, the professor has to face the fact that transmission of ideas and transgression of truth are mixed together. The story touches as much on the alienation and narcissism of Chinese intellectuals in end-of-the-century Hong Kong as on the dissemination and promiscuity of information in an age of postmodern technology.

With examples drawn from mainland China, Taiwan, Hong Kong, and overseas sources, I have identified three directions in the development of contemporary Chinese fiction. These *three directions* are familiarization of the uncanny, the manifestation of the epic through its lyrical other, and flirtation with China.

First, in their effort to re-present China through defamiliarization, Chinese writers must confront the paradoxical result of familiarization of the uncanny. For them, any literary endeavors to take the real and "make it strange" may turn out to be a painful laying bare of the real. The absurdities and horrors contained in the recent history of China are so unbelievable that they make their mimicries take on the modes of the uncanny.

Second, writing in an era of post-History, contemporary Chinese writers can make sense of history only by evoking its lyrical other. This lyrical inclination seems to take us full circle to the point almost nine decades before where the first generation of modern Chinese writers reformed literature by proclaiming their subjective vision. But unlike their predecessors, who posited a collective historical subjectivity—in the name of the epic—as the goal of their lyrical discourse, contemporary writers' negation of that subjectivity as well as its formal manifestation constitutes the most intriguing aspect of their end-of-the-century writings.

Third, breaking with the obsession with China, contemporary Chinese writers find in flirtation with China a better way to instantiate the circumstances in which they write and the strategies that they have developed to cope with these circumstances. With its playful, erotic overtones, flirtation with China refers to a discourse that recognizes its own theatrical or figurative quality and therefore refuses to fall victim to the allures of hard-core realism.

All three directions have significantly undermined the traditional approaches to China and Chinese literature, approaches that were bound by a mimesis-oriented canon of realism, a yearning for a total knowledge of History at the expense of a first understanding of the self, and a desire to prescribe the national discourse before local voices have learned how to speak. In stating these new directions, I am not offering a transcendental view of the nature of end-of-the-century Chinese fiction, much less prescribing what path it should take. I want only to convey the wonder and pleasure that any reader must feel when suddenly aware that a literature is on the verge of recovering itself, of letting all its voices speak—as if the departing century had at last learned from its painful experiments.

LIST OF

CONTRIBUTORS

Editors

David Der-wei Wang received his Ph.D. in Comparative Literature
from the University of Wisconsin at Madison. He has taught
at National Taiwan University and Harvard. He is currently
Associate Professor of Chinese Literature in the Department
of East Asian Languages and Cultures of Columbia Universi-
ty. His most recent publications include *Fictional Realism in
Twentieth-Century China: Mao Dun, Lao She, Shen Congwen*
(New York: Columbia University Press, 1992), *From May
Fourth to June Fourth: Fiction and Film in Twentieth-Century
China* (coedited with Ellen Widmer; Cambridge: Harvard
University Press, 1993), and *Xiaoshuo Zhongguo* [Narrating
China] (Taipei: Ryefield, 1993).

Jeanne Tai received her degree in law from the University of Michi-
gan. She practiced law in New York and taught modern Chinese literature at Harvard University before becoming a freelance translator. She is the translator and editor of *Spring
Bamboo* (New York: Random House, 1989), a collection of
Chinese stories of the eighties.

Translators

Kirk Anderson received his master's degree in Chinese Literature from Harvard University. He is a freelance translator based in Boston.

Jeffrey C. Bent has lived, worked, and travelled extensively in East Asia. He is currently an MBA candidate at the Johnson School, Cornell University.

Amy Dooling is a Ph.D. candidate in the Department of East Asian Languages and Cultures at Columbia University.

Randy Du is a software developer, independent translator, and editor living in Quincy, Mass.

Ann Huss is a Ph.D. candidate in the Department of East Asian Languages and Cultures at Columbia University.

Andrew F. Jones received his B.A. in East Asian Languages and Civilization from Harvard University in 1991 and is currently a Ph.D. candidate in Chinese literature at the University of California at Berkeley.

Charles A. Laughlin is a Ph.D. candidate in the Department of East Asian Languages and Cultures at Columbia University.

Kristina M. Torgeson is a Ph.D. candidate in the Department of East Asian Languages and Cultures at Columbia University.

Michelle Yeh received her Ph.D. in comparative literature from the University of Southern California. She is now teaching at the University of California at Davis. She is the author of *Modern Chinese Poetry: Theory and Practice Since 1917* (1991) and the editor and translator of *An Anthology of Modern Chinese Poetry* (1992), both published by Yale University Press.

Zheng Da is a Ph.D. candidate and lecturer in the English Department at Boston University and an accomplished translator and writer.

About the Authors

A Cheng (1949–) won enormous acclaim in the mid-eighties for his three "King" novellas ("Qiwang," "Shuwang," "Haiziwang," or "Chess King," "Tree King," "Children King"); these tales made him one of the founders of the "root-seeking" movement, a nativist movement that prevailed in the mid-eighties. An extremely meticulous writer, A Cheng has since produced only a handful of short stories and sketches, all characterized by his patent lyricism and linguistic economy. He is now living in Los Angeles. "Holiday" [Jieri] appeared in *Nuxingren* [W. M.], vol. 3 (1990).

Gu Zhaosen (1955–) is by profession a medical doctor in New York, but he has also been a familiar name over the past decade in literary circles. His works focus mostly on the drastically changing manners and morals of Chinese immigrants in American cities. "Suyue" [Suyue] was the winner of the fiction contest of *Lianhebao* [United Daily] in 1991.

Li Peifu (1950–) is a writer based in Henan Province, China. His works represent a good example of the "sketch-style" fiction (*biji ti xiaoshuo*) that was widely practiced by local-color writers in the late eighties and early nineties. Li's works can be seen in major mainland Chinese literary magazines such as *Shanghai Wenxue* [Shanghai Literature]. "Adultery" [Zhuojian] was included in *Zhongguo xiaoshuo yijiujiuling* [Chinese Fiction of 1990] (1991).

Mo Yan (1956–) is perhaps one of the best-known new-generation mainland Chinese writers in the West, thanks to the translation of his novel *Honggaoliang jiazu* [Red sorghum] into English and

French, and to the worldwide release of the movie version of the novel. A prolific writer, Mo Yan has published dozens of short stories and four novels, touching on a wide range of genres from family saga to grotesque exposé, from parodic revolutionary romance to outlandish fantasy. "Divine Debauchery" [Shenpiao] first appeared in *Lianhe wenxue* [Unitas], vol. 3 (1992).

Su Tong (1963–) first caught critics' attention for a series of works recollecting the pre–Communist Revolution days. He has an unusual ability to evoke a decadent, mysterious historical ambiance, one in which political chaos, sexual transgressions, and irrationalities thrive and play against one another. Contrary to People's Republic of China literary formulas, his critique of the past, if any, derives from his deep fascination with it. Su Tong is a superb storyteller; his narrative is charged with baroque imagery and sensuous symbolism, indicating his command of the Chinese language and his indebtedness to traditional Chinese fiction. "Running Wild" [Kuangben] was included in *Nanfang de duoluo* [The fall of the south] (1992).

Tang Min (1956–) is a writer based in Fujian Province, China. "I Am Not a Cat" [Wo bushi mao] was originally published in *Nuxingren* [W. M.], vol. 3 (1990).

Xi Xi (1938–), fiction writer, essayist, poet, critic of fine arts, translator, editor, and movie reviewer, is one of the most talented and versatile people in contemporary Chinese literature. Her achievements, however, have been unfairly overlooked as writings on the margin of China (Hong Kong) by mainland-oriented critics and readers. Her style is highly experimental and changeable, while unfailingly suggestive of its roots in a Chinese experience. Xi Xi started writing in the sixties, her early works in many ways anticipating the avant-garde trends in China in the eighties. Few Chinese writers today can emulate Xi Xi in terms of originality, imagination, and compassion. "Mother Fish" [Muyu] appeared in *Muyu* [Mother fish] (1990).

Yang Lian (1957–) was regarded as one of the most promising young

Chinese poets before the Tian'anmen Incident. He left China on the eve of the incident and has since exiled himself successively in Germany, Austria, the United States, and New Zealand. His poetry and other creative writings can be seen in newspapers and journals in Taiwan and Hong Kong and in overseas Chinese publications. Some of his poems have been translated into English and published under the title *Masks and Crocodile* (Honolulu: University of Hawaii Press, 1991). "Ghost Talk" [Guihua] appears in *Nuxingren* [W. M.], vol. 4 (1990).

Yang Zhao (1963–) started publishing fiction in the early eighties. He has published four collections of short stories and one novel, all acclaimed for acute political awareness and lyrical sensibilities. Yang Zhao is now studying for his Ph.D. in Chinese history at Harvard University. "Our Childhood" [Women de tongnian] was included in *Dubai* [Monologue] (1991).

Ye Si (1948–), poet, short-story writer, and art critic, has been a well-established literary figure in Hong Kong for the past fifteen years. His poems, vignettes, sketches, and short stories present a lively *tableau vivant* of life in Hong Kong, decorated with fantastic touches and sarcastic humor. Ye Si is now teaching comparative literature at Hong Kong University. "Transcendence and the Fax Machine" was included in *Bulage de mingxinpian* [A postcard from Prague] (1990).

Yü Hua (1960–) is one of the most controversial writers in Chinese fiction of the early nineties. His penchant for eerie, macabre subjects, his radical experiments with the Chinese language, and his seemingly capricious modes of writing have resulted in a series of highly idiosyncratic stories and novellas. These works offend, baffle, or fascinate readers, pointing to an environment that is absurd in appearance yet hauntingly suggestive of China's immediate past. "One Kind of Reality" [Xianshi yizhong] was included in *Shibasui chumen yuanxing* [Leaving home for a long trip at the age of eighteen] (1990).

S.K. Chang (1944–), one of the most popular writers among Taiwan and overseas Chinese readers, has published more than a dozen collections of short stories and novels in the past two decades, though his professional title is Professor of Computer Science at the University of Pittsburgh. Zhang is noted for comic fiction on gender issues and science fiction, replete with black humor and biting sarcasm. "The Amateur Cameraman" [Shaqi] appeared in *Shazhu chuangi* [Legends of male chauvinist pigs] (1991).

Zhong Ling (1945–), poet, short-story writer, and jade connoisseur, received her Ph.D. in comparative literature from the University of Wisconsin at Madison and now teaches at National Sun Yat-sen University in Taiwan. Often inspired by ancient tales or gothic legends, Zhong Ling's stories explore the unfathomable desires and frustrations of women trapped in a male-centered world. Her style is characterized by a daring inquiry into female sexuality and a persistent interest in sensuous symbolism. "The Isle of Wang'an" [Wang'an] was included in *Shengsi yuanjia* [A destined couple] (1992).

Zhu Tianwen (1956–) started out being a popular middlebrow fiction writer in the early eighties. She made a remarkable breakthrough with *Shijimo de huali* [Fin-de-siècle splendor] in 1990, a collection of stories that envisages Taipei as a glittering, decadent metropolis, peopled by a "new species" of citizens, torn between end-of-the-century desires and despair. Zhu Tianwen has also been scriptwriter for the internationally renowned Taiwan film director Hou Xiaoxian. "Master Chai" [Chai shifu] was originally included in *Shijimo de huali* [Fin-de-siécle splendor] (1990).